Praise for *The Berlin Apartment*

"Bryn Turnbull brought the two sides of the Berlin Wall to life in a way that made me feel like I was there. Immaculately well researched and fast-paced, this book is an absolute must read!"

—Madeline Martin, *New York Times* bestselling author of *The Keeper of Hidden Books*

"Turnbull tackles tough questions of loyalty, patriotism, and the test of true love as a country divided erects the infamous wall that pitted brother against brother. An utterly fascinating portrait of East and West Germany, the old regime versus the new, and a world on the brink of change. I devoured this gripping and romantic novel in one sitting!"

—Heather Webb, *USA TODAY* bestselling author of *Queens of London*

"Bryn Turnbull weaves a tale of intrigue, betrayal and redemption... At its core, *The Berlin Apartment* is a novel that shows the importance of forgiveness, and of following your heart. Highly recommend!"

—Eliza Knight, *USA TODAY* and internationally bestselling author of *The Queen's Faithful Companion*

"With impeccable research and evocative writing, Bryn Turnbull has a true gift for immersing the reader in the past. *The Berlin Apartment* is a poignant story of love and hope in a world that has been cruelly divided, and where danger lurks at every turn."

—Christine Wells, internationally bestselling author of *The Paris Gown*

"An enthralling meant-to-be love story crushed by the cruel circumstances of the cold war. I couldn't put it down—I read it all in one sitting and wanted more."

—Lecia Cornwall, author of *That Summer in Berlin*

Also by Bryn Turnbull

The Woman Before Wallis

The Last Grand Duchess

The Paris Deception

BRYN TURNBULL

The BERLIN APARTMENT

MIRA

MIRA™

ISBN-13: 978-0-7783-0545-3

The Berlin Apartment

For questions and comments about the quality of this book, please contact us at CustomerService@Harlequin.com.

Mira
22 Adelaide St. West, 41st Floor
Toronto, Ontario M5H 4E3, Canada
MIRABooks.com

Printed in U.S.A.

To those who were separated, and those who found each other again.

prologue

DECLASSIFIED on the orders of the Bundesbeauftragter für die Unterlagen des Staatssicherheitsdienstes der ehemaligen Deutschen Demokratischen Republik (Stasi Records Agency) on December 22, 1994.

19 JULY, 1962

My darling Uli,

The world can change in the space of a heartbeat. That's what I recall telling myself on the day that you proposed. I think about that day so often, and it seems both more and less real to me than my life now: a moment spent on the precipice of joy and despair. In that space between your question and my answer, time seemed to slow, somehow: thinking on it now, I could swear that the sound of traffic outside the window fell silent; that the rain hung, suspended, over the stopped cars on Bernauer Strasse.

I suspect it must have been agony for you, sitting there

with the ring between us, waiting for me to respond. But there was something in the silence I longed to savor: the possibility, I suppose, of what your question held for us both. The endless hope I felt in the moments before it all became real.

Perhaps I wanted to remain there because real life carries risk…real love carries pain. Bittersweet heartbreak. For isn't that what lies at the heart of love, Uli: the inevitability of betrayal, in one form or another? Betrayal by infidelity, by apathy—by sickness, or death. A beginning contains, at its very core, an end.

I wonder. Is the risk of love worth it?

But I wasn't thinking about any of that on the day you proposed. All that I could think about was wanting to live in the sweetness of that moment: in the space between question and answer.

I suppose, then, that there's some justice in love.

Because I've lived in that unbearable purgatory every day since.

Yours always,
Lise

UNDELIVERED. Intercepted by the East German Ministry for State Security on 20 July, 1962.

Part One

1

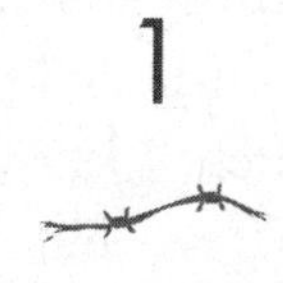

11 AUGUST, 1961

The apartment was on the topmost floor of a shrapnel-dusted building on Bernauer Strasse, an incongruous prewar oddity with plaster-molded windows and narrow hallways, which, in comparison to its newer, wider neighbors, felt unexpectedly quaint. With its marble floors and papered walls, it seemed as if the building had seen all the joys and horrors of the past and taken them in its stride: it rolled out an impersonal, dusty welcome to all who'd passed through its doors before, secure in the knowledge that they would one day pass their way out once again. The cast-iron lift clattered a hello to those who chanced its dodgy mechanics, but the stairs were the more reliable option, the once-shimmering marble dulled beneath thousands of footfalls.

As she walked upstairs, smoothing her hand along the banister, something about the building's shabby state spoke to Lise, promising a future that she could see with crystal clarity—but then, that sense of joy might have had more to do with the young man who held out his hand to her on the landing.

They stopped outside the fourth door to the left, and as Lise watched him jiggle the key in its rusted lock, her mind narrowed in on one single, giddying thought.

He's going to propose. Uli Neumann is going to propose!

The door gave way with a groan and Uli turned with a smile. "Remind me to bring some oil for the hinges," he said. "Watch that floorboard, it's a little loose..."

Lise stepped inside, craning her neck to admire the faded wallpaper that crept up to curlicued plaster trim.

"It doesn't look like much, I know," Uli continued with a shrug of his narrow shoulders, "but with some new paint and furniture—a television, perhaps..." He grinned and ran a hand through his dark hair. "Just tell me you don't hate it, that's all I ask."

"Hate it?" Like so many of the remaining Mietskaserne apartment blocks in Berlin, this one had survived the devastation of the war on luck alone, and it was luck that Lise chose to see in the apartment: luck, rather than the hard work that she and Uli would have in bringing the place up to standard.

To the right of the modest entrance hall was a kitchenette, the cupboards painted a cheery shade of eggshell blue: a slapdash conversion, Lise suspected, of what had once been half a bedroom. She opened the door closest to the entrance—what she had assumed to be a hall closet—to reveal a bathroom and smiled, her suspicions confirmed.

She continued down the hall, averting her eyes from the bedrooms opposite the kitchenette with a sudden, absurd attack of modesty. What was there to be modest about, when this apartment was a declaration of the commitment she and Uli had expressed to each other in everything but words?

"I love it," she said finally, meeting Uli in the sitting room at the end of the hall. She smiled as he fussed over the placement of secondhand furniture around the fireplace, and pictured the room as it would be when she and Uli were finished with it, with colorful, fresh wallpaper and a new living room set from KaDeWe department store, porcelain mugs hung from the painted trim of the kitchenette's pass-through window. She thought of Uli, mixing drinks for their guests from a bar cart while she checked on the progress of a roast dinner; the sound of a baby screeching in its bassinet.

He finished nudging the ottoman in place and looked up. "You're not just saying that, are you? You wouldn't prefer some impossibly expensive new build near the Ku'damm with functional plumbing?"

"Functional plumbing would be a draw," Lise replied lightly, pulling aside the dusty curtains to flood the room with sunlight, "but no. This is ours. It feels like us."

"I was hoping you'd say that." He stepped forward to wrap Lise in his arms, and she allowed herself to fall into his kiss. Would she ever tire of Uli's irrepressible optimism? The brightness in Uli's soul seemed purpose-built to illuminate the darkness in Lise's own, drawing her out of her tendency toward gloom and bringing her, willingly, toward joy.

Uli pulled back, his gray eyes sparkling behind the glass of his horn-rimmed spectacles. Tall and slender, with rounded shoulders and a mess of dark hair that looked as if it had never made the acquaintance of a hairbrush, Uli resembled, to Lise's mind, Buddy Holly, but for the deeply scored laugh lines that gave rare distinction to his wide smile.

He led her to the window, nestling his chin in the hollow of her collarbone as they looked out onto bustling Bernauer Strasse. Below, cars and trucks trundled along the rain-soaked street as people wandered the sidewalk in groups of twos and threes, occasionally disappearing beneath the leafy canopy of slender saplings before reappearing further down the pavement. From here, she could see past the parkette on the opposite side of the road where green-clad Grenztruppen patrolled their rigid routes, past the bombed-out remains of several apartment buildings on

Schönholzer Strasse and into the darkened, postage-stamp window of her family's apartment on the top floor of 56 Rheinsberger Strasse.

"I know how hard it's been for you to think about leaving," Uli said, his breath warm on her cheek. "I hope that by being only a few streets away, you won't feel you have to choose."

She stared at the windows of her family apartment, picturing her father, Rudolph, as he'd been that morning, leafing through a medical reference book in the living room; Paul, finishing a coffee before reporting for his shift at the police station. Between Rheinsberger Strasse and the center of Bernauer Strasse ran the invisible divide between East and West Berlin, and though she'd grown up in the East, West Berlin was the side of the city that truly held her heart. It was here, in West Berlin, where she attended university, hoping to follow in her father's footsteps as a doctor; here, where she spent her time with Uli.

She smiled. "And you'd be all right, would you, living a block away from my father? From Paul?"

"I get along well with your dad. As for Paul… We've just not spent enough time together. That's all."

Lise bit back a response. It was so much in Uli's nature to think of Paul's opposition to him as a matter of persistence: to think that time and charm could lessen objections that Lise knew went beyond personality alone. But persistence was one of Uli's great attributes—an attribute or a flaw, depending on one's perspective. Uli's persistence had brought them together in those early days of their courtship when he would dash out of his engineering lecture early so he could wait outside the medical building to walk Lise across campus; when he would brush aside the complications that faced them in dating from opposite ends of the politically divided city. It was persistence, now, which had led him to find an apartment that was both close to Lise's neighborhood and still in West Berlin—one which would allow Lise to live the life she wanted with those she loved on both sides of the border.

Lise twisted in Uli's arms to run her hands down his shoulders, his back, as she pressed her lips to his. She could feel the heat of him, intoxicating and heavy, and drew closer.

They lay together in a tangle of sheets, listening to the sounds of Bernauer Strasse below. She shivered as the perspiration on her skin cooled, and Uli pulled the blanket up over her shoulder, snugging her close.

"Remember the night we met?"

Lise laughed, recalling the night her life had changed: the warmth of the nightclub, the sound of the band. "Inge told the maître d' some ridiculous lie to get us through the front door. She'd been so set on meeting an American."

"And then I turned up and you spent the whole night talking to me and my friends instead," Uli replied, not missing a beat in the well-worn cadence of their story. "I hope Inge forgives me one day."

"Seeing as she ended up dating Wolf for three months, I don't think she's held it against you." The club had been packed with tourists and American GIs and British soldiers, all dancing to the strains of a jazz band. It had been almost impossible to hear Uli over the sound of the music, but she'd liked the look in his kind eyes so she let him buy her and Inge a drink. "You were so handsome…standing there in your suit and tie like a proud schoolboy."

"A *schoolboy*?" Uli growled. "I'll have you know those threads are still very much the style, but seeing as you East Berliners don't know the first thing about fashion, I'll let that comment go. And as I recall, you were the one carrying textbooks."

The nightclub had been in the American sector, close to the Free University where Lise studied medicine but far from her home on the east side of the city—too far to bother dropping off her books and then making the journey back. In those early days of studying in West Berlin, Lise had seen what life could be beyond the strict confines of the German Democratic Republic: the university had provided a window to the wider world.

When she met Uli, that window had become a door, and she was ready, now, to run through it.

Lise turned in the sheets to face Uli, running a curled finger along his bare chest. "A very *handsome* schoolboy," she conceded.

"I graduate in less than a year," Uli pointed out. "And then I'll be a very handsome *civil engineer.*"

"And I'll be finishing my studies." She pictured her life in a year's time: still attending classes at the Free University, living with Uli in the West; visiting Papa and Paul, only a block away. Perhaps after she finished her studies, they would leave Berlin, travel somewhere far-off and send postcards back home—or perhaps they would stay here and raise a round-cheeked daughter who would learn the route to Papa's house.

Uli propped himself on one arm and reached into the bedside table.

"I suppose this is as good a moment as any," he said, letting a note of trepidation slip into his voice.

She sat up against the iron headboard, her heart fluttering as he presented her with a small velvet box.

"Uli," she whispered.

"You know why I bought this apartment—why I brought you here," Uli said. "You know what my intentions are, and they haven't changed from the first moment I set eyes on you. I love you, Lise." He paused, his voice trembling. "A lifetime would never be long enough, but I…I want to spend my lifetime with you." Carefully, he unclasped the box and opened it to reveal a simple gold band topped with a modest, emerald-cut diamond. "That is, if you'll have me."

She could scarcely remember to breathe. *This is it,* she thought as she allowed him to place the ring on her finger. *This is the moment my life begins.*

She held up her trembling hand and let out a choked laugh at the perfect fit. "How did you know—?"

"Your ring size?" Uli grinned. "Inge helped me."

She sat forward and kissed him urgently, joyfully, with such force that Uli overbalanced and they tumbled back together against the mattress.

"Is that a yes?"

"It's a yes. *Yes!*" Lise raised her voice in the hopes that she could be heard through the closed window over the sounds of the traffic, her happiness traveling across the rooftops of Mitte and Wedding to the ends of East and West Berlin and beyond. "Yes, Uli Neumann, I will marry you!"

Some hours later, Lise opened her eyes, noticing how far the sun had crept along the ceiling. "I ought to go home," she whispered as she nudged Uli awake. "Paul will be home from work soon and he'll want to leave for the *datsche* as soon as we can."

Uli groaned, rolling to bury his face in the pillow. "You are home," he muttered, his voice muffled by feathers. "Stay. Stay with me. We can go out with our friends, share the good news."

She rolled out of bed and set her feet on the floorboards: *carpet*, she added to her list of requirements for the flat.

"You know I wish I could, but I have to go. I promised." She found her Dederon pantyhose tossed in the corner: after retrieving them, she perched back on the edge of the bed. "You know this will change everything."

He let out a sigh. "I know." At a time when East Germans were fleeing the GDR with alarming regularity, Lise's decision to move to West Berlin, to marry a West Berliner, would raise eyebrows amongst the more fervently socialist amongst her friends and family. As a communist nation, the German Democratic Republic—the GDR—subscribed to the notion of a planned economy: each citizen was a member of the workers' and peasants' state, and was afforded the same basic rights—income, health care, housing—in exchange for putting their skills and abilities at the disposal of the economy.

In some respects, the system worked; in far too many others, it didn't. Unlike many of her peers, who had been funnelled into apprenticeships and factory jobs after finishing secondary school, Lise was lucky to have been granted permission from the State Secretariat for Higher Education to pursue postsecondary study. But the government dictated what kind of education Lise would receive, and from her cohort the economy needed more scientists than doctors, so she'd been offered a place at Karl Marx University to study physics.

The offer, however, had come with a warning. If Lise refused to accept it, she would be barred from pursuing higher education entirely.

She'd applied to the Free University in West Berlin as a last resort, and had been elated when she'd been accepted into their faculty of medicine. She'd intended, at first, to return to East Berlin after graduation, but her studies had opened her eyes to the limitations of life in the GDR: here, in the West, Lise could pursue the studies—and the life—she liked. In West Berlin, she met people from all over the world who'd traveled far beyond the short list of approved socialist brother countries sanctioned by the Reisebüro, servicemen and women who told her of their homes far beyond the Iron Curtain.

It was intoxicating, and though her brother pursed his lips with disapproval when she returned home at night with stories of what life was like in the capitalist west, Lise knew, beyond doubt, that she wanted to live there permanently.

If she'd not met Uli, Lise was certain that one day she would have simply packed a suitcase and made her way to the refugee center in Marienfelde, claimed asylum from the GDR and the limited future it promised. After all, it was an easy journey to make from one side of the city to the other: a walk or a ride on the S-Bahn into West Berlin was simple, given the city's open borders. And with Uli, Lise's future in the West was legitimate: she would become a West German citizen through marriage, but her family in East Berlin would be only a few blocks away.

Uli sat up, scratching a pink trail along his bare chest. "When should we tell them?"

The news would be a shock, Lise knew: less so to Papa, who approved of Uli, but certainly for Paul.

"We're leaving for the *datsche* as soon as Paul gets home," Lise said, rolling up her tights as she worked out the logistics in her mind, "and perhaps it will be a good thing to have a family weekend away, just me and Paul and Papa. On Sunday, you can come over for dinner, and we can tell them together…or—" Lise grinned at her sudden burst of inspiration "—you could ask Papa's permission."

Uli frowned. "Isn't that terribly old-fashioned?"

"Yes, but Papa would be so touched by the gesture. Besides—" she leaned forward and planted another kiss on Uli's lips "—you already know what my answer will be."

"So, we'll tell them on Sunday," Uli concluded once Lise broke away. "Are you sure you don't just want to elope tonight? Find a nice ship's captain or an unfussy priest, make it official…"

"We'll tell them on Sunday," Lise repeated, laughing. "My love, we only need to be patient for two days. And after that—" she smiled, thinking of their bright future together "—we will have all the time in the world."

2

One of the many advantages of Uli's new apartment was its proximity to Siggi's, a dark and long-loved *kneipe* for Uli and his friends, given that Jurgen, Uli's former flatmate, was related to the owner. Despite its distance from the Free University, this familial connection had made it a preferred destination for after-class drinks because Agatha, Jurgen's red-haired aunt, could often be coaxed into sending along a round of beer on the house. It was a perk that more than made up for the pub's dark corners and elderly clientele; its Formica-topped tables encased in a layer of grime that, despite Agatha's best efforts, never seemed to come clean.

Tonight, Agatha arrived at the table with a celebratory round of pilsner and kissed the top of Uli's head as she set them down.

"I knew she was a good one," she said, beaming, before returning to the bar.

"Thanks, *Tante*." Jurgen raised his mug, its foamy head clinging to the sides of the glass. "To Uli and the woman of his dreams!"

Four glasses lifted to meet his, creating a small eruption of foam as the drinks clashed together.

"To Lise," Uli replied, meeting his friends' smiles: Wolf and Jurgen, wedged into the corner of the pub's vinyl booth, their shoulders touching; Inge and Axel, perched on the edges of the banquette. The only one missing was Lise, and Uli rested his hand on the soft depression in the seat that she usually filled. "Thank god she said yes!"

"Come now, Uli, was it ever really in question?" Inge lifted her eyebrow with a knowing smirk, her stunning features yellowed in the light of the bulb swinging overhead. "She was head over heels from the moment we met you. She didn't call you back for nearly a week because she didn't want you thinking she was too interested." She let out a tinkling laugh. "I told her she was being ridiculous. It was obvious from the start, you two are a true love match."

Uli felt himself redden at Inge's approval. "And I'll be forever grateful to you for pleading my case with her."

Inge's smile broadened. Uli had been friends with her for as long as he'd known Lise, and he suspected that Inge had played a bigger role in his relationship with Lise than he knew. The two of them had been inseparable ever since Inge transferred to the Free University from her native Sweden, and they shared the kind of frank, open connection that blossomed amongst women who regarded each other as something more akin to sisters than friends. Had Inge disapproved of him, Uli was certain that he wouldn't have gotten far with Lise.

"Marrying an *Ossi*..." Axel grinned, infusing his tone with a playful note of scandal. Like Lise, Axel lived in East Berlin and studied at the Free University—art history, with a specialization in Renaissance portraiture. "What did your parents say when you told them?"

Uli quietened, recalling Father's silent disappearance behind the pages of his newspaper; Mother, cupping Uli's cheeks in her hands. *If you're sure*, they'd said, and Uli couldn't help wishing they'd been more effusive in their approval. But then, they'd never been the happiest of couples. Had they ever felt the way Uli did now—as though his heart would burst with joy?

"Oh, you know," he said finally as Axel shifted out of the banquette in search of another round. "They worry we'll have difficulty with her emigration. So many Easterners are trying to get across to West Germany, they think it'll be more complicated than we expect."

"It might be." Jurgen exchanged a look with Wolf. "My brother and sister-in-law live in Bernau, and they tell me that the border guards are getting antsy. Holding up trains, checking passports, questioning anyone going west..." He lowered his voice. "Karl and Brigit want to come across and claim asylum at Marienfelde, but Karl's been followed home from work the past couple of days. They've decided to wait."

Uli took a slow sip of his beer. The East German secret police—the Stasi—were, it was rumored, capable of tracking every person, every action, every thought within East Germany. If half of what Uli had heard about the Stasi was true, they already knew about Jurgen's brother and his desire to move to the West—the only reason Karl had seen them was because they wanted him to know they were wise to his plans.

He set the mug down with a thump, unease twisting in his stomach. If the Stasi were as skilled at surveillance as people believed them to be, they already knew about Lise's engagement to Uli—knew, and no doubt disapproved.

"Is that wise?" Wolf offered, as Axel returned with another beer-laden tray. "Did you hear Ulbricht's address on the radio the other day? He keeps going on about the border..."

"He's always going on about the border," Axel replied, "but what can he do? East Berlin, West Berlin...it might be two countries, but it's still one city."

"Even so." Wolf patted Jurgen's arm, the casual gesture a familiar shorthand in their relationship. "You might want to let Karl know that if he's making plans, they might be easier accomplished sooner rather than later."

Jurgen's sunny expression dimmed. "Lise's brother is a Vopo, right? Has he told you anything?"

Uli turned his mind to Paul: tall and stern, his blue eyes always bright with scrutiny beneath the brim of his police cap. Paul and Uli had never gotten along, despite Uli's efforts to win him over: he was an ideologue, staunchly supportive of the GDR in a way that Uli simply couldn't understand. Paul would disapprove of their engagement, of that Uli had no doubt. Even if he liked Uli as a person—even if Lise was only moving a hair's breadth past the invisible border between East and West—Paul would object.

East and West Berlin, East and West Germany…what did it matter, if Lise and Uli loved each other?

But Jurgen had asked about something entirely different.

"Paul doesn't say much to me," Uli replied with a shrug.

"Perhaps Lise will be able to shed some light on the matter when she's back from Lake Flakensee," Inge concluded, tossing her white-blond hair over her shoulder. "But if the GDR is planning to make it more difficult to cross the border, it's all the more reason for a short engagement."

"I'd marry her this evening if I could." Uli set down his beer. "I want to spend the rest of my life making her happy."

A strange smile flickered across Inge's face. "I think you've just written the start of your wedding vows," she said, and Uli smiled back, allowing himself to set aside all the complications—his parents, Lise's family, the border—and simply think of Lise in a white dress, standing opposite him at a registry office.

Axel drained the last of his beer and stood. "Speaking of East Berlin, I ought to get going before the trains stop running for the night." He clapped Uli on the shoulder. "Congratulations, my friend. I look forward to hearing how it goes with Lise's family."

He slung his rucksack over his shoulder and departed, elbowing past the elderly men who propped up Agatha's bar top with laughter and loud jokes.

"I suppose it's sweet to be asking her father's permission," Inge was saying as Uli turned his attention back to the table, "but I think it's silly to negotiate over women as if they're livestock."

"It's tradition, Inge," Wolf replied with an exaggerated roll of his eyes. "Uli's hardly asking for a dowry. He's just being respectful."

"And she's already said yes," Uli added.

Jurgen smirked. "But what if Rudolph says no?"

Wolf socked him lightly on the arm—*"Jurgi!"*—and Jurgen put up his arms in mock surrender.

"Well, if that's all the stupid questions out of the way, I suppose I'd best be off, too." Inge got to her feet and slung her handbag over her shoulder before leaning to kiss Uli on the cheek. "Congratulations, Uli. I await my appointment as maid of honor with bated breath."

3

12 AUGUST, 1961

The shores of Lake Flakensee were packed with people, holidaymakers from Berlin carrying baskets and blankets, calling after dogs who splashed joyfully into the water on the heels of children in bright bathing suits. Carrying a wicker basket of her own, Lise found an unoccupied stretch of beach and spread out a checkered blanket; beside her, Paul set down a small cooler they'd packed with beer.

He straightened, casting his gaze down the beach before pulling off his shirt to reveal a taut, tanned chest. "Are you coming in?"

Lise followed his gaze down to the water, where a young woman was watching Paul with ill-concealed interest. She stifled a smile: her cocky brother never could resist an admirer. "I want to warm up first," she replied, then squinted past the woman at another, bulkier figure. "Isn't that Horst in the water?"

Paul's poorly feigned surprise made it clear to Lise that this was more than a coincidence. "Why, so it is. Should I tell him to come join us?"

"You can tell him whatever you like, but you know I won't say yes to a date," Lise called out as Paul crashed into the lake, knowing that her brother wouldn't be so easily dissuaded. He'd been hoping to set Lise up with Horst for years, cheerfully bringing Horst along to family gatherings and parties in the hopes that, one day, Lise might overcome a lifetime of indifference and finally fall for his best friend. Even Lise's relationship with Uli hadn't dissuaded Paul from his mission: though he behaved cordially toward Uli, Paul clearly preferred to think of him as a temporary obstacle, rather than a future brother-in-law.

If only he knew. She stretched out long on the blanket, replaying in her mind the moment that Uli had proposed. *My fiancé.* In less than two days' time, the announcement would be official: how would Paul react? She knew that his objection—and he *would* object—would be to the thought of Lise leaving the GDR, more than Lise getting married. Unlike Lise, who viewed East Berlin as an increasingly stifling social obligation she longed to give up, Paul believed wholeheartedly in the state: as a card-carrying member of the Socialist Unity Party and the Volkspolizei police force, he upheld the laws of East Germany with a fervency that Lise, despite sharing an upbringing, simply didn't posess.

Paul emerged from the water and waved Horst over before making his way back to Lise. Tall and broad shouldered, Paul shared Lise's blond hair and downturned eyes; as children, their classically attractive features and motherless upbringing made them objects of affection and pity to all the neighborhood mothers. Whereas Lise was introspective and academic, Paul was charismatic and athletic—a charming rogue who'd left behind a trail of broken hearts as long as Stalinallee—but while he never lacked for female company, Paul always made time for Lise. On these weekend trips to their family datsche near the shores of Lake Flakensee, Lise and Paul would stay up late into the night talking, and it was this time that Lise valued most: time spent with her brother, her best friend.

Paul reached into the cooler, pulled out three bottles of beer, and handed the first to Lise. She took it, making more of a fuss over finding the bottle opener than was strictly necessary.

The thought of upsetting Paul with news of her engagement hurt Lise more than she cared to admit. Would there still be late-night conversations and trips to the datsche once she moved to West Berlin?

"How's your father?"

She looked up as Horst collapsed onto the blanket next to her and took the second bottle of beer. Horst was impressively built, a broad and muscle-bound man who'd been Paul's best friend since the time they were scrawny kids in the Free German Youth, but where Paul had charisma, Horst had all the charm of a brick wall. But despite their differences in temperament, Paul and Horst were brothers in nearly every sense, even serving together in the Volkspolizei to patrol the streets of East Berlin side by side.

In her more judgmental moments, Lise wondered whether Horst's dull nature was his very appeal: he allowed Paul to shine.

"Papa's been a little absent, recently," Paul replied, lifting his beer bottle to his lips. "Nothing to be concerned about. He's got an appointment with the doctor next month."

"I worry it's anemia," Lise offered as she dug into the picnic basket and pulled out an orange. They'd left Papa at the datsche to putter in the raised vegetable plot that Paul had built outside the small cabin, tall enough for him to weed in his wheelchair. Papa had always been a thoughtful sort, but these days he seemed more lethargic, more absent-minded, than usual. Not for the first time, she wished she was a little further along in her medical studies so that she could take a more active role in Papa's welfare. Was it his wartime wounds acting up, or was there something else at play?

"It might be," Paul said with a nod. "You can ask the doctors, they'll set him right."

"Of course they will. We have the best medical system in the world," Horst added, his dark sunglasses glinting as he looked out over the water. "And one day you'll be among their number, Lise."

Lise smiled thinly as she peeled the orange. The compliment matched Horst himself: bland and automatic. Did he truly think she hoped for a career in an East German hospital, when she'd been denied the chance to study medicine at an East German university? When West Berlin paid so much more for qualified physicians?

She held out segments of the peeled orange and Horst took one before flopping back on the sand; Paul, however, hesitated.

"From your *Wessie* boyfriend?"

Lise pulled her hand out of his reach. *My Wessie fiancé.* "Well now, if you can't be nice about him, you don't get any," she said tartly.

"I was only asking," Paul protested, twisting to reach for the orange. Though fruit was available in abundance in West Berlin, flown in by American airplanes from Florida farms, the shops in East Berlin had lacked oranges for months, now. Bringing fruit across the city from West to East was, technically, a criminal offence, but East German border guards could usually be convinced to turn a blind eye to such petty smuggling.

It was smuggling things *out* of East Berlin that the border guards truly disapproved of: Westerners coming east to take advantage of East Germany's low prices. They would buy products in bulk to sell them at an exorbitant markup in the West, and though Lise preferred West Berlin to East, even she could see the injustice of such transactions. Once, she'd watched a customs officer pat down a woman on the S-Bahn who'd been attempting to smuggle no less than twenty-two Greußener salamis beneath her girdle.

"He wants to be your friend," Lise said. "Won't you give him a chance, for my sake?"

"I just don't want you getting hurt," Paul replied. "Particularly not by some Western capitalist with long hair…"

Lise laughed. "His hair isn't that long." She rolled over on the sand and propped herself up on her elbows, the sun warm on her back. "I love you, you know," she continued, "but I can make up my own mind. On Uli, and on everything else."

Paul sat upright to toss his orange rind into the lake. "Just don't set anything in stone," he replied. "Men can change their minds…particularly when they're used to getting the newest and brightest."

"What's that supposed to mean?"

"He's a *Westerner*," Paul said. "They think differently than we do. Take this new apartment you told us about…what was wrong with the old one? That's the difference between them and us—they're always looking to change things, to find what's new and exciting."

"And you think that's the way he is with women?" Lise replied incredulously.

Paul shrugged. "Not necessarily. But what's to say he won't tire of you?"

Lise shoved him, knowing both that Paul was teasing, and that he would soon be proven wrong. "Are you calling me boring?"

He laughed, rolling away from her attempts to beat him with her orange peel. "I'm just saying that men can get tired! Particularly ones who are used to novelty every day of the week." He grinned and drew close again. "What about Horst? He thinks you're pretty…"

Lise glanced at Horst, who was snoring peacefully in the sand. "You're trying to put me off, but I won't let you," she replied. "Why are you so determined to hate him?"

Paul settled back into the sand, nestling his head in the crook of his elbow as he basked in the sun. "I don't hate him. Truly, I don't. I just—" he grinned, revealing a row of perfectly straight teeth "—don't like him."

"You don't like him?" Lise took a bite of her orange. "Or you don't like where he was born?"

Paul let out a lighthearted sigh, lifting his hands in the air in a gesture of surrender. "If he moved to the GDR, I would never say another word against him."

"He'd never do that." Lise deposited the orange peel back in the basket. "He remembers those days at the end of the war... what the Russians did to his family." Lise trailed off, knowing how fortunate she was to have no memories of 1945. Her memories of childhood were of playing in the ruins of the Berlin that had been, of sitting in bombed-out classrooms where teachers explained that their current circumstances were the result of fascist ambition and capitalist greed. "He would never move to the GDR, never."

Paul's sigh grew exasperated. "Good thing the GDR isn't Russian, then," he shot back. "We live in a German state. Run by Germans."

"A German state still beholden to Russia."

"To the Soviet Union," Paul replied, though to Lise's mind the technical distinction made no difference. "It's people like him who won't let us move on. Why must he bear old grudges?"

Lise smirked. "He could say the same about you, you know."

"Hardly. My grudges are legitimate." He looked up at Lise, faintly imploring. "I have nothing against him personally. He's just so...flashy all the time. Flaunting his money. It's part of his Western capitalist agenda, bringing presents, acting like we're some kind of charity case."

Lise flinched at the characterization. "He's just generous."

"Yeah, well, we don't need his generosity." Paul propped himself up, looking cross. "We have everything we need, right here. Why can't you see it? We don't need some capitalist pig coming into our lives, trying to turn your head."

"It's too late for that. My head's already been turned," Lise replied, and Paul's frown deepened.

"I told Papa he should never have let you study in the West," he muttered. "I knew nothing good could come of it."

She glanced at Horst, still snoring away. Paul could—he *would*—argue for hours, if Lise let him. Like Uli, Paul had memories of his own from 1945, and those memories had shaped the man he was today: a police officer, duty and honor bound to protect those he loved. And who did he love more than Lise? Paul had protected her from the time they were children, when their father was in the hospital and they'd had to fend for themselves; he'd worked hard and was grateful to the state for giving them everything he couldn't provide with his own two hands.

He'd never stopped protecting her, in his own way.

She thought once more of the ring on Uli's nightstand and tomorrow's dinner with Papa. *Let him think he's won the argument.* This was Lise's last weekend at the datsche, before her life changed for the better. What good would it do to fill their remaining hours with bitterness?

She eased herself back onto the blanket and closed her eyes, letting the sun warm her skin as she reached across the sand and took Paul's hand.

"Uli's coming for dinner tomorrow, and I want you to be nice to him." She squeezed his fingers. "Promise you'll be nice. Don't set anything in stone."

Sunday morning dawned bright and sunny, and out the window of the datsche Lise watched as butterflies and bumblebees tripped lazily over the heavy rosebushes in the garden. The datsche, like so many other summer homes that surrounded Lake Flakensee, was tiny, with two small bedrooms and a claustrophobic loft which Paul, despite being the tallest among them, had long ago claimed as his own. Some weekends, when Paul brought a girl along and Horst turned up for dinner, the datsche could feel cramped, and they would wheel Papa's chair out into the garden for a candlelit dinner at the long picnic table, but this morning Lise moved at a leisurely pace. Paul and Horst had been unexpectedly called back to Berlin late last night, and Lise was content to putter as Papa tended to his vegetables.

She scrubbed last night's dishes, watching through the window as Papa wheeled himself around the raised garden beds. As a young man, Papa had objected to serving in Hitler's army, choosing to preserve life rather than take it. He'd been a surgeon at one of Berlin's top hospitals and had been halfway through a gallbladder removal when an American bomb flattened the building, trapping Papa beneath a pile of rubble for two days: when he'd finally been rescued, Papa was paralyzed from the waist down and left with a permanent tremor in his right hand.

In the garden, Papa called out a hello to their neighbor, Frau Bottcher, and shifted closer to the shared fence to exchange pleasantries.

Lise was often amazed at how sanguine her father was: how gracefully he moved through life. He never seemed to look back with bitterness at his life, nor hold on to anger about the war that had taken his wife, his job, his mobility. Instead, he raised his children, shared his expertise as a professor of medicine at Humboldt University of Berlin and tended to his gardens. He lived a good life—comfortable and quiet, never seeming to want more than he already had.

She set a dripping wet plate aside to dry, thinking about Paul's characterization of Uli the day before: *Men can get tired… Particularly ones who are used to novelty every day of the week.* It wasn't a fair thing to say, not when Uli had proven to be the opposite in every way. Still, the conversation irked her. Would Paul ever overcome his scruples?

Perhaps a good meal would help to ease tensions between the two. In her mind, she ran through the list of groceries they would buy for tonight's dinner once they were back in Berlin:

stewing beef and carrots, onions and barley. Uli would bring wine, of course, and the ring, in the inner pocket of his dinner jacket…

She plunged her hands back into the soapy water, then caught sight of Papa wheeling up the ramp to the datsche, his peaceful expression suddenly stormy. She opened the door with the dish towel as all thoughts of dinner fled from her mind, replaced by a sudden sense of misgiving.

"What's going on?"

"Turn on the radio," Papa said without preamble. "Something's happened."

Lise dried her hands and flicked on the wireless, already tuned to a news channel. Through the gravelly static, the broadcaster's voice sounded distant and bewildered.

"Under direct orders from First Secretary Walter Ulbricht, the National People's Army have erected an Antifascist Protection Barrier across the country to protect the East German citizenry from Western incursion," he said, and Lise met Papa's shocked expression. She opened her mouth, but Papa lifted a trembling hand and she fell silent. *"As of midnight on the thirteenth of August, the border between East and West Germany has been sealed."*

4

13 AUGUST, 1961

Uli stared out his apartment window, his pulse beating wildly in his ears. Seven stories below, a tangle of concertina wire ran the length of Bernauer Strasse, bisecting East Berlin from West: onlookers on both sides of the wire watched, muttering, as green-uniformed Grenztruppen, separated from the East German citizenry by a line of Volkspolizei, jackhammered the cobbles to fix stakes into the ground and carted in more spools of barbed wire, rolling it out with gloved hands.

Was it war? He studied the faces of the border guards, searching for an indication of panic, of fear, but they looked measured and resolute. Was it a planned operation, then? A provocation?

He needed to find Lise. He pulled on a shirt and trousers and descended into the fray.

Outside, the sound of jackhammers was a relentless snarl that drowned out the fury of Berliners on both sides of the wire, shouting their ire. In the East, a mishmash of soldiers—police officers and border guards and members of the People's National

Army—stood with their backs to the west, shoulder to shoulder, as guards hammered stakes in place.

"Uli!"

He wrenched his attention away from the barbed wire to see Jurgen's stocky, sandy-haired figure. "Have you spoken to Lise?"

Uli shook his head: across the street, a scrum of people had formed around a nearby telephone box. "I only just came outside. I'm still trying to piece together... What's going on?"

"Ulbricht's sealed the border."

"Sealed it?"

"Yeah." Jurgen bit his lip, and Uli knew that he was thinking of his family, his brother and sister-in-law and niece, living in Bernau. "People kept saying he was going to do something, but I never thought..." He trailed off. "You've not seen Lise?"

"Not since Friday." Uli searched for a higher vantage point—a bench, the bonnet of a car—and gestured for Jurgen to follow him toward a rusting Mercedes, parked on the opposite side of the road. "Have you spoken to your brother?"

"I tried telephoning Karl, but they've cut the wires. I heard they've sealed off the U-Bahn and S-Bahn as well... I don't think anyone can make contact."

Uli jumped onto the bonnet of the Mercedes. What purpose did it serve to cut the telephone lines? He gave Jurgen his hand and tugged him up on top of the car: from here, they could see past the guards and jackhammers to the bewildered East Berliners beyond.

"Lise was out of town, wasn't she?" Jurgen muttered. In the empty streets beyond Bernauer Strasse, Soviet tanks rolled in and out of view in the direction of Brandenburg Gate: Where was the answering military presence from the West? He turned, hoping to see British or American troops: on a far-off corner, a pair of French soldiers watched the growing crowd but made no attempt to move closer. Surely, they had to intervene?

Uli turned back to the barbed wire and his heart lurched:

there, coming down Brunnenstrasse, was Lise. He shouted her name and waved to catch her attention: she turned and lifted her arm in response.

Uli leaped down from the car and made his way toward the wire. He muscled past men and women with Jurgen in his wake, rising onto his toes to keep Lise in his sights.

A shout rang up behind him—*"Fascists!"*—and the crowd surged forward. He stumbled, and a West Berlin police officer caught him before he hit the ground.

"Watch yourself."

Uli straightened. "My fiancée. She's in the East," he began, hearing in his voice the panic he was trying, and falling, to quell. On the opposite side of the wire, Lise was pushing forward too, her pale head visible as she tried to reason with a *Grenztruppe*. "I need to speak with her, if you could just let me through, she's right there—"

The officer's expression was pitying and fearful in equal measure. "I have my orders. No one is to approach the barrier," he said. Across the wire, a second *Grenztruppe* turned his head, listening to their conversation over his shoulder. "They're operating within East Berlin, we have no jurisdiction to intervene—"

"They're tearing the city apart!" Uli shouted, his rational mind reeling against the sheer absurdity of what was in front of him. He took another step, searching for a break in the wire. "If I could just *talk* to her—"

The officer's grip on Uli's arms was mercilessly hard. "If you want to start the next world war, keep going," he hissed, before shoving Uli back. "There's nothing I can do, mate. Take it up with Walter Ulbricht."

He stumbled into Jurgen, trembling with a rage he'd never felt: an impotence, a helplessness that he'd not experienced since he was a boy.

"Easy…this might only be temporary," Jurgen said, his hand steady on Uli's shoulder. "We ought to go to Brandenburg Gate.

We might learn more about what this is—there will be reporters, politicians—"

On the other side of the wire, he watched as Lise's own attempts to reason with a border guard failed: she stepped back, looking distraught. "If Ulbricht really is sealing the border, we need to act now. We need to find a way to get to Lise—bring her across—"

"I know."

Uli broke off midsentence, wrenching his eyes away from Lise. Jurgen stared at him, resolute, and his steadiness gave ground to Uli's panic, helped him think beyond his own fear, his own anger.

"We need to act now, but whatever we do, it can't be here," Jurgen continued. He was right: they couldn't push through, not here, where there were so many people, so many sets of eyes. "We find a break in the wire—a gap..."

"They can't be everywhere all at once," Uli said.

"Further along," Jurgen whispered back, and Uli's heart quickened. Across the wire, Lise stared at him, and he jerked his head, knowing that Lise would understand—she nodded, and melted back into the crowd.

"C'mon," he muttered, and he and Jurgen took off down the street.

5

Lise made her way toward the corner of Brunnenstrasse and Bernauer Strasse, relieved to have gotten back to Berlin but horrified to see in person what she'd hoped wasn't real: a barrier guarded by a long line of soldiers; Kalashnikovs and trucks and barbed wire, spooling out in an endless metal tangle. Driving home from the *datsche* with Papa, Lise had flipped though radio stations, listening to flint-voiced reporters describing what she was now witnessing with her own eyes: the severing of West Berlin from East Germany; the amputation of one half of the city.

"Surely, it's a temporary measure," Papa had said as Lise navigated their Trabant through the outskirts of the city. "Too many East Germans have used Berlin as a means of fleeing to the West: all they need to do is walk into Wedding or Kreuzberg and before long they're on a plane to West Germany. Ulbricht is just making a point. This will all be over before the end of the month."

Did Papa truly believe that, or was he simply trying to calm her down?

She pictured the map of Germany, already segmented into

West and East; West Berlin, an island of capitalism one hundred and sixty kilometres within East German territory. Until now, there had always been free movement throughout the city, and it was unfathomable, audacious, to think that the East German government would allow West Berlin to be so cruelly set adrift, cut off from the countryside and from East Germany itself. But still, there was some solace for those on the opposite side of the wire: West Berlin had an unbreakable connection to the Allied powers: to America, Britain and France. It had airports and radio stations, freedom of thought and freedom of movement.

West Berliners were the ones being cut off from the countryside by a wall that snaked through the city. So why did Lise feel like she was the one being imprisoned?

Perhaps Papa was right—perhaps it was only a temporary measure—but when Lise finally dropped him off and went to Bernauer Strasse on foot, the endless coils of barbed wire between the apartment blocks felt terrifyingly permanent. A small group of East Berliners had congregated near the armed guards, but the crowd on the opposite side of the wire was larger.

She stood on her toes, searching. Where was Uli?

Finally, she caught sight of him waving at the corner of Brunnenstrasse, head and shoulders above the crowd on the hood of a car with Jurgen beside him. She raised her arm in response, relief and anxiety filling her with equal measure: of course Uli was here, searching for her just as she was looking for him. But what guarantee did she have that she could get any closer to him than this?

Uli and Jurgen jumped down from the car, elbowing their way toward the wire. She followed suit, glancing at the border guards, hoping to find someone who could help her. She was a citizen of East Berlin but a student of the West, engaged to a West Berliner: surely, there would be some allowances made for someone in her situation?

She approached a border guard with the barest shadow of unshaven stubble, wishing that he was Paul or Horst: a friendly face of authority, rather than a blank slate. This, no doubt, was the reason they'd been called home from the countryside: to do their duty and help the border guards with this baffling operation. But everyone who stood before her in uniform was a stranger, standing firm with a machine gun in hand.

"Excuse me, officer." She smiled, hoping that a show of courtesy would help her cause. "I wonder if you might be able to help me. You see, my apartment is just across the street, in Wedding—"

"You're a West Berliner?" The guard looked past her shoulder, squinting into the sunlight. "You'll have to go to Bahnhof Friedrichstrasse, there's a designated crossing through the Antifascist Protection Barrier for your kind."

"No, you misunderstand." Lise dug through her handbag and pulled out her passport. "I'm East German, but I study at the Free University. My fiancé lives in West Berlin, if you turn around you can see him, just there—"

"You're a *grenzgänger*, then." The guard's measured expression congealed into a scowl. "So you're the reason we have to contend with all of this."

"Excuse me?" Lise stepped back. "Studying in West Berlin is hardly a crime."

"And I suppose living off the backs of your fellow citizens isn't a crime, either, is it? You border-crossers are all the same—you use all the advantages of our socialist system—our free health care, our cheap rents—then throw your lot in with the capitalists rather than stay here and contribute to the workers' and peasants' state..."

Lise glanced over the guard's shoulder: across the barbed wire, Uli's attempts to reason with a West Berlin police officer seemed to be going equally poorly. "What about love?" Lise tried, her sense of panic growing. "What about my fiancé? He's just on the other side of the road, if I could only speak to him—"

The guard slowly shifted his gaze down to Lise's bare hand.

"You wouldn't believe how many times I've been told that same story today, and yet no one ever seems to have an engagement ring."

Lise blinked back tears. "It's…it's at home, we…we haven't—"

The guard sighed. "You've applied for your marriage license, haven't you? You'll have to go to a border checkpoint and make your case there. But whether you'll be allowed to cross is another matter."

Lise stepped back, the enormity of the guard's words hitting her with the force of a tidal wave. She could petition the government to let her cross into the West, but without Uli's ring, what proof did she have that she was truly engaged? It had all happened so fast. *We didn't have time,* she thought, tears stinging her eyes as she watched Uli across the wire. *We didn't have time for the marriage license, for the announcement…*

"Stupid," she muttered, wiping her cheek with the back of her hand. Tomorrow, the border checkpoints would be flooded with applications to cross to the West, written by people just like her and Uli: lovers separated by a quirk of geography, or else people fabricating love stories in the hopes of getting where they wanted to go. Without documentation—without a ring—what hope did Lise have of being taken seriously?

She'd lost sight of Uli: panicked, she looked round and found him and Jurgen standing, now, on the outskirts of the West Berlin crowd. Uli stared at her and jerked his head before taking off down Bernauer Strasse with Jurgen in tow.

Lise patted her eyes dry and glanced at the border guard she'd been speaking to. Satisfied that he'd turned his attention elsewhere, she followed in the direction Uli and Jurgen had taken.

Lise strode along the sidewalk, her fingers tightening over her handbag. She didn't turn her head to look directly at Uli and Jurgen, walking a parallel path on the far side of the wire: not when there were so many guards, so many Volkspolizei and soldiers who might take an interest in her movements. Instead, she slowed her stride, letting Uli and Jurgen race ahead so she could watch them out of the corner of her eye: up ahead, a Vopo watched them, his expression impassive.

Slow down, Lise thought, mentally urging Uli and Jurgen to be less obvious in their haste. What good would it do, to draw attention to themselves? She swallowed her own urge to run, knowing that time was of the essence: with every passing hour, the barrier between East and West would grow higher and more impregnable, a prison built by the hands of its own prisoners.

For that was what the barrier was: a prison, built to keep East Germans in, locked and beholden to the state. No matter Ulbricht's attempts to dress it up as a protective measure, there was nothing "protective" about splitting Berlin in two, nor in preventing people from living the lives that they wanted.

She crossed Wolliner Strasse, fighting the urge to turn and see whether the Vopo was still watching. Here, blocks away from the busy intersection at Brunnenstrasse, the number of guards had thinned: though concertina wire still ran along the road, held in place by heavy wooden posts, it was clear that the guards were concentrating their efforts on more densely populated streets.

Half a block away, the wire took a sharp turn into an abandoned railway yard: a barren stretch of scrubby wasteland, twenty years' worth of weeds and wildflowers growing up between the cracks and crevices of rubble deposited here at the end of the war. Uli and Jurgen turned to follow the wire and Lise followed suit, recalling the countless hours she'd spent here as a child, playing with Paul in bombed-out buildings that served as the backdrop to imaginary adventures.

Even the railway yard hadn't been spared the indignity of the barrier: clearly, teams of workers had toiled through the night to clear a path through the rubble for a barbed wire fence, ugly and hastily made, strung with overlapping tendrils of sharp, glinting steel.

To Lise's right, the rubble rose in a short, steep hill, which shielded her from view of Prenzlauer Berg beyond. She glanced behind her, relieved to find herself alone: the border guards, it seemed, were more concerned with fortifying Bernauer Strasse than with keeping an eye on the rail yard. Ahead, Uli and Jurgen had begun to attack the wire, pushing hard in an attempt to make a hole big enough for Lise to slip through.

She broke into a run, her handbag swinging at her side as she caught up to them. She thought with regret of Papa and Paul, leaving them without a word, but she knew that Papa, at least, would understand: hers was a decision that had to be made now, in this split second before her chance was gone.

"Uli, I—"

"I know." Uli stared at her, his chest heaving with exertion as Jurgen forced down a line of wire. The wire was strung four and five layers thick, and as Lise plunged her hands in to help, it felt as though each quivering strand conspired with the next, snapping mercilessly tight as they fought to loosen it. Jurgen grasped the nearest post with two hands and Uli got to his feet to try and help him dislodge it.

"It's not budging!"

"It's buried too deep—"

From behind Lise, a shot rang out and Uli looked up, his gray eyes wide.

"Hurry!"

Uli and Jurgen abandoned their efforts with the post and dropped to their knees, trying once again to ease a hole in the wire. Lise cursed as the barbs scraped her bare arms bloody, wishing she had a knife, a set of pliers—anything to help snap the wire loose. She could hear the sound of footsteps behind her, people shouting as they raced down the slope.

Finally, the wire began to give way. Straight-armed, Jurgen pushed down on the bottommost wire with all his strength, and Uli lifted the one above it, then held out his free hand.

Lise took it, and the adrenaline pumping through her veins was enough to block out the searing pain of the barbs as she ducked under the wire. All she could feel was Uli's hand in hers, and images flickered through her head—she saw herself standing with Uli at a registry office, exchanging vows; holding a baby in her arms; graduating from medical school—

Rough hands grasped her from behind. She tightened her grip on Uli's hand, but Uli, his other arm trembling from the strain of holding up the wire, had only so much strength to give: if he and Jurgen lost their hold on the wire they would bring it snapping down on Lise's head.

She screamed as her grip began to falter. *"No!"*

She lost hold of Uli's hand and was pulled back through the wire, into the arms of a burly pair of Vopos; behind them, a soldier stood with his Kalashnikov raised, pointed at Uli and Jurgen.

"Lise!" Uli's face and shoulders streamed with blood as he struggled to reach her, but Lise knew that they'd lost: that Uli would tear himself to pieces on the wire if he continued to fight. She could hardly see him through her tears, but she watched as Jurgen pulled Uli back, their figures shrinking as the officers carried her off.

30 AUGUST, 1961

To the office of Konrad Adenauer, Chancellor of West Germany:

I write to you as a citizen of East Germany, but as a student of West Berlin. My name is Lise Bauer, and I live at 56 Rheinsberger Strasse in Mitte. I am engaged to Ulrich Neumann, a West German citizen living in Wedding, and we have been separated by the East German Antifascist Protection Border. Before the border closure, I studied medicine at the Free University, and had made plans with my fiancé to move to West Berlin at our earliest possible convenience. I write to you in the hopes that your office can grant me a West German visa so that I might continue my studies and marry the man I love.

Chancellor Adenauer, we might live in two separate countries, but we are all of us Germans. I hope that your administration can come to an arrangement with East Germany to allow for free movement between our two countries once again.

With appreciation,
Lise Bauer

UNDELIVERED: Intercepted by the East German Ministry for State Security on 31 August 1961

6

SEPTEMBER 1961

The postcard had been slid through the letterbox a week ago and Uli had carried it in his breast pocket like a talisman every day since. On the front, it portrayed a photograph of East Germany's Elbe Sandstone Mountains—a craggy, alien outcropping of uneven pillars which Lise had chosen, Uli knew, because of his love of all things geological, as beautiful as it was baffling. The edges of the postcard had grown frayed from constant perusal and he flipped it over, tracing his fingers along the short message, which had been overlaid with a heavy stamp that marked the postcard as having been read and cleared by the East German postal system.

I'm safe. I love you.

He looked at the date Lise had written at the top of the card. She'd sent it three days after the border closure: three days after she'd been hauled away by the Volkspolizei, carried over the rail yard rubble and out of sight.

He studied Lise's scant script, picturing the hands that had written it: her short, unvarnished nails and long thumbs; her crooked middle finger, the topmost knuckle tilted from years of holding pens and pencils too tightly. After so many days of carrying it, the postcard had lost the faded fragrance of her perfume, and he wished he knew the name of the scent he associated with no one but her.

How many times had he looked at the postcard? He was desperate for news of her, desperate to know more: was she safe, still? But Uli knew that the postcard was more than he could have hoped for: had Lise been more verbose, Uli doubted it would have passed the East German censors.

He stepped out onto Bernauer Strasse and glanced at the empty road. The barbed wire had been cleared days ago to make way for heavy concrete panels, set down and cemented in place between the East German apartment buildings that faced onto Bernauer Strasse: the border guards, it seemed, had decided to use the buildings themselves to create the barrier, their doors and lowermost windows bricked over as the buildings' upper-floor inhabitants, doubtless watched closely by border guards stalking the halls, looked out at West Berlin.

At least Uli had his own view into the East from the window of his apartment. From there, he could see past the parkette opposite his flat into Lise's window, and he'd made a habit of leaving the light on when he was home in the hopes that she might see it, and know he was thinking of her.

He tucked the postcard back into his pocket: back where it belonged, close to his heart. He missed Lise so much that the ache felt physical, and even as the deep barbed wire cuts on his chest and arms healed painfully he knew he would have endured them a thousand times over if it had meant Lise's safe arrival in the West.

In the days that had followed the border closure he and Jurgen had attended fiery rallies with West Berlin's mayor, Willy Brandt, who took to the microphone and implored Ulbricht to see sense; he'd cheered on the American vice president, Lyndon

B. Johnson, who'd railed against the GDR's actions near Brandenburg Gate. Buoyed by messages of hope, he'd stood in long lines outside police stations and government offices, pleading with officials to help him bring Lise across the wire. But despite his stubborn efforts—and the outrage of the Western world—there was little to be done: the GDR was its own independent nation and could do as it wished, even if it was to the detriment of its own citizens.

He snugged his book bag over his shoulder and carried on down Bernauer Strasse: though the world had changed his studies hadn't, although the Free University's campus, now devoid of a significant portion of its student body, felt deserted. He passed a small crowd of people, nodding a greeting as he went: groups had taken to gathering outside the boarded-up apartments on the opposite side of the street as if they were attending a vigil, passing out petitions which Uli duly signed, privately suspecting they would make little difference.

He glanced up at the building and met the distant gaze of an East German sentry standing on the roof, his hand casually resting atop his machine gun as he patrolled back and forth. Uli paused, staring daggers at the sentry until he stepped back, disappearing out of sight beyond the building's eaves.

Good, he thought. *Let him be ashamed for the part he's playing in all this.*

A flicker of movement two stories down caught his eye and Uli froze, watching as a double-hung window on the fourth floor slid open to reveal a middle-aged man who poked his head out to study the cobbles below.

There was a flurry of silent movement from the assembled onlookers as they shifted down the road toward the building, their faces craned up as they whispered encouragement.

"Jump!"

Uli joined them, watching as the man disappeared back into

the apartment momentarily before reappearing with a duffel bag in hand.

"It's too high," Uli whispered to no one in particular as a woman raced toward them with a wool blanket in hand. "He'll break his neck."

But the woman pushed a corner of the blanket into Uli's hand and he helped the onlookers stretch the blanket out to break the man's fall.

"Jump! Now's your chance, *jump*!"

The man seemed to hesitate before throwing down the duffel bag, and Uli's heart raced as he watched him edge out onto the windowsill. He thought with dread of the sentry, only three floors away: surely, there were more guards in the building? But maybe they didn't think anyone was mad enough—desperate enough—to leap from forty-five feet in the air.

"Jump!"

The man swung his legs out the window, then paused. He looked as if he was losing his nerve, and Uli couldn't blame him. From his vantage point, the blanket they were holding to catch him would look little bigger than a postage stamp. What guarantee did he have that he would land in the safety of the blanket—or that the blanket would even hold his weight?

"Jump!"

Suddenly the man twisted violently, and from the open window Uli could hear the sound of raised voices: border guards, bursting into the apartment. He'd run out of time, and Uli joined the chorus of West Berliners urging him to take the leap.

But the man's nerves failed him: he slid down the window frame, no doubt trying to lessen the drop, until he was hanging from the sill by his fingertips. Uli and the rest of the onlookers shuffled the blanket forward, eyeballing the best place to stand so they could catch him, but the sentries were now at the window, and the man let go of the sill a moment too late:

in the split second after he released his hold, a sentry leaned out the window and grabbed his wrist.

He hung, legs dangling, and the sentry struggled to keep him from falling before a second sentry stuck his head out the window, grappling for the man's other hand.

Uli held his breath, watching as the man fought against his captors midair. *He could still fall*, he thought wildly, and for a brief instant he saw Lise there, kicking against the bricks in an attempt to free herself—but then the second sentry leaned out of the window far enough to grip the man's upper arm, straining against the weight of his quarry.

Slowly, shouting, the man was pulled back through the window and out of sight.

27 SEPTEMBER, 1961

Lise,

I don't know whether this note will find you but I received your postcard so I suppose I can hope.

Things aren't the same without you here—an understatement, I know, but it's true all the same. I'm doing everything I can to find answers for us: a loophole, maybe, or some exception that might apply to us as an engaged couple. So far I've not had much success but I'm not going to give up.

Until then, stay safe, and be patient. So long as we're patient, we'll find a way.

All my love,
Uli

UNDELIVERED: Intercepted by the East German Ministry for State Security on 29 September, 1961

7

OCTOBER 1961

Lise stared down at the letter she'd received from the State Secretariat for Higher Education, her brain a dull roar of thoughts.

Your application to transfer your studies in medicine to Humboldt University of Berlin has been denied, she read, staring hard at the words as though she might change their meaning. The letter was blunt and to the point, and provided no explanation for the devastating decision, but Lise was well aware of why she'd been denied entry: as a Western-educated student and grenzgänger—a border-crosser—she posed a risk to the ideological purity of the young minds on Humboldt University's campus: a dissident, whose stories of Western excess could contaminate the body politic and create rot from within.

Perhaps, in light of her chosen field of study, the university might have been persuaded to overlook her Western education—if it hadn't been for her recent detention by the East German police after her attempt to reach Uli in the rail yard.

She crumpled the letter and stood. From the kitchen, she could hear the steady drip of the faucet—a rhythmic, incessant tapping that had been a background noise in her life for years—punctuated by the occasional sound of a cough, a utensil scraping against cast iron as Papa sorted out dinner.

She'd long grown used to ignoring the peculiarities of the small apartment: the damp spot on the bathroom ceiling and the kitchen's leaky faucet; the hum of neighbors' voices through the paper-thin walls. Today, however, the sound was enough to set her teeth on edge and she crossed to the living room's front window, wishing she could drown it all out.

Outside, the impossibly sunny day had deepened into the rich, golden glow of an unseen sunset, and she watched the far-off square of Uli's apartment window for signs of movement: the flick of a curtain; the quick illumination of a lamp. These days, watching at the window for glimpses of her fiancé had become her sole source of hope, but today the apartment window was dark.

Was he at the university? At his parents' house? Drowning his sorrows at Siggi's with their friends?

She shifted her gaze down to Bernauer Strasse, where workers continued their steady fortification of the barrier. In the past few weeks, the barbed wire fence had disappeared, replaced by hulking concrete blocks: heavy panels topped with barbed wire fenceposts which arced out on either side in the shape of a Y. Watched over by border guards, white-clad workers bricked up the uppermost windows in the apartment buildings that directly faced Bernauer Strasse—the better to discourage, Lise knew, those desperate few prepared to jump to freedom. But that path, like so many others, was quickly disappearing: people who lived in the apartments directly on the border were being rehoused, forced to different enclaves of the city. Heavy iron grates had been placed throughout the sewer system and police boats patrolled the River Spree, all to dash the hopes of those longing to reach the West.

Lise would have been among their number, jumping from

apartment windows or swimming across the Spree, if she'd not spent the first 72 hours of the border closure in a police station.

Six weeks on, it felt as though the initial panic of the border closure had abated: East Berliners, it seemed, had resigned themselves to their new reality. People went about their days, taking circuitous routes to avoid straying too close to the Wall, as some had started to call it: to avoid any paths which might put them in the crosshairs of suspicious border guards, or worse, bring them to the attention of East Germany's terrifying secret police.

The lack of official discussion about the border closure unnerved Lise. In the past several weeks, she'd tried to find out who might be able to grant her an emigration visa, but her efforts had turned up nothing but more questions: she'd gone to the library and the local prefecture, but hadn't received a straight answer from anyone. In desperation, she'd even dropped a letter in the postbox addressed to the West German chancellor, hoping to stir his sympathies—but had the letter even reached his desk?

She could feel the days slipping through her fingers: lost time with Uli, lost time for her studies. Her application to Humboldt University had been a last resort in her efforts not to fall behind in her classes, but she knew now that she would have to retake her semester once she returned to the Free University.

If she returned to the Free University.

She crossed her arms, fingers tracing along the healing scars left by her ordeal as she looked back at Uli's apartment.

If only he would come to the window.

If only she'd had the courage to plunge through the barbed wire when she had the chance.

If only she'd accepted Uli's ring when he'd offered it, run without hesitation to a registry office and presented their marriage as a *fait accompli.*

She let her hand drift to her stomach, counting each one of the forty-two days since she'd last seen Uli: forty-two days of heartbreak and anguish.

Forty-two days of waiting for her period which, she knew, wasn't coming.

"You look so serious, standing there."

Lise turned, hastily drying her eyes as Papa entered the room. He wheeled past the dining table, glancing briefly at the mess of papers she'd left strewn across the table runner, and she felt the corners of her mouth lift in response to his gentle smile. These past several weeks had been awful, but at least there was some consolation in knowing that she still had Paul and Papa to rely on as she adjusted to the new reality that they seemed to have accepted with ease.

She pictured life on the other side of Bernauer Strasse: living with Uli, staring down at that same border, missing Papa and Paul as badly as she was missing Uli now. Would she be just as miserable if she'd made it across?

"Dinner's nearly ready." Papa rested a hand on Lise's arm and followed her gaze out beyond the barbed wire. "Your brother will be home soon. The boiler's playing up again so I'm afraid he's in for a cold shower when he arrives—the sooner our petition for a new apartment is granted, the better." He gave Lise's forearm a reassuring squeeze. "Would you help me set the table?"

She crossed to the kitchen and pulled out a handful of cutlery, grateful for Papa's quiet, tacit support; that, despite her tears, he'd chosen not to pry. It had always been Papa's way. Whereas his surgeon friends let professional bluster and bravado bleed into their dealings with friends and relations, Papa's compassionate manner put people at ease: a skill that he'd found useful both as a surgeon and as a professor. But much as she longed to retreat into the silence that her father was offering her, she knew that some conversations were better brought out into the open.

Papa, clearing up Lise's papers, held up the crumpled remains of the letter from the State Secretariat with an inquiring look. "May I?"

She nodded, her throat too tight to respond as she watched

Papa's face crease with disappointment as he read it. "Oh, my dear." He held out his arms and Lise collapsed into his embrace, sobbing. "My darling. I'm so sorry."

She took a breath and spoke into the rough linen of his shirt. "I thought, perhaps, given your position at the university..."

"If we lived in the West, maybe my position would have helped you." He sighed. Though Papa was a well-regarded academic, most university places in East Germany were given to students with proper proletarian credentials—not to children of the intelligentsia. "But there are so many considerations, I suppose, for the university to take into account."

"That's not all." She drew back. "Uli and me, we—when we got engaged..." She trailed off, unable to look Papa in the eye. "I'm—I'm expecting."

Papa pulled Lise back into his arms, resting his chin on the top of her head. "We'll find a way through this, somehow," he said. "We always do."

Lise stared up at the ceiling, too restless to sleep. She'd told Paul about her pregnancy at dinner, and though she suspected that the news wasn't particularly welcome to either one of her family members, they'd both taken it with good grace.

Still, there was little joy in the thought of having a baby without its father to share in the experience of parenthood: still less, knowing that her life as a mother would now be defined by her inability to pursue her chosen profession. Much as the thought of leaving her family pained her, there was no doubt in her mind that her future lay in West Berlin—West Berlin, West Germany, or beyond, with Uli by her side.

Surely, she'd not yet exhausted all her options in finding a way across the border?

She kicked herself free from her bedsheets and crossed to her desk to pull out a pad of paper and a pen, tucking the crumpled letter from the State Secretariat beneath a blank sheet. She'd heard of people petitioning the East German government for emigration visas, although she wasn't sure exactly which ministry to petition. If she pleaded her case properly, surely, they'd have to listen?

She stepped into the living room and turned on the light, surprised to find Paul sitting in the darkness with a glass in hand.

He looked up at Lise's approach. "Couldn't sleep, either?" He tilted the glass to his lips, the ice clinking gently with the movement. "I would offer you vodka, but given your condition..."

She lowered herself into the chair opposite. "I suppose you're furious with me," she said as Paul studied the clear contents of his glass. "Although if it's any consolation, technically I was engaged at the time."

"You think I care about some petit bourgeois notion of whether he compromised your virtue?" He planted his elbows on his knees with a smirk. "Give me a little more credit than that. You're a modern woman, and you know your own mind. Although I would be lying if I said you've chosen an easy path."

Lise tucked her feet beneath her, relieved to have overestimated Paul's disapproval. "It would be easier if I had my husband with me," she replied, smoothing her hand over the pad of paper in her lap. "Tell me honestly, Paul. Is there really no way to get to West Berlin?"

"No." Paul stood and crossed to straighten the lampshade that Lise had set askew when she'd turned it on, his blond hair glinting in the lamplight. "This—this border measure. I know how difficult it is, but you must know that it's for our own good."

"For our own good..." Lise couldn't help allowing a note of sarcasm to slip into her voice. "Because we can't be trusted to stay."

"Lise." Paul's answering tone was firm. "I may not be a border guard, but I've worked closely enough with them over the years to see what we're up against. The Westerners were taking advantage of us. They would come across to our side of the city with their Western money, devaluing our currency, depleting our stores of the food and supplies we need for our own citizens. Luring our labor force away from the factories…" He trailed off, looking genuinely troubled, and Lise knew where his lecture was going: any moment now, he would start talking about *the means of production.* "Don't make the mistake of thinking we're overreacting to a few cases of smuggling. That border is the first line of defence against Western aggression. Human trafficking, espionage… I've seen it all. But you don't, because my comrades in the police force and the People's Army do their jobs well."

He might have had a point, if it wasn't for the letter in Lise's hand.

"And I'm supposed to just—just give it all up? Give up my husband, give up my education, my career, for the good of—of what, the state?"

He didn't answer.

Disappointed, she held up the notepad. "I thought if I could send a petition to the People's Council, explain why I ought to qualify for an exit visa—"

Paul sighed. Illuminated from behind by the lamp, his face was in shadows, but Lise could tell that he felt hers was a question better left unasked. "Lise, please don't make a mistake you can't take back."

"Why would it be a mistake?" Lise looked up, letting the frustration of the day out in a hiss. "Because I'm such an asset to East Germany? They won't let me study medicine, Paul. I can't be a doctor—everything I've worked toward, all my education—worthless. But don't worry—" she waved the rejection letter at him bitterly, not caring that she was speaking loud enough to wake Papa "—the dressmaker in Mitte is in need of an assistant."

"And would that be so terrible?" Paul shot back. "It's skilled work. Be grateful for it. You could have been assigned to work a production line in some factory." He paused. "You're to be a mother, Lise. How did you expect to keep up with a postgraduate course load with a baby to take care of?"

"The same way every other working mother does." She shook her head, incredulous. Was he really so obtuse? "Mitte can find another seamstress. I can't find another husband."

"But he's not your husband, though, is he?"

Lise's incredulity fused into a bright, burning fury. "That's not fair."

She stared at Paul, daring him to respond, but he remained silent, and finally, she slammed her pad of paper down on the coffee table. Paul wasn't going to help, and it was clear that he wasn't intending to leave, but Lise pushed his bottle of vodka out of the way and began to write her petition, hardly registering her words as she transferred them to the page.

She heard, rather than saw, Paul return to the couch, his footsteps heavy on the creaking floor.

"I'm sorry." He dropped back onto the couch and refilled his glass. "Truly, Lise, I am. But you must know that whatever you do…it won't make a difference." He leaned forward to address her without meeting her eyes. "This—this notion of writing a petition, it won't do anything to further your case. All you would be doing is making life more difficult for yourself. And the more you push, the more you risk for all of us."

Her pen stilled on the page.

"You've already jeopardized your future once by trying to run. What about Papa's future? What about mine? Do you think Papa's petition for a new apartment will be granted if his daughter is branded a dissident?" The heat had drained from Paul's tone, leaving his words unbearably matter-of-fact. "You recall that promotion Horst received last week? Why do you think I didn't get it?"

"I'm so sorry," Lise replied bitterly. "Poor Paul, passed up for a promotion."

Paul let the insult stand as he drained the last of his drink. "I will always be here for you," he said. "And I intend to take care of you—you and the baby both. Papa and me, we'll do everything we can to support you...and, for what it's worth, to make sure that you're happy." He tilted his chin to look at Lise directly, and she could see her own petulance, her own childishness reflected in his eyes. "But you have to understand that your actions put us at risk, too."

Lise's fingers twitched on her pen. "What if I don't care? What if I try to leave anyways?"

"Then you should know the border guards have been given clear orders. They shoot to kill."

He stood, the sound of the ticking clock growing louder in the wake of his words.

"You're going to be a mother, Lise. Don't make stupid choices." He leaned over and kissed the top of her head, his fingers tight on her shoulder. "Not now that yours isn't the only life at stake."

8

A fog of cigarette smoke hung over Siggi's bar, clouding the faces of the ancient regulars who held forth loudly by the jukebox.

Wedged across the table in the vinyl booth, Jurgen and Wolf raised their steins, and Uli responded in kind, tapping his glass against theirs with a belated smile. These days, their booth felt cavernously empty, without Lise tucked beside him; without their classmate Axel, stranded in the East Berlin neighborhood of Treptow, pulling up a stool opposite.

He looked up as Inge slid into Lise's empty seat, pushing back a curtain of ice-blond hair as she shrugged out of her overcoat. "Any news?"

Uli took another sip of his beer and shook his head. He'd not heard from Lise since that first postcard, and he doubted she'd received his letter in response.

"Scheisse," Inge muttered, as Wolf lifted a lanky arm to signal for another round of drinks. "You know I'd be happy to cross the border to see her. It's only you Wessis they're trying

to keep out. I could take a letter for her, or some keepsake—her engagement ring—"

Uli forced a smile. "I appreciate the offer." It was true that Swedish passport holders could still cross the border into East Germany—the border closure was a measure specifically directed at East and West Berliners—but secondhand news from Inge felt like a poor substitute to seeing Lise in person; to having her here where she belonged, amongst her friends, in his arms.

Inge squeezed his arm, her lips pursed in sympathy. "If there's anything I can do," she said, before turning her attention to Jurgen. "How about your family, Jurgi?"

Jurgen shrugged, looking as miserable as Uli felt. "Not since they made it illegal to wave across the Wall," he replied. "It was Willa's third birthday yesterday. We were supposed to be all together to—to celebrate..." He broke off, his face flushed. "It's bullshit."

Uli let out a breath as Wolf swung a bracing arm around Jurgen's shoulders. He shared in Jurgen's frustration: he felt it every day, each time he stood at the window to watch Lise in her apartment, so close and so desperately far away. Much as he missed Lise, he couldn't imagine the pain of being cut off from an entire branch of his family.

But Jurgen had Wolf—that, at least, was something.

Agatha arrived with a fresh round of beers and Inge lifted her glass. "To Willa," she said solemnly, and Jurgen managed a smile. "Happy birthday."

They clinked their glasses.

"It isn't right." Inge set down her beer and planted her elbows on the table. "We live in a modern world, a modern democracy... Surely, there's something we can do."

"What do you suggest?" Uli replied. "Petition writing? Protests? We've tried, Inge, and they all amount to nothing. East Germany is a Soviet satellite state, they don't respond to—to international finger wagging."

Jurgen pulled a newspaper from his jacket pocket and set it on the counter, jabbing at an article on the front page: *Nine Escape GDR*. "We do this," he said, lowering his voice. "A group managed to get across at Zehlendorf—nine people. They drove a truck straight through the border crossing." He nodded, his shoulders rounded as he let the sound of other drinkers mask his words. "They totaled the truck, but they all made it across. Not a single fatality. We could do that."

Uli's heart sank as he considered the sheer practicalities involved with such a plan. How many times had he been startled awake in the middle of the night by the sound of gunshots echoing over the Wall?

"We can't," he concluded. "It's too risky."

"We've talked about this," Wolf added, the note of exasperation in his voice indicating that Jurgen had raised this idea more than once. "It would be suicide to attempt something like that, especially when it's exactly what the border guards expect people to do. And with Willa to consider..." He shook his head. "We can't put your niece in that kind of danger, Jurgi."

"Then what do you suggest?" Jurgen shot back. "I'm sick of sitting here talking when we could be doing something. We could rent a truck, drive it across—"

"With whose license?" Wolf replied hotly. "They won't let West Berliners across the border."

"We forge passports," Jurgen replied, and Wolf scoffed aloud.

"Of course. With that impeccable skill for forgery you've been honing all these years."

"Wolf's right," Inge interjected. "We hear about the successes, but what of the failures? How many people have died trying to cross? How many arrested? These escapes are all PR coups for the West, but we all know they're only telling us what we want to hear. If they truly cared about the safety of East Germans, they wouldn't sit back and let people put themselves in danger.

They would be working toward systemic change, forcing the UN to act—"

"And it *isn't working.*" Jurgen tapped the newspaper again with the blunt tip of his finger. "Individual action—that's what will change things. People taking their fate into their own hands."

"And what happens to those people when the Stasi catches up to them?" Wolf shot back. "When they discover the—the car with the reinforced bumpers, or the forged passports, or the luggage packed and ready to go at the front door—"

Uli let their bickered conversation fade into the background as he pictured Lise, white-knuckled behind the wheel of a car careening at full speed toward the concrete barrier; Lise, dangling from a window over Bernauer Strasse. The thought of her risking her life to cross to West Berlin was enough to make Uli ill. She was athletic enough, he knew, to make it across if everything went according to plan—but for every success there were ten failures. How could Uli live with himself if it all went wrong?

"There must be some way we can bring people across the border without putting them at risk," Uli said. He looked up and Jurgen paused, his eyebrows raised as he listened. "The biggest risk is detection, is it not? What if there's some way for us to do all the work—to find a route, or create one, without even letting people in the East know it's happening until the last minute? A—a secret path, a trail—"

Wolf let out a heavy sigh, and squeezed his eyes shut. "And how do you suggest we do that? The sewers?"

Uli shook his head, the plan revealing itself to him step by step, even as he spoke. "The sewers have been blocked," he replied slowly, "and the Spree is too dangerous..."

Jurgen looked up. "A tunnel?"

Uli smiled. "A tunnel," he replied, meeting Jurgen's gaze with sudden conviction.

"Insanity." Wolf set down his drink and leaned back against

the banquette. "A tunnel would take months to dig, maybe years."

"But it would be the safest option," Jurgen pointed out. "We could bring entire groups through. Children, the elderly..."

"That's supposing the entire thing doesn't come collapsing down on us." Wolf shook his head. "It would have to be enormous. Hundreds of metres long."

"Not if we dig in the right place." Uli looked up, his heart beating fast at the sudden satisfaction of feeling a plan fall into place: of having something to do, rather than sitting in miserable impatience. "Jurgen and I are both engineers, we know enough to keep the tunnel from collapsing."

"That is, if we dig somewhere with the right soil composition," Jurgen added, excitement dawning on his freckled face. "And Inge—you can travel to East Germany, you can make contact with my family—with Lise and Axel, with everyone we want to get out."

Inge drained the last of her pint. "Naturally," she said, and Uli felt a rush of affection for Lise's stalwart friend.

Wolf shook his head, but it was clear that he felt himself outnumbered. "I still think it's a real risk," he said. "And we'll have to find somewhere to—to dig this monstrosity. While keeping on top of our studies, I might add..."

"Of course it's a risk," Inge replied. "But what they're doing is an injustice. And if we sit here and do nothing, we'll never forgive ourselves."

Wolf let out a breath and raised his glass to his lips. "Well, then," he said, and Uli's smile came easier than it had done since August. "We'd better get started."

22 OCTOBER, 1961

Uli,

I can't believe I don't get to tell you this news in person, nor see your face when you hear it. Will you be happy, to receive this letter? Or will you be as scared as I am?

I'm pregnant. It's not how we imagined it to be, but it's how it is. I'm not sure why it's come as such a shock to me. It feels as though our engagement—our entire life together—took place in a dream, but upon waking there's still this undeniable proof of our commitment to each other. More real than the promises we made to each other. More substantial than the ring I wish I still had on my finger.

Papa and Paul are wonderfully supportive about it all, but they're no substitute for you. Papa's arranged for me to have an interview for a position with a dressmaker—I think he feels it would be better for me than sitting alone with my thoughts. And all my thoughts are of you, Uli.

With each passing day it feels as though the life we planned together slips further and further from my grasp, but knowing that I have this piece of you—this life we made together—keeps you close.

All my love,
Lise

UNDELIVERED: Intercepted by the East German Ministry for State Security on 23 October, 1961

9

Die Nadel und der Faden—The Needle and Thread—was a dressmaker's shop located on the first floor of an ancient apartment building on Oderberger Strasse, tucked between a busy café and a municipal swimming pool. Low ceilinged and dark, it was dominated by a large cutting table surrounded by tall bolts of fabric, illuminated by a sliver of light falling through the narrow front window: durable, heavy polyesters; gauzy ersatz linens and thick polyvinyls, standing like four-foot soldiers ready to be pressed into service.

Across the table Gerda Hespeler lowered her reading glasses and looked up from Lise's résumé with bright eyes. "Well," she said, fitting the ear of her spectacles in the corner of her mouth, "Perhaps you'll do. Do you have any training?"

Lise clasped her hands in her lap. "No, but I'm a quick study."

"I believe it. Medical school isn't for the faint of heart." Gerda's gaze flickered to Lise's midsection. "But I suppose with a baby on the way..."

"I want to earn rather than study." The lie stuck in Lise's

throat, but it was better than admitting to being a dissident—better than being forced to accept a job in a textile factory, like so many other *grenzgängers* now looking for employment. "The baby's father is—he's unavoidably detained."

Understanding dawned in Gerda's eyes. "Children are a blessing, dear, no matter how they come into the world."

Lise took a shaky breath, overwhelmed by Gerda's tactful kindness. She had few memories of her mother, but she hoped that she had been like this: stern and compassionate. Lise cleared her throat, determined to steer the interview back into more professional waters.

Gerda was an older woman, sturdily built with a fashionable jacket that, Lise suspected, had been copied from a couturier in Paris. "I—I recognize the cut of that gilet," Lise offered, recalling conversations with her stylish friend Inge. "Givenchy, no?"

"It's my own design," Gerda replied, snugging down on the jacket's hem, "but yes, it's inspired by Givenchy. I applied for a visa to go to Paris four years ago to view the spring collections—Givenchy and Dior, Balmain and Balenciaga. I'd not been to Paris in…oh, not since I was a girl. To see the city in all its glory…" She smiled, roses filling her cheeks, and Lise could see a glimpse of the young woman she'd been—but then Gerda snugged her reading glasses back on her nose. "But of course, now we have all the inspiration we need here in East Germany."

She paused meaningfully, and Lise nodded. "Oh—of course," she replied, jarred by Gerda's swift shift in tone. "I always consult the pages of *Sibylle* to know what's in style."

"As do so many of my clients." Gerda slid a magazine across the table, its front cover showing a glossy image of a woman dressed in a blue jacket and shawl. "They bring me the patterns from the magazine and I use them as inspiration to create one of a kind pieces." She smiled. "We might all share in the common goal of building of our workers' and peasants' state, but no woman wants to go to the State Opera and see someone else wearing the same dress."

Lise took the magazine and flipped through the pages. *Sibylle* was the most widely read women's magazine in East Berlin: the arbiter of taste for anyone who wanted to wear clothes beyond those offered at state-run stores. She paused at a picture of two women dressed in smart skirt sets, with rounded collars and cloche hats. "I particularly like these ones."

Gerda arched an eyebrow. "Do you? What would you do differently with them?"

She bent over the picture to scrutinize the outfits closer. "Perhaps I would switch out the Peter Pan collar for something a little sharper...and I'd alter the length of the skirt so that it hits at the knee, rather than mid-calf."

"Depending, of course, on the shape of the woman. I tailor the dress to the client, Fräulein Bauer. Despite what the German Fashion Institute might lead one to believe, not every woman is slender." Gerda set aside her glasses, and Lise felt as if she'd passed some kind of test. "Well, my dear, your father did me a good turn during the war years, so I suppose I'll give you a chance. But I'll expect hard work, you understand? You can start at eight o'clock tomorrow morning."

"I'm not afraid of hard work. Thank you, Frau Hespeler."

Lise left the shop, feeling disappointed and relieved in equal measure. She'd gotten a job, yes, but it felt like she'd capitulated, in a very real way, to the limitations placed upon her. It felt like a betrayal of Uli, too, but after her late-night conversation with Paul she'd recognized that she had little choice but to abandon her petition to move to the West: not when her actions reflected directly on her father and brother; not with a baby on the way. But as hard as it was to start building a life for herself in East Berlin, it seemed that her surrender was already bearing fruit: just yesterday, Papa had received a letter from the Ministry of Housing granting his petition for a new apartment.

She turned at the corner, thinking of the new apartment, in a gleaming white building just off Stalinallee, white-tiled and tiered like a wedding cake. It was an undeniable improvement from their current prewar flat: the wider hallways would be easier for Papa to navigate in his wheelchair. But the new apartment had one distinct disadvantage: it was a forty-minute walk from Bernauer Strasse, far from Lise's perch where she could see Uli at a distance. How would she stand it?

At least the job would give her some distraction from her worries. Gerda seemed an all right sort—smart and disciplined, with a clear passion for her work. She thought back to Gerda's expression as she talked about the French designers from whom she'd drawn inspiration. Would she be willing to tell Lise more about her time in Paris?

Lise knew better than to ask—not when such questions could be interpreted as enthusiasm for Western culture.

She knew she was lucky not to have been assigned work on some factory floor: in a textile manufacturing facility or a food processing plant, where talk about the West was strictly forbidden. She'd heard that such places had eavesdropping foremen, tasked with monitoring their workers for antisocial sentiments: that the wrong comment, made at the wrong time, might result in a visit from the secret police. Was Gerda the sort to pass on confidences to the Stasi? Or would she and Lise develop, in time, a genuine friendship?

She turned down Schwedter Strasse, lost in her thoughts, when someone across the street whistled. She looked up, nearly stumbling across the curb at the sight of a familiar flash of platinum hair.

Inge crossed the street, tucking her hands in the pocket of her tweed overcoat as she fell into step with Lise. "Did you miss me?"

"*Miss* you?" Lise sputtered. At a café patio across the street, a man twitched down his newspaper to watch as Inge pulled Lise into a hug. "What are you doing here? How did you manage—?"

"I'm Swedish. I can get a day pass," Inge replied. "I was waiting for you on Rheinsberger Strasse, but I popped over here for a sandwich...what timing! Where were you?"

"Never mind all that. How are you?" Lise glanced once more at the man with the newspaper, who was still watching them, and she chivied Inge down the street. "How's...how's school? Your classes? I can't tell you how much I miss them—"

"School?" Inge smirked. "*School* is just fine. Your *classes* are missing you just as much as you're missing them."

Lise could feel the smile stretch across her face and she didn't fight it: how could she, when Inge was nearly as wonderful a surprise as Uli himself? "I didn't—I don't want you to think I only care about—"

"What do you take me for? It's only natural for you to ask." Inge slipped her hand into the crook of Lise's elbow as they carried on. "He's missing you, of course. Desperately."

A knot formed in Lise's throat and she allowed Inge's grip to steady her as a wave of anguish surged and subsided. "If only there was a way—"

"There is." Inge spoke without looking at Lise directly, allowing the sound of passing traffic to cover her words. "We're digging a tunnel, Lise. To get you out."

Lise could feel her knees turn to water, but she willed herself to keep walking. "Is it safe?"

"Uli's digging it. What do you think?" Inge replied dryly. "Between Uli and Wolf and Jurgen, we've enough engineers among our number to make it as safe any other route across the Wall. Safer than climbing it, certainly."

Lise blinked back tears, feeling the knot in her throat loosen. She knew that Uli would never have forgotten about her, but she felt absurdly relieved at this concrete proof that he was still fighting for her: that he'd not seen their situation as hopeless.

But what did it say about her that she'd resigned herself to her fate so quickly?

"We're looking for the right entry point from the West," Inge was saying, "and an egress point in the East. Somewhere with the right soil composition, where we can avoid water mains and sewer lines…"

"The less I know about it, the better." Lise squinted up at the apartment blocks on either side of the road, feeling invisible eyes upon her: was it her imagination, or had a curtain in an upper window just twitched shut? "But you ought to know… Uli needs to know. I'm pregnant."

Inge paused, her rosebud mouth dropping open into a perfect O. Impulsively, she leaned in and gave Lise a swift kiss on either cheek. "Congratulations."

"It's less than ideal, I know—"

"We'll make it work." Inge squeezed Lise's hands in her own. "I'm so pleased for you both. Really, I am. It—it complicates things, but truly, Lise. I couldn't be happier."

Lise wished she could share in Inge's happiness. "I'm two months along," she said slowly, "and I think I ought to come through while I'm pregnant."

"I agree."

Inge squeezed Lise's hands again, and Lise could see the wheels turning in her mind.

"Do you think the tunnel could be completed in time?"

Inge hesitated. "It might not be particularly comfortable, but yes. You ought to come through before your third trimester."

Though neither of them said it aloud, Lise knew that they were thinking the same thing. Were she to have her child here, it would be an East German citizen, as subject as Lise to the laws that prevented her from leaving the country. The thought chilled her to the bone: *A mother can be separated from her child.*

"We'll dig quickly," Inge promised. She stepped back and pulled off her glove: although night had begun to fall, Lise could see Inge's finger sparkle in the light of a streetlamp. "I'm sorry, but it was the only way to bring it across," she explained, pulling Uli's engagement ring from her finger. "He wanted you to have this."

Lise slipped the ring on her finger, feeling as though the universe, shifted so far off course, had clicked slightly back on track. "It's going to work," she said. "Tell Uli I love him, and that this is going to work."

10

Uli crouched on the fireplace surround with a matchbox in hand, his knees digging uncomfortably into the cracked marble as he struck a match against touch paper. The match erupted into flame, and he set it against the twists of newspaper he'd piled beneath splinters of wood, then stood, satisfied, to watch the fire crackle to life.

"Uli?"

Inge rushed toward him as smoke began to pour out of the fireplace and into the living room, gray and roiling. She dropped to her knees and snaked a hand up the fireplace, hardly noticing the burgeoning flames as she fumbled in the grate. Uli heard the heavy clunk of iron against iron, then Inge sat back on her heels as the smoke began to properly draw up the chimney.

He offered his hand to help her to her feet, and she gripped it with sooty fingers. "I'm an idiot. I didn't think—"

"The flue was shut," Inge explained.

"I didn't even notice. It's the first time I've used it—"

"Uli. It's fine." She pulled away, brushing ash from her hands. "No harm done. Shall we get to work?"

She retreated to the rickety dining table beneath the kitchen pass-through to join Wolf and Jurgen as they pored over an unfurled map.

Uli swept his hand along his stubbled chin as he strode into the kitchenette, kicking himself for his lack of foresight. *What sort of idiot lights a fire without checking the flue?* Lise would have checked the flue: she would have made sure there were clean glasses on the pass-through before inviting guests over; she would have banished the dust bunnies that had congregated beneath the table. He opened the refrigerator door, revealing a pitiful assortment of contents that did little to disabuse himself of the notion he was less than a functioning adult: a crate's worth of beer bottles and a jar of pickles alongside a slowly moldering block of cheese. Was this truly the home of a father-to-be?

He pulled out four pilsners and rejoined his friends in the living room.

"...This is the right location for a tunnel: here in Bernauer Strasse," Jurgen was saying as Uli slid into the chair opposite. He pointed at their location on the map: a detailed rendering of the city's waterlines and underground infrastructure, quietly pilfered from his apprenticeship at the municipal waterworks. "The soil is composed predominantly of clay, so it's less prone to collapse."

"But it will make for a harder go of things," Uli muttered, his shoulders already aching at the thought of carving heavy soil out of the ground. *Perhaps if we rig up some sort of cart to carry the soil back out of the earth...* "And we need to find a suitable starting point."

"We already have one," Jurgen replied. "I've spoken to Aunt Agatha and she's agreed to let us use the basement of Siggi's."

"Can we trust her?" Inge asked, frowning. "The Stasi has

informants everywhere...what's to say they're not in West Berlin, too?"

Jurgen nodded. "My brother Karl was always her favorite, and she dotes on Willa. She's as sick as I am about being separated from them. And Siggi's has a separate entrance to the basement, down a back alley off Stralsunder Strasse, so we won't be seen going in and out."

Inge's doubtful expression eased.

"If Jurgi says we can trust her, then I do," Uli said, "but we'll need to figure out a way to get the earth out of the building."

Wolf narrowed his eyes as he studied the map. "Leave that to me," he said. "What about her staff? We ought to consider the possibility that people might talk."

"If that's the case, we'll have to buy their silence. The pub is our best option. There's nothing suspicious about a group of friends frequenting a pub." Jurgen grinned. "Perhaps Agatha will give us free beer for our efforts, too."

"We'll *need* free beer if we're to carry this off," Wolf muttered. "How are we to pay for this? Bribing bar staff? We'll need supplies—wood for shoring up the tunnel, shovels, pickaxes... And that's not to mention the sheer amount of time involved. We're supposed to be graduating this year."

"I've decided to defer," Uli replied. He met Inge's eyes, and it was clear the news wasn't a shock to her. "I can't sit in a classroom while Lise waits for me—I just can't. I don't expect the rest of you to put your lives on hold, too, but..."

"I'm deferring, too," Jurgen cut in. "We're getting my family out as well. It's too important for us to wait."

Uli smiled, his throat tight. He'd expected as much from Jurgen, though it felt good to hear it aloud.

Wolf set down his glass and let out a sigh. "I'm in, too."

Jurgen shot him a glance. "You're sure?"

"Why not?" Wolf smirked. "We'll call it a practical engineering internship."

He turned his attention back to the map, and Uli listened as Inge and Jurgen raised the issue of proper ventilation in the tunnel. It was clear that Wolf wasn't as enthusiastic about the plan as Jurgen and Uli—but then, it was Jurgen and Uli who had the most compelling reasons to believe in their success.

Nonetheless, Wolf was here and helping. Whether he voiced his doubts to Jurgen in the privacy of their home didn't matter to Uli: not when too many others in West Berlin had chosen to ignore what was happening in the East.

"We still need an exit point," Jurgen said, tracing his finger along the map. "Somewhere not so far from the Wall that we'll be digging forever, but not so close that it would be difficult for people to get to."

"They've emptied buildings all along the border," Uli added, recalling the harrowing image of the man who'd been dragged back into his fourth-floor apartment. "The Vopos don't want any more out-the-window escapes. We'll have to go back at least a block to be safe."

"I'll go to Mitte this weekend to scout for a suitable place." Inge took a deep, unladylike swig from her beer bottle. "Perhaps if I can talk to Lise, she'll have a few ideas."

"So we have a hypothetical entrance, a nonexistent exit and a possible need for bribery." Wolf squeezed Jurgen's hand with a resigned sort of laugh. "Have I just about covered it?"

11

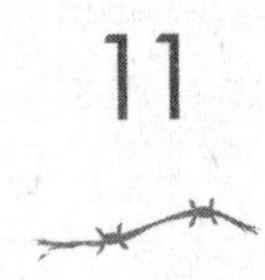

NOVEMBER 1961

Lise unhooked the first of the heavy curtain rings from the window overlooking Rheinsberger Strasse, coughing as a cloud of dust billowed from the thick fabric. In her long years of living at the flat, it had never occurred to Lise that she or Paul might have taken the curtains off their rods and beaten them clean of dust. It was the sort of task that their mother, who'd chosen the curtains nearly thirty years ago, might have taught them, if they'd been a little bit older when she died.

She finished pulling the curtain down, thinking of the few sparse memories she still had of her mother: a figure remembered mainly on the edge of sleep, in a glimpse of brown hair or a kind voice, whispering just out of earshot. With the prospect of motherhood now firmly in her own future, Lise regretted all the moments she'd not been able to share with her own mother: her dreams and plans, her academic success, her first period, her first heartbreak.

Uli, and the life they'd created.

Mother, it seemed, was on everyone else's mind as well. In

his bedroom, Papa was nearly silent as he packed the dressers she'd once filled with knitted sweaters; on the other side of the living room, Paul reverently wrapped the few decorative pieces on the mantel that had survived the bomb blast that had sent all the dishes crashing to the floor in '45. Here, Mother lived on in the dark corners of the apartment, breathing life into each tablecloth and piece of furniture and painting she'd chosen, long ago. Would she still be there, in the accumulated belongings of their lives, when it all sat in the new apartment on Stalinallee?

She opened the window and shook out the curtains, sending two decades worth of dust clouding into the street below. Her mother had died at the beginning of the end, when the Russians had poured into Berlin with a wide-eyed menace that lived on in the silence of the women old enough to remember. Lise, thankfully, had no memories of those dark days: whether she'd been too young or had simply pushed them out of her conscious mind, she wasn't sure, but she'd overheard, in tearful conversations years later, what had happened: how, while Papa was trapped beneath the rubble of his operating room, a gang of soldiers had kicked down the door to their apartment, unmoved when the young Jewish woman Mama and Papa had sheltered for years in the crawlspace between the kitchen and bedroom (*Ellie*, a voice in the back of Lise's mind whispered) had pleaded for mercy for them both; how Paul had tried, with childish bravado, to fight them off, and had been struck so hard on the head he'd woken nearly a full day later.

The kitchen door swung open and Anna came through, carrying a cardboard box. "That's all the dishes," she said brightly, depositing the box on the dining table.

Paul finished wrapping a candlestick in paper and swept Anna into his arms.

"You're a wonder," he declared, firmly planting a kiss on Anna's cheek. Paul and Anna had met nearly a month ago, and she'd knitted herself into the fabric of their family with a speed that Lise found disconcerting. These days, Anna was always underfoot, dressed in some sensible outfit from Präsent 20 with a bright smile and a cheerful insistence upon her own method of doing things. She seemed to be clinically incapable of uttering a critical word, and had a stubborn streak that rivaled Lise's own.

It irritated Lise to no end: did Anna truly expect the world to bend around her?

"I'm only doing what I can," Anna replied, wrapping her slender arms around Paul's neck. She was built like a plank of wood, with cropped hair and pale eyes made larger by her hollowed cheeks: too skinny, in Lise's opinion, to be beautiful. But she'd captured Paul's attention in a way no other woman—those more beautiful, more unique, more challenging, to Lise's mind—had, so Lise supposed that had to count for something. "Besides, I like packing."

"Of course you do," Lise muttered, before realizing she'd spoken aloud; she looked up to see Paul and Anna staring at her with matching puzzled expressions. "I only mean that Anna is so efficient."

Anna's wan smile broadened. "I packed enough pup tents during my days with the Thälmann Pioneers to know how it's done." She tapped her hand to her forehead in a slanted salute and recited the Pioneers motto. *"Always ready!"*

Lise stopped herself from rolling her eyes as she pulled the curtain back through the window: of course Anna had been a Pioneer. She pictured Anna with the regulation kerchief tied around her neck, running through the woods and spouting revolutionary slogans turned into catchy songs by Party functionaries.

"My productive princess," Paul said, planting a soft kiss on Anna's cheek before returning to the mantel. Though the thought of Uli giving Lise such a bland compliment turned Lise's stomach, she knew that Paul meant it as the highest of compliments. "Always ready to lend a helping hand."

As if in illustration, Anna strode across the room and picked up the trailing ends of Lise's curtain. "It's easier to do it like this," she said with a smile, and Lise bit back a snarky retort as Anna started folding it with brusque efficiency. She knew she was being unfair: Anna was making an effort, and the job of packing up the apartment would have been so much more difficult without her help.

"I'm afraid I won't be able to stay much longer," she continued as she wrested the folded sheet from Lise's hands. "I've got class this afternoon... Anatomy, you know."

This was another reason for Lise's disdain: Anna was in her second year of studying medicine at Humboldt University. Could Paul truly not have found anyone else?

She gave Anna a tight-lipped grimace. "Well, we'll simply have to carry on without you."

Anna's smile faltered, but she bid Lise a kind goodbye nonetheless.

"You could make more of an effort with her," Paul muttered as he followed Anna downstairs with the box of dishes. "She only wants to be friends."

By the time night fell, the apartment was almost entirely empty. Papa had gone ahead to unpack in the new flat, while Paul, who'd staunchly refused to allow Lise to pick up anything heavy in her condition, shuttled back and forth with the moving truck. Lise, meanwhile, had offered to stay in the old apartment with the last of their belongings, and was waiting for Paul to return for the final few boxes.

She pictured the new flat, with its shiny appliances and scrubbed windows. Paul and Papa were both enamored by the apartment's bright hallways and laminate countertops, the Sprelacart shelving unit in the living room and the nursery they'd painted in a cheery shade of yellow for Lise's baby.

"What more could you ask for?" Paul had declared when they'd arrived with the first of their boxes.

But it doesn't have this. Signaling to the West was forbidden, but Lise switched on the lights and moved to the window. Across the Wall, Uli's apartment was dark, and Lise pressed her lips together, determined not to succumb to disappointment. She'd hoped for one final glimpse of him before she turned in the apartment's keys.

Perhaps he'd already begun to dig: perhaps at this very moment, he was knee-deep in soil, slowly making his way toward her.

That, surely, was the easy part. The difficulty would lie in finding someplace safe in East Berlin where they could break through; where Lise could slide, unnoticed, beneath the watchful eyes of the border guards and the Volkspolizei.

She stepped away from the window, regretting how little control she had over her own salvation. Lise had always been a practical sort, accustomed to making her own way in the world: it had been Lise who'd decided to study in the West; Lise, who'd looked to fulfilling her own dreams. If it had been her in the West and Uli in the East, Lise would be digging a tunnel of her own, but there was little she could do here beyond wait for others to be the heroes.

She spun Uli's engagement ring on her finger. Perhaps there was something she could do, if she was smart about it: she could put out the word, quietly, to others living in East Berlin—to Axel and to Jurgen's family, others who might share in Lise's dream of escaping to the West. It was hardly practical, after all, for Inge to travel to East Berlin on a regular basis, not when such frequent trips might bring her to the attention of the border guards. But Lise could work within the GDR itself to lay the groundwork for the escape, and make sure that when the tunnel was operational, it would be worth all Uli's efforts in building it.

"Lise?" Paul stood at the apartment's open door with two stacked boxes in hand. "This is the last of it. Are you ready to go?"

"All that's left are the keys," she replied, and Paul shuffled the boxes into one arm to reach into his pocket.

"Leave mine, too," he said, tossing Lise two set of keys. "And

Papa's." He cast a wistful eye over the empty room. "End of an era, isn't it," he said softly.

"The end of an era," Lise agreed.

She expected him to disappear down the hall, but Paul leaned against the doorframe, balancing the boxes on his knee. "You know the beauty of a new apartment? It's not just in the fact that the water will run hot when you want it to, and that the windows won't leak heat." He shot her a meaningful look. "It's that there are no ghosts there. No unwelcome reminders of the past."

Lise's heart broke at his sincerity. "I know that packing up this place has been difficult for you," she began, but Paul waved away her words.

"I'm not talking about my ghosts. Those will follow me wherever I go. But yours... That window." His gaze shifted past her and she knew that he was looking at Uli's window. "Think of this as a fresh start, Lise. That's what this new apartment is going to be. For all of us."

A fresh start. Did Paul really think it could be that simple?

"You go on ahead. I'll be down in a minute."

She stood in the apartment for a moment longer, savoring the lingering silence of the home she'd known as a child. Out the window, she watched the dark square of Uli's flat, weighing the three sets of keys in her hand: keys to the flat, to the front door and to the building's basement storage rooms.

With one more glance out the window, Lise turned and walked out of the apartment, working two keys free from two different rings: the front door key from her own set and the storeroom key from Paul's. *Keys go missing all the time,* she thought as she locked the apartment door and dropped the keys back through the mail slot. *Who's to say we didn't lose them years ago?*

She wasn't sure where the entrance to Uli's tunnel would be—but the next time Inge visited, Lise would be able to offer a possible exit.

~~Lise,~~
~~My darling Lise~~

Dearest Lise,

Inge told me the news and I don't know whether to laugh or cry. We spoke so often about children that it feels as if the universe is fulfilling my most deeply held wish, in the worst possible circumstances.

What scares me isn't the thought of the baby. It's the thought that I might not get to be part of it all. It kills me that I'm not there to hold your hand through this. Was it irresponsible, doing what we'd done countless times before? It didn't feel irresponsible at the time. But it does now, knowing everything that's happened since.

I know that if I were to send this letter to you, you'd never receive it. So, I've resolved to keep my thoughts in this journal for you and for our child—to write down everything I wish I could say, until I can say it all to you in person.

Love,
Uli

12

Uli opened the door to his parents' apartment, knocking snow from his boots before shouldering his way into the hall, his arms laden with bags of groceries. From within the depths of the apartment he could hear the sound of pots and pans, a metallic clanging that cut through the current of the Blue Diamonds single playing on the hi-fi. Mother's warbling hum joined in at the chorus, and he slipped his boots off one at a time before crossing through the living room, where wall-mounted bookcases displayed hundreds of records in a dizzying, kaleidoscopic riot. Though his parents didn't share the sort of closeness that Uli had with Lise, music had long been the thread that tied the Neumann family together, coloring Uli's memories from the time he was a boy.

He walked through to the kitchen, where Mother was pulling a perfect-looking roast from the oven. Unlike his apartment on Bernauer Strasse, Mother and Father's flat was gleaming and new, devoid of the sort of complaints that Uli wrestled with on a daily basis: the stubborn window latches; the groaning hinges that had settled too long ago for the doors to ever close properly. Here in his parents' kitchen, an avocado-green fridge hummed beside painted cupboards, and Uli thought ruefully of his own feeble culinary adventures at his flat, so often derailed by the finicky stovetop or the temperamental fusebox.

"Uli, *liebchen*. I didn't hear you come in." Mother set the roast on a hot plate and wiped her hands on her apron, raising her voice above the music. "Franz, Uli's home."

"I know." Father leaned against the kitchen door, a newspaper tucked beneath his arm. He stowed his reading glasses away in the breast pocket of his shirt with a smile. "How are you, my boy?"

Before he could answer, Mother had come forward to inspect the groceries, pulling jars and wrapped packages of meat from the bags with a disapproving cluck. "You shouldn't be spending your money on us," she said, but Uli could see she was pleased by the gesture. "Take all this back with you when you leave after dinner."

"I like spending my money on you." Uli lifted the lid on a pot of stewing carrots, letting their earthy scent mingle with the roast as he tried to identify the herbs Mother had used on the meat. Rosemary?

"Your mother's right, son." Father uncorked a bottle of wine as Mother swatted Uli's hands away from the stove.

Her lined face creased with worry. "You're not eating."

Uli stepped back, thinking of the waterworks map strewn across his dining table; the shovels and pickaxes and buckets he and Jurgen had amassed, now sitting in the living room. The spare bedroom, now home to a bassinet he'd bought secondhand, repainted and filled with peachy soft blankets. "I've been busy."

"Busy with school?" Father said with a meaningful glance. "Or with other matters?"

Uli pulled a serving tray from the cupboard and set it on the counter without answering his father's question, and Mother sighed. "Go and sit down, liebchen, before it gets cold."

Uli followed Father into the dining room, which had been set with Mother's fine china—plates on white chargers and rows of cutlery, neatly lined up beneath the glassware: cut crystal goblets for red wine, white wine, water and port. Mother had bought it all after the war, after the devastation and humiliation that had followed Germany's defeat; after Father's return from the Canadian POW camp where he'd been sent early in the war. She'd had to: all the family heirlooms had been lost in the chaos that followed the Red Army into Berlin, smashed or stolen by soldiers who blamed Berlin's women for the pain that the city's men had inflicted upon the world. Uli suspected that his parents' love of clutter had been borne out of that deprivation: that they'd filled their home with things, with music, to replace the people they'd lost—including, Uli suspected, parts of themselves.

Uli could still recall the day his father arrived home from the prisoner of war camp in 1952: how Mother had greeted him not with a kiss, but with a smile. After their long years apart they'd become strangers to each other, bound, in those early days of reunion, by their love for Uli and now by habit. How could Uli stand by and let that same relentless wear of time make strangers of him and Lise?

Uli sat down as Mother came in carrying the roast, dressed with carrots and sprigs of fresh rosemary, and set it before Father's seat.

"We're so glad you were able to join us tonight," she said, clasping her hands in her lap as Father began carving the meat. "We've seen so little of you recently."

Uli poured Mother a glass of wine. "As I said, I've been busy."

Mother and Father exchanged a glance without speaking.

"Uli, your father and I—we want to know whether you'd consider moving back home," Mother began, as Father slid a ladened plate down the table. "Whether you might like to—to have your old room back. To help us around the house. We thought you might like the company."

Uli took a sip of his wine: red, sweet and too heavy for his taste. "You want me to move back in with you," he repeated, and Mother's smile weakened.

"You spend all your time in that flat of yours." Father fixed Uli with a meaningful stare. "We worry, son, that you're spending all your time thinking about—about something you can't have."

"Lise." Uli set down his glass. "You can say her name. *Lise.*"

"Lise." Mother reached across the table and placed her hand over his. "Of course we can say her name. Darling, you must understand, it's been months, and there's no reason to believe that East Germany is going to relent. This border might be permanent. And if that's the case, we want you to start thinking about your future."

"A future without her, you mean," Uli replied. "She *is* my future, Mother."

"Be reasonable, Ulrich," Father snapped. "There's no visa for hopeless romantics. You're twenty-one years old, and the girl is an infatuation. Don't waste your life building up some expectation of a life you can never have."

"An *infatuation*?" Though Uli was furious he felt oddly calm, unwilling to give his parents the satisfaction of his anger. "I love her, and we'll find a way to be together. Whether it takes months or—or years—"

"Years spent living in a memory!" Mother cried. "I don't doubt your feelings, but you're too young to be throwing your life away in wait." She exchanged a pained look with Father. "We weren't thrilled with the thought of you marrying to begin with, and now you have an opportunity to think better of your actions. We were far too young for marriage, your father and I, and we worry you're making the same mistake we did."

"You're unbelievable. Do you know that?" Uli got to his feet, trembling. "Lise hasn't left me for some other man. This isn't a question of *whim*. We've been separated by—by circumstances beyond our control—"

Mother, too, stood. "Circumstances that don't show any signs of changing!"

"Circumstances that *must* be changed," Uli shot back. "You're the ones who got us into this mess. You're the reason we have these borders, we have this—this hell keeping us apart. Your generation won't do the right thing, but mine will." He exhaled heavily, wishing for more understanding than his parents were willing to give. There was no point in telling them what he'd come here to say: that they would soon be grandparents. Why bother, when they clearly cared so little for his happiness?

He looked down and realized he was still clutching a napkin in his fist.

"I think we'd be best to have dinner some other night," he muttered, as Mother wilted back into her chair. "Thank you for the invitation."

Father cleared his throat and Uli circled around the table to press a kiss to the top of Mother's curls before stalking out of the room.

Father trailed after Uli, waiting until they were in the hall before addressing him in an undertone. "We're only trying to help."

"Then *help.*" He took off his glasses and squeezed his eyes shut, too exasperated to continue fighting. "Lise is pregnant, Dad. I'm not just fighting for her. I'm fighting for my child. Help me get her back. Help me get her out."

Father frowned, and Uli braced himself for another argument: for Father to tell him that it was too risky, too reckless; that nothing was worth risking the wrath of the Stasi.

He nodded. "What do you need?"

13

25 DECEMBER, 1961

Music piped through the apartment, thin and tinny through the speakers of Paul's hi-fi, and Lise strained to hear the sound of Hartmut Eichler's band above the voices of guests arrayed beneath the blue glow of tinsel strung in blowsy loops from the ceiling. She would have preferred the velvet-smooth voice of Elvis Presley, but she knew better than to retrieve his album from beneath her mattress: although she suspected that everyone here could sing along with the chorus to "Stuck on You," Presley's music had been banned, along with all the other Western artists that Lise loved.

She picked up an empty tray of appetizers, relieved to have found an excuse to retreat to the kitchen. Papa's Christmas party was an annual tradition that Lise endured with good grace, but this year the comments from family friends she preferred to see only once a year had become particularly pointed: *A baby—what a joy! When are you due?... Such a shame you've given up your studies, but motherhood will suit you... What a delight to know we have a new dressmaker to let up the hems of our skirts.*

She opened the refrigerator to retrieve a plastic dish filled with sliced sausage, listening as Paul's laughter rang out above the din. All evening he'd held court by the Christmas tree, surrounded by women with bouffant hair and men in their sharpest suits, everyone turned out in their finery to celebrate the holidays—and to toast to Paul and Anna. She stood by the pass-through window and watched as Paul threaded his fingers through Anna's, the light catching on Anna's engagement ring. He looked for all the world as though he'd never been happier.

So why couldn't Lise share in his joy?

She opened the dish to refill the empty tray, her stomach turning slightly at the smell of sausage and mustard—and at the unbearable feeling that she was spending Christmas on the opposite side of a fun house mirror. Everyone in the living room had friends and family in West Berlin, people from whom they'd been cut off, just like Lise herself. How could they all stand about smiling, acting as though this was a Christmas like any other?

Papa wheeled into the kitchen with a second empty tray on his lap, a line of blue tinsel strung around his shoulders like a feather boa.

"Quite the turnout this year," he said brightly, his cheeks flushed with overindulgence. He set the tray on the counter and let out a contented sigh as he began refilling it from Lise's sausage dish. "Couldn't get another jar of pickled carrots for me, could you, *liebchen*?"

She circled to the pantry. "I think it's the new apartment," she replied, opening the pantry to reveal jars of preserved vegetables they'd made from their garden at the *datsche* earlier that year. "They all want to see it. And Paul's new fiancée, of course."

"They want to see you, too," Papa said as Lise returned to the counter with the carrots.

"To see if I really did get myself pregnant with a Wessi's baby," she scoffed, then fell silent at the look on Papa's face.

"Please don't disparage yourself," he said gently. "Everyone here just wants you to be happy."

She planted her hands on the counter, but didn't respond, and Papa's wheelchair creaked as he came closer.

"I know you're holding out hope that one day you and Uli might be together again, and I'm not asking you to put that hope aside. But I know only too well what it feels like when life is stopped in its tracks and, my darling, I don't want you to waste your days in wait."

Lise stayed silent, thinking of her last meeting with Inge only weeks earlier, when she'd handed over the keys to her old apartment block on Rheinsberger Strasse. If all went to plan, Lise wouldn't be waiting much longer—but she couldn't say as much to Papa.

He rested his hand atop hers. "No matter where you are in the world—in Berlin, or Germany, or anywhere else—life is only ever going to be what you make of it. So please, my darling, make it your resolution this year to try and be happy."

Several hours later, Lise slipped out onto the balcony, letting the chill of the evening air bring down the heat in her flushed cheeks. She stared out over the city: several blocks away, the bright streets of West Berlin were visible as a glow in the distance.

She smiled as the faint sound of music reached her ears: from an open apartment window somewhere not too far away, some incautious person was listening to a West German radio station.

Does your memory stray
to a bright summer day
when I kissed you and called you sweetheart?

How irksome it must be to the authorities, she thought, to know that despite official disapprobation radio waves couldn't be censored.

Tell me dear, are you lonesome…

The sound drifted into silence, and Lise knew that whoever had been listening had succumbed to common sense—but she appreciated the small gift nonetheless.

She rubbed her bare arms, feeling as though her composure hung on the balance of one shaky breath. She had been so caught up with thoughts of leaving East Berlin that she'd neglected to think about the impact her actions would have on her family: how Papa would wake up one morning, mere months from now, to find her gone. If all went to plan, this would be the last Christmas she'd spend with Papa and Paul—perhaps forever. Did she really want to spend it moping?

"Have you a light?"

Lise turned around to find that Horst had joined her. With his bottle-brush haircut and browline glasses, Horst looked as though he was always on duty, even in his tailored suit. He held out a packet of cigarettes, its tricolor label muted in the darkness, but Lise declined.

"You know, studies show that cigarettes are terrible for your health," she commented, resting her forearms against the balcony railing.

He studied the packet in his broad mitt of a hand a moment longer, then tossed it over the balcony railing. "Then I won't smoke them."

She lifted an eyebrow. "Just like that?"

"I've never particularly cared for the smell. Aren't you cold?" Before she could answer, Horst removed his jacket and draped it over Lise's shoulders.

"Thank you," she replied, surprised at his casual chivalry. Given Horst's build, the jacket was cartoonishly large on her narrow shoulders, but she appreciated the gesture.

"Do you miss it?"

"Miss what?"

He nodded at the yellow glow of the far-off streetlamps. "The West."

She took her time replying. Though she'd known him her whole life, Horst was still a member of the Volkspolizei, as committed as Paul to realizing the socialist paradise that they believed the GDR to be. "I miss aspects of it," she replied finally. "The movie theaters. The shopping."

"We have all those things here too, you know." Horst's glasses glinted in the reflected streetlights as he turned his head to face her with a half smile. "Perhaps you spent too much time over there to realize it."

When she didn't reply, Horst sighed. "I know it's more than that, Lise. Of course it is. You miss your friends. Your fiancé. Paul tells me these things. It's been difficult for you." He hesitated. "I just want you to know that you have friends here, too."

It was the same thing Papa had said to her earlier, in as many words.

Perhaps it was time she started believing it.

She slipped Horst's jacket from her shoulders and handed it back to him so she could return to the party. "Merry Christmas, Horst."

"Merry Christmas, Lise."

14

Uli turned the radio dial, letting the sound of Elvis's deep voice flood the cold air of the pub's cellar. Overhead, he could hear the sound of revelers singing along to carols. This late on Christmas Eve, they would be too far in their cups to realize there was music playing beneath the floorboards, and Uli closed his eyes to listen, gripping the handle of his shovel.

Elvis had always been Lise's favorite singer. It was a bone of playful contention between the two of them: Uli was always eager to broaden Lise's musical tastes while Lise preferred to sing along to the billboard hits she loved best. How many times had they fought over the selections on the pub's jukebox, Lise grinning with triumph when "Blue Suede Shoes" came over the speaker?

It ought to have been their first Christmas together, their only Christmas as an engaged couple. Uli pictured the season as it should have been, dancing in front of a small tree in their apartment, kissing beneath the mistletoe. But instead Uli was here, listening to his fiancée's favourite singer as his breath clouded in the cold air.

Elvis's voice faded into nothingness, and a disc jockey took the microphone.

"That was Elvis Presley with "Are You Lonesome Tonight," here on RIAS," the disc jockey said, and Uli bowed his head over the shovel handle, hoping against hope that Lise had heard it. He had no way of knowing for certain whether she'd been listening to the radio or whether his special request to the radio station had been a wish sent out into the ether. He would have preferred to give Lise something better than a song for Christmas, but a song was all he could send—a song would have to do.

He felt a hand on his shoulder and hastily wiped tears from his cheeks before he turned to face Jurgen.

"No need to hold it in, mate." Jurgen tucked his shovel into the crook of his arm, then dug in his coat pocket to pull out a flask. "Not with us."

Uli shifted his gaze. Behind him, Wolf, removing the last of the jackhammered chunks of the cellar's cement floor, gave a solemn nod. He straightened and set the rubble aside before giving an experimental kick to the hard-packed earth he'd exposed.

"If we want to turn back," Wolf said, "now's the time."

Uli met Jurgen's determined gaze. Thanks to Father's sizable investment, Uli, Wolf and Jurgen had the funding they'd needed to defer their school year and commit their time to the tunnel. It was a venture that would take the three of them months, digging in round-the-clock shifts to meet the unavoidable deadline of Lise's due date.

He tightened his grip on his shovel. "There's no turning back."

From across the room, the door to the cellar creaked open and Uli twisted round with alarm, heart pounding in his chest as a slender figure slipped through the door, carrying a large rucksack filled with bottles of beer.

"You didn't honestly think you'd be doing all the work without me, did you?"

Wolf let out a breath. "*Scheisse*, Inge. You nearly gave me a heart attack."

"What are you doing here?" Uli stepped forward. "You're not helping us with the digging, it's too dangerous."

"Like hell I'm not." Inge had stayed quiet when Uli and Jurgen had come up with their plan, and nodded when they'd explained her role to her: she was to be a courier, making contact in the East once the tunnel was close to completion. But here she was, dressed in a cable-knit sweater and a pair of dungarees, and she stepped forward to take Jurgen's shovel, daring the three of them to object. "Besides, I'm the only one among us with medical training. Given what you're planning to do, it makes sense to have me helping in case something goes wrong."

Uli glanced at Jurgen, who shrugged. It was no more a risk for Inge than it was for the rest of them, and the work would go quicker with four.

He looked back at Inge. "Let's get to it, then."

As one, they sank their shovels into the earth and began to dig.

Part Two

11 MARCH, 1962

To my dear sister,

It's the evening before my wedding, and while you know I've never really been one for sentimentality, there's something about reaching one of life's important milestones that makes it feel appropriate to take stock of things: to tally up life's wins and losses, and look at them from the perspective of what truly matters.

When I think about all the important moments in my life—all those wins and losses—you've been there for every one. Cheering me on, holding my hand, or being that voice of reason on those (few) occasions when I've needed it. I can't tell you how meaningful that has been to me.

Tomorrow, Anna becomes my voice of reason. But I want you to know that no matter what, I'll always strive to be yours.

You've had a terrible time of things, over the past several months. But whatever the future holds, know that you'll never have to face it alone.

Paul

15

JANUARY 1962

Lise sat at the top of the long table that bordered three edges of the community hall, watching as Papa, beaming, lifted a glass of Rotkäppchen.

"To Paul and Anna," he said, and Lise dutifully lifted her glass. She met Horst's eye across the narrow table and fixed a belated smile to her face before taking the smallest possible sip. Though she'd spent the five long months of her pregnancy abstaining from alcohol, she knew better than to incur the wrath of old superstitions by refusing to drink in the newlyweds' honor.

Horst lowered his glass and Lise looked away, her cheeks unbearably warm as the assembly of guests tucked into the wedding feast. At the front of the room, Paul snugged his chair closer to Anna to whisper something that made her laugh, and Lise's smile softened. Even she could admit that Anna looked beautiful: her thin hair had been teased into a modest bouffant held back by a satin headband that matched the pale fabric of her tea gown—designed, naturally, by Gerda. The dress was a triumph, beautifully tailored to Anna's slender figure, with three-quarter sleeves and a full skirt that lent Anna the illusion of natural curves. Lise had helped Gerda with the making of it, cutting the fabric and sewing the straight hems while leaving the more difficult aspects of construction—the pleating, the bodice, the tempering of Anna's expectations—to Gerda's expert ministrations. Lise couldn't help feeling a tinge of secondhand pride as Anna smoothed her hands across her waist.

She turned her attention to Paul. She was glad Anna had talked him into wearing his best suit for the occasion, rather than his Volkspolizei uniform: he looked more relaxed, more himself, and happier than Lise could ever remember seeing him. Theirs was true love, of that Lise was certain: as he gazed at Anna, she could see in Paul's expression an echo of what she felt for Uli, and though the comparison broke her heart, she shelved it away in the back of her mind, determined to put on a smile for her brother's big day.

After dinner, the tables were pushed to the corners of the room to make room for dancing, and Lise nursed a cup of coffee on the fringes of the dance floor, watching as Anna spun Papa's wheelchair on the dance floor in a modified version of the Lipsi.

Horst dropped into the seat beside her. "You don't feel like dancing?"

She rested a hand to her belly. "I don't, but the baby does."

Horst glanced at Lise sidelong. "Is it—is it kicking?"

Wordlessly, she took Horst's hand and pressed it against her, watching his expression transform as the baby fluttered in her abdomen.

"Does it hurt?"

She released Horst's wrist and sank back in her chair with a sigh. "It's more tiring than anything else, these days."

Horst, too, leaned back—an oddly relaxed movement, so at odds with his rigid bearing. "Well? What do you think of your new sister-in-law?"

Despite Paul's efforts to find common ground for the two of

them, Lise still struggled to forgive Anna her inadvertent transgression of achieving what Lise had been denied: her schooling; a happy marriage. With the turn of the new year Anna had surpassed where Lise had been in her studies, and now she sat late into the night with Papa discussing the intricacies of her classwork, like Lise had done before the border closure—and though Papa did his best to draw Lise into their conversations, she couldn't stand listening to Anna wax eloquent about the world she'd been forced to give up.

She thought of Uli's tunnel, knowing, with quiet satisfaction, that she would be able to resume her studies soon. At least Anna would bring Paul solace once Lise slipped back into the West.

"She makes Paul happy," she said finally. "What more could I ask for than that?"

Horst turned to her, the glass in his spectacles momentarily occluded by the hall's bright lights. "But do you like her?"

Lise allowed herself a thin smile. "She makes Paul happy," she repeated, "and that makes me happy."

Horst smirked and lowered his voice. "Between the two of us, I find her something of an acquired taste."

Lise let out a huff of laughter, surprised that Horst had noticed Anna's pleasant yet relentless ability to get her own way. It was the first time she'd heard Horst voice an opinion that wasn't a carbon copy of Paul's, and she liked him better for it.

"She's moved her things into the apartment. I give her three days before she's reorganized the kitchen cupboards based on strict adherence to socialist principles." She took a sip of her coffee, watching Horst for signs that he was about to shore back up again—that her little joke about the system had been a bridge too far—but he only chuckled.

Across the room, Paul, now waltzing with Anna in his arms, looked up and caught Lise's eye. He looked from Lise to Horst and his expression brightened.

It's just a conversation, she thought irritably. Paul could be so terribly obvious.

"...Though it's only natural for her to want to make some changes," Horst was saying, and Lise drained the last of her coffee. "You can hardly begrudge her the opportunity to make the place her own."

"It's not *hers*, though. It's Papa's apartment."

"Spoken like a true bourgeois," he replied, but his tone was playful rather than scolding.

"East or West, there are only so many bedrooms," Lise pointed out. "Surely, they've applied to the Ministry of Housing for a place of their own. They won't want to keep living with Papa and me, particularly not when the baby arrives."

Horst shot Lise a puzzled glance. "Paul submitted the application for the apartment, not Rudolph," he said. "I thought you knew."

Lise glanced at Papa, chatting easily with Gerda at the edge of the dance floor. Why hadn't he said anything about it? Why hadn't Paul?

"I suppose it doesn't really matter," she said, shaking off her unease for Horst's benefit. "We all rub along well enough."

"Quite right." He lifted his coffee to his lips once again.

Though Horst didn't seem particularly troubled by it, Lise was unsettled by the notion that Papa's application for new housing had been ignored while Paul's had been granted. She thought back to her conversation with Paul after she'd been arrested at the Wall. Had Papa's failure been her fault?

The music shifted to a gentler ballad by Gerhard Wendland, and Horst set down his empty cup. "How are you feeling now? Would you care to dance?"

Lise nodded and allowed Horst to help her out of her chair. There was something gallant in the way Paul had allowed Papa to take credit for the new apartment—in how he'd never given Lise reason to believe she and her child would ever want for a roof over their heads. And it was a comfort to know that Papa wouldn't be left on his own, once she'd traveled to the West. But if Papa's application had been denied because of Lise's actions, what would it mean for him—for Paul, for Anna—if Lise fled across the border?

Horst gripped her waist, spinning her gently. "I hope I've not spoken out of turn," he said, his broad chest rumbling as he spoke. "Not that it particularly matters. After all, housing is allocated on the basis of collective need."

She suppressed a sigh, staring at the knot of Horst's tie. *There he is*, she thought. *Horst the automaton, back again.*

"But even I can see that collective need sometimes doesn't account for breathing room. And four adults and a baby…that's a lot, even in an apartment as spacious as yours." Horst slowed, and Lise craned her neck to meet his gaze. "I want you to know that if you ever need room of your own—if you ever decide you want something more—"

Lise stepped away. "Horst, you misunderstand—"

"Please, just let me finish. Raising a child on your own will be difficult, even with a supportive family." He paused, as though waiting for Lise to argue the point, but she stayed silent. What was there to say, when Horst was discussing a hypothetical that would never come to pass? "Your family is growing, and soon Anna and Paul will have children of their own. And when that happens, your apartment will feel very small."

But by then, I'll be back where I belong.

"I've always been fond of you, Lise, and I want you to know that I would be happy—honored—to be part of your life in a more meaningful way. Part of your child's life, in a more meaningful way."

Lise could feel a red flush rising in her cheeks, and she glanced away, unable to bear the look of hope on Horst's face a moment longer. God knew she'd never given him encouragement toward anything other than friendship—and even that was for Paul's benefit. She didn't want to embarrass Horst, but how could he think this was an appropriate conversation?

She took a deep breath, hoping that he believed her hesitation to be something other than what it was: mortification, plain and simple. She knew better than to reject Horst outright. It was dangerous to give him any reason to think she was planning to raise her child anywhere other than here in East Berlin. He was a member of the Volkspolizei, trained to think with a suspicious mind.

She smiled and squeezed Horst's hand. "Thank you," she said, trying to sound as though she meant it. "Truly, Horst. Today is Paul's day, and I wouldn't want to complicate it by making plans without fully considering them. But I promise to think about it."

His troubled expression cleared, and he bent down to press a kiss to her cheek. "Good," he replied.

2 MARCH, 1962

Lise,

We've been digging for months now, and as exhausted as I am I spend my days thinking of you—you, and our child. I know I'm taking my life in my hands, digging this tunnel, but there's something about the work that I find almost liberating, if that's the right word—or rather, I have somewhere to focus my efforts. Somewhere concrete, which can draw my attention, if only to stop my mind from wandering to darker places.

All my love,
Uli

16

Uli stepped into the pub's basement, breathing in the mineral rich scent of freshly dug earth. Listening for distant sounds of industry below, he unbuttoned his shirt and changed into the pair of mud-stained dungarees he'd left hanging on one of the nails that Jurgen had hammered into the wall, tucking a dirt-encrusted pickax into an empty belt loop.

Three months into digging, the pub basement had gained permanent signs of its temporary occupants. Dozens of buckets stood stacked against the walls, emptied each evening by Wolf, who'd modified the shocks of his NSU Prinz to carry the hundreds of pounds of earth he drove out of the neighborhood under cover of darkness. They'd smuggled shovels and pickaxes into the cellar by way of the service door in the building's courtyard, shielded from sight from the East German guards perched in their sentry posts.

Uli approached the unsightly hole that served as a platform from which to dive into the depths of the ground beneath Bernauer Strasse, and, bare chested, climbed down the ladder.

The tunnel was twelve feet deep—deep enough, Uli hoped, for them to remain undetected beneath the shallow foundations of apartment buildings, but not so deep as to disturb the city's water table.

At the bottom he got to his hands and knees, fingers curling over the dense, moist earth that had become the sole concern of his subterranean existence. He began to crawl, his knees aching at the uncomfortable familiarity of his crouched position: at only three feet square, the tunnel would be claustrophobic to anyone who wasn't part of their digging team, but to Uli it had become a second home. His fingers caught on the smooth iron rails for the narrow-gauge railcar that Jurgen had built to help transport earth out of the ever-lengthening tunnel, mechanized to pull itself along cables with the flick of a switch. It was a mercy, now that the tunnel was nearly seventy metres long, but Uli never complained about the distance. Every foot of track laid down was a foot closer to Lise, and Uli measured his work in inches, lit by the bare bulbs that Wolf had hung along the wooden struts that helped the tunnel keep its shape.

He let out a breath that fogged his glasses, listening to the sounds above that indicated he was beneath Bernauer Strasse, where heavy cars shook sawdust loose from the support beams. He could hear the muffled sound of conversation from pedestrians overhead, the occasional bray of laughter from the hundreds of tourists who congregated to see the Wall and shout abuse at the border guards who turned their backs to the West.

He paused to look up at a small, block letter sign that was fixed to the support beam: YOU ARE NOW ENTERING THE TERRITORY OF THE GERMAN DEMOCRATIC REPUBLIC. He smirked: the sign had been Inge's contribution, nailed to the board which the diggers suspected lay directly beneath the Wall itself. They'd broken through this barrier nearly two months ago, and it had been a solemn, momentous moment. From here, any conversation within the tunnel was made at barely a whisper, given that the East Germans had listening devices dug deep into the earth to detect tunnels like theirs. It was sheer luck that they'd not been caught out, that the earth above them hadn't collapsed in an explosion brought on by a hand grenade thrown by a border guard who'd heard their scratching.

After several more minutes of crawling, Uli reached the end of the tunnel where Inge crouched with a trowel in hand beside the miniature railcar that ran along the narrow-gauge track. He smiled, satisfied at the progress they'd all made. The diggers worked in teams of two—Uli and Inge, and Wolf and Jurgen, switching off every five hours—and Inge had arrived early, no doubt to install a new segment of the ventilation shaft that she'd run from the tunnel's entrance to ensure a steady supply of fresh air.

He rested a hand on Inge's ankle so as not to startle her, and she shifted, contorting to allow Uli to crawl to the tunnel's end. He pulled the pickax from his belt loop, got to his knees and began chipping away at the earth, stopping occasionally to flex blood back into his fingers while Inge filled the railcar. Though the tunnel itself was damp and cold, theirs was heavy, hot work made harder by the soil's claylike composition, and soon Uli was covered in a sheen of sweat that slicked the pickax from his hand.

After an hour, Inge rested her hand on Uli's shoulder and they switched positions, Inge shoveling while Uli filled the railcar. His back ached from holding such a cramped position for so long, and he stretched out along the tunnel's floor to ease his pains, measuring his progress by the distance they'd managed to eke out from Inge's ventilation shaft: they'd extended the tunnel by another foot, and Uli's fingers brushed against Inge's as they shifted in the close space.

After another hour's silent work, Inge glanced back sharply.

"Uli," she whispered, and Uli looked up from the nearly full railcar. She tapped against the tunnel's end with her trowel, scraping away a layer of dirt to reveal the long-hidden foundations of a building.

He frowned. "It's too soon." They'd been digging in the direction of Lise's apartment building on Rheinsberger Strasse, careful to avoid the foundations of buildings in their path, but according to Uli's calculations they were still several weeks away from breaking through to the correct cellar.

They crawled back out of the tunnel without speaking, but Uli knew that Inge was as concerned as he was. Once they emerged in the cellar basement, Inge crossed to the pile of maps they'd brought down from Uli's apartment and rolled them out on the cellar floor.

"I don't understand," she muttered, dropping to her hands and knees to inspect the maps. "We've been digging south-southeast from the cellar for weeks, measured the length…" She planted a finger on the map, situating the block between Bernauer Strasse and Rheinsberger Strasse. "The blockage is here, beneath Schönholzer Strasse. Could it be an old foundation? Something left over from before the war?"

Uli hissed out a curse. Like so many of Berlin's city blocks, Schönholzer Strasse was composed of old tenement buildings, Mietskasernen, which had been built and added on to over the years to become rabbit warrens of rooms stacked on rooms in increasingly smaller courtyards. Perhaps one of those additions had been built differently from the rest, its foundation dug deeper than its fellows.

Inge sighed. "What does this mean? Do we break into this building instead of the one on Rheinsberger Strasse?"

Uli shook his head. "It's too risky." He didn't know a thing about the building itself, other than that it was a block closer to the Wall—and thus subject to more scrutiny from border guards. "We'll have to go around it."

His back cracked as he straightened to pace around the small cellar. They'd made it so close to their goal—only a few more weeks of work and they would have hit Lise's cellar with time to spare before Lise's due date. How many more weeks of digging would this complication cause?

Inge rolled the maps and looked up at Uli, her blue eyes seeming brighter than normal above her dirt-stained cheeks. "It's a delay, Uli. It isn't an ending."

He could feel himself trembling. So many months of work, so many long days spent underground, digging toward a future that had been snatched from his grasp. He dropped down beside Inge and buried his head in his hands, not trusting himself to voice his despair without shouting. "Damn it. *Damn it.*"

"I know." Inge rested her head on his shoulder, but her words were scant comfort as he tallied up the cost of the delay in days, in inches and feet of lost time. "We'll talk to Wolf and Jurgen… see if there's some solution—"

The feel of her head on his shoulder was suddenly more than he could stand, and he jerked away from her with a swift shrug as he got to his feet. "What solution could they possibly have? Christ, Inge, this is going to add weeks to the job—weeks Lise doesn't have."

"You think I don't know that?" Inge, too, stood. "You think this isn't as frustrating to me as it is to you?"

"Of course it isn't," Uli spat. "She's my fiancée. She's pregnant with my child. You couldn't possibly know—"

"And she's my friend." Inge looked as furious as Uli felt. "You're upset, but don't you dare take this out on me. I'm here, every day, working just as hard as you are."

Uli's anger evaporated as quickly as it had come. "I'm sorry." He removed his glasses to rub at the aching spot on his temple. "I know, Inge, and I'm so grateful for you. I just… I forgot myself, for a moment."

The floorboards creaked beneath Inge's feet. "Thank you for saying that." She drew close to him once more, gripping her arms tightly around her middle. "What we're doing is difficult, Uli, but we can't start sniping at each other. We just can't."

"I know." Instinctively, Uli pulled Inge, still cross-armed into a hug, her elbows sharp against his chest. "Forgive me, Inge. Please."

For a moment longer, Inge bristled, but then she relaxed into his arms. "It's forgiven." She pulled back, her blue gaze full of conviction. "We're so close to the end. We're going to make it, Uli. I promise."

26 MARCH, 1962

Dear Uli,

The snowdrops have begun to bloom in the garden outside my building, and it always seems such a marvel to me when those first shoots appear—to realize that the soil which has seemed so barren and cold for so many months has in fact been hard at work, creating the right conditions so that new life might thrive.

Yours always,
Lise

17

It was unseasonably warm inside the dressmaker's shop, and Gerda had opened the front window to let a spring breeze caress the bolts of fabric that stood lined against the wall. Bent over the ancient draper's table, Lise lifted her head and inhaled deeply, thinking of chestnut trees and the balmy warmth of summer sunlight. The long, slow evenings of July were still months away, but the breeze carried on it the green promise of spring, and she allowed herself to bask in the prospect of lilacs before turning her attention back to her work.

She ran her hands along the gray-blue polyester that lined the table, thinking wistfully of the vibrant hues of a summer sunset. She'd worked with this drab fabric more times than she could count—it was a hardy, economical blank canvas to turn into smart skirts and jackets, an ideal uniform of sorts for the neighborhood's working women. Today, she'd laid the polyester out in service of a new commission: a skirt suit for the wife of some Party member or another, who'd pulled the latest issue of *Sibylle* out of her handbag to show a photograph to Gerda for inspiration.

She'd watched as Gerda tried to coax Frau Becker into choosing a color more suited to her complexion than the blue-gray—something in raspberry or plum, classic and elegant with the client's dark coloring. She had glanced longingly at a bolt of beautiful magenta linen while Gerda was taking her measurements—Gerda must have purchased it long ago, before the border closure—but Frau Becker shook her head. Party members gave themselves special treatment, Lise knew, treatment which would easily extend to choosing the more luxurious fabrics that Gerda had on offer in the back of the shop—but what message would it send if the wife of a Party member allowed herself to look like she could afford such fineries?

Lise pulled a measuring tape from around her neck and began calculating the yardage, glancing at the open pages of the magazine that the client had left behind more out of curiosity than for inspiration. The photograph that the client had referenced was of a model wearing a tailored skirt and jacket combination, with three-quarter-length sleeves and a midcalf hemline—ideal, Lise supposed, for cocktail functions full of self-congratulatory *apparatchiks* who stuffed themselves full of the kinds of food and drink impossible to find at Konsum grocery stores.

Like peaches, she thought longingly, and her stomach clenched with the craving she'd been unable to satisfy since the start of her pregnancy. She'd not seen a peach since her days at the Free University: she doubted she would until she returned to the West.

Until then, apples would have to suffice.

She rested a hand on the rise of her stomach, knowing that the date of her departure was fast approaching. She'd not heard from Uli or Inge in weeks, but she knew how hard they'd been working: each time she walked along Rheinsberger Strasse she pictured Uli digging beneath her feet, coming ever closer to the cellar of her old apartment building.

She longed to breathe the air of West Berlin, but she couldn't deny that with each passing day the escape became riskier. Seven months into her pregnancy, she was uncomfortable and ungainly, and worries about how she would traverse the narrow confines of the tunnel plagued her anxious mind. What would happen if she got trapped beneath Bernauer Strasse? What if the stress of the escape brought on an early labour? She'd woken more times than she could count from nightmares about having a breech birth halfway through the tunnel, and though she knew upon waking that the journey would take mere minutes, how could she be sure she wouldn't slow down her fellow escapees?

There were so many factors to consider; so many things that could go wrong.

And yet...

She looked once more at the pages of *Sybille*, thinking of the promises it offered. Unlike previous editions of the magazine, which showed models stiffly positioned against elegantly draped backdrops, this model had been photographed out and about in East Berlin: striding along the wide boulevard of the recently renamed Karl-Marx-Allee; dancing beneath the dappled foliage of Volkspark Friedrichshain.

In another photo, she lounged on a bench at a U-Bahn station. The effect was effortlessly sartorial: even if the outfit skewed somewhat dowdy for Lise's tastes, the model looked modern and carefree, as though she was waiting for the train to whisk her anywhere she wanted to go.

These days, riders on the U-Bahn avoided each others' eyes as they rocketed past the boarded-up stations that had once dropped passengers in West Berlin. It wouldn't do, to meet a stranger's eye and show any emotion that might be mistaken for a longing to return to the way things were, back when the trains let out passengers at all the stations. Not when a frown or a stifled smile could result in a visit from the secret police, tipped off by someone eager to show their loyalty to the state.

East Germany could make all the empty promises it wanted, but Lise could see the limitations of the world around her. She would do whatever it took to return to where she truly belonged.

Once Lise had finished measuring and cutting the length of fabric she needed, she laid out the pattern pieces that Gerda had made based on Frau Becker's measurements and started pinning the pieces to the fabric in a jigsaw-like fashion. *Supraspinatus*, she thought as she pinned the yoke front pattern piece to the polyester, recalling her anatomy lessons from the Free University. She picked up the pattern piece that she would use to cut out the jacket's shoulder. *Subdeltoid bursa.*

From behind her, Gerda let out a satisfied huff. "Very nice."

"Thank you." Lise straightened, letting the measuring tape slide between her swollen fingers. "It's a pretty pattern. Frau Becker will be pleased with it, I think." She reached for the next pattern piece—the center back seam—and laid it over the polyester. *Trapezius. Levator scapulae.* "It's a shame she chose the blue-gray. She's so much better suited to rose tones."

Gerda hesitated before answering. "She'll look just as lovely in the blue." She reached into the pocket of her smock apron and pulled out the shop's keys. "I've an appointment at my daughter's school this afternoon. You wouldn't mind closing up, would you?"

"Of course not."

Gerda laid the keys on the table and chuckled. "School appointments, trips to the doctor's office, recitals... It won't be long before your little one keeps you running about the city on their behalf, too!"

Lise smiled, picturing her baby wailing its tiny lungs out in Uli's apartment. "I look forward to it."

"At least you'll have help," Gerda continued. "There's nowhere else on earth better for a single mother than East Germany. Have you registered with the local nursery yet?"

She looked up. "Not yet."

"Well, it won't be too difficult to manage. I found the state nurseries were so helpful when I had my Frida. She was so well cared for that I was back at the shop and contributing to the economy in no time."

Lise waved Gerda out the door before returning to her task. Their conversations could be so jarring, shifting from natural to forced in a manner that Lise found exceedingly frustrating. Why did Gerda suddenly sound like she was reading off a prepared placard?

It was several more hours before Lise finished cutting out the pieces for Frau Becker's outfit, and by the time she left, the afternoon breeze had become an evening chill. She collected the off-cut scraps of polyester and left the outfit's many pieces on the draper's table, ready to be pinned to a dressmaker's figure tomorrow. She swept the floor clean and pulled the curtains across the front window, then paused as something wedged between the window frame and the wall caught her eye.

It was a small round of plastic, barely visible but for a slight buckle in the drywall that had pulled the window frame a centimetre or so out of alignment. With the curtains pulled open, the thing was completely concealed, and she frowned, reaching out to pull it loose before she thought better of her actions. Could it be a listening device?

If so, Lise knew better than to disturb it. Unnerved, she shut the curtains and turned out the light before locking up.

Stasi, she thought, her blood chilling at the notion that everything she and Gerda said was overheard, documented by some faceless spy. She thought back to conversations she'd had with Gerda about their clients, petty gossip and overheard observations, shared intimacies that had been meant for an audience of one. Did Gerda know the shop was under surveillance? Did she suspect?

"Lise."

Lise had been so deep in thought that she'd nearly passed by

Inge without noticing her, and though her heart leaped at the prospect of what Inge's visit signified, her presence, following so quickly on the heels of Lise's discovery, was decidedly unwelcome.

"Not here," she hissed. "Weinbergspark, five minutes."

From the corner of her eye she saw Inge nod, and she quickened her steps, allowing Inge to melt away behind her.

Perhaps she was being overly dramatic. But if the Stasi had her under surveillance, she couldn't be too careful. Listening devices were the stuff of silver-screen intrigue and Bond novels, bugged hotel rooms where spies and terrorists plotted coups over bottles of poisoned whisky—not for monitoring conversations about hem lengths and polyester yardage. The very idea that she and Gerda were worthy of such scrutiny seemed absurd. But then she thought back to the letters she'd sent after the border closure, and her brief detainment in August.

Uli's tunnel.

Republikflucht, she thought, giving name to the crime she was planning to commit. The simple fact that she was here, walking through the neighborhood, meant she'd not been found guilty of premeditation—not yet. Was the listening device evidence that the Stasi was mounting a case against her? Or was it the sort of deterrent meant to scare anyone who might come across it?

She pictured some spook in an overhead window as she scuttled into the park and resisted the urge to look up.

She ordered a coffee at a glass-fronted café and sat at a vacant table on the terrace, watching as children played tag on the sloping lawn below. When she'd been their age, this park had been little more than a rubble yard, and the parents of the children Lise had played with shouted warnings as they clambered up piles of rebar and concrete. It hadn't been long before she and her friends had been put into Young Pioneer programs, where they'd been taught to salute to socialism under the watchful eye of platitude-spouting troupe leaders.

All to encourage the right sort of thinking, she mused, swirling milk into her coffee.

But then, if the state was so good at indoctrinating its young citizens, why did it feel the need to monitor their conversations?

She didn't dare smile when Inge sat down at the table beside hers; didn't dare look up and acknowledge Inge's presence openly, not while paranoia still crept along her spine. "How are you?"

"I'm well. And yourself?"

Lise chanced a glance and was surprised at how pale Inge had become in the few months since they'd last seen each other; how digging had burned away the curves she'd once had. Had Uli been similarly transformed by the work?

"I'm better for seeing you," she said. Following so closely on her discovery, consorting with a Westerner felt reckless, but Lise couldn't help it—Inge felt like a lighthouse in a storm, calming her jangling nerves. "Is it time?"

Inge reached into her bag and opened a book, skimming the pages with practiced concentration. "Not yet."

Acid dropped into the pit of Lise's stomach. "What do you mean?"

"There's been a—a complication. We're now a month away from—from delivering." Inge looked up, her blue eyes darting to meet Lise's. "I'm sorry. We're moving as quickly as we can."

Lise blinked back the sudden sting of tears. Another month of waiting. How could she endure it?

She swallowed back the knot that had formed in her throat. "I understand," she muttered, and out of the corner of her eye she watched as Inge fought back the urge to say more, to offer the sort of sympathy that would have caught the attention of too many others.

"If you need us to delay further—to wait until after the baby's arrived—"

"No. Tell me what I can do. How can I—" She broke off,

resisting the urge to slam her fist on the table. The notion of coming across the border seven months pregnant had been hard enough to contemplate, but the thought of another month worth of waiting—the thought of crawling beneath the city of Berlin *eight* months pregnant—was enough to turn her stomach. Still, it was her only option. How could she crawl through a tunnel with a newborn in arms? "What can I do to help?"

"There's a couple in Bernau, Jurgen's brother and sister-in-law. I've not been able to tell them about the change in timing." Inge took a slip of paper and positioned it within the pages of her book, then set the book down as she rummaged in her pocketbook for Ostmarks to pay for her coffee. "Make contact with them and let them know about the delay."

"I will." She looked past Inge's shoulder at a man reading the newspaper with studied concentration; at a woman who'd taken too long over her jam and toast. Lise met Inge's eyes a second time, and though she longed for more conversation—for news of Uli—she knew they'd lingered long enough.

Inge stood. "Lise," she said in an undertone as she arranged a beige scarf around her neck. "What we're doing… If the Stasi catch wind of it…" She trailed off. "No one would blame you if we were to stop now. Before we can't go back. We could wait a few months, a year, until your baby's stronger…"

Lise thought of the microphone in Gerda's shop and shook her head once, slightly, as if dislodging a fly from its perch. "This is our only option," she replied. "Tell Uli I'll see him soon."

"I will. Take care, Lise."

Lise didn't dare watch as Inge strode out of the café, and she waited a moment longer before standing herself, arranging the folds of her overcoat just so as she slipped the book Inge had left atop her bill into her sleeve jacket, knowing that she would find the address of Jurgen's brother concealed within the pages.

18

APRIL 1962

Uli stood in his bedroom, listening to the muffled sound of the shower across the hall. He stared at his reflection in the mirror he'd hung on the back of the closet door, taking stock, for the first time, of the transformation that months of digging had wrought on his body. He'd always been slim but working underground had carved out hollows in his stomach that Uli had never seen before, his muscles lean and wiry beneath layers of grime. He rubbed at his arm, revealing a stark shock of pale skin: when was the last time he'd properly enjoyed the sun?

He crossed to the kitchen and pulled a bottle of beer from the refrigerator, listening to the faint sound of Inge humming some song in the shower. After every shift in the tunnel, he and Inge returned to his apartment to clean themselves up before continuing on with their respective days. He'd given Wolf and Jurgen a set of keys so they could do the same—it aroused less suspicion than letting his friends travel halfway across the city caked in mud.

It also made the apartment something of a train station. Duffel bags of clothes and equipment were piled next to the bassinet in the nursery room and behind the sofa, while the refrigerator was full of food Uli hadn't bought. Most afternoons he came home to find Jurgen asleep on the couch or in the bed, or Wolf in the kitchen, preparing something to eat; whenever Uli switched on the television, it was tuned to Inge's favourite channel. There was something in it all that pulled at Uli's heartstrings—their company made the place feel more like a home to Uli than it had since Lise's departure.

He returned to the bedroom and collapsed onto the mattress, waiting for his turn in the shower. He balanced the beer bottle on his stomach and tried to identify the song Inge was singing. "Twist & Shout"? He closed his eyes, and imagined that it was Lise in the shower, singing so shockingly off-key.

In another few weeks, it would be. How would his life change, once Lise was back? He could see it all, playing out like the start of a film. They would live here, in this apartment, properly furnished with Lise's input; they would return to school, the pair of them, to finish the degrees they'd put off. They would walk hand in hand to their classes, stop on their way home for romantic dinners…

He opened his eyes, the smile fading from his lips. His life with Lise would be nothing like it had been before the Wall. How could Uli think of returning to school once he had a baby to care for? He would have to find a job, once Father's loan ran out—and a good job, too, one which would allow them to hire a nurse so Lise could resume her studies. But what sort of job would that be?

He wasn't the same man he'd been last summer, and Lise couldn't possibly be the same woman. Would she still want the same life they'd dreamed about when she'd accepted his proposal?

He heard the bathroom door open, and Inge, wrapped in Uli's

house robe with her hair piled high in a towel, padded barefoot into the bedroom.

"What's wrong?" She reached into the bedside table where Uli kept a pack of cigarettes—more for Inge's benefit than for his own. She sat on the end of the bed, her pale eyes ghostly without her usual mascara.

Uli got to his feet and crossed to the kitchen. "Nothing at all." He pulled a bottle of pilsner from the refrigerator for Inge and knocked off the cap before returning to the room and handing it to her. "What makes you think something's the matter?"

She shrugged. "You have that look about you, that's all."

"What look?"

She lit the cigarette and leaned back against the mattress, propping herself up with an elbow. "That look you get whenever we're in the tunnel," she replied. "When you're there, but you're not really *there.* You know what I mean?"

He drummed his calloused fingers along the neck of his bottle. "We're days away from breaking through, and I—I suppose it's finally all becoming real," he said finally.

"Oh?" Inge exhaled, her sharp features pulled back further by her terry cloth turban as she studied him through a billow of smoke. "How do you mean?"

"I mean..." He fumbled to put his feelings to words. "Lise is *pregnant.*"

"I know," Inge replied, amused. "She's positively glowing. Are you worried about bringing her through the tunnel? I promise, we'll get her through safely."

"It's not that." He played with the label on his beer bottle, prizing up the edge with a dirt-crusted nail. "It's just...what happens after? I've been so focused on getting her here, I've not stopped to think about what it will be like once she *is* here. Our lives are going to be so different from what we thought they were going to be. What if we realize we no longer...no longer fit together like we used to?"

He glanced up, watching as Inge shook her hair loose from the towel. Twenty minutes ago, it would have been hard to mistake her for the mud-stained creature who'd emerged from the tunnel; twenty minutes from now, it would be hard to mistake this scrubbed-clean student for the glamorous woman who would leave the apartment. Before the Wall went up, Uli had considered Inge to be Lise's friend, first and foremost: the glittering, impractical contrast to Lise's understated charms. But their long hours spent together had unearthed a friendship that Uli hadn't fully expected—one where anything less than honesty would have felt cheap.

She clamped her cigarette between her teeth as she raked out tangles from her hair with her fingers. "Is *that* all? Uli, what if she'd never left? What if you'd gotten married a year ago, and come to that same realization?" She must have seen the look of alarm on Uli's face, because she smiled, then tapped the ash from her cigarette into an empty teacup on the nightstand. "I'm not saying this to upset you, but to make a point. You might decide you're ill-suited, after all. But the fact of the matter is that it's her choice to make."

He didn't entirely know how to respond.

"Look, you love her, yes? So, no matter what happens to the two of you, you've done the right thing. She's not coming to the West for you alone. She intends to be a doctor. To give her baby the kind of life she wants for it. The way I see it, all you're giving her—all *we're* giving her—is a choice. To live life on her own terms. And if those terms include you, all the better for it." Inge looked up, her easy manner shifting into something steelier. "But if you're doing this in the expectation that Lise will owe you her freedom, then you're no better than the Stasi."

He'd never thought of it that way: he'd never had to, and the realization was an uncomfortable one. He looked down, chastened. "I suppose you're right."

She shifted off the bed and collected the damp towel in the

crook of her arm. "I know I am. But the fact that you're worrying about all this does you credit." She hesitated, and a sudden red flush rose in her cheeks. "I can't promise that everything will be hearts and roses for the two of you. That's the nature of any marriage, I'm afraid. But for what it's worth, I know you and Lise are meant for each other." She crossed the bedroom to rest her hand on Uli's shoulder, and Uli felt some of his doubts ease. "You take risks, loving the way you do. I admire that, you know. But I promise, Uli, it will all be worth it in the end."

19

APRIL 1962

Lise stepped out of the train station, squinting up the sunlit street as passenger-stuffed Trabis trundled up the road. Across the street, medieval half-timber buildings stood next to stern Socialist blocks and building sites, the distant spire of an ancient church looking incongruously quaint against the stark rooftops of sparkling new apartment buildings.

She walked away from the old city center through the city's winding streets, silently reminding herself of the address Inge had scrawled for her in the pages of a paperback novel.

Like so many of the suburbs that hemmed in East Berlin, Bernau was a dizzying contradiction of old and new, monolithic stretches of sturdy apartment blocks and ancient city walls, gray concrete buildings with whitewashed windows that stood in such close proximity to their neighbors that Lise could picture their inhabitants leaning over the narrow span of air that separated the balconies to pass judgment on each others' new curtains and dinner sets.

But perhaps that was exactly the point: to know that one's

actions were under scrutiny even within the walls of one's own house; to know that privacy, like freedom, was an illusion.

Finally, she stopped outside the address she'd memorized. The building was identical to its neighbors, a recently constructed *plattenbau* made of the same slabs of concrete that comprised stretches of the Wall along Bernauer Strasse.

She walked through the door and was halfway up the staircase when her stomach clenched, dizzyingly tight.

She gripped the banister. *Braxton Hicks*, she thought, rubbing a hand over her abdomen. *Not yet, little one.*

In the fourth-floor corridor, florescent lights fizzed above orange carpeting that had already worn thin beneath the heavy traffic of the building's inhabitants. She thought of the microphone in Gerda's shop, carefully wedged in the ancient windowsill: the Stasi wouldn't need to resort to such tactics here, in a building where they could install whatever listening devices they pleased behind the fresh new drywall.

She reached the third door to the left of the elevator and knocked twice, plastering a smile to her face as she heard faint footsteps approach the door.

It was opened by a willowy stranger with a small, wild-haired child clinging to her hip.

"Brigit, darling!" Lise held out her hands and the woman, with admirable presence of mind, pulled her into a hug.

"So good to see you." She stepped back, and though her tone matched Lise's note for note in enthusiasm, a look of bemusement rippled across her beautiful features. "My goodness, how long has it been…?"

"Since Tomas's birthday party," Lise said, reciting the words that Inge had instructed her to say, and the woman's expression cleared. "Siegfried and Wilma got tipsy and fell into Marchenbrunnen Fountain, remember that?"

"How could I forget?" Brigit replied without missing a beat. "Siegfried wanted to kiss the statue of Cinderella."

Lise let out a breath, feeling the tension dissipate between them. *Jurgen's sister-in-law*, she thought, and slid her gaze to the child in Brigit's arms. *Willa.*

"We've so much to catch up on, and this little one is in need of some fresh air," Brigit said, bouncing Willa with an affectionate squeeze that made the child beam with delight. "Why don't I get her coat and we'll go to the park?"

An hour later, Lise climbed into a half-empty compartment on the S-Bahn and navigated toward an empty seat. *There*, she thought, exhilarated, as the train pulled away from the station. She'd relayed all the information she'd needed to Brigit in a whisper: where and when she would send word that the tunnel was complete; how Brigit would be able to identify the person who would lead her and her family to the tunnel's entrance.

Find a woman by Berlin Nordbanhoff station, and if she's wearing red it's safe to follow, Lise had instructed, but it was clear Brigit wanted more details than Lise was able to give. She knew better than to divulge the location of the tunnel's entrance to Brigit—she had no doubt that Brigit was sincere in her wish to cross the border, but who was to say that she wasn't being monitored by Stasi agents? That her husband—Jurgen's brother—hadn't been compromised at work, or that some listening device wouldn't pick up on a conversation between the two of them, at home where they might feel safe enough to speak about such matters? Information could be extracted in any manner of ways, and Lise was only too aware of how one single false move could put the entire operation—and everyone who hoped to escape—in peril.

Even Lise didn't know the true extent of the escape, only what Inge had told her—and Inge, Lise suspected, hadn't told her everything. But there was something galvanizing in the realization that there was a network of people like her—people who knew one or two scraps of information, which they would soon knit together into a map out of East Berlin.

She closed her eyes, letting the train's rocking movement lull her into a daydream. What a relief it would be, to be able to speak openly once more.

The train's brakes screeched as it neared Friedrichstrasse station, and Lise opened her eyes. She gripped the handrail and got to her feet as the train slowed, squealing, to a halt, then pushed the compartment's door open to step out onto the platform.

She knew what was going to happen before it did, the world slowing to a crawl as her heel snagged in the grate of the compartment's sliding door. She tipped forward, but her heel remained stubbornly in the grate and she tumbled down the steps, hearing cries of alarm, footsteps, as she crashed forward.

"Help!"

She felt her wrists crack as she hit the ground, instinctively throwing them forward to protect the baby, but she landed on her stomach nonetheless and the impact was hard enough to rip the air from her lungs. *No*, she thought as a searing pain gripped her so tightly that the world turned black. She felt a sudden rush of warmth between her legs as unseen hands guided her onto her back, and she shuddered as the wave of a contraction took hold, and then another—too intense, too quickly, to be Braxton Hicks.

It's a month too soon, it's too early—

"Are you all right?"

"Someone call an ambulance!"

She blinked her eyes open and the world slid into focus to reveal a Vopo officer hovering above her, his square jaw clenched as he pressed a hand gently to her shoulder. "Stay where you are, fräulein. Help is coming."

"It's too soon," she said, choking on her words. She could feel her body going into shock, blood staining her skirt dark, and she fought to stay conscious. "It's too soon, the baby—"

"Help is on the way."

She closed her eyes, picturing Uli's face, Uli's hands, holding her close as she was bundled into a stretcher and borne away.

20

Uli stood in the damp of the tunnel, squinting in the darkness as he and Wolf scraped carefully at the earth overhead. According to his calculations they were within striking distance of the cellar floor, and they didn't dare to illuminate their way while they were working: not here, where their lights might shine through floorboards and give them away.

He held his breath, his shoulders aching after hours of silent, painstaking work. Though the rest of the tunnel was shored up by overhead braces, there was nothing now between him and the earth: one wrong move could cause a collapse that might suffocate them both. It was why Uli had asked for Wolf's help in excavating the tunnel's entrance, rather than Inge's: this, and the potential that the Stasi might be waiting overhead, listening to every scrape of Wolf's trowel.

Superstitiously, Uli reached back to touch the pistol he'd tucked into the back of his trousers. It had been procured by Jurgen from some black market or another, and some strange fit of gallantry had prevented Uli, Jurgen and Wolf from mentioning its existence to Inge.

Wolf grunted as a small shower of clay fell to the ground, and Uli swallowed his frustration as the trowel revealed nothing but more earth. He hoped beyond hope that he'd not miscalculated: it had been his decision to dig upward here, hollowing out a narrow shaft which at first had been barely tall enough to crouch in, and now required the use of stout rungs, embedded securely in the shaft's clay walls. If all went to plan, they would be able to schedule the escape this week...but if he was off, even by a few feet in his calculations, they might find themselves sitting ducks in the middle of the apartment building's courtyard—or worse, beneath the concrete of the sidewalk outside.

He listened for the sound of movement overhead—footsteps, car wheels, the distant snippet of a radio—but all was mercifully silent, and they continued scraping. In such close quarters, he kept bumping against Wolf, and he found himself missing Inge: they knew how to work seamlessly together, moving in small spaces without being on top of each other. But Inge had left early that morning to East Berlin to do a final sweep of Rheinsberger Strasse.

Finally, Uli's trowel hit against something harder than dirt. He glanced at Wolf, seeing his own excitement—his own terror—reflected in his friend's face as he replaced his trowel with his fingertips to feel the underside of a wooden floorboard. Carefully, quietly, Uli scraped away at the wood, feeling his way along the grooved planks of a cellar floor.

He continued scraping, elation giving him renewed energy as he cleared a fist-sized section of board. Finally, Wolf tapped him on the shoulder, and Uli glanced back to see him shake his head: *Enough*.

Much as it irked Uli to stop, he knew Wolf was right: though they'd cleared a small section, to hollow out any more of the ground beneath the floorboard risked detection from someone—

a caretaker or handyman or building manager who might step in exactly the wrong place. The final push would have to be made during the escape itself.

Wolf held up a sturdy piece of wood—the same kind they'd used to brace the tunnel along its length—and Uli shifted out of the way so Wolf could prop it at an angle beneath the cleared floorboard. With luck, no one would step on that particular section of floor anytime soon, but if someone did, he didn't want their foot going through and giving them away.

They crawled back to West Berlin, Uli timing the journey as they went: it was seventeen minutes end to end, and as he and Wolf emerged in the cellar he couldn't help letting out a whoop of triumph.

"Finally!" He swung Wolf into his arms, and Wolf laughed, taken aback by the unexpected gesture. "Call Jurgen. Call Inge. We've got work to do, we need to set a date, the sooner the better—tomorrow, if we're lucky. We need to let—"

"Uli." Inge emerged through the door, her odd tone putting an abrupt end to Uli and Wolf's impromptu celebration. She wore a blue jacket over a minidress, her legs sheathed in white stockings and Mary Janes, looking impossibly clean amidst the dirt of the cellar.

She stepped over a discarded shovel, wearing a smile that looked as if she'd pulled it from the bottom of a well. "Congratulations, Uli. You're a father."

21

Lise stared up at the seafoam ceiling of the hospital room, blinking back the tears of a thousand emotions: joy and relief; exhaustion and pain. She looked down at the red-faced infant that lay dozing in a bassinet beside her: little Rudi had arrived faster than Lise had ever anticipated, the whirlwind terror of her fall bringing on an early labor that, thankfully, hadn't harmed the baby.

The same, unfortunately, couldn't be said for Lise. She looked down at her plastered arm, listening to the beeps and bustle of the hospital around her. She'd lost a lot of blood during labor, more than usual, and she'd broken one of her wrists in the fall from the train carriage. From somewhere beyond the morphine fog, she could feel the far-off panic of what her situation signified. The doctor had assured her that she would make a full recovery, but how could she crawl through the tunnel with a broken wrist and a newborn?

She laid her head back on the pillow and dropped her good hand ("merely a sprain," according to the doctor) into the bassinet. Rudi was sleeping, looking far too peaceful for someone who'd arrived in the world in such a dramatic fashion: peaceful and perfect, admittedly on the small side but mercifully healthy. She smoothed a finger over his warm cheek, feeling the entire axis of her world shift to orbit around him.

My son. All the long months of her pregnancy she'd been so focused on escaping East Berlin that she'd not thought of the baby as anything other than a complication: a stomach to be accommodated, pains to be eased. But now that he was here, she couldn't fathom that the world had ever existed without him: without his Uli-like mop of sparse black hair and his pointed, Lise-like nose.

Why hadn't she allowed herself to enjoy all those months when he'd been a part of her?

She listened to the shallow tide of his breath as he took small gulps of air, his lungs working out the business of how to properly breathe.

There was so much to learn, out here in the real world: so much to risk, now that he was no longer in the safety of Lise's womb.

"I'll teach you," she murmured drowsily, allowing her eyes to shut once more.

"Lise?"

She opened her eyes and let the world swirl back into focus as she met Papa's anguished gaze.

"Thank God. When we heard what had happened…how are you feeling?"

Lise struggled to push herself upright, wincing as she put weight on her sprained wrist. Across the room, Paul stood with Rudi in his arms, murmuring into the baby's ear.

"We're fine," she said as Papa pressed a kiss to her cheek. "Both of us, we're fine."

"I've had a word with your attending physician, and we both agree that you're to remain here under observation, for the time being. How do you feel?" he repeated, as though he'd forgotten that he'd already asked the question. "Your blood pressure, any dizziness?"

"I already told you, I'm fine," Lise replied. She dropped her head back to the pillow. "Beyond feeling like an absolute fool."

"You *were* an absolute fool," Paul whispered, rocking baby Rudi in his arms. He must have been summoned directly from his beat; he was still wearing his gray-green uniform, his peaked cap discarded on a nearby table. "How could you have been so reckless? You could have killed yourself! What were you doing at Friedrichstrasse station?"

"I know," Lise murmured. "My heel got stuck in the grate."

"But what were you doing at the station in the first place?" Paul pressed. "If you had errands to run, you could have sent me or Anna rather than traipsing halfway across Berlin—"

"It's my fault, I'm afraid," Papa interjected, lifting a hand to dispel the start of an argument. "I asked her to take a book I'd borrowed back to Frau Bottcher."

Lise looked up in surprise, but Papa's expression was guileless. Even in her delayed state, she knew that Papa was covering for her absence—did he know what had really taken her to Friedrichstrasse station? Did he suspect?

Finally, Paul let out an impatient sigh. "Don't you ever scare me like that again."

"There will be time for all this later," Papa replied. "For now, I want to meet my grandson."

Paul brought the baby forward and gently laid him in Papa's arms, and Lise swallowed back tears as she watched Papa gently press a kiss to Rudi's forehead.

"Hello, my boy." Papa looked up at Lise, his eyes brimming with tears. "Oh, my dear… Ever since we lost your mother, our family has felt incomplete, but now it feels as if we're finally whole again."

Lise could feel it, too: the baby fit in Papa's arms like a long-lost puzzle piece, his joy—*their* joy—filling the room with a serenity she'd never felt before.

A puzzle piece he'll soon lose. Though Papa felt their family was complete, Lise knew that it could never truly be complete without Uli. One day soon, she would have to leave half of her heart here, and though she'd reconciled herself to the impact her own departure would have on Papa and Paul, Rudi's arrival—and his imminent departure with her across the Wall—had thrown her decision into painful relief once more.

She'd just made Papa a grandfather. How could she rip that delicate new bond away from him so soon?

Paul circled to the other side of her bed and pulled up a stool. He put an arm around her shoulder and offered her a handkerchief; to her surprise, she realized she was crying.

"I'm sorry," she said, dabbing at her cheeks. "I've taken you both for granted for far too long, and I—I want you to know how much I love you both, how much I love—"

"We know," Paul replied steadily, and Lise could feel her heart break all over again. "We're so proud of you, Lise. So proud."

She pulled back, folding Paul's handkerchief along its sharp creases. "I'm sorry," she said again. "Look at me, falling apart. It must be the hormones... I'm not normally so—so sentimental."

"If you can't be sentimental when welcoming a new soul into the world, when can you be?" Papa rocked the baby gently in his arms. "What's his name, then?"

There would be time, in the days to come, to grieve over the pain she would have to inflict upon her family but for now, she let out a shaky breath and met Papa's gaze. "He's named after you, Papa. Rudolph Ulrich Neumann. Rudi. For his grandpapa."

The next afternoon, Paul and Papa returned for visiting hours, along with books and flowers to cheer up Lise's hospital room. Sometime after noon, Paul wandered down the hall in search of coffee, and Papa edged his wheelchair closer to Lise's bed. "You had a visitor at the apartment," he murmured, staring down at Rudi's sleeping form. "A friend of yours from the old days... your Swedish classmate."

Lise looked up, alarmed. "Papa, I—"

Under the guise of settling the baby, Papa eased Lise's objections. "I told her what happened. I didn't want her to worry." He looked up, meeting Lise's panicked gaze. "I didn't want *him* to worry, either."

Though Papa had proven his discretion with Paul, his words felt risky, reckless: a stolen moment of candor that made Lise feel as if she might still be dreaming under the effects of the morphine. "Papa, I—"

He glanced at the hospital room's open door. "You're making decisions as a parent now," he whispered. "Whatever you decide, know that you'll have my full support."

22

Uli's apartment was dimly lit, the music on the hi-fi lending slight credence to the illusion that the four people gathered within had been invited for a party. In the kitchen, he pulled beers from the refrigerator as Inge assembled toasts Hawaii on a baking sheet. On the sofa, Jurgen and Wolf sat side by side, trading puffs from the same joint.

He opened the oven door so Inge could slide the toasts beneath the broiler, mildly surprised at the realization that this was the first time he'd used the oven since signing the lease. These days, his diet consisted mainly of tinned ravioli and whatever was served in the nearest *Wirtschaft*—or whatever Wolf or Inge managed to rustle up from the cans in his cupboard. But surely this was an appropriate occasion for proper cooking, given that his friends had gathered to help him celebrate the arrival of his newborn son.

His son. The words sounded dizzying and wonderful and altogether unreal to Uli: to know that there was a child of his, out there in the world. Did he look anything like Uli, or had he inherited Lise's blond features?

Inge slid the baking sheet into the oven and straightened, wiping her hands on a tea towel that Uli realized was in need of a wash. "You okay?"

Just a few hours ago Inge had been in East Berlin, and though Uli was grateful for the news she'd brought back, the realization of what had happened—the image of Lise tumbling, pregnant, to the ground—terrified him.

He glanced back to make sure Wolf and Jurgen were still distracted on the couch, then let out a shaky breath. "I almost lost them, didn't I?"

Inge was silent for a moment. "You almost did. But you didn't."

There was something steadying in Inge's matter-of-fact tone, and Uli nodded. "I didn't lose them today," he replied, "but what if—what if—"

Inge rested a hand on his arm. "Asking *what if* will only lead to sleepless nights."

He met her eyes. "What if we don't succeed?"

She squeezed. "Then we try again." She glanced down at the oven, where the scent of caramelizing pineapple and cheese had begun to fill the room.

We try again. Uli watched as Inge topped the toasts with maraschino cherries, slid them onto a plate, then followed her into the living room to find that Wolf and Jurgen had set out small glasses filled with schnapps.

He traded Jurgen a beer for one of the shot glasses, his throat tight as he remembered the last toast that Jurgen had given in his honor.

Jurgen lifted the glass. "To Rudolph Ulrich Neumann."

Uli lifted his glass, feeling their mission more keenly than ever. "And to the tunnel that will bring him home."

He drank deeply, the liquor burning his throat as he swallowed. How strange to be wetting the baby's head without having met him. He wondered whether Lise's brother and father were doing the same thing tonight: Did they share in his sense of injustice at a father being kept from his son?

"To the tunnel," Wolf repeated. He picked up a piece of toast and bit into it, ravenous, no doubt, after his afternoon of digging. "Given our accomplishment, I think it's fair to toast to us as well. Tell me, Uli, how is this going to change our timing?"

Jurgen groaned. "Jesus, Wolf, give him a minute—"

"No, no," Uli replied. "It's a fair question. What do we do now?"

Inge sighed, crossing her legs as she leaned back in her armchair. "I'm afraid you're the only one who can answer that question," she said. "Whether we wait until Lise has regained her strength, or we continue on tomorrow as planned and try to find some other way to bring her and the baby across later—"

"No." Uli looked up. "We've come this far, we can't leave her behind. We can't leave *them* behind."

"That's as may be, but she's just given birth," Inge replied. "You expect her to crawl through a tunnel after *that*?"

"And we may not have a choice," Wolf added. "We hollowed out a hole beneath the cellar. It's only a matter of time before someone finds it."

Uli could feel a red heat rising in his cheeks. "Not without Lise," he repeated. "We've not even broken through the floorboard, so long as no one steps on it—"

"Be reasonable, Uli!" Wolf slammed his beer down on the table, causing an eruption of bubbles up the neck of the bottle. "You aren't the only one trying to get people out. We've twenty-six other passengers. Jurgen's family. Axel. You think we ought to make them wait any longer than they already have?"

"I know." Uli nudged his fingers beneath the glass of his spectacles to rub his eyes, the frustration and exhaustion of the day suddenly washing over him. When was the last time he'd gotten a decent night's sleep? "I know. But we've only got one chance with this. Once we break through to the cellar, we start a ticking clock: it will only be a matter of time before we're discovered. I intend to get everyone through safely before that happens, but we're not going to start that clock until Lise and the baby are ready to come, too."

"Then we'll be waiting some time," Inge said. "Her father told me that Lise will be in the hospital at least a week. The birth was quite traumatic, and she broke her wrist on top of it all. She'll need time to heal... The baby will need time to grow." She shook her head. "Bringing an infant through the tunnel... we didn't plan for that."

She stretched a long arm over the back of the chair, looking as tired as Uli felt. How many times had she ventured into East Germany these past months? How often did she fear for her own safety? The delay would mean more trips to East Germany for Inge, contacting their passengers as Uli, Wolf and Jurgen remained in relative safety in the West. How could he ask her to continue putting herself in peril?

He thought once more of his newborn son, growing up in a country where he would be expected to sing socialist nursery rhymes; a boy taught to think the way the Party wanted him to think, and pursue a career the Party told him to pursue.

What choice did he have?

"So, we plan for it now," he said. "We take the time Lise needs—another month, six weeks, however long it is—and we make sure the tunnel is as safe as it can be." Inge still didn't look entirely convinced, and Uli pressed on. "We always knew it was going to be a possibility that Lise might give birth early. Jurgen, what do you think?"

"If it were Brigit in that situation, I'd want to wait," Jurgen replied carefully. "We've put too much work into this—Uli's put too much work into this. We can't do it all a second time. We need to make sure that we get everyone across at once." He took a breath and clapped Wolf on the knee. "I say we postpone the escape. We can use the time to strengthen the tunnel, improve the ventilation, add waypoints, perhaps. We put first aid kits throughout. We might even recruit more passengers."

Uli beamed at Jurgen, grateful for his support. "Inge? What do you say?"

She inhaled deeply. "From a medical perspective, it's risky," she said carefully, "but it's manageable. I say we wait, too."

Uli smiled. "Thank you," he replied. "Well, Wolf?"

Wolf didn't smile back. "Another month of waiting is another month where we might get found out," he said. "I would feel better going tomorrow. But if Jurgen says we should wait..."

Uli got to his feet and reached across the table to offer his hand to Wolf. "Thank you, my friend," he said. "So, we're agreed? We wait?"

Jurgen lifted his beer bottle, and Wolf took Uli's hand. "We wait," he replied.

4 MAY, 1962

Dear Uli,

I am writing to inform you of the birth of Rudolph Ulrich Neumann, born 17 April, 1962.

Mother and child both well.

Regards,
Paul Bauer

23

The apartment was dimly lit, candles along the length of the dining table putting Lise in mind of long nights spent over open bottles of wine at the datsche. Sitting on the sofa with one ear listening for any signs of movement behind the closed door of Rudi's nursery room, Lise watched Paul and Anna bustle past the pass-through window in the kitchen. Lise had asked whether she could help with dinner, but she'd been quickly disabused of the notion: with one of her arms still in a cast, she knew that she would be of little use.

She and Rudi had been brought home from the hospital two days ago, and though Rudi had adjusted quickly to his new surroundings, Lise felt as though she was ready to burst. She'd weaned herself off painkillers in order to breastfeed, and her wrist constantly ached as a result. It was a pain exacerbated by knowing that she was still here, in East Germany: that, through her own clumsiness, she'd caused yet another delay in reuniting with Uli.

It was enough to make her scream, even without Anna's constant, anxious attempts to fluff her pillows.

Paul emerged from the kitchen, carrying a covered bowl.

"Voilà," he said, removing the napkin from the bowl with a flourish as Anna crept up behind him. "Canned peaches."

"Oh, Paul." Lise shifted upright. "You shouldn't have."

"He went to three different Konsum shops to find them," Anna offered as they slid onto the sofa. "He was determined to have them for you as a welcome home present."

Lise lifted a slice to her mouth, touched by the lengths he'd gone to in order to secure her this sweet taste of sunshine. "Thank you," she said, letting her irritable mood melt away. "Papa will be sorry to have missed these."

"He's perfectly happy at the opera," Paul replied, easing onto the sofa.

"Oh, I've news about that," Lise replied, adopting the low, conspiratorial tone that she and Paul had used since their days of sharing playground gossip. "You know who else is at the opera tonight? Gerda."

"No," Paul replied with a gleeful grin.

"Yes. She stopped by with a *kuchen* earlier and told me she was going to be there." Gerda had been filled with the joys of spring when she'd sat with Lise earlier that afternoon—more so than any evening at the opera warranted. She recalled how Gerda had brightened further when Papa had come through the front door, then thought back to how they'd sat together at Paul and Anna's wedding. If what Lise suspected was true, she was thrilled for them—they'd both been long widowed, and deserved happiness.

Paul nudged Anna. "I told you there was something different about Papa," he said before turning his attention back to Lise. "What do we think? Is it serious?"

It was a refreshing thing, to have a secret that she was able to share with her brother.

"I don't know," Anna cut in, snuggling herself into the crook of Paul's arm. "I always pictured your father with someone more matronly than Gerda."

"More 'matronly'? Why's that?"

"I don't know." Anna wrinkled her nose. "Gerda seems a little unreliable, that's all. Rudolph deserves someone steady."

Lise bristled. "Gerda *is* steady," she began, but Paul lifted his hand to quell the start of an argument.

"Well, if it's true, and she makes Papa happy, then it's wonderful news," he said, pressing a kiss to Anna's temple. "Everyone deserves to feel as happy as I do when I look at you."

Anna's giggle filled Lise's throat with bile. "Not in front of your sister, *liebling*."

Despite her efforts to swallow her feelings, Lise still managed to be irritated by Anna at every turn. Why shouldn't Gerda be good enough for Papa? Her time in the hospital had even felt like something of a respite when it came to Anna, but now that she was back at home, the true test of Lise's patience was about to begin. How long would they be able to share a roof before she throttled Anna in front of her brother?

"How about you, Lise?" Paul was saying as Anna got up to check the oven. "Have you *gone to the opera* with anyone lately?"

She snorted, fiddling with the rough edge of her cast. "You know I haven't."

"How about Horst?"

"Be serious."

"I am being serious." Lise looked up to find Paul staring at her, his blue eyes steady. "He told me what you two spoke about at the wedding—that you'd promised to give his proposal some thought. Have you?"

In the kitchen, the sound of clattering pots and pans had quietened, and Lise knew that Anna, too, was listening. "I've been in the hospital, Paul. I've had other things on my mind."

"And now you're out of the hospital. With a baby, no less." Paul leaned forward and rested his elbows on his knees. "Horst has always carried a torch for you. Hasn't Rudi put things in perspective? He deserves to have a father."

It was all too preposterous for words. "He has a father." Lise shot back. "He has three. Uli, Papa and you."

"That's as may be," Paul replied, "and you know that we'll always be here for Rudi, but you need to start thinking about your future. You need to start thinking about Rudi's future."

"I *am* thinking about my future." Lise pictured Uli, standing at the door to their apartment on Bernauer Strasse, and her heart lurched with sudden longing. "I just—I just don't feel that way for Horst. And I don't have the—the space to feel that way for anyone else."

"For anyone but Uli, you mean." Paul hadn't said his name since the border closure, and there was something in it that Lise hadn't heard before: a brittle edge of contempt. "You must see that you're living in a fantasy, Lise. I know this is difficult for you to hear, but this is the reality of your life now. You're not going to reunite with Uli. You're not going to be able to cross the border. No matter what you do, your life is here. You need to start living it."

Lise stared at him for a long moment, rattled by the certainty he had about the future that lay before her. "What are you trying to say, Paul?"

He studied her for a long moment. From the kitchen, Anna began clattering about once more, and the sound of her sudden movements made her eavesdropping absurdly clear.

"What I'm trying to say is that I want you to be happy," he said finally. "And I think that Horst could make you happy, if you'd let him." He glanced down as Lise's engagement ring caught the candlelight. "I'm not asking you to put your past aside. But you need to start thinking about your future. Please."

24

The lift clattered up toward the fourth floor, the sound of its iron mechanics echoing down the stairwell as they went. Though it was frequently out of service, the lift, when working, performed a blessed function after so many worn-out hours in the tunnel, and to Uli it almost felt worth the risk of being stuck between floors not to have to climb.

The lift stopped at the top floor and Uli opened the door, letting Inge exit first. Though they weren't excavating any more of the tunnel, they were steadily making it safer: reinforcing the joists that kept it from caving in; improving the lighting and the ventilation shaft to increase the flow of fresh air from the cellar.

It was all going well, but to Uli it felt like so much busywork. The fact that they'd reduced the number of hours spent below ground reflected the fact that there was little else to do but wait for news that Lise was well enough to travel.

The apartment was empty when Uli and Inge walked in, and the silence felt unusual after so many months of trading off shifts with Wolf and Jurgen.

"They must have gone home for the night," Inge said in response to Uli's unasked question.

"Good for them." Uli kicked off his shoes. "They deserve it."

Though Wolf and Jurgen spent all their time together in the tunnel, Uli worried about the impact all this work was having on their relationship. Too much time spent together could be as harmful as too much time spent apart, and Wolf and Jurgen rarely saw eye to eye, even at the best of times. With any luck, they were enjoying each other's company somewhere far from the concerns and stresses of the work that filled their days.

"They brought in your mail," Inge commented as she picked up a small pile of envelopes and a newspaper from the dining table. She flipped through the letters, then looked up at Uli with an apologetic smile. "It doesn't look like any of these are from East Berlin."

"Thanks." Though he'd not truly expected any letters from Lise, he couldn't help feeling a twinge of disappointment, nonetheless. He dropped into an armchair by the empty fireplace, allowing himself a moment to sink into his bone-deep exhaustion.

"I'll go across this weekend," Inge offered.

Uli lifted his head as she tossed the newspaper in his lap. She looked as worn out as he felt.

"You don't need to," he said. "Lise won't be ready to travel, not yet, and there's really nothing new to relay to our other passengers. Why not take the weekend off? You could go out, maybe go dancing?"

She grinned, perching on the edge of the sofa to untie her boot laces. "Dancing," she scoffed. "With who?"

"With whoever you like." Uli lifted his head, allowing himself to voice the opinions of a younger, more carefree, version of himself. "As I recall, you're particularly good at talking your way into the best clubs in town. Remind me, did you wear your wimple before or after getting through the front door?"

She laughed. "Lise was the one who impersonated a nun, not me," she replied. "Remember?"

"How could I forget? You and Lise," he murmured, recalling the night he met them both: how radiant Lise had looked; how intimidated he'd been, crossing the dance floor with Wolf, back before Wolf had fallen for Jurgen, beside him. "Unstoppable, the pair of you. Trouble."

"We'll be making plenty of trouble soon enough, don't you worry." Inge eased herself upright with a groan. "Mind if I take the first shower?"

"Help yourself."

He listened to the sound of her footsteps as she crossed the apartment, then the creak of the door followed by the steady sound of running water. Sighing, he opened the newspaper, skimming the headlines for news about East Berlin—it had become a habit of his, to monitor the pages for news about any successful escapes across the Wall.

A short article on the second page caught his attention, and he read with solemn interest about a young man who'd been shot dead in the border zone. He'd jumped over the fence of East Berlin's Charité Hospital and made a run toward the Wall—was it a planned escape, Uli wondered, or was it a decision he'd made on the spur of the moment?

Perhaps he'd been walking in the area and thought he was alone. Perhaps he'd been desperate enough to take the chance.

What a tragedy, for him to make such a gamble.

The article hadn't named this latest victim of the Wall—Uli doubted he'd been properly identified by authorities. But the names of all the other East Germans who'd tried and failed to make it into West Berlin echoed in Uli's mind, and these were the names that kept him awake in the early hours of each morning, haunted by the sound of gunshots outside his window. Ingo Krüger, who drowned in the Spree trying to reach his fiancée; Bernd Lünser, who missed the fireman's rescue net only a few blocks away from here on Bernauer Strasse. Günter Litfin, one of the first victims of the new regime, shot dead in the water at Humboldthafen; Udo Düllick and Werner Probst, both drowned in the waves of the Spree.

He stood and made his way to the window to look down at the battlements that now comprised the Wall. It had been nearly a year since the first spools of barbed wire were rolled across the city, and though Uli dug beneath the Wall every day he'd grown immune, somehow, to the sight of it outside his window: to the buildings across the street, their windows bricked all the way to the top; to the concrete slabs that ran across empty intersections. Gun-toting soldiers patrolled from square observation posts that loomed over wire and concrete, aided by blinding spotlights, staring down at the empty city blocks that comprised the hollow heart of the East German capital.

He'd made peace long ago with the idea that he might not survive his attempt to breach the Wall—that he might soon join the growing list of victims of the East German regime. But the idea that his actions—his tunnel—might be the cause of someone else's demise haunted him. How would he ever live with himself if Lise or Rudi didn't survive the attempt? If one of their other passengers didn't make it?

Inge emerged from the bathroom, wrapped in a house robe. "Do you mind if I sleep here tonight? I'm absolutely beat."

Uli glanced back at her, grateful for the distraction from his dark thoughts. "Of course." He stretched his arms overhead, easing the tension from his tight back. "You take the bed. I'll sleep on the couch."

"Are you sure? I'm happy to take the couch, it's really no trouble."

"I wouldn't dream of it," Uli replied. "You take the bed. Let me just grab a pillow first."

She shot him a weary smile. "Thanks."

Once Inge had gone to sleep, Uli turned out lights in the

kitchen and made up his bed on the sofa. He lingered at the window, watching as a light went on in the postage-stamp square of Lise's old apartment, and though he knew she didn't live there anymore his heart lifted out of sheer habit.

They all knew the risks of what they were about to do—Lise, Uli suspected, more than most.

"It has to work," he whispered, staring at the lamp across the Wall. "It has to."

He wasn't sure what would become of him if it didn't.

25

JUNE 1962

Lise pushed Rudi's carriage down Karl-Marx-Allee. She looked up as an ambulance drove past, its tidy blue siren blaring, and within the creamy cotton bed of the carriage, Rudi, swaddled in a crocheted blanket, stirred. She reached in to rest a hand atop the rounded rise of his belly, and he settled at her touch as the ambulance drove off, the noise of the siren replaced by the blank buzz of conversation from diners at nearby patios.

Lise smiled. Her insistence on taking Rudi through East Berlin's most bustling neighborhood at nap time baffled Papa and Paul, but she knew that having a resilient baby, able to sleep through anything, would soon serve her well.

She bumped across Berolinastrasse and made her way toward a newsagent's stand to peruse the magazines on offer. Beneath the shaded awning of the stall, newspapers and tabloids were stacked in rainbow abundance, their covers revealing a dizzying display of titles: *Berliner Zeitung, Die Neue Zeit* and *Neues Deutschland*, among so many others. Lise lifted magazine after magazine, each one condemning, in only slightly different terms, the death of border officer Reinhold Huhn at the Berlin Wall. His brigade had uncovered a tunnel, Lise knew, under Zimmerstrasse, and he'd been shot in the line of duty—however, Lise questioned the basics of the argument. Had Rudolf Müller, the tunnel's East German architect, truly shot first? Or had he killed Petty Officer Huhn out of self-defense?

It was hard to know, when every media outlet in the country received their talking points from the government.

She continued past the newsagent's stand and stopped outside a butcher's shop, running over the evening's menu in her mind—roast pork and potatoes—as she navigated Rudi's stroller up and over the steps.

Within, a handful of people waited at the counter, and Lise joined the crowd, watching as a paper-hatted butcher selected cuts of meat from behind a glass-fronted case. She caught his eye and he smiled, his familiar grin putting her in mind of long nights at Siggi's bar. Like Lise, Axel's life had changed immeasurably after the border closure: as a grenzgänger, he, like her, had been barred from pursuing higher education. She thought back to the nights he'd spent waxing eloquent about Renaissance portraiture over steins of beer. Had he kept up with his studies, or had his new life become too busy for extracurricular learning?

She reached the counter and Axel leaned over to admire Rudi, still sleeping in his bassinet. "Look at you," he said fondly, then turned his attention to Lise. "Little mother. How are you?"

"We're doing well." Lise flexed her fingers: though she'd had her cast taken off a few days ago her wrists still ached after a day of carrying Rudi. "It was a difficult delivery, but we came through it."

"I'm glad." Axel glanced at the other customers and cleared his throat. "What can I get you?"

"A roast of pork, please."

"Of course. Special occasion?"

"Oh, you know." She met Axel's eye. "We're taking a short holiday. To Hungary."

Axel wrapped the roast in paper and handed it across. "How nice."

"It is." Lise held out a twenty-mark banknote. "I'm sorry I don't have anything smaller."

Axel turned to open the register, and Lise watched as the small handwritten note she'd hidden beneath the bill disappeared up his sleeve.

He turned back and dropped her change into her hand. *"Danke, fräulein."*

She tucked the roast into the wire basket beneath Rudi's stroller and continued out of the shop, her heart thrumming. *Another passenger booked*, she thought. The note she'd left had given Axel all he needed to know about the escape, scheduled for tomorrow afternoon: he was to meet Inge at the corner of Schwedter Strasse and Choriner Strasse at three o'clock, and tail her to the tunnel's entrance.

Inge had visited her a week ago, and Lise had been steadily making her way across the city ever since, notifying the handful of people she'd been assigned to tell about their upcoming trip. She suspected that Inge had recruited messengers to contact others who'd expressed interest in escaping to the West—after all, the tunnel wasn't hers alone. It had been a secret she'd held on to for nearly a year, turning it over in her mind like a lucky stone in those darkest moments when she doubted whether she'd ever return to Uli; now, with the date set for her departure, she was content to hold on to the secret for a little longer.

She passed the U-Bahn station and Rudi wriggled himself loose from the blanket, letting out a howl of indignation at the sudden chill on his bare legs.

"Stop wriggling and you won't get cold," she admonished, tucking Rudi back into his swaddle. *I'll have to dress him in layers*, she thought, adding another line item to her to-do list as she imagined the damp chill of the tunnel. She needed to consider every eventuality: every possible discomfort that might make Rudi cry out in the dark. Though she was terrified at the prospect of bringing Rudi through, she knew that the older he got, the more difficult it would be to transport him to the West. At ten weeks old, he could be carried, passed from hand to hand while still asleep: to Rudi, she hoped, their escape would be nothing more than a dream. But it was a dream that depended on his silence as they slipped beneath the feet of border guards: any sound whatsoever, a cough, a sneeze, might be enough to raise the alarm.

"It's only a seventeen-minute journey," Inge had assured her on her last visit to East Berlin. All that stood between Lise and Uli was seventeen minutes of good luck. Surely, she and Rudi could endure seventeen minutes for a better life.

She ran through a list of final preparations in her head, knowing that she would be unable to bring anything to the West other than the bare essentials: her identification card; a change of Rudi's diapers. She'd sewn a photograph of Papa and Paul into the lining of the skirt she intended to wear, carefully mending the seam with an invisible stitch that Gerda had taught her, but she knew better than to bring anything else. If she was stopped by Volkspolizei on the street tomorrow, anything sentimental or important on her person would be taken as proof of her intent to leave.

She paused at the corner of Otto-Braun-Strasse and waited for the light to change, and as she watched candy-colored automobiles slide past she fought the urge to cry. Her emotions seemed to sweep over her in tidal pulls these days. She pictured Papa returning home to an empty apartment, his worry and unease growing with every passing hour as Lise and Rudi failed to turn up for dinner. She knew her departure wouldn't be a surprise to Papa, but it would be a shock to Paul—and a disappointment to them both.

Papa would forgive her. But Paul…

One day she would write to them and explain herself. Until then, her actions would have to be explanation enough.

The light changed and she carried on down Karl-Marx-Allee, her wrists aching with the effort of pushing Rudi's carriage past Alexanderplatz.

Tomorrow, everything will be different, she thought, looking up at the impossibly blue sky.

Tomorrow, my life begins again.

She was so caught up in her reveries that she didn't notice a van that had pulled up behind her until it was too late. Rough hands grabbed her from behind and bundled her into the darkness before she could scream.

26

The living room was dark, the curtains drawn against the afternoon sun. Uli, Wolf and Jurgen stood shoulder to shoulder, and Inge held out her hands, presenting the tips of three white straws behind her long fingers.

"Short straw wins," she said, and Uli knocked Jurgen's hand out of the way to pull out the middle straw; he held it up, disappointment coursing through him as Jurgen let out a whoop of triumph.

It's my tunnel, he thought bitterly, even though he knew that wasn't true. Drawing straws was an admittedly childish way of choosing which among them would be the first to break through to East Berlin, but they all had equal claim to the honor, and they all, with the exception of Inge, wanted to lead the breakout of their friends and family.

Inge touched the breadth of her hand down on either side of Jurgen's neck. "I hereby appoint Jurgen our commanding officer," she said, and Uli swallowed another wave of resentment. "His orders are to be obeyed without question, is that understood? We need a clear chain of command in case anything goes wrong." Her smile wavered, and Uli's stomach lurched unexpectedly at the sight. "I don't want to have to come down there myself to clean up any of your messes."

Jurgen let out a chuckle, and Uli offered Inge a half-hearted smile as Wolf hefted a heavy duffel bag onto the dining table. He unzipped the duffel to reveal an array of tools and began setting them out on the table one by one: a slender saw, hunting knives, a coil of rope, electric drill, hammer, pickax.

"Here we are: everything we need for a bank robbery," he said, his offhand delivery belying the seriousness of their task. In a few short hours, their tunnel would finally be put to use, and they all knew better than to risk breaking through to East Berlin unarmed.

Looking at the array of weapons, Uli was grateful that Inge was staying behind. After her last visit to Lise, they'd all concluded that Inge's luck had just about run out: she'd visited East Berlin too often, asked too many questions. Instead, Inge had recruited her cousin Sigrid to act as a courier in her place: someone with a new face and a spotless visa to help ferry East Berliners west.

Uli circled to the bookcase and reached behind his anthology of works by Goethe to pull Jurgen's pistol from its hiding place. He added it to the small arsenal, hoping fervently that they would have no occasion to use it.

Inge stepped back, her eyes large. "Where did you get that?"

Wolf threw her a rakish smile. "A friend on the black market owed us a favor," he replied.

Inge let out an incredulous huff. "Must have been some favor," she said. "Jesus, Uli, have you had that *thing* with you the entire time we—"

Jurgen pointedly cleared his throat, and Inge fell silent. "If you'll indulge me a moment..." He looked down at the weapons on the table, and despite his excitement Uli couldn't help feeling something else—trepidation?—settle in the pit of his chest. "Assuming all has gone to plan so far, Sigrid is in East Berlin as we speak and will be making contact in the next—" he checked his watch "—five minutes to let us know whether it's safe to proceed." He looked at Uli, Inge and Wolf in turn, uncharacteristically solemn. "I hardly need to remind you all that we're breaking serious laws. We will have four hours total to get our passengers out of East Berlin—two of those, I wager, we'll spend expanding the hole beneath the floorboards. That leaves us two hours, more or less, to get our passengers out."

None of what Jurgen said was news to Uli; none of it could be, given that they'd all agreed upon the plan together. Two hours to ferry twenty-seven people through to West Berlin seemed to Uli to be both plenty of time and not enough: an eternity and a blink of an eye.

Twenty-eight, with the addition of baby Rudi.

"Uli, I want you with me in the tunnel for the breakthrough as my second in command. Wolf, you'll be in the tunnel at the halfway mark, to assist any of our passengers who might need help."

Wolf glanced up. "What? You don't want me there with you?"

Jurgen gave him a soft look. "If it were up to me, you'd stay here, where I'd know for certain you'd be safe," he replied, "but we need Inge at the exit. With her medical training she can perform any first aid that might be needed." His eyes flicked to Uli, and Uli knew that he was thinking, first and foremost, of Lise and little Rudi.

Jurgen picked up the pistol and stowed it in the back of his jeans, flipping the tail of his plaid shirt to cover the pistol's butt as Uli returned the rest of their equipment back to the duffel.

Jurgen straightened, and to Uli he seemed more authoritative than usual: as if Inge's imaginary knighthood had bestowed upon him an additional measure of courage. "This is it. This is our chance to reunite with friends and family. Safely, God willing."

"God willing," Wolf echoed. "What do we do if things don't go according to plan?"

He was voicing a concern they all shared, but to Uli the question seemed dangerous, somehow: as if to ask it risked courting the peril they all hoped to avoid.

Uli spoke up. "We'll be in a tunnel. What else will we be able to do but retreat?"

Jurgen looked as if there was something else he wanted to add, but then he cleared his throat. "I just want you all to know that whatever happens, I'm proud of what we've accomplished." He paused, reddening as if at his own sudden burst of mawkishness, and consulted his watch. "We best start looking for Sigrid's signal. Inge, perhaps you might take a look. It could seem suspicious if we're all at the window."

Wolf and Jurgen drifted into the kitchen for a private word as Inge twitched open the window's curtain, leaving Uli at the dining table. He glanced at Jurgen and Wolf through the pass-through window: they drew closer, Jurgen's arms around Wolf's neck as he pulled Wolf close. The sight of their embrace calmed Uli's jangling nerves: by this time tomorrow, he and Lise would be standing in that very kitchen, Rudi between them.

His family, whole.

Though Uli wasn't religious, he wished at this moment that he possessed faith in some higher power: something he could pray to for Lise's and Rudi's protection, a god, a patron saint. But as soon as he had the thought, he pushed it away. He would be bringing Lise and Rudi home through his actions, not his prayers.

He crossed to the window where Inge stood, watching for Sigrid. From here, he could see over the Wall, past the remains of the old buildings on Schönholzer Strasse to the window of Lise's old apartment, now occupied by new inhabitants. They'd timed the escape for the early evening, in the hopes that their passengers would blend in with the crowds of people returning home from their factory jobs, but now, just past midday, the sidewalk was sparse, peopled by a few Volkspolizei and an elderly woman pushing a walker. If all had gone according to plan, Sigrid would turn up on the bench at the corner of Rheinsberger Strasse and Ruppiner Strasse within a matter of minutes. If she tied her shoelaces, it would mean she planned to bring passengers to the tunnel; if she opened a book, then Uli and his friends would know that she'd deemed the escape too risky. What would they do if Sigrid called off the operation?

With her arms crossed tight over her chest, Uli could see that Inge shared in his trepidation. He breathed in the scent of Inge's perfume—something floral and pretty, a scent he'd come to find comforting in the dark of the tunnel.

He stepped back, struck by the realization that he would miss Inge's quiet camaraderie, in the days to come.

"We'll have to have you and Sigrid over for dinner," he said as Wolf and Jurgen's conversation grew quiet behind them. "Once everyone's settled. It will be a—a celebration."

Inge kept her gaze trained on Rheinsberger Strasse. "I expect you'll be far too busy for company for quite some time."

"Not too busy for you." He hesitated, not sure how to put his clunky sentimentality to words. "I hope you know how grateful I am. For your—your friendship."

Inge let out a dry laugh. "Well, what's a bit of dirt between friends?"

Uli fell silent, feeling oddly cheated by her indifference. They *were* friends—they'd become friends over the past year, friends beyond their joint connection to Lise. They'd shared a mission, broken bread, divulged their fears and confidences in a way that Uli, at least, had found meaningful—and yet, he could feel her withdrawing, retreating into the casual detachment of a stranger.

Uli had always known that the rapport between him and Inge would change once Lise came across the Wall: it would soften, would wear and fade with time as Lise once more became their shared center. But there was something tender in this moment that he wanted to hold on to; some urge to mark one last moment of honesty between them.

He reached for Inge's hand and she flinched, snatching her fist away as if he'd touched her with a lit match. She met his gaze, alarmed, before snapping her attention back to the window.

Shit. "Inge—"

"There," she said, loud enough to draw Wolf's and Jurgen's attention. "It's Sigrid."

His cheeks burning, Uli turned his attention back to Rheinsberger Strasse, where a small figure in a red dress walked along the street. She sat down on an empty bench and leaned forward to fumble with the laces of her shoes.

Inge stepped back. "It's safe to go. The escape is on."

27

Lise woke up on the floor of a small room filled with the relentless hum of a fluorescent light. Panicked, she pushed herself upright, her weak wrist aching. Where was Rudi?

Dizzy and alone, but unharmed, she got to her feet, shivering in the icy blast from an air conditioner. The room was small and narrow, with faded, patterned wallpaper in the sort of quaint print that she might have expected to see in Papa's old apartment: set against the glossy right angles of a Sprelacart desk and a locked cabinet, the wallpaper looked out of place, a startling glimpse of home in sinister surroundings.

The cold light flooding in from the window was bright but occluded, giving no indication as to how long she'd been here—or indeed, where she was. She fumbled for her watch and found that someone had removed it. Had today become tomorrow in the time she'd been knocked out?

If so, the escape might already be underway.

From somewhere beyond the room's patterned walls, she

could hear the distant cry of a baby, and the sound froze her to her core. Where was Rudi?

After an endless wait, she heard the click of a door handle and swung round as a short man holding a manila folder stepped in. Like his suit, his features were bland and unremarkable: neither handsome nor ugly, he had brush cut hair that was beginning to gray at the temples, and horn-rimmed glasses that cut heavily across his eyebrows.

He didn't need to introduce himself for Lise to know what he was.

Stasi.

He smiled and strode to the far side of the desk. "Good. You're awake." He sat down in a fabric-backed chair and indicated a stool opposite the desk for Lise. "How are you feeling? How's that wrist of yours? Would you like me to have someone take a look at it for you?"

She sank onto the stool, cradling her weak wrist in her lap. "Where's my son?"

He leaned back in his seat, studying Lise with a look of genuine concern. "He's fine, Lise. He's being well taken care of. But before I can take you to him, I need you to answer some questions." He opened the manila folder, taking pains not to reveal its contents before sliding a photograph across the table. "Do you recognize this woman?"

Lise shivered, her polyester blouse inadequate protection against the chill of the room. "No."

He pushed the photograph closer. "Please take a proper look for me, fräulein."

She glanced down, already knowing what it would show.

"I don't—don't know her," Lise replied. "Please, my son, Rudi—if I could just see him, to know he's okay—"

His tone was maddeningly calm. "You'll see him once you give me the information I need."

Knowing Inge wasn't a crime, in itself. She looked closer:

Inge was wearing an outfit that Lise hadn't seen before, a coat that reached to her thighs and white stockings, her white-blond hair concealed beneath a patterned scarf. She was waiting at a street corner, one leg crossed over the other, looking like any other young woman one might find in a city center.

There was nothing in the photograph to connect Inge to Lise. But surely, the agent had more than that in his folder.

"I told you, I don't know who she is." Lise let out a breath. From somewhere within the complex, she heard a baby cry again, and her heart seized at the sound. "Please, if I can just—"

"You're lying, fräulein." He reached once more into the folder and pulled out a second photo and a third: Lise and Inge, walking a few paces apart down Schwedter Strasse; Inge, lifting a coffee cup to her lips, the photograph taken, undeniably, from behind Lise's shoulder. "Inge Olsson is wanted in relation to an ongoing investigation, and you've been seen in illicit contact with her." He leaned back, his tone easy, cajoling. "There's no reason this should be a hardship for either of us. Tell me what I need to know, and you and your son can leave today."

Lise's composure cracked. "Please," she said again. "He's just a baby. If I could just see him, I'd be able to—to tell you—"

"That's not how this is done." He leaned forward, and for the first time she could hear a sliver of menace in his voice. "We know that Inge Olsson is part of a network of subversives that is planning to kidnap East German citizens. If we don't stop her, her criminal actions will put lives at risk. Tell me what I need to know."

Don't say a thing. Lise's mind whirled as she thought through her options. How much did he know? She'd tried to so hard to be discreet, but the photographs before her were proof that she'd failed in that regard. How many more photos were in the envelope, and what did they reveal of her actions? Had she been seen passing a note to Axel? Meeting with Brigit?

Still, the fact that she was here and not languishing in some prison cell was proof that the Stasi, despite their reputation for omnipotence, didn't know the full extent of the escape plan.

The agent looked at her, his eyes brimming with sympathy. "We know it's not your fault, fräulein. These imperialist aggressors…they'll say and do anything to undermine our socialist republic. What did they promise you? Money?" He sighed, and the gesture felt artificial, as if he were reading lines from a one-man show. "The sad fact of the matter is that these capitalist networks never deliver on their promises. How do you intend to care for your child once you're in the West?" He leaned forward, his bland features twisting with subtle malice. "They'll bring you across the border, then turn around and ask for payment for their troubles. You'll be in a country with no family, no friends and no prospects. Were you to throw your lot in with them, you and your child would end up penniless, begging on the street." He sat back, surveying Lise from behind his thick glasses. "Here, we recognize the value of our citizens. We can offer you safety, security. Work with us, and we'll offer you even more."

Lise met the Stasi agent's eyes, a bright red flush of impatience on his cheeks undermining his silky words. Her gaze slid to the window, the brilliant light outside still giving no indication of the time. Had Uli broken through the floorboards? Had they begun ferrying people through? She and Rudi would not be leaving East Germany tonight: that much, she knew. But if she could keep this agent in the room, asking questions—if she could keep him from discovering where the tunnel was for as long as possible—perhaps she could give Uli the chance to get as many others to West Berlin as he could.

"I don't know anything," she repeated. "I—I was approached by Fräulein Olsson, it's true, but I never agreed to anything, never agreed to work with her—"

"And Uli Neumann? We know that Olsson is collaborating with your former fiancé." He pulled yet more photographs from the file with a sly smile. "Lise, I'm sorry to be the one to have to tell you. Fräulein Olsson has been seen in Herr Neumann's apartment in various states of undress."

Lise felt as though she'd been struck across the face: she looked down at the photographs, taken, no doubt, with a telephoto lens from across the Wall, perhaps even from the same window where she'd once stood waiting for Uli to turn on the light: a grainy image of Inge in a towel, her hand on a shirtless Uli's shoulder.

She felt her legs turn to water, and she lifted the photo to inspect it closer. *It's not real*, she thought, as the Stasi agent's voice became a distant hiss. *It can't be.*

The agent sat back and folded his hands over his midsection. "He's clearly mended his broken heart, but have you done the same? Tell me, Lise. Is a man like this really worth your love?"

She gripped the photo tighter. "Go to hell."

His expression darkened. "If you think you're doing yourself or your child any favors with your attitude, you might want to reconsider your actions," he began, but then the phone on the desk began to ring. He picked it up, his expression ugly as he listened to a muffled voice on the other end.

He stood, and despite her terror, Lise couldn't help feeling a twinge of satisfaction as he stalked out of the room.

She let out a shaky breath, knowing that his departure didn't signify an end to her ordeal. She looked down once more at the picture of Uli and Inge: despite her show of bravado to the agent, the image was disconcerting, to say the least.

She set it aside. There would be time for questions later. But for now, she needed to focus on getting herself out of her predicament—her and Rudi, both.

The door opened once more, and Lise resisted the urge to turn—to show any sign of fear to the agent whose footsteps sounded heavier than the last. He took a step forward, and another, and the scent of his cologne grew stronger, strangely familiar—

Paul sat down in the Stasi agent's unoccupied chair and spread his broad hands across the table, his wedding ring glinting in the light.

28

The sound of the electric drill was low but maddeningly loud—excruciatingly so to Uli, who had spent so many quiet hours working down here in the dark. To him, it sounded like a beacon, alerting every border officer in the area to the presence of intruders in their midst: surely, some Stasi listening device had picked up the noise by now? Over the past two hours, he'd worked with Jurgen to remove the bracing beneath the cleared floorboard and hollow out a proper entrance to the tunnel, carving away the earth, quickly, quietly. Now, with the noisy intrusion of the electric drill on the underside of the floorboards, they were fast approaching their goal.

Jurgen finished drilling pilot holes in the floorboard, and Uli rummaged through the duffel bag for their keyhole saw. Barely breathing, he watched Jurgen fit the blade into the pilot hole and begin to saw, slowly at first and then quicker, creating a thin sliver of light along the join between floorboards, no larger than the width of a pencil. Without looking back, he held out his hand and Uli, feeling like an emergency room nurse, exchanged the saw for a small hand mirror. Jurgen slid the mirror through the crack, rounding his back to look through at the reflected cellar; after turning it to inspect the other side of the cellar, he withdrew the mirror and nodded.

Ulli nearly sagged with relief: the cellar was empty. No Stasi agents or Volkspolizei; no border guards with their rifles trained at Jurgen's and Uli's heads.

He passed the keyhole saw back to Jurgen, knowing that his relief would be short-lived. The real challenge was yet to come, in the next hour when their passengers would start arriving. He spared a thought for Sigrid, leading the first of the passengers to the tunnel: she would be bringing seven groups to Rheinsberger Strasse, twenty-seven people in total, in groups small enough so as not to attract attention, with enough time between each group to ensure safe passage through the tunnel.

Including Lise.

He closed his eyes in the darkness and pictured Lise, her blond hair shining, arms wrapped around a child that looked blissfully like her. He'd set aside thoughts of love, buried them deep within himself so that he might meet the challenge of bringing her back.

Their year apart had been so much stolen time, but now their lives would start anew.

Inge's voice reassured him in the dark: *You and Lise are meant for each other.*

Nothing else mattered but that.

He heard a clunk overhead as Jurgen finished sawing through the floorboards and opened his eyes to relieve Jurgen of the saw. After checking again with the hand mirror, Jurgen lifted the square of floorboard, setting it to one side before climbing up and through, into the light.

They'd broken through to East Germany.

Whether they'd broken into the right cellar remained to be seen.

29

Lise stared at Paul, feeling as though the floor had given way beneath her. "Paul," she said, the words souring in her mouth like bile. "How could you?"

He took a breath, meeting Lise's outrage with a look of resignation. She was so used to seeing him in the crisp uniform of the Volkspolizei that the sight of him in civilian dress, midday, was jarring. He wasn't even wearing a jacket: his shirtsleeves were rolled to the elbow as if he and Lise were about to work the gardens at the family datsche.

"So what, you've been—you've been informing on me, this whole time—?"

"I'm not an informant." A small muscle in his jaw tightened. Only the night before, Lise had teased him about the golden glow of stubble she'd seen when he'd turned his head at dinner: he'd laughed and made some joke about long shifts walking his beat with Horst. "And I'm not a police officer. I'm an agent with the Ministry for State Security."

Lise fell silent. Paul, an agent of the secret police? She knew that he believed wholeheartedly in East Germany and its government—that she and Paul didn't see eye to eye on many things, least of all the socialist state—but this was her brother: her trusted confidant.

Her friend.

He threaded his hands on the tabletop, his words spilling quickly, urgently, as if he was being interrogated alongside her. "Lise, I know this is a shock, but you must listen to me. The Ministry has been building evidence against you for months, and their case is very strong." He paused. "We know about the tunnel."

She stood, trembling with a sudden, boiling rage. "How could you?"

"How could I not?" He stared at Lise with the same look of brittle frustration he wore whenever she'd bested him at a board game or Papa had argued some point at the dinner table. "For God's sake, Lise, I'm trying to protect you. We know that Uli Neumann has dug a tunnel under Bernauer Strasse. We need to know where it leads."

"How long?"

He swore. "We don't have time for this."

"No, Paul, I think we do." She paced the small room, her mind whirling with new suspicion. Microphones in her workplace; informants, trailing her steps. Had Paul sat back and listened through the bedroom wall as she sobbed herself to sleep every night? Did he rifle through her room, make pointed observations to his superiors about each new development in her pregnancy? "You could at least have the decency to look contrite. How long have you been spying on me?"

"You've been under surveillance since you attempted to illegally cross the border last year. I was brought onto the case when you were found to be having illicit contact with a Westerner—Inge Olsson." He looked up, his fingers tightening on the edge of the desk. "This is what I do, Lise. I investigate cases of attempted Republikflucht. What else was I supposed to do, when my own sister was found to be part of a Western conspiracy?"

Lise blinked back her tears. "You could have spoken to me, Paul."

Paul's expression slackened, and just for a moment she could see how heavily the weight of his transgressions hung on him—but then he hardened once more.

"Hate me if you must, but you need to understand the gravity of your situation. I'm going to do everything I can to save you now, but you need to cooperate with us. Tell us where the tunnel is, and I can protect you and Rudi both."

Rudi. Beyond the walls of the interrogation room, the halls were silent: had it been Rudi, crying for her? Or had the sound only been in her imagination?

"There is only one outcome to this conversation. You tell me the location of the tunnel and the date for the escape." He held up his hands. "A location and a date. That's all. You give me a location and a date, and you get to walk out of here with Rudi in your arms."

30

Jurgen climbed out of the tunnel, disappearing into the yellow light of the cellar above. For a moment Uli stared up at nothing, listening from the base of the ladder to Jurgen's heavy footsteps as he did a sweep of the cellar—then his face appeared in the square of light above.

"We're clear," he whispered, and Uli began to climb.

The cellar was a small, utilitarian space lit by a single fizzing lightbulb: a room for mops and brooms, the forgotten detritus required to maintain some measure of cleanliness in any shared living quarters. Half a dozen buckets were stacked in one corner, in front of a shelving unit filled with bottles of cleaning products; in another, vacuum cleaners stood lined against the wall like soldiers.

Uli glanced back at the hole they'd made, small and square. They'd managed to break through in the far left corner of the room, near a dripping puddle left by a mop on a hook.

Jurgen checked his watch. "Our first passengers should be arriving any minute," he whispered. "I suppose we ought to make sure we've broken into the right building."

"Only one way to find out."

Uli's heart thrummed as he made his way down the short hallway outside the cellar. To one side, an open door led to a line of washing machines and dryers, none of which appeared to be in use; to the other, a marble staircase led up to the building's lobby.

He gripped the balustrade, memories flooding his mind as he climbed to the top of the stairs: listening to the echo of Lise's footsteps from the fifth floor to the first as she ran down to meet him; riding up the clattering caged elevator with Lise's father, Rudolph, following a sunlit picnic in the Tiergarten.

He smiled, thinking of the first time he'd come here to pick Lise up for a date: he'd stood awkwardly at the foot of the stairs as he waited for her to arrive, looking for figures in the peeling wallpaper like a child might find creatures in a cloud. He'd brought roses for her, that first evening: hothouse roses in shades of red and pink, which Lise had insisted upon carrying up to put in water before they left for the movie theater. Paul had rolled his eyes at the display of extravagance, but Rudolph had smiled and told Uli as Lise filled a vase that he'd done the same for her mother when they'd first started courting.

Uli had admired how close Lise had been to her family: how happy they seemed together, how dissimilar her rapport with her father was to Uli's relationship with his own distant parents.

What would Rudolph think, when Lise wrote to him from West Berlin?

From some distant upper floor Uli heard a door open and he started: time was too short for him to bask in old memories. He crossed to the double front doors and pulled Lise's keys from his pocket to unlock them, hoping that the building's inhabitants would conclude that the security breach was nothing more than an oversight on the part of a neighbor. He opened the door a crack to peer at the sidewalk he'd once known so well: outside, children played in the streets, men and women chatting amiably as cars ambled past. With any luck, the after-work activity would provide a bustling cover for their passengers.

He was about to close the door when a family walking down the street caught his attention. There was nothing special about them, nothing particularly distinctive, but Uli knew without being told that they were coming here, for him. He crossed back to the staircase and vaulted down it, listening as the door clicked open above: footsteps, nearly in unison, as they made their way down the stairs.

He met them on the basement's landing, his heart pounding as he took the measure of them: the man's ruddy face and stocky build, the woman's vicelike grip on a toddler with dark, candy-floss hair.

"Good evening," he said, and the couple met his eyes with twin, tense expressions. Neither he nor they had any guarantee that the other was who he purported to be, and Uli could see himself through their eyes: a Stasi plant, come to round them up, mother, father and child.

Finally, the man leaned close and spoke in barely a whisper. "Eurydice sends her regards."

A sudden lump in Uli's throat caused him to choke out his response. "We—we hadn't expected to hear from her until May."

He'd laughed, when Inge had told him the code name that Lise had given herself for the operation: "A bit heavy-handed," he'd told her. "I suppose I ought to get myself a lyre." Whereas Inge had chosen to call herself Freya, the warrior goddess of old, Lise's reference to Greek myth had seemed altogether fitting: for what else was Uli but a modern-day Orpheus, traveling though the underworld to find her?

Hearing Lise's code name was a comfort that would sustain him until she arrived herself. She had sent these people, trusting Uli to help them make their way to a better life.

"Well," he whispered, watching as their worried expressions cleared. "We'd best get on with it, hadn't we?"

He led them to the cellar and opened the door. Jurgen looked up: he stilled, then ran across the small room to pull the man into a tight hug.

"Uli." He drew back, his eyes brimming with tears. "I'd like you to meet my brother."

31

Lise leaned against the wall of the interrogation room, her wrist throbbing with pain. As a child, she had suffered from nightmares of falling rubble and firestorms, hazy-faced men who'd kicked down the door to her bedroom with malice in their eyes. How many nights had Paul awoken to her screams, tiptoed across the hall to her bedroom to take her in his bony arms and soothe her back to sleep?

Don't respond, she told herself. *Don't give him the satisfaction.*

Paul nodded at her wrist. "I can get you something for that," he offered mildly, and Lise stared at him with such disdain that he looked away.

"Why would you do this to me? To Rudi?"

"I don't expect you to understand. My loyalty is to something bigger than family. Stronger than blood." His square jaw twitched. "The capitalist West is attempting to gain supremacy over our republic by bleeding us dry, and people like Uli Neumann are willing to be martyrs to their cause in order to let it happen. I'm doing this for the survival of our country. Our way of *life*."

He sounded so blank, so automatic, that although there was nowhere to go, Lise found herself pacing, powerless against a line of argument based on ideology. "And what of *my* survival? What of my son's survival?"

Paul's gaze flickered to the door. "Your survival will depend on what you tell us."

She looked up, alarmed by the chill in his voice. Paul had always known the worst and the best of her, accepted her without judgment or ridicule, seen their differences in outlook as something to laugh about, then shrug off.

When had he decided that their difference in politics mattered more than their love for each other?

"I'll tell you what we know, how about that? And you can fill in the blanks for us." He leaned back, tapping his pen lightly on the table. "Uli Neumann is digging a tunnel under Bernauer Strasse, from the basement of a pub at the corner of Bernauer and Strelitzer Strasse. According to our sources, Neumann has three accomplices, Inge Olsson among them. Olsson has traveled to East Berlin five times on a Swedish passport and has made contact with you on three separate occasions." He looked at Lise, his mouth twitching with incredulity. "Surely you see the danger, Lise. Digging a tunnel beneath city streets? How could you consider putting yourself and Rudi in such a dangerous situation? How many collapsed tunnels do you think I've seen in my line of work? It's a miracle this one hasn't caved in."

He leaned back in his chair, studying Lise with his steady gaze. "He always was reckless, but your absence seems to have made him even more so. He's putting lives at risk. He's willing to put *your* life at risk. Yours and your son's. How many others?"

"Uli would never put us in danger," Lise shot back. Desperation drove people to carelessness, but Uli was never careless; he *wouldn't* be careless, not about this.

Would he?

A faint smile flickered across Paul's face. "Surely I don't need to tell you that even if Uli Neumann never steps foot in the German Democratic Republic, you can still be held accountable for your actions." He held up his hand, ticking off Lise's transgressions on his long fingers. "Attempted illegal border crossing. Illicit contact with a Western organization intent on harming our citizens. Illicit contact with a Westerner. These are serious offences, Lise. People have been sent to prison for less."

Rather than chastening her, Paul's words filled Lise with a sudden, furious courage. "If you know about the tunnel, why arrest me now? You could have waited, followed me to it and locked us all away."

Paul looked pained at the suggestion. "You know why," he replied. "There's still time for you. Time to think better of your actions."

"I take full responsibility for my actions," she snarled.

"Then you'll face the full consequences for them," he snapped back.

She met Paul's gaze but didn't respond, her indignation melting away as quickly as it had arrived. She'd always known that her actions carried risk—she'd known from the outset. But what would it mean for Rudi if she were locked away for her crimes?

Paul pulled a typewritten sheet of paper from beneath his legal pad. "I've thought this through from every angle, and there's only one course of action available to you. This is a statement swearing your allegiance to the East German government. If you tell us what we need to know, then your involvement with Uli Neumann disappears."

Although Lise had no intention of signing the statement, she found herself sinking back onto the stool to read it. "You want me to become an informant?"

"A secret collaborator," he corrected her. "As a collaborator with the Ministry of State Security, everything you've done—

your contact with Inge Olsson, your involvement with the tunnel—it all becomes legitimate, in the eyes of the State. Do this, and you won't face any consequences for your actions. But Lise." He leveled a very even look at her. "We have to act now. Do you understand me?"

32

Jurgen clasped Willa in his arms as Brigit made her way down the ladder, holding the child so close it felt as if he was making up for all the time he'd lost with her. How much had she grown in the past year, Uli wondered: how many of his niece's "firsts" had Jurgen missed in their time apart?

Brigit reached the bottom of the ladder and held up her hands for Willa, and Jurgen pressed a kiss to her wild curls.

"You're going on an adventure, now," he whispered. "I want you to be brave for me."

Willa leaned out from Jurgen's arms to study the tunnel. "Is it cold down there? I don't like the cold."

Uli's heart seized at the sound of her clear, childish voice, ringing out on the cellar's stone walls like a bell.

"It's a little chilly, but that's why you brought your sweater," Jurgen whispered back, giving a playful tug to Willa's collar.

Her smile wavered. "I don't like the dark..."

"Your papa will be right behind you," Uli whispered from behind Jurgen's shoulder. Keeping Willa calm was of the utmost importance: a panicked adult would be better able to control themselves in the tunnel, but a panicked child—screaming, crying—would put not only herself but the entire operation at risk. "Do you remember the story of Alice in Wonderland?"

Willa nodded.

"Remember how she fell through a rabbit hole?"

She nodded again.

"This tunnel is just like the one to get to the White Rabbit's house. And when you reach the other side, Alice will be there to say hello." He smiled, thinking of how delighted Willa would be to see Inge in her blue dress, waiting at the other end of the tunnel. "All you need to do is stay quiet and follow the White Rabbit."

33

The words of the statement of allegiance swam before Lise's eyes, letters swirling and recomposing as she read it. *An informant.* The idea that she could even consider betraying Uli was unthinkable, unconscionable. Signing the document would mean giving up everything she'd ever wanted, ever worked for: a life in the West, a life with the man she loved, with the father of her child.

But that future was closed to her now; that much was certain. There would be no West Berlin for Lise; not now that she was here, in the hands of those who would never let her leave.

The realization that she'd been under surveillance from the very first days after the Wall went up chilled her, coloring every interaction in her memory: her conversations with Gerda; her meetings with Inge. Had they arrested Brigit and Karl? Axel? Or had her friends slipped past the net that Paul and his Stasi underlings had thrown around her?

If she refused to sign, she would be put in prison—of that she had no doubt. What could she salvage from the wreckage?

A life with Rudi.

She glanced past Paul's shoulder to the cold light from the window beyond, wishing once again for some indication of how long she'd spent here: minutes, hours, or days. Had Uli broken through the cellar floor? If she could stall, he might succeed in bringing the rest of the travelers through, in which case her betrayal would mean less.

Not nothing, but less.

Keep him talking, she thought, counting each passing second by the throbbing in her wrist. *Just keep him talking.*

"How could you do this to me? To us?"

"How could *you*?" Paul looked at Lise with unconcealed disdain. "You're a subject of East Germany, accountable to East German laws. Everything the State gives you, every opportunity, every security... Fidelity is the price that you pay for it. It's the price we all pay."

"What if I don't want it?" She pictured the map of Berlin: but for a quirk of geography, but for a game of bureaucratic chess, she and Paul might have been on the Western side of the city, bound by different laws, different circumstances. "I don't want what the State gives me. I don't want its opportunities. I would give them all back if it meant I could be with Uli."

"And what of Papa? What about the opportunities the State gives to him?" Paul shot back. "His physiotherapy, his medical treatments? Do you really think the government will continue providing him with what he needs if his daughter is convicted of treason?"

Lise shot Paul a bitter smirk. "You seem to have connections, Paul, I'm sure your friends in the Politburo can give him a hand."

"Be serious, Lise." For the first time, Paul looked rattled. "Do you really think I'll be allowed to keep my position if my sister is sent to prison?"

She narrowed her eyes, realization crystallizing in her mind. "I see. This is about you. Your position, your place."

"I don't give a damn about my position. What I care about is our family." He leaned across the table. "If you're convicted, everything I've built—everything I've worked for—vanishes. You know nothing of the sacrifices I've made, the choices and sleepless nights... *Nothing.* Why else do you think I've been allowed to come here and talk you out of doing something stupid?"

An uneasy thought cut through Lise's anger. If Paul was spying on Lise, who was spying on Paul?

"You've spent the past year thinking of nothing and no one but yourself, while I've done what was needed for our family," he continued harshly. "If you run, we're all lost. You, me, Papa, Anna. And Rudi." He looked up—no longer the Stasi agent, but her desperate brother, once more. "I love you, Lise, and I will do everything I can to protect our family. But my position won't be enough save you, nor will it save Papa." His voice broke as his hand brushed across the tabletop, pushing the statement of allegiance closer to her. "And that's to say nothing of Rudi."

34

It had been an hour and a half since they'd broken through the cellar floor, the minutes measured by the growing ache in Uli's clenched jaw. Where was Lise? They'd brought twenty-three people through to West Berlin already, but Uli's family had not been among them.

He could hear the distant shuffle of the last group of passengers—a grandmother, a factory worker and a teenage boy with an intensely fragile face—as they made their way through the tunnel. Uli didn't know whether they were related, but the grandmother had given the teen a reassuring squeeze on the shoulder before he'd descended: Would they go their separate ways once they reached the refugee camp at Marienfelde, or would they have each other to rely on as they rebuilt their lives in the West?

Perhaps they would be reuniting with family tonight—the teenager's parents, maybe—or else they might simply have decided to go it alone. Whatever their circumstances, Uli wished them well.

The grandmother had pressed slices of coffee cake into Uli's and Jurgen's hands before she'd slipped into the tunnel with surprising spryness for a woman of her years. "Please thank Eurydice for us," she'd said, and Uli had promised he would. But where was Eurydice herself?

Halfway through finishing his slice of cake, Jurgen lifted his head. "Footsteps," he whispered, then stepped out into the hall to head them off.

Uli held his breath as he tried to listen to the muffled voices outside the door, then let it out in a frustrated exhale as Jurgen pulled Axel into the room.

"Thank God." Axel pulled Uli into a hug, gripping the back of Uli's collar. "I can't tell you how glad I am to see you. Took you long enough!"

"Yeah, well, we weren't sure we wanted you back," he joked, clapping Axel genially on the arm. He drew back, letting the grin fade from his face. "Haven't heard from Lise today, have you?"

"Not since yesterday morning." Axel lowered himself into the tunnel as he spoke, clearly not intending to spend any more time in East Berlin than strictly necessary. "Said the escape would be happening today, told me to meet the Swedish bird outside the pub." He paused, his fingers curled around the ladder's rounded rung. "Why, has something gone wrong?"

"Of course not," Jurgen replied. "Now get a move on."

Once Axel was out of sight, Uli shot Jurgen a meaningful glance.

"I'm not sure it signifies anything," Jurgen said. "She's still got time."

Uli fingered the hilt of the hunting knife in his pocket. "I'm going to find her."

"Out of the question." Like Uli, Jurgen was whispering, but his tone was firm. "We're on borrowed time as it is. What if you get delayed? Or arrested? We're safest here, Uli. No heroics."

Uli gritted his teeth. "If I can only—"

"No heroics." Jurgen shot Uli a hard glare. "Need I remind you that we've a duty of care to every one of our passengers? That you agreed to follow my orders until we're back in West Berlin? I need you here, not out on the street where your actions might compromise us both." Uli nodded, but Jurgen stepped closer, his ruddy face grave. "She might still turn up. And if she doesn't, tomorrow's another day. We might be able to arrange for a new escape... But only if we get out of here without drawing anyone's attention."

"Then I'll stay behind," he replied fiercely. "I won't miss this chance. I'm not leaving without them."

Jurgen looked pained. "I can't leave you here on your own," he began, but then he fell silent.

Uli heard it too: a muffled cry from deep within the tunnel. Had something happened to Axel?

Jurgen swore as Axel cried out again. "Where's Wolf? Go and see what's happened," he said. "Please, Uli. Once we've gotten everyone else through, we'll find Lise together."

Uli swore too, then climbed down the ladder. Although the interruption had put a stop to their argument, it hadn't, in Uli's mind, ended it. *We're not an actual military unit*, he thought with a huff as he crawled. *I'm staying behind whether he wants me to or not.*

He found Axel partway down the tunnel, past the bend around the old apartment building foundation at Schönholzer Strasse.

"I can't...can't seem to move." Axel was trembling, his eyes squeezed shut as he crouched, frozen in place. He let out a pinched laugh. "I don't usually have trouble with small spaces, it's just that it's—it's suffocating down here."

In the yellow-lit distance, Uli could see the bracing board that indicated the demarcation point between East and West Berlin. The Wall was so close: only a few steps more, and Axel could make all the noise he liked.

"I know," he whispered. He gave Axel a reassuring pat on the back, unsure how else to move him along. Where was Wolf? "But the only way out is through."

Still rigid with fear, Axel nodded. "The only way out is through," he whispered.

After what seemed like an eternity, Uli looked past Axel and saw Wolf crawling in his direction. He nearly sagged with relief: Axel was Wolf's problem, now. He could return to the East and begin his search for Lise.

With some difficulty, Uli turned around, making his way past the Schönholzer Strasse bend. How much time had passed since he went into the tunnel? Would there be another group of passengers in the cellar, waiting for him to emerge?

He closed his eyes and carried on down the tunnel's familiar trail, hoping against hope that he would find Lise and Rudi waiting in the cellar with Jurgen.

Please, he prayed to a god he didn't believe in. *Please let them be there—*

He'd almost made it to the end when the sound of a gunshot shattered his fragile faith.

35

Lise began to tremble. "I want to speak to a lawyer."

Paul let out a hiss of breath. "Be *reasonable*," he said. "It's only a matter of time before my operatives find the tunnel. And once that happens, any leverage you and I have is gone. There will be nothing I can do to help you. We're running out of time."

"I—I need a moment, I need to *think*—"

"What do you think happens to the children of traitors?" Fear lifted Paul's voice to a harsh whisper. "If you get charged with treason, do you honestly think you'll ever be allowed to see Rudi again?"

He's bluffing, she thought uneasily. But if that were the case, why did he look as scared as she felt? "You'd raise him," she replied. "You and Anna, or Papa—"

"If you get sent to prison, we're all guilty by association," Paul shot back, and in the still air between them, she could hear the faint sound of crying once more. "He'll be sent to an orphanage, placed in the home of some Party member, if he's lucky. You'd never *see* him again, Lise."

Lise squeezed her eyes shut, desperately wishing for news of Uli's success: that he'd ferried everyone else through the tunnel; that he was safely back in the West. She pictured him waiting at the tunnel's entrance, listening for the sound of her voice; for the cry of his son.

There's another way, she thought hopelessly. *There has to be.*

"Even if I were to let you walk out of here right now into that deathtrap of a tunnel your friends have built, do you really think I'd allow you to risk my newborn nephew's life in that way?"

She could feel her resistance crumbling, the prospect of losing Rudi chipping away at the foundation of her own conviction.

"*Think*, Lise. Is Rudi's welfare worth all of this?"

Somewhere, far in the distance of her mind, she could hear the hypocrisy in Paul's words. He was concerned for his position, for his own safety. But that didn't make what he was saying about Rudi any less true.

He pushed the document toward her.

"The longer you delay, the harder it will be for me to protect you. And I *am* trying to protect you, Lise. You and Rudi both."

Uli meant the world to her, but Rudi was her universe.

How was she supposed to choose between them?

"I swear I will protect you both until the day I die, and that's what I'm doing now. Help me keep Rudi safe, Lise. Help me keep the two of you together." He placed the pen on the table, delicately, hesitantly. "Tell me what I need to know. Help me protect your son."

36

Uli scrambled back along the tunnel, the calloused skin of his palms tearing on grit and stones. At the bottom of the ladder, he looked up and caught sight of a flash of blond hair.

"Lise!" He vaulted up the ladder and scrambled into the cellar on his hands and knees, his glasses slipping from his nose as he slammed against the floor. Cursing, he jammed his glasses back in place and tried to make sense of what was happening: Jurgen, barricading the cellar door; a woman—a stranger—standing petrified in the corner.

He got to his feet and shot to Jurgen's side, slamming his weight against the door as it gave another shuddering bang.

"Border guards," Jurgen grunted, his forehead slick with perspiration.

Uli shot a look at the woman in the corner. "Did she—?"

"No, she's Brigit's sister, I can vouch—" Jurgen broke off as someone shouted from the corridor. "Get her out of here, I'll hold them off as long as I can."

Uli looked up, horrified. "I'm not leaving you alone."

"It's not a request." Jurgen was pale but resolute; he gripped the gun, his finger sliding to slip the safety off the trigger. "My family is out. Yours isn't. If you stay here, you'll never see Lise."

"But Wolf—"

"Wolf will understand." Jurgen cocked the gun. "Go. I'll be right behind you."

They ducked as a volley of gunfire splintered the door's hinges, and Uli scrabbled to the tunnel's entrance. Brigit's sister stood on the ladder, her fingers frozen to the rung as she watched Uli push over one of the cellar's shelving units to give them cover from East German bullets.

"What are you waiting for? *Go!*" The door gave one final, almighty crack, and Uli looked up to see Jurgen, his pistol raised aloft as he dived behind the bookcase.

Uli jumped down into the tunnel, his ankle twisting horribly as he thudded and rolled on the hard ground. Out of the corner of his eye he could see the flash of Brigit's sister as she ran, doubled over, down the narrow tunnel. He scrambled clear of the ladder, waited for Jurgen—

He froze as the sound of gunfire echoed from the above.

Uli twisted round to return the ladder, his ankle screaming as he crawled, but then a green-jacketed figure dropped into the tunnel, got to his knees and lifted his submachine gun.

Instinctively, Uli pulled the hunting knife from his back pocket and whipped it at the guard. The guard reared back, screaming, as the knife embedded itself in his cheek, but not before he'd pulled the trigger and sent a short spray of bullets rocketing through the air.

They thudded into the tunnel's earthen wall wide of where he'd intended them to go, but Uli was launched backward as a single bullet found him, sending a blinding pain through his shoulder. Overhead, the tunnel's line of lights flickered—cut, no doubt, by another stray bullet—and plunged Uli into darkness. One armed, he struggled back upright, feeling a hot flow of blood down his side.

Overhead he could hear voices: more border guards, ready to infiltrate the tunnel. Where was Jurgen? Was he still alive?

In the dim light cast down from the cellar, Uli could see the guard lying in a heap at the foot of the ladder, his fingers twitching over the handle of his gun. Horrified, he edged forward and kicked the gun loose from the guard's limp grasp, retching as his gaze traveled uncontrollably, sickeningly, to the knife hilt lodged deep in the guard's face.

Slowly, the guard's eyes flickered open, slivers of hazel against the red flood. Uli shouted and scrabbled back, his heart thudding an accusation as the guard held his gaze.

You did this. You did this.

"Move!"

Another voice emerged in the darkness, breaking Uli free from his frozen state: Brigit's sister. She'd returned for him, and the sound of her voice brought him back to their present danger: to the sacrifice Jurgen had made to see them both safely out of East Berlin.

Together, crouched double, they raced west.

37

Lise collapsed into Paul's arms, sobbing. She couldn't bear to look past his shoulder at the desk, where her statement of allegiance to East Germany—copied out in her own shaking hand—sat signed; couldn't bear to think of what she had done, the secrets she'd divulged.

"Good job," said Paul, and behind her she could hear the interrogation room's door open, followed by the soft sound of Rudi's rasping breath: a chorus of relief and guilt and pain. "You did the right thing, Lise. Trust me."

38

Uli crawled out of the tunnel, his shoulder screaming as a pale-faced Wolf helped him to his feet.

"What happened? Where's Jurgen?"

The cellar beneath Siggi's was full: though most of the passengers who'd come through the tunnel had already left, Axel, Brigit, Karl and Wolf had stayed behind—waiting, no doubt, for a proper reunion. Brigit's sister raced into her arms, sobbing, as Willa dozed on a pile of blankets in a corner.

Uli winced as Inge rushed forward to inspect his shoulder. "I—I don't know—"

"Border guards found us." Brigit's sister looked up from the refuge of Brigit's arms, and it was only in looking at her that Uli realized he, too, was trembling. "We were waiting for Uli to come back out of the tunnel when they found us. I swear," she added more forcefully as tears began to stream down her cheeks, "I swear I didn't betray you, I swear—"

Wolf's frantic gaze shot from her to Uli. "Jurgen? What about Jurgen?"

Uli couldn't bear to look at him; beside him, Inge began to weep. "They got into the tunnel and I—I couldn't go back." His words sounded weak, even to his own ears as Wolf began pacing the cellar, his long hair shielding his angular features from view. "I—I tried to get to him, Wolf, I—"

"Jesus *Christ*." Wolf started down the ladder, ready to return to the East. "He needs us, he needs our help."

"Wolf." Inge sobbed as she knelt beside him, tugged on his arm. "It's too late, we can't go back. It's too late."

He paused and looked to Uli, his eyes wide, and Uli, sickened by his own cowardice, nodded. "There were—there were too many of them," he croaked. "One of them made it into the tunnel, he—he blocked the ladder or else I would have been able to get to him—"

Wolf was out of the tunnel and back on solid ground in the blink of an eye, and he crossed to the corner of the cellar and slammed his fist into the wall so forcefully he left a hole in the plaster; behind him, Axel watched, grave-faced. "What the *fuck* were you doing in the tunnel in the first place? You should have been there with him! You should have—"

"That's not helpful." Inge sat back on her heels, and the look of pity she threw at Uli was worse, somehow, than Wolf's rage.

There was nothing Uli could say; nothing he could do to make things right. Not here, not now. "I—I tried—"

"Yeah, well there are no points for trying when you're sentenced to life in an East German prison." Wolf squeezed his eyes shut and began pacing again like a caged lion. *"Fuck."*

"It's my fault, isn't it?" Axel looked from Wolf to Uli, stricken. "I panicked. It's my fault."

"It's not your fault," Inge replied, her voice too tight, too small. "We'll figure out our plan in the morning. We—we'll go to an embassy, see what they can do, but for now we need to get Uli to the hospital, I c-can't get the bullet out, not on my own."

"Yeah, well, of course we'll tend to Uli first. It's what you've done right from the start, isn't it, Inge?" Wolf shot her an acid glare and ran a hand over his stubbled jaw before opening the cellar door. He paused, and though he addressed his parting words to Karl and Brigit, Uli knew that the bitter remark was meant for him and him alone. "Welcome to the West."

39

JULY 1962

Television cameras lined Rheinsberger Strasse, jostling for prominence in front of the small stage that had been erected in front of number 56. Freshly lime-washed, with new green paint adorning the windows' plaster moldings, the building looked better than it ever had when Lise lived there: but then, she supposed, it was natural to scrub up for a funeral. On the stage, a modest podium stood amidst immense stands of floral arrangements, complemented by smaller bouquets wrapped in cellophane: while the large wreaths of lilies and roses were clearly the work of the government, the more modest contributions had been made by individual citizens of East Berlin: people who'd brought them in sympathy and support for the young man whose life they mourned here today.

Or at least, that was what the Party wanted people to think.

Lise looked up at the immense photograph that hung from the building's third and fourth story windows, the canvas gently billowing in the summer breeze. Sergeant Uwe Spranger had been blond and baby faced, with the sort of full lips and soulful expression that suggested he might have been a sensitive sort—a teacher or philosopher, perhaps, once his days of mandatory service were behind him.

Now that day would never come. Lise's gaze traveled down past the flag-draped coffin that stood beside the podium to the border guards—Spranger's former regiment—who flanked the stage, then to the two black-veiled women who stood arm in arm before the casket. Panic rose from deep within her at the sight of them and she bowed her head, hoping that the crowd would take her trembling to be a sign of grief for the departed soldier. But the fact of the matter was that the sight of Spranger's pregnant wife and mother was too unbearable for Lise to face when she'd been the cause of their pain.

Anna, standing beside her in a black dress, nudged Lise's side. "It's about to start," she whispered, and Lise looked up as Erich Honecker, East Germany's Party Security Secretary, took to the podium.

Short and broad shouldered, with heavy black glasses and graying hair, Honecker looked like a man who might have been prone to smiling, if the circumstances of his life had played out differently. As it was, he had a stern bearing made sterner still by the events of the day: he gripped the podium and surveyed the assembled crowd, letting the fluttering clicks of camera shutters fade before beginning his address.

"It's a dark day for our nation when we must bid one of our brave defenders farewell," he announced. "Uwe Spranger was one of those defenders—one of the many chosen sons who safeguard our way of life against those who would seek to destroy it." He paused to adjust his glasses, his expression shifting with fervent conviction. "Spranger lived his life in accordance with socialist ideals, and he died in defence of those ideals."

From behind Honecker, Spranger's mother let out a keening wail. From the other side of the coffin, Paul, standing in a long line of Party members and border guards, broke ranks and crossed to comfort her, bracing her in a sidelong hug as he pulled a handkerchief from the breast pocket of his dark suit.

Lise's stomach lurched at the sight of them together: Paul, playing the dutiful friend; Spranger's mother, lost in grief. From the press scrum, cameras flickered to life at the tableau the pair of them made: did they know Paul had been the one who'd sent Uwe Spranger into that cellar? Lise doubted it, but when photos of Paul comforting Spranger's family made their way into East and West German newspapers tomorrow, it would prove to Uli, beyond any doubt, that Lise had been the one who'd betrayed them in the tunnel.

She pressed her lips together, fighting the flood of tears that threatened to undo her. Paul had kept the promise he'd made in return for her cooperation on that horrible day: Lise hadn't suffered any consequences, nor endured any official punishment for her role in the events that had claimed Uwe Spranger's life. But he'd insisted on her attendance here today, and it was punishment of a different kind to have to stand and listen to the cries of a family that she'd bereaved.

Honecker finished speaking and stepped back from the podium, inclining his head in a dignified nod as an honor guard of border officers stepped forward to lift the coffin aloft. From the opposite side of the street, a children's choir wearing Thälmann Pioneer neckerchiefs began to sing the national anthem as Spranger's coffin was borne from the podium and through the silent crowd.

Was Uli watching from his apartment above Bernauer Strasse? Lise couldn't bring herself to look up and see.

Once the podium was clear of mourners, the crowd began to disperse—some to follow in Uwe Spranger's wake, and many more to return to the factory jobs from which they'd gotten leave to attend the service.

Lise reached down to release the brake from Rudi's carriage, then straightened to find Anna studying her with maternal concern.

"Such a tragedy to see a young life cut short." She threaded her hand through the crook of Lise's arm and drew her close. "Such a brave young man...his mother must be so proud."

Something heavy in the back of Lise's throat prevented her from answering. How much had Paul told Anna about the night of the escape?

Given how skilled Paul had turned out to be at keeping secrets, perhaps he hadn't said a word.

"There's no pride in an early death," Lise said finally, quietly.

She watched the procession turn onto Ruppiner Strasse, the black-topped figures of Uwe Spranger's wife and mother still visible in the distance, Paul's blond head between them. She'd never wanted this: she'd never wanted to sacrifice another woman's son in exchange for her own. She'd never wanted to be the reason that Uli would spend the rest of his life not knowing his own child; that Jurgen was on trial for murder, and that Inge's young cousin was facing prison, too.

So much collateral damage; so many lives ruined by her hopeless desire to follow true love.

Anna snugged Lise closer, and Lise allowed her to steer them in the wake of the procession, one shuffling foot after another. They followed the coffin around the corner, and Lise didn't need to resist the urge to look back at the Wall, nor to cast her gaze up to the window where she'd once pinned all her hopes and dreams. It no longer signified, whether Uli was there watching for her or not; it was all immaterial when she knew that she would never be able to bring herself to return to this part of town ever again.

There was nothing left for her on Bernauer Strasse but the wreckage of what might have been.

It would be too cruel to allow herself to continue playing in the ruins.

40

It was near to closing time at Siggi's, and the raucous crowd of drinkers who filled the vinyl seats on weekend evenings had thinned out, leaving behind the same old handful of barflies who flirted with Agatha as she pulled pints behind the counter.

As the only remaining party under the age of sixty-five, Uli and Inge had taken their usual booth by the window: a perfect vantage point, to Uli's inebriated mind, from which to study the line of bowed backs at the bar. His hand skittered along a litter of empty steins as he reached for the dregs of what had once been a pint of lager.

"Look at them," he muttered, adjusting the knot of his sling. "Which one do you think it was?"

Inge steadied her head in her cupped hand and followed his crooked gaze across the room. "How d'you mean?"

Uli's drunken suspicion hardened into drunken conviction. "It had to have been one of them. Didn't it? They must have seen us going—going downstairs, maybe followed us one night. Someone here sold us out to the *Stasi*!"

He shouted the last word and a few of the barflies turned on their stools, their eyebrows raised at his outburst, but Uli didn't care.

"Someone betrayed us," he muttered again. "Someone betrayed *Lise*."

Inge put a hand on his arm. "S'not worth it," she replied dully. Uli squinted at her in the dim light, registering her hollow eyes and lank hair: had she, like him, not slept since the night of the escape? Every time he closed his eyes, Uli saw the face of the man he'd killed in the darkness of the tunnel—killed or let die, he wasn't entirely sure which. How could he drift off to sleep not knowing whether Lise and Rudi were safe? Instead, he walked the streets of West Berlin plagued by thoughts of Jurgen and Sigrid, thrown in some East German prison. Had Lise suffered the same fate? Had she been arrested on her way to the tunnel?

He couldn't know—he wouldn't rest—until he found the son of a bitch who'd betrayed them all.

He pulled his wandering attention back to Inge, who was wiping her cheeks with the patterned sleeve of her dress.

"Stop it." He slid a paper napkin across the table, fixing his gaze on the tabletop. Inge cried at the smallest provocation these days and the sight of it pained him, though he couldn't say why: only that if she continued to cry, he would start as well, and then where would they be? "Stop crying, it's—it's—"

"I'm sorry." Inge hiccuped, dabbing at her running eyeliner. "It's just that when I think of—of Sigrid... I should have been there. It should have been me..."

She trailed off and Uli excused himself, lurching out of the booth as the room swirled around him. He adjusted his sling once more, thinking of those terrible moments after they'd left the cellar, when Inge had taken him to the hospital to repair his shattered shoulder: how he'd been visited by the West Berlin police, who'd quickly put two and two together about the tunnel and dragged them all to the police station to interrogate them. Uli had read countless stories in the newspaper about tunnelers just like them who'd been feted as heroes for bringing people across the Wall, and yet he and Inge and Wolf had been treated like criminals, berated for actions that, but for one misstep, should have been seen as nothing short of heroic. They'd even informed Uli that he was the subject of an extradition request from East German authorities, who wanted him in connection to the death of Sergeant Uwe Spranger.

It had only been thanks to an intervention by his parents in the form of a highly paid lawyer that the extradition request had been denied—but Uli hadn't gotten off lightly for his efforts. Jurgen and Sigrid were still in prison, awaiting show trials for their roles in the escape; Lise and Rudi were unaccounted for.

He slumped on the bar, wishing there was some way to wash away his anguish.

He looked up as Agatha slid two large glasses of water across the wooden tabletop. "That's all you need at the moment, young man," she said. The *kneipe* had been crawling with reporters and rubberneckers ever since the escape attempt had hit the newspapers, distracting Agatha from the hard work of running her establishment.

Another selfish consequence of his actions.

"Sorry," he mumbled, and the barmaid's expression softened.

She pulled two packets of peanuts from beneath the bar and set them beside the glasses. "On the house. I know you were only trying to help your girlfriend."

He stuffed the peanuts in his pocket. "And look where it got me."

He balanced the glasses of water in the crook of his elbow and turned around to find that someone else had slipped into the booth along with Inge.

Guilt slowed his steps. He'd not spoken to Wolf since the night of the escape, but Uli knew that while he'd spent time licking his wounds, Wolf had been busy trying to rally support for

Jurgen and Sigrid. They'd been vilified in the East German press as criminals, but Wolf had helped to raise their profiles in West Germany and beyond as folk heroes: he'd arranged for candle-light vigils at Brandenburg Gate and spoke to the media about Jurgen's heroism, Sigrid's sacrifice. He'd set up Jurgen's family in a flat in West Berlin, encouraged them to speak to journalists about Jurgen's good heart, his compassionate nature.

All while Uli had done nothing but feel sorry for himself.

He set the glasses on the table and sat back down; without preamble, Wolf slid the latest edition of *Bild* across the table, the pages flipped open to show a series of East German photographs from the funeral of Sergeant Spranger.

Uli flinched. The spread featured a prominent picture of Spranger, looking so young, so resolute in his uniform, and while the photograph had been reproduced in black-and-white, Uli couldn't help but recall the brilliant hazel of his eyes.

Somewhere beneath his self-pity, a thin spark of anger kindled in his chest. "So…so what, Wolf? You want me to feel worse about it than I already do?"

Like himself and Inge, Wolf was a mess, his handsome features ragged from lack of sleep, and something darker. His hollowed cheeks were dusted with stubble, and he narrowed his dark eyes, his lip curling with disdain. "See anyone you know?"

Uli frowned; beside him, Inge stiffened.

Wolf stabbed a finger at a smaller photo embedded in the article, depicting two women in black, supported by a tall, familiar man.

"Do you want to explain why Lise's brother is at the funeral of the man we killed," Wolf hissed, "or do you need me to enlighten you?"

"No." Uli felt as if the table was slipping away beneath him, and he gripped the edge, his mind reeling. "No, there must be some mistake."

"A mistake?" Wolf's voice lifted with incredulity, attracting the attention of the barflies over his shoulder. "Her brother is Stasi. She betrayed you! Betrayed *us*!"

Bile rose in Uli's throat but he swallowed it down, trying to make sense of what he was looking at: Paul, standing between Spranger's wife and his mother; Paul standing beside Erich Honecker as they followed the coffin down the street.

"Maybe it—maybe she didn't know about Paul. She couldn't have known. I spoke to her so many times," Inge began, but Wolf turned his fierce glare on her and she faltered beneath it.

"You told her everything she needed to know," he snarled. "She was the only one who knew where the tunnel's entrance was, beyond Sigrid and Inge. She was the only one who didn't turn up… Jesus Christ, she must have been laughing as we worked ourselves to the bone. You trusted her—*we* trusted her—and now a man is dead!"

He rose from the table, his voice hoarse with grief. "Jurgen's in prison, and I don't know whether I'll see him again thanks to that—that *bitch*—"

In a flash, Uli was on his feet. He didn't remember striking Wolf, didn't remember anything beyond boiling rage, but then his vision cleared, and Wolf was on the ground as Inge screamed behind him, and all he wanted was for it all to stop—for the pain to stop, the confusion, the fury—

Strong hands gripped him from behind, sending a blind bolt of pain up his arm before the barflies threw him out, sprawling, onto the street.

He groaned on the pavement, clutching his shoulder as the door to Siggi's creaked open once more. He could hear the thud of Wolf's feet, then felt a wad of spittle hit his face.

I deserved that. He listened as Wolf walked off into the night and opened his eyes, staring up at the dark sky above. A lamppost flickered nearby, obliterating any chance he might have had of seeing the stars—but what use were stars tonight?

The door opened once more, and Inge stepped into his line of vision with a wet rag in hand.

"Are you okay?"

Uli sat up as Inge leaned forward, neither of them quite as unsteady as they'd been moments ago. She held his jaw and wiped his cheek with the rag before running her hands down the rise of his neck toward his shoulder, ensuring the bandages that the hospital had so painstakingly wrapped around his wound were still secure.

"Don't listen to him," she continued as she cleaned gravel from his bleeding elbow. "He's upset about Jurgen."

"With good reason." Without Wolf shouting accusations, Uli could hear the truth in what he'd said; he took off his glasses and ground the heel of his palm into his eyes, willing himself to stop the sudden river of tears. "How could she do this to me?"

He didn't realize he'd spoken aloud until Inge gently guided his hand back down to his lap. "She might not have had a choice," she replied. "Not if her brother really is what Wolf says he is. Don't be too quick to judge."

"Tell that to Jurgen and Sigrid."

They sat together under the lamplight, listening to the muffled sounds of the kneipe carrying on—Uli had given the barflies plenty to discuss over another round of drinks. He could feel the adrenaline starting to fade from his system, leaving him tired and trembling.

He looked down to find that Inge's fingers were still wrapped around his and realized that he was grateful for it: her steadiness was a comfort, giving him something solid to cling to.

It had been a year since he'd felt the warmth of another person; a year since he'd looked into someone's eyes and seen honesty, compassion, reflected back.

It broke his heart to know that he didn't deserve it.

He let out a ragged breath. "Why are you here, Inge?"

Beneath the glow of the streetlamp, Inge's pale features blurred, then came back into focus. "I just don't think you should be alone right now."

Slowly, tentatively, Uli turned his hand so that he could thread his fingers through hers and met her eyes with a steady, direct question. He leaned close, resting his forehead against Inge's for a brief, quiet moment, then pressed his lips to hers.

He'd never imagined that she would kiss him back—but then, he'd never dreamed of kissing her before. But Inge responded to him first with hesitation, then enthusiasm, and he buried his hands in her hair.

They were both drunk—both heartbroken, and somewhere in the back of his mind Uli knew that in the morning they would both add their actions tonight to a long list of regrets. But as he got to his feet to lead Inge across the street and back to the apartment, he could hear the distant roar of his howling grief fall silent.

Part Three

41

OCTOBER 1958
FREE UNIVERSITY OF BERLIN

The lecture hall was large and imposing, an echoing, no-nonsense space with long lines of desks arranged, amphitheater-style, around an empty podium. Hefting her book bag higher on her shoulder, Inge walked up the shallow steps toward the desks, avoiding the gaze of students who swiveled in their seats to watch her progress. She breathed in, the scent of cologne and sweat revealing what she didn't need to see: men, their half-stubbled faces slack with surprise at the sight of a woman in their classroom.

Eyes down, she told herself. As a female student of medicine, Inge was used to the incredulous stares of others—and as a strikingly beautiful woman, she was used to gazes of a more aggressive nature, from men who felt she owed them her attention and from women who viewed her as competition, or worse. She'd known when she was accepted at the Free University that she would be only one of a handful of women in her course, and though she'd grown a thick skin for being the center of attention, she couldn't help feeling as though she was an insect on display, pinned into place to receive the scrutiny of others.

She glanced up, catching sight of an empty seat next to a young woman—one of the only other women in the room, who, like Inge, had arranged her smooth features into a blank mask as she stared down at the chalkboard. Inge hesitated: in her experience, women could be more vicious than men, particularly when they had something to prove.

Don't be so cowardly. She swallowed her trepidation and made her way down the row of seats. She was here to listen and learn, and she would have an easier time of doing that next to a woman rather than a male student who might want to flirt.

She slid into the empty seat, and the woman offered her a perfunctory smile before turning her attention back to the podium. It was clear that she, like Inge, wasn't interested in making friends, and that suited Inge just fine. Instead, Inge glanced at her watch: there were only five minutes before the lecture was slated to begin, and she busied herself with arranging her notebook and fountain pen on the desk before a gentle tap on her shoulder interrupted her preparations.

She turned and met the glance of a handsome young man sitting behind her, his stubbled cheeks and rumpled oxford shirt indicating long hours spent in the library.

"Excuse me," he said with a perfect smile. "Do you have a pen I might borrow?"

"Sorry, no." Inge turned her attention back to her book bag.

He cleared his throat, and Inge suppressed a sigh. "You probably think I'm an idiot, not having one of my own," he continued. "I'm not usually so unprepared, it's just...first day of lecture, and all. You're sure I can't use yours? I'd be happy to share my notes after class."

She shot him a cool smile. "I prefer to take my own notes, thanks."

The young man's smile hardened, and he leaned forward.

"Come on, don't be so difficult. It's not like you really need to take notes." He winked. "Unlike you, I'm actually going to practice medicine. You're just here wasting time before marriage."

Inge turned fully, properly, in her seat to face him. "You might be learning how to practice medicine, but I'm here to learn how to perform it," she shot back. "And when you misdiagnose a woman's heart murmur as hysteria, I'll be the one they come to for a correct treatment plan."

She watched, satisfied, as a beet red flush rose in his face. "There's no need to be such a bitch," he muttered.

"When you stop being an asshole, I'll stop acting like a bitch. How about it?"

She turned back to her notebook without waiting for a response.

Beside her, the woman leaned over. "That was glorious," she said in a low voice.

Inge allowed herself a proper smile. "It's not the first time I've had to do that, and I doubt it will be the last," she replied. "How about you? Any bad behavior from the others so far?"

She shot Inge a sardonic look. "What do you think? If I had a mark for every time someone's offered to explain the course syllabus to me, I'd be a rich woman."

Inge chuckled. "Five minutes into our studies and we're already having to deal with men who think we belong at home," she replied. "Surely, there are easier ways to find a husband than embarking upon a rigorous academic career."

"They'll argue it was all part of our plan. We enrolled at one of the best universities in Germany so we could meet and marry the smartest guys in the room."

"*Marry* the smartest guy in the room? I plan to *be* the smartest guy in the room."

The woman's smile broadened. "So do I." She held out her hand, and Inge took it. "So we agree that's our goal? To become the smartest guys in the room?"

Inge shook her hand, knowing that despite her efforts to the contrary, she'd just made a friend for life. "I'm Inge."

"Lise. It's a pleasure to meet you."

5 SEPTEMBER, 1961

Uli,

I know that nothing I can say will make up for what occurred that night in July. I wish with all my heart that things had turned out differently. But know that my hand was forced, and the decisions I made that day were made solely for the welfare of our son.

Paul has agreed to have this letter sent to you without passing the censors. It was a condition of my cooperation. He's agreed to send more letters to you for Rudi's sake, but I don't know how often I'll be able to write.

It has always has been my dearest wish to be with you, but I realize now that such a future is no longer within our grasp. We simply must make the best of our lives apart.

I will always love you.

Lise

42

MAY 1959

The tram clattered its way through Köpenick Forest, the vivid new growth on the pine trees putting Inge in mind of summers spent beneath the shade of the mighty spruces that surrounded her childhood home. From the front of the tram, a passenger cracked open a ventilation window and she breathed in the fresh air, then turned to smile at Lise. Though they were only an hour's journey from the center of Berlin, it felt to Inge as though they were a world away from darkened libraries and lecture halls, here in the bucolic green enclaves of East Germany.

"I love taking the tram," Lise said, a beam of sunlight hitting her through the window as they emerged from the forest into the white suburbs of Woltersdorf. "We usually drive when we come out here."

Inge had been studying at the Free University for seven months, and she'd not spent much time beyond West Berlin's city center: she'd been too busy, too focused, to spend her time sightseeing. Besides, the thought of venturing into the East Germany proper seemed intimidating, given the border guards and police officers in East Berlin who constantly asked for papers, harrying any Westerners who ventured into the socialist paradise. But when Lise had invited her to her family's datsche for the weekend, Inge had jumped at the opportunity: it was a chance to see East Germany with a friend, one for whom the country and its idiosyncrasies were second nature.

But as they passed pebble dash houses and quaint storefronts, Inge wondered why she'd worried. It was all so common, so familiar: women walked with their dogs down the same cobbled streets as in the West; men dashed across the same town squares to meet them. The currency might have been different, and the uniforms were different, but to Inge's untrained eye it was all Germany, and marks of its common past persisted.

Perhaps one day the country would be united once more.

The tram pulled in at its final stop, and Inge followed Lise out into the warm sunlight. A handful of people had gotten out of the tram along with them, and as they all drifted off to their own destinations Inge caught sight of someone across the street, who lifted his arm to wave Lise over.

She elbowed Lise in the side as they waited to cross the street.

"Lise," she whispered. "You never told me your brother was so *handsome*!"

Lise smirked. "I never have to," she replied. "My friends always insist on telling me so."

Inge's heart flipped giddily as they crossed the cobblestones. Though it was clear that he and Lise were siblings, Paul's features were a refined, masculine version of hers: he was tall, broad and blond, with an aquiline nose and soft, downturned eyes that were the same blue as a cloudless sky.

He wrapped Lise in a hug, then turned his breathtaking smile onto Inge.

"I'm Paul," he said, holding out a warm hand. "It's a pleasure to meet you."

"Inge," she replied.

He took Inge's and Lise's suitcases and placed them in the boot of an idling Trabant. "Shall we?"

The datsche was a small cottage, with rough-hewn beams in the kitchenette and mismatched windows that overlooked a sweet little garden in bloom. To Inge, the place felt like a reflection of the Lise she'd come to know in her time at the Free University: relaxed and unpretentious.

Paul carried their suitcases toward a set of twin beds nestled beneath a loft.

"Papa prefers the daybed," Lise explained as Paul swung the suitcases onto the bed. "He's visiting friends—we'll say hello when he's back."

"Who painted the swallows?" Inge asked, admiring the hand-painted birds that danced along the rafters.

Lise cleared her throat. "I believe her name was Heidi, was it not, Paul? Or Freida?"

"An ex-girlfriend of yours?" Inge asked playfully.

Paul shot Lise a cartoonishly overdrawn glare. "*Heidi* was a talented artist," he replied, though his response was entirely devoid of venom.

Lise glanced at Inge over her shoulder. "Paul's girlfriends tend to leave little souvenirs," she explained as he stalked, red-faced, out to the garden. "So that he invites them back."

Watching the two of them, it was clear that theirs was an easy rapport, one based on shared humor and history: a relationship unique to siblings who genuinely enjoyed each others' company.

Inge couldn't help feeling a pang of longing. As an only child, she'd never experienced the sort of friendship that could only come from a lifetime spent together.

Dinner that evening was an alfresco affair, hearty dishes of pickled vegetables and roast pork laid along a groaning harvest table set between the raised garden beds. Across the table, Paul's face was illuminated by the flickering light of mismatched candlesticks set amidst the wildflowers that Inge had been tasked with collecting in jam jars, and music floated from the datsche's open window.

At the head of the table, Lise's father, Rudolph, lifted his glass. "We're so thrilled to have you here with us," he said, twinkling a smile at Inge. "Lise has spoken of you so often. I'm so pleased she's found a real friend at school."

"So am I," Inge replied, casting a grateful glance at Lise. "She was the first person I met in Berlin, and she's still my favorite."

Lise lifted her glass. "Smartest guys in the room," she quipped, and Inge lifted hers in response.

"What brought you to West Berlin?" Rudolph asked, lifting his glass of Rotkäppchen to his lips.

Inge hesitated. How could she tell them, these socialists who were sharing their table, about her upbringing? She pictured the immense rooms of her childhood; the peaceful stables and painted relatives, staring down at her from ornate frames as she ran through halls that demanded stately paces; the mountains of silverware on long oak tables, polished by unseen hands.

"I grew up quite...differently than I live now," she said carefully. "My parents, they don't approve of some of the choices I've made."

She could see in Rudolph's expression that this was a battle Lise had never had to fight. "How so?"

"They don't approve of my studying medicine."

Inge could feel the incredulity in their silence as they stared at her across the table.

"They—they don't approve?" Paul asked.

"They don't approve." Inge offered Lise a grim smile, knowing how ridiculous her past would sound, here in the company of Lise's lovely family. "I'm from an old family in Sweden. Inherited wealth, and all that... My parents believe that women are best employed in sustaining old family lineages."

Rudolph set down his drink. "You mean—?"

"They intended that I would marry the boy from the estate

in the next village," Inge explained. "It was all neat and tidy. He was an only child, I was an only child... And I ought to say that it wasn't Sven's fault. We were friends, really, but it wasn't what I wanted. When I told my parents I would rather study medicine I'm afraid they reacted rather badly."

She recalled the argument that had preceded her departure from the family estate—Mother, wailing, Father, yelling. They'd expected her to fall into line, to marry for connections, for money, rather than for love—to walk the same worn path they'd trod as newlyweds, dutiful but despairing, ground down beneath the expectations of nobility and estate duties. But such a life took a toll that Inge had recognized even as a girl: Mother, increasingly reliant upon her bottles of valium; Father, never without a drink in hand.

"When I was little, we would summer in Europe, and I remember being struck by how many people lived in poverty," she continued. "It made no sense to me, why we had so much and they had so little. I wanted to do something with my life to help people, rather than sit in some vast country house and rot away. So, I decided to become a doctor."

Paul let out a long breath. *"Scheisse,"* he said finally. "You sure you're not a socialist? It sounds like you'd fit right in, here in East Germany."

She shot Paul a sardonic smile. "I wouldn't go that far," she replied, "but to hear my parents tell it, I'm practically a communist."

Rudolph reached across the table and patted Inge's hand. "We like ambitious women in this family," he said, and Inge felt something soften within her at his fatherly kindness. "It's why I was so pleased when Lise was accepted at the Free University."

"She could have gone to Humboldt," Paul began, but Lise shot him a withering glare and he relented. "Well, I suppose it's a good thing she went to West Berlin," he said, turning his beautiful blue gaze onto Inge, "because if she hadn't, we wouldn't have met you."

★★★

Sleep came fitfully to Inge that evening, the sound of Paul snoring in the loft above her putting too many distracting thoughts in her mind for her to dream. Finally, she threw off her covers and tiptoed out into the garden, bringing a crocheted blanket along with her to keep her warm.

If she wasn't going to sleep, she might as well enjoy the stars.

She sat on a bench between two of the raised garden beds, craning her neck to admire the night sky. Here in the dark suburbs, more stars sparkled overhead than she ever saw in Berlin and she hadn't realized in those long months of study how much she'd missed them. To see them now felt like reuniting with old friends: the Winter Road, sprawling like cream along the darkness; *Karlavagnen*, arcing gracefully across the sky.

She glanced back at the datsche at the sound of the door creaking open, and pulled her blanket tighter over her shoulders as she watched Paul's tall shadow wander down to meet her.

He eased onto the bench beside her and pulled a package of cigarettes from his pocket, holding them out in a wordless offer, which Inge declined.

"Couldn't sleep?"

"No."

He pulled a flask from his other pocket and unscrewed the lid. "How about a drink?"

"Why not?"

They sat in silence for a few moments, passing the flask back and forth between them. This was it: the moment where she and Paul would share midnight confessions and a moonlight kiss. If this were a romance novel, she and Paul would declare their love in the darkness and Inge would join this perfect little family, spend all her weekends here, with them.

How many of Lise's friends had fallen prey to that same dizzying fantasy?

"Can I ask you a question?"

Paul nudged the flask into her hands. "Of course."

"Why didn't Lise tell me about your father?"

Out of the corner of her eye, she could see Paul turn to look at her and she knew that this was not the question he'd expected. "What about him?"

She handed him back the flask. "His condition. She didn't mention the wheelchair."

Paul took a sip. "I suppose neither of us feel it's really worth mentioning."

Inge conceded the point with a shrug, then turned her attention to the raised garden beds: tall enough for Rudolph to tend to, unaided. They shared the same angular construction as the *datsche*, and Inge realized that Paul must have built them.

It was another point in his favor.

"I can appreciate that," she replied. "It must be easier for him, to have the two of you."

Paul was quiet for a moment, and the sound of cicadas in the trees buzzed louder in the silence. "I give thanks every day that I have him," he said finally. "Papa and Lise both."

Paralysis was a condition that could come on in so many different ways, but given Paul and Lise, Inge suspected that it had come to Rudolph later in his life. "How did it happen?"

Paul took a long drink from the flask. "The war," he replied, dropping the flask into his lap. "He was performing a gallbladder operation, and his hospital was bombed. It took them days to find him under the rubble...he was one of very few survivors."

It was a terrible story, and as Paul gave Inge the flask she was loath to ask more questions. As an officially neutral nation, Sweden had been spared so many horrors of the war—not all, but many. Since moving to Berlin, she'd reflected countless times on how fortunate she'd been, not to grow up shadowed by such atrocities, nor to contend with the family members, friends and neighbors who committed them.

But her family had been indifferent to the suffering of others, and that brought with it its own kind of guilt.

"I'm so sorry."

"Yeah…well." Paul planted his elbows on his knees, the graceful curve of his back a shadowed bulk in the darkness. "He was the lucky one. What happened to my mother was worse."

Inge didn't want to ask, but it was clear that Paul wanted to talk, so she handed him the flask and listened.

"You know we were all…put into service, at the end. All us kids." He looked down and played with the lid of the flask. "When Berlin fell, I—I was given a rifle. Me and the rest of the boys in my youth group. We were told we were the last line of defense; us, and the grandfathers in the Home Guard. We'd learned for—oh, for a few years by then—how to load a machine gun, and I was in charge of preparing rounds of ammunition for the older boy who—who fired it."

He lowered his head as Inge tallied the math in her head. Paul was only a few years older than her and Lise. He would have been nine or ten at the time.

"When the boy manning the machine gun got shot, I remember being pushed into his place by my troupe leader. The Russians were advancing, and I—I don't even think I aimed at anything, not properly. I just closed my eyes and pulled the trigger."

He closed his eyes, lost in the memory, and Inge wondered how long he'd held this all in—whether he'd ever spoken of it before, whether he'd told this story to anyone else.

But then, every other German his age had the same story to tell.

"Finally, we ran out of bullets and we were told to—to go home. It was clear we'd lost. Russian tanks were rolling past us, and they didn't even bother to stop and shoot. But there were soldiers in the streets, and fires, and bombs going off… My troupe leader took a pistol from the nearest dead body and pushed it into my hands. Told me to go home and defend whoever I found there."

She could picture him there, a child in a khaki shirt, and the image filled her with a deep, heavy sadness.

Paul sighed again. "Anyways, I was… I was too late. When I got home, soldiers were already there."

He didn't elaborate, and Inge didn't need him to. Not when the truth of what had happened was so clearly written in his face.

"Lise didn't speak for a full year after that," he continued. "Not even when Papa came home from the hospital. She'd become this…this shell of herself. When she finally did start talking again, she told me she couldn't remember anything that had happened, that she—she blacked it all out, or something. But she didn't speak for an entire year." He sighed and leaned his head back against the garden fence. "She was only five."

Five years old, to face such horrors. Inge handed the nearly empty flask back to Paul, childishly embarrassed by her own conduct at dinner, whining about inherited wealth and dutiful proposals. How could anything she'd ever faced in her privileged little life compare to what Lise and Paul had gone through?

"Anyways, she doesn't know the extent of what happened, and she never will. Not from me, at least." Paul straightened, and his voice took on an edge she'd not heard before. "I promised myself that day that I'd never let anyone hurt her ever again." He looked down, grave faced. "I've kept that promise, as best I can. And I'll continue to keep it until the day I die."

It was the most heartbreaking thing Inge had ever heard: a childhood vow, made in the darkest, most tragic, of circumstances.

She put her hand on his arm and Paul started, as if he'd forgotten she was there.

"You're not being fair to yourself," she said gently. "You can't protect her from everything. No one can take on that kind of burden."

Paul stared grimly into the darkness. "I can protect her from most things," he replied. "From the worst this world has to offer."

1 MAY, 1963

Uli,

Enclosed is a picture of Rudi on his first birthday. We took him to the Tierpark Zoo for the afternoon, and he enjoyed it. He particularly liked the monkeys.

He's toddling now, and has begun to speak. It's wonderful to see his development. His first word was "spot," and he enjoys playing with his toy cars.

He's the tallest boy in his nursery class. I think he's going to be tall like you.

I tell him bedtime stories about his brave papa, who lives far away and loves him as much as I do.

Yours always,
Lise

43

NOVEMBER 1959

Inge handed her jacket to the cloakroom attendant, listening to the brush of a snare drum as she made her way through a long line of revelers waiting for entry to the nightclub. A quick glance at her watch told her that Lise was late, but that was hardly a surprise: Lise seemed to be in a perpetual struggle with the clock, always rushing into the lecture hall at the last minute, always the last of their crowd to arrive at Siggi's. She tended to explain her tardiness away as the fault of East German police, constantly questioning her need to be in West Berlin; Inge, however, suspected that Lise simply had poor time management.

She approached the maître d' stand, where a short man in a dark suit stood barring the way to the ballroom, perusing a thick book of reservations before a closed set of double doors. He glanced up and Inge shot him a dazzling smile: she'd not made reservations, but she'd had a lifetime of practice sliding past society's gatekeepers.

"Good evening," she said, and his eyes widened, barely perceptibly, as she rested her hand on the edge of his table. "I wonder whether you have space for my friend and me? She's just on her way, and we'd love to stop in for a drink..."

The maître d' glanced down at his ledger. "I'm terribly sorry, but we're not seating anyone without a reservation. We're entirely full. You'll have to try another night."

Inge had expected as much, but she wasn't so easily beat. She pursed her lips in a moue of disappointment and made a show of glancing at his name tag. "Magnus, is it? That's such a shame, Magnus. My friend will be so disappointed, seeing as it's her last night of freedom." The maître d' frowned, and Inge pressed on. "She's taking her vows," she explained. "As a novitiate, tomorrow afternoon."

The maître d's gaze flickered to the long line of people behind Inge. "Your friend has decided to become a nun," he replied dubiously.

Inge let out an overdrawn sigh. "Well, does one ever truly decide to become a nun, Magnus? It's a calling from God. I was just as surprised as you are when she told me, but I suppose they don't all enter the Abbey as saints. I'll miss her, of course, once she's joined her sisters, but I promised to support her in whatever she chooses to do. It's only that she wanted one last night out. One last night of secular freedom, so to speak, before she begins her new life."

The maître d' still didn't look convinced. "Your friend has decided to become a nun, and wants to spend her last night before entering the nunnery here?"

Inge tilted her head, and held his gaze with a wide-eyed, guileless stare. "Well, wouldn't you?"

He hesitated a moment longer. "Let me see what I can do."

Inge stepped back, satisfied, as Lise drew up beside her. "Sorry I'm late," she said, fixing her heavy book bag over her shoulder.

Magnus came out from behind his stand. "I presume this is the novitiate herself?"

Inge rested a hand on Lise's arm, ignoring the look of sheer bemusement on her face. "Yes. It really means so much that you can squeeze us in, to make one last memory. I can't tell you how much I'll miss her, once she takes her vows."

Lise stared at the maître d' for a blank moment, until Inge squeezed her elbow in a silent urge for her to play along.

"Um… Peace be with you," Lise stammered as Magnus opened the double doors into the ballroom.

Arm in arm, they followed him into an explosion of sound. The nightclub was an old survivor from the days of the Weimar Republic, with deco etchings high on pink marble columns and chrome palm trees that arched languorously over banquette tables. It was packed with people dancing wildly in time to a ten-piece jazz band arrayed on a far-off stage: uniformed GIs and bank managers and students like Lise and Inge, blowing off steam after classes.

Lise leaned close as Magnus wove them past tables stuffed with diners and drinkers. "Did you tell that man I'm becoming a nun?"

Inge shrugged. "They didn't have any availability. I had to come up with something."

Lise let out a huff. "You can talk the hind legs off a donkey, do you know that?"

"What can I say? It's a gift." She raised her voice as Magnus pulled out a chair for her at a small, round table set on the edge of the dance floor. "You're a darling, Magnus. Thank you."

"Just…say an Ave Maria for me when you're there, would you, Sister? Enjoy your evening."

They waited until he was out of earshot before bursting into laughter. "Do you think he really bought it?" Lise asked.

Inge leafed though the drink menu. "Does it matter? It worked." She lifted a finger to call over a waiter before casting an eye over the crowd. "What do you think? Shall we find ourselves some company?"

"I suppose if I'm a nun in training, I ought to behave myself," Lise replied with a smirk. "Honestly, Inge..."

"There's a way into every room," Inge replied. "The challenge is simply to find it."

A waiter came over and after Lise ordered them both glasses of champagne, she watched him retreat with interest. "He's cute."

Inge shrugged. "I suppose so, but I'm not looking for a local." Across the dance floor, a tall soldier shot Inge a broad smile, and she shot one back. This was the reason she'd wanted to come to this particular ballroom, in the American sector of the city: to meet some handsome Yank who could tell her about his travels in North America and beyond.

"You and your wanderlust," Lise said, shaking her head. "Where would you most like to go in the world?"

"Africa," she replied. "Tanganyika, maybe. I'd love to go on a safari and see Dar es Salaam."

"Maybe if you end up joining *Médecins sans Frontières*, you'll have an opportunity to go," Lise offered as the waiter returned with two tall flutes. She took a sip of her drink and returned her attention to the dance floor.

Inge hesitated. "How about you? Have you thought of traveling?"

Lise shrugged. "Of course I have. It's just a little more difficult in my situation."

The question might have come across as callous, if Inge and Lise didn't know each other so well. East Germany rarely granted travel visas, and even then it only allowed its citizens to travel to countries that shared its socialist ideals. But Lise spoke so often about the life she planned to live: one with a scale of ambition and independence that often felt at odds with the strictures of her country.

Inge leaned across the table. "Have you ever thought of... just staying in West Berlin? Going to Marienfelde and making a claim?"

Lise's expression was even and unequivocal, her words barely audible beneath the sound of the band. "What do you think? I'd go tomorrow if it wasn't for my family."

Inge had never considered her fractured relationship with her parents to be an asset, but looking at Lise, she could appreciate for the first time the dilemma involved in being part of a loving family. For Inge, it had been easy to make the decisions that had led her to the Free University, and which would, she hoped, lead her to a life of adventure. The only person she had to take into account was herself. But Lise had Rudolph and Paul, and Inge knew only too well the loneliness of a life estranged from family. Even if it was for the life she wanted, how would Lise ever manage leaving them behind?

Lise straightened in her chair. "Incoming," she murmured, and Inge looked up as two men made their way across the dance floor.

Inge studied them as they walked over, straightening their ties. "They go to the Free University, too. I've seen the shorter one on campus."

"Shorter's a relative term. Look at him, he's easily six feet tall." Lise's smile grew as the shorter one—the one wearing thick black glasses and a lopsided smile—stopped in front of their table. "Hello, there."

"Hello, yourself," he replied, and Inge glanced at Lise, rolling her eyes in a wordless conversation: *German*, she thought, disappointed. "We noticed you walk in, and Wolf thinks we all go to the same university. I'm Uli. May we sit down?"

Lise shifted her chair to make space as Uli went to get chairs, and Inge shifted her attention to his friend—taller and angular, with sharp features and piercing eyes.

Perhaps it's not a complete loss, she mused as Wolf shot her a look that promised nothing less than trouble.

She leaned back in her chair and offered him her hand with a wicked smile. "I'm Inge. My friend here is Lise. She's joining a nunnery tomorrow, so you two really ought to buy the drinks."

14 SEPTEMBER, 1963

Uli,

I'm writing to tell you that I am getting married. His name is Horst Kammerer. He's a family friend. I've known him for years, but in recent months we've grown closer. He's good with Rudi, and I believe that we can be happy together.

I want you to know that this was not an easy decision for me to make, but I think it will be good for both Rudi and me. Rudi is in need of a father figure, and Horst has been a steady influence.

I told you that we both needed to make the best of our lives, and this is my attempt to do that.

I hope that you can understand.

Affectionately,
Lise

44

MAY 1961

A bell tinkled above the shop door as Inge stepped in out of the rain. She set her dripping umbrella in a stand near the door, letting her eyes adjust as she listened to the muffled sounds of the showroom: the handful of customers who stood, murmuring at various glass-fronted display cases; dark-suited attendants, their faces cast in shadows by the bright lights that illuminated the sparkling wares.

From beside a case in the back corner, Uli looked up, relief etched on his features as Inge drew closer. "Thank goodness," he said, leaning forward to kiss her cheek. "I'm in far over my head. Thank you for coming."

Inge stepped back and pushed her hands in her pockets, then immediately pulled them out, self-consciously worried that the watchful security guard in the corner might have misinterpreted the movement and thought she was pocketing the goods.

"Well," she said, "it's not every day you help pick out your friend's engagement ring."

Lise and Uli had been dating for over a year, and when Uli

had asked Inge to help him with the ring, it had felt less like a surprise than a logical conclusion. She was happy for Lise: it was clear that Lise was head over heels for Uli, and that Uli was doting and kind. Still, she had her reservations about it all. Lise had worked so hard to be top of the class, and to Inge it felt like a defeat of sorts for her to do the very thing the boys in their year had accused them both of being in school to do. She'd met a man. She was to become a wife.

But Inge knew better than to voice her concerns aloud.

"So? Has anything caught your eye yet?"

Uli ran a hand along his jaw as he studied the glittering rings in the display case. He wasn't Inge's type—she'd always gone for Vikings, burly and blond and broad shouldered. Indeed, Uli was the opposite of Inge's ideal man: dark haired and lanky, with a tendency toward slouching to hide his height. But there was something about him that even Inge could concede she found compelling: a charm, perhaps, that was entirely his.

"I was hoping to ask for your opinion first," he was saying. "All the cuts, all the options..." He looked up and straightened his glasses, which had slipped down his nose. "You're her best friend. Do any of these—do any of them look like her?"

The question was oddly phrased, but Inge was touched by the sentiment behind it. The ring she'd been given by Sven, her childhood intended, had been a massive family heirloom, ugly and heavy, something she never would have chosen for herself: a rock meant to cement her in place.

To Sven, her opinion about the ring—about the estate where they were to live, about the life she wanted to have—hadn't mattered. Not, at least, above the wishes of the family. Her own marriage would have been luxurious and impersonal, a suffocating capitulation.

But here was Uli, taking Lise's preferences into consideration from the very start.

She leaned over the jewelry case. "She's not going to want something ostentatious," she began.

Uli let out a snort of laughter. "Don't worry about that. I can't afford anything ostentatious." Out of the corner of Inge's eye, she could see the shop attendant shift on his feet. "Will she want gold or silver?"

"Gold." Inge had always been partial to silver herself, but Lise, with her warmer coloring, was clearly better suited to gold. "She wears those earrings of her mother's almost every day. She'll want something that goes with them."

"And the stone, fräulein?" The attendant opened the display case with a practised movement.

She glanced at Uli. "Has she ever mentioned a preference to you?"

"She hasn't," Uli replied, "but I've always thought she'd look wonderful in diamonds. D'you think she'd like diamonds?"

Inge grinned. "They're a girl's best friend."

"Excellent." The attendant began choosing several rings from within the display case and set them on a velvet-covered tray. "We have many different styles to choose from. Would the lucky lady prefer a solitaire or perhaps a trilogy ring? Or an eternity band?"

"A—a solitaire, I think," Uli murmured, with a confirming glance at Inge.

"Excellent. And the cut? Baguette, brilliant, cushion, emerald, pear…?"

"We'd like to see some options."

"Of course. And her ring size?"

"Seven," Inge supplied. She turned to Uli. "I borrowed a ring of hers the other day to make sure."

A short while later, Inge and Uli had chosen a beautiful yellow gold band with an emerald-cut solitaire. As the attendant left to sort out the paperwork and pack the ring into a small box, Inge turned to Uli.

"Where will you live, do you think?"

"It depends on Lise," Uli replied, watching the attendant's

retreating figure. "I've bought an apartment in Wedding, not far from where her father and brother live. But I suppose we'll move, if Lise's studies take us elsewhere."

Inge paused. "You'll not ask her to give up her studies?"

"Of course not." Uli shot her a smile that bordered on incredulity, as if the very question was preposterous to him. "She's a brilliant woman, and she's going to be a brilliant doctor. What sort of husband would I be if I asked her to give up the work she loved?"

Inge turned her attention back to the display case, feeling her cheeks warm as she stared down at the rings. She'd come to believe that marriage was a prison, something that would trap a woman in a life without choices.

She could see now that marriage to the right person could be an entirely different thing.

How wonderful that Lise had found a love like that.

Once the attendant had presented him with the ring, Uli escorted Inge out of the shop. "It's really happening," he said. "Thank you, Inge, for your help."

"It was my pleasure," she replied, and though she'd not been entirely convinced at the start of the appointment, she found she truly meant it. "How do you feel?"

He glanced down at the bag, gripping the handle with both hands. "Like my life is beginning again," he said fervently. "I love her, Inge. I'm going to spend the rest of my life making her happy."

Inge thought back to the day she'd given Sven back his priceless heirloom; to the day she'd packed her bags, listening to her parents' tirades as they drove her to the train station.

She'd chosen her own happiness over marriage, but she could see in Uli's eyes how such a union could bring a happiness all its own.

She stepped closer and kissed Uli on the cheek. "I know you will," she said, "and I love you for it. Thank you for being so good to my friend."

22 JANUARY, 1964

Uli,

I've asked Paul to do me one final kindness in sending this letter to you. I've waited years for a reply from you—whether for me or for your son—and the meaning in your silence is plain.

I know that you will never forgive me for what I've done. You must also know that I will never forgive myself, either. I've tried, but I know now that I never will.

Even in my marriage I've held on to some small spark of hope that you and I might one day find each other again. But I need to let you go.

I wish you happiness, my darling Uli, in all the days ahead.

Always,
Lise

15 APRIL, 1964

Dearest Lise,

I don't know how to write this letter (nor even if it will reach you) but you deserve to hear the news.

Uli and I are getting married.

This isn't the future that any of us had planned. Not you, not Uli, and certainly not me. But Uli and I have become close, over the past several years—closer than either of us ever thought possible. He's a good man, and we've built a good life together.

We share a daughter, Gretchen.

I don't pretend to speak for Uli when I say this, but I don't believe that his love for me has made his love for you any less. I'm not sure whether that helps to soften the blow, or whether the blow needs softening at all, not when what we went through together feels so far in the past now. But I have no doubt in my mind that, had things turned out differently, you and Uli would still be together. I hope that you have someone in your life who makes you as happy as he did. Someone whose love for you has made the past a cherished memory, rather than something to continue turning over in your mind.

I think of you often. Not about those days after the Wall, but back when we were at the Free University together, taking on the world. Back when we were sisters.

I hope that you can be happy for us, as I would have been happy for you.

We miss you, and hold you and your son in our thoughts.

All my love,
Inge

Part Four

45

MARCH 1972

Uli stepped out onto the Kurfürstendamm, glancing up at the ruined remains of Kaiser Wilhelm Memorial Church as he opened his umbrella against the drizzling rain. Despite his aversion to organized religion, the church, bookended by a modern, lipstick-tube bell tower and powder-box octagonal nave, was one of Uli's favorite landmarks in West Berlin: a perfect juxtaposition of past and present, old and new.

He wandered west along the broad boulevard, his shoulder aching from his old injury as he held the umbrella aloft. As he walked, he watched handfuls of tourists with less foresight dash for cover from the rain in the stores that lined the street, their windows displaying the latest fashions from New York and Paris; housewares and jewelry and everything else that might tempt passersby.

Even in the rain, Uli enjoyed the commute home from his office. There was something energizing about wandering through West Berlin, and he often found himself incorporating aspects of the city—its architecture and its people—into the bridges he designed. The perfect round sunglasses he'd seen on a busker two summers ago had given rise to the distinctive curves that adorned a cantilevered bridge he'd designed in Bonn, while the wide avenue of trees along the Ku'damm had inspired the look of an award-winning truss bridge in Munich, its struts arching like a canopy of leaves over the deck.

Once he reached Halensee, he turned off the main boulevard, letting the bustle of the Kurfürstendamm fade behind him, his thoughts on dinner. They were having roast lamb tonight and he ducked into his local wine shop to pick up a bottle of Sicilian red, knowing that Inge would appreciate the fact that it was a Nero d'Avola from the winery they'd visited last year to celebrate their seventh wedding anniversary. Unlike Uli, Inge was a natural with languages—a real asset given her frequent travel with Mèdecins sans Frontières—and she'd had enough Italian to converse easily with the vintner while Uli trailed behind them, enjoying the fruits of the vintner's labor.

Seven years married. *Eight, now*, he corrected himself. He measured his marriage in terms of his daughter, Gretchen, grown tall and gangly and so much more mature than Uli could ever remember being. He thought briefly of his eldest child, Rudi. He was almost ten years old, now. What sort of boy had he become?

Uli carried on to the elbow-crook turn of Halberstädter Strasse, the short residential street where he'd lived with Inge since their wedding. Their apartment was a lovely new build, with oak floors and wide windows.

Inge hadn't questioned Uli's reluctance to live at the apartment on Bernauer Strasse—she didn't need to. But Uli had never been able to bring himself to sell it: instead, he rented it out, hoping that one day Gretchen might decide to live there and make happy memories that would erase the terrible ones.

He reached into his pocket to pull out his keys, nodding a

polite hello to the man in the wheelchair who waited outside the steps.

"Uli Neumann?" He looked down, and the man's lined face broke into a smile. "Yes. I thought that was you."

"Herr—Herr Bauer?" Lise's father looked smaller and grayer than he'd done in the past, but it was unmistakably him. "What are you doing here?"

Rudolph nodded at the bottle in Uli's hand. "Perhaps it's a question better asked over a glass of wine, young man."

Uli settled Lise's father at an empty table outside a nearby restaurant before going inside to order drinks. He hadn't wanted to bring Rudolph into the house—not so much for Inge's sake but for Gretchen's, who might ask questions that Uli wasn't yet ready to answer.

He glanced over his shoulder as he waited: outside, the wide leaves of the chestnut trees cast dappled shadows onto Rudolph's face, making him look both more and less like a figment of Uli's imagination.

Rudolph Bauer, here. Following the signing of the Transport Pact this past May, travel and communication between East and West Berlin had become slightly less strained, particularly for pensioners—retired East Germans could now travel to West Berlin, but working-age East Germans were still barred from entry in all but the most exceptional circumstances. He knew full well why the GDR was willing to allow its elderly citizens to journey west: were they to lose a pensioner to Republikflucht, it would mean one less strain on the country's resources.

But that didn't answer the fundamental question. Why had Rudolph sought him out?

He returned to the table with a bottle of wine in a bucket of ice, and Rudolph straightened to read the label. "Chablis," he said approvingly. "And here I thought you were a beer man."

Uli hadn't touched beer since the night he found himself sprawled across the cobbles at Siggi's. "I lost the taste for it."

"You've grown out your hair," Rudolph commented as Uli poured him a glass. He motioned to Uli's face. "And the beard. I like it."

Uli lifted a self-conscious hand to the close-cropped bristles that covered his chin. "The older men in the office think I look like I belong in San Francisco," he offered, and Rudolph laughed.

"Like one of those hippies you see on the television. But I hope you've managed to make more of your life than some of the young tourists we get on our side of the city. Always blathering on about world peace without lifting a finger to achieve it." He raised his glass in a genteel toast before taking a sip, then closed his eyes as he let the wine linger on his palate.

"Bliss," he concluded. "It's been eleven years since I've stepped foot in West Berlin, but this glass of wine makes it all worth it. All we get on our side is Georgian wine, and while I've had a decent *saperavi* in my day, nothing compares to a good French vintage." He opened his eyes. "When I was granted a travel visa, I thought I would take myself on a little tour. Visit my old haunts, go down memory lane, so to speak." He smiled. "Imagine my surprise when I found myself searching for your name in the telephone book."

"I'm as surprised as you are." Uli set down his glass of wine. "Why did you want to talk to me, Herr Bauer?"

"Call me Rudolph, please." He spread his hands across the tabletop, the fingers on his right hand shaking with a familiar tremor. "After all, we were very nearly family, not so long ago."

"It was a lifetime ago."

"When you've lived through as much as I have, a decade becomes nothing more than a blink of an eye," Rudolph replied solemnly. "I'm here to talk about Lise. But I'm sure you came to that conclusion on your own."

Uli focused his attention on a nearby chestnut tree. "What about her?"

"That...that business with the tunnel." Rudolph hesitated. "She wrote letters to you, tried to explain, but I—" He broke off and studied Uli with a more critical eye. "Did you receive them? You never wrote back so she couldn't be sure."

Uli shifted, thinking of the envelopes he kept in his bedside table: unopened, but not discarded. It still hurt him, to think of Lise: the pain she'd caused, her betrayal and his frustrating, stubborn love for her, all tangled together in his mind. "One or two," he conceded. "But I don't see the point in dredging all this up again."

"Perhaps not."

Rudolph fell silent and took another sip of his wine, looking past Uli at the other diners: men and women enjoying baskets of bread, bottles of pilsner.

Uli bristled at Rudolph's casual demeanor. Why were they sitting here in silence?

Finally, he cleared his throat. "How's Rudi?"

Rudolph leaned back in his wheelchair. "He's a happy little chap." He reached into the pocket of his coat and pulled out his wallet to unearth a small photograph. "Talks like you wouldn't believe, and curious like a cat." He held out the photo, and Uli bit back an uncharitable thought as he took it.

He couldn't have just given me a school photograph. Lise and Rudi were sitting together on a checkered picnic blanket, Lise shielding her eyes from the sun, one arm wrapped around her knees, looking as blindingly beautiful as she had on the day Uli had met her. Beside her, Rudi was a reedy, beaming boy, with Uli's dark hair and Lise's freckle-dusted nose. He was squinting, but

Uli wasn't sure if it was because of the sun: had he inherited Uli's poor eyesight?

He cleared his throat, indicating the sliver of gold around Lise's finger. "How…how long has she been married?"

"Lise and Horst got together six—seven?—months after Rudi was born. They married in '63." Rudolph sighed, and indicated with a wave of his hand that Uli could keep the photograph. "He's been good for Rudi. Gives him some structure."

He looked down at the photograph again, studying Lise's face. "Is she happy?"

The question, it seemed, was a difficult one to answer. After a lengthy pause, Rudolph spoke. "She's a good wife and mother."

He pushed his empty glass across the table and Uli, realizing he'd lapsed in his duties as bartender, refilled it. There was a small, bitter part of Uli that felt vindictive pleasure at the thought that Lise was less than content with her lot in life; that she deserved such a fate, after everything she'd done.

He pushed away the bitterness almost as quickly as it came. Despite everything that had happened between them, Lise was the mother of his child. Should he not want the best for her?

"And how about yourself? Are you happy?"

Uli considered the question, his unhesitating answer giving him even more reason to feel badly about his moment of petty weakness.

He *was* happy—he and Inge had built a good life together, and while theirs wasn't the passionate, desperate joy he'd felt for Lise, it was a love built on companionship and a shared commitment to their daughter.

"I'm happy," he replied, "and I hope that Lise is happy, too."

Rudolph cleared his throat and nodded at the photograph. "You'll notice I've written my address on the back of the picture," he offered. "If you felt you might like to—to keep in touch. With me, or with her."

Uli tucked the photograph in his pocket. Inge made him

happy. What good was dwelling on what might have been, when he was content with what he had?

"I don't think that's a good idea," he replied. "But I hope you'll send her my regards."

Rudolph's smile carried disappointment at its edges; nevertheless, he raised his glass once more. "I understand," he replied, and tapped his glass to Uli's.

46

The kitchen smelled of boiled potatoes and broiled chicken, and as Lise dumped a spent cutting board in the overflowing sink she paused, smelling something acrid, burning, beneath the fragrant meat.

Cursing, she hastily dried her hands on a dish towel and rescued a pan of onions she'd left on the stovetop—they were meant to be caramelized, but at this point they'd passed irretrievably into the territory of burnt. Lise had never been the world's best cook: she'd never learned the skill, not properly. All throughout her childhood she'd been told that living in a socialist society meant she could expect an equal distribution of labor both at work and at home, and as much as Horst ascribed to such mantras in theory, he'd made it clear, over nine long years of marriage, that he felt women were best suited to the business of housekeeping.

She glanced through the kitchen's pass-through window to the dining table—set for four, neat and tidy. Still, she couldn't shake the suspicion that she'd forgotten something, some small element that would become an obvious lack once they'd all sat down to eat…

Flowers. Yes. The dahlias she'd grown in large pots on the balcony would be perfect. She got up on a chair to open the cupboard above the refrigerator, rummaging past plastic egg cups and mixing bowls, bypassing the cake bell she used once a year for Rudi's birthday cake to find the ceramic vase she used for special occasions.

From the other side of the kitchen wall, she heard the front door open, followed by the twin thump of shoes.

"In the closet, please!" She got down from the stool, vase in hand as she listened to the slide of the closet door.

Rudi entered the kitchen first and he ran to pull her into a spindly-armed hug. She kissed him atop his untidy mess of hair and sent up a wish that he would never outgrow his childish habit of wanting a hug from his mother every time he came home.

"How was your troupe meeting?"

Rudi beamed. "We learned how to forage for mushrooms in the woods!"

Horst leaned against the doorframe and pulled a pipe and a packet of tobacco from his pocket. "But that wasn't all you did, was it, Rudi? Go on, tell your mother what happened."

Lise suppressed a sigh. When Horst had enrolled Rudi in his troupe of Thälmann Pioneers, he'd presented it as an opportunity to bond with his stepson. But Horst and Rudi were chalk and cheese, and every day, it seemed, the pair of them wrote a new chapter in the book on how not to get along.

A flush rose in Rudi's cheeks, and he began pawing at his blue neckerchief. "We—we went hiking in the woods, and Peter Fischer and me, we—we had a bet? To see who could get closest to the Wall? But it was only a joke, you can ask Peter—"

"An extremely dangerous joke." Horst finished packing his pipe and exchanged a meaningful look with Lise. "It took nearly an hour to find the two of them, and the entire troupe lost their ice cream privileges because of it, didn't they?"

Rudi's little face crumpled. "We just wanted to *see*!"

Lise crouched down and rested her hands on Rudi's narrow shoulders. "Your stepfather is quite right." She could feel Horst's eyes on her, burning a hole into her back. "The barrier is there for our protection, and the guards defend us for our own good. It's dangerous to get in their way. Do you understand?"

Rudi let out a watery sniff. "The guards protect us from Western imperialist aggression," he said dully, and Lise swallowed a sudden lick of fury. The Thälmann Pioneers was a youth group made popular by their outdoor excursions, but the price of those excursions was the sort of indoctrination that had boys like Rudi spouting propaganda. Couldn't they just let kids be kids?

Horst sent a thick plume of smoke into the kitchen. "Quite right. Now what do we do when we've misbehaved?"

Rudi sighed and drew himself up to his full height. *"We Thälmann Pioneers love our socialist fatherland, the German Democratic Republic,"* he recited. *"In word and deed, we will always defend our workers' and farmers' state, which is a firm part of the socialist community of nations..."*

Horst ruffled Rudi's hair when he'd finished. "Very good, son. Now go clean up for dinner, your grandfather is going to be here very soon."

Together, Lise and Horst watched as Rudi disappeared into his bedroom, and Lise let out a breath as he slammed the door.

"He didn't get close to the Wall, did he?"

"We were miles from it." Horst bent to rummage in the refrigerator for a bottle of beer and straightened before doubling back to pull a second one out for Lise. "He needed to learn a lesson, that's all. He can't just leave the group like that." He handed Lise the bottle, the glass cold on her fingers. "This is what you get from indulging him, you know. He's too headstrong for his own good."

It's a trait he gets from his father, Lise thought, but she knew better than to say it aloud.

Horst sighed at her silence, then pressed his dry lips to her cheek. "I'll go clean up as well," he said. "Dinner smells nice."

Lise stared at her dahlias throughout dinner, allowing Papa and Horst to dictate the flow of conversation—mainly about the wild extravaganza that was the new variety program on television, *Ein Kessel Buntes.*

She looked down at the slim band of gold that encircled her finger, thinking back to the day she'd agreed to marry Horst. She'd done so at Paul's behest, thinking it the best course of action: a sturdy marriage to a sturdy socialist, in order to put any questions about her allegiances to rest. And Horst was nothing if not sturdy. She supposed him to be a decent enough husband, though the cracks in their relationship had begun to form even before the wedding: they were too incompatibly different, too set in their own soil, to ever properly grow together.

It wasn't that Horst wasn't nice, or even that he was inconsiderate. It was simply that he lacked passion in all respects: passion for life, for happiness, for her. Though Lise had tried to find some common interest to draw them together—painting, cooking, dancing—each activity fizzled out shortly after it began. These days, Horst's dry pecks to Lise's cheeks were the extent of the affection they showed each other, and they were enough to set her teeth on edge.

She recognized that she bore no small part of the blame for the problems in their marriage, but she knew that if she were ever to go to Horst with her concerns, he would genuinely believe that things were fine between them.

Their differences had only become more apparent as Rudi grew older: Rudi, who was restless and curious, as different from Horst as it was possible to be. Lise did her best to occupy the middle ground between them, but it was a difficult thing to do when she found her husband so unrelentingly dull.

She looked across the table at Rudi, who'd recovered from his earlier dressing down and had gotten to his feet to regale Papa with an impression of one of the variety show's hosts. He shared his father's irrepressible optimism, as well as his handsome features: in the tilt of his head, the set of his jaw and his bright eyes, all Lise could see was Uli. It was a beautiful cruelty, to have such a constant reminder of him—a source of pain for her and Horst both, she knew, in their own ways.

Try as she might to make the best of her present, Lise found it so very hard to do when her past was sitting across the table.

"How about you, Grandpapa?" Rudi was saying as he collapsed back in his chair, breathless after his vigorous performance. "Did you do anything interesting this weekend?"

"As a matter of fact, I went to West Berlin," Papa replied, and Lise looked up.

"You *did*?" Rudi wriggled like a puppy in his chair. "What's it like? Do they all have guns? Is everyone a criminal? Is everyone a *capitalist*?" He said the word like one might say "cockroach," spitting it out with disgusted glee.

Horst offered a hesitant smile. "I'm not sure this is an entirely appropriate topic of conversation."

Lise stared at Papa, thunderstruck.

Was Uli still living there? With Inge? The news of their marriage had come as a bitter betrayal, but no more a betrayal than the one she'd visited upon him so long ago.

She'd written to him a handful of times, but never received anything in return. Did he ever think of her and Rudi? Was he still furious at her, all these years later?

"I hardly think it's inappropriate. They're our neighbors, after all." Papa turned to Rudi, his brown eyes twinkling. "To answer your question, dear boy, it's not all that different from here. I met lots of lovely capitalists, and none of them had forked tongues or lizard eyes. They were all perfectly, perfectly normal."

She cleared her throat, hoping that she sounded more nonchalant than she felt. "Did you—did you see anyone we knew?"

Papa lifted his glass of beer. "I'm afraid not, my girl."

47

"Lise's father?" Inge glanced at Uli through the reflection of her dressing table's mirror, but before he could make sense of her expression, she carried on with her nighttime routine of imported creams and salves, which, she believed, contributed to her still-luminous complexion. Much as Uli rolled his eyes at the cost, he had to admit that perhaps the routine worked: at thirty-two, Inge's skin was as unlined as the day he'd met her. "What did he want?"

Uli flopped back onto the mattress. "I'm not sure, exactly. To talk about Lise." He studied the waterfall of white-blond hair down Inge's back, recalling what she'd looked like back in the days when she and Lise had been joined at the hip: Lise the radiant sun, and Inge the luminous moon. Back then, they'd consulted the same fashion magazines for the same inspiration, wearing matching bouffants and bright fabrics in complementary colors.

He thought once more of the photograph that Rudolph had given him of Lise, dressed in a patterned blouse and trousers, looking prim and pretty but conservative in her sense of style. In recent years, Inge, by contrast, had taken to dressing in long, flowing dresses, eschewing heavy makeup and stiff undergarments for a carefree, bohemian look that put Uli in mind of Brigitte Bardot.

Inge and Lise had once shared everything, including a fashion sense. How else were they different, after ten years apart?

Inge turned in her seat, wrapping her fingers around the upholstered chair back. "I'm sorry. That must have been difficult for you."

"It was." He stared at a crack in the ceiling paint, a thin trail snaking out from the chandelier his parents had given them as a wedding present. "I don't think she's happy. I think that's what he wanted to talk to me about. He asked if I would consider writing to her."

He could hear Inge's measured silence. "In what sort of capacity?"

"I don't know."

Still staring at the ceiling, he felt the mattress dip as Inge sat beside him, and he reached over to run a hand along her thigh. How far they'd come since that night outside Siggi's bar.

After their drunken night together had resulted in a pregnancy, he'd resolved to do the right thing and offered her a modest silver ring with a question he'd been reluctant to ask, and she'd been reluctant to answer.

They'd grown closer in the months after his proposal, the prospect of a baby—their baby—providing a comforting balm over the painful memories of the months that had come before.

He'd held her in his arms on the night she miscarried, and the thought of that terrible moment still made him squeeze his eyes shut: how he'd held Inge in his arms as she sobbed; how she'd twisted the ring from her finger to release him from his obligation.

That had been the night he'd proposed to her in earnest. He'd taken the ring and offered it again, told her that they could build a life together based on more than obligation—one based on friendship and respect.

On love.

Inge looked down at Uli, her blue gaze steady. In eight years of marriage, Uli had never been unfaithful: he'd never strayed, nor had the inclination to, either in thought or in deed. But *Lise…* It wasn't fair, bringing this sort of angst to his wife. But how could he not, when Lise had been a constant, unspoken presence in their lives?

"In what sort of capacity would you be comfortable writing to her?"

"As a father." He sat up, sweeping back the bedsheets to climb in properly. Although West Berliners had been granted the limited ability to travel to East Berlin in 1971, Uli's brush with the Stasi made him ineligible for a temporary visa. But even if he could go to East Berlin to see Rudi and Lise, he wasn't entirely sure he had the strength to do it. "Gretchen is the most wonderful thing that's ever happened to me. I know that the East German authorities would never let me cross the border to meet Rudi, but if I could know that he's doing all right…"

He trailed off. Was it a betrayal of his life with Inge to admit that there was something missing—the loss of a child he didn't share with her?

Inge removed her robe and set it atop the dressing table chair. "It never sat right with me that you've not spoken to her." She crossed the room again and Uli propped himself against the headboard, lifting his good arm to allow Inge to curl into the hollow of his chest. "Even if you can't forgive her, you owe it to your son to write."

He switched out the light as Inge settled against his chest, gently pressing his lips to the crown of her head. This was the thing he appreciated most about their relationship: they shared an honesty, one born in dark and disappointment, forged into something beautiful.

"You'd be comfortable, would you, if I spoke to her?"

"I think you should." Inge tilted her neck, her eyes glinting in the dark. "Rudi is one reason, yes. But you've always blamed her for what happened in the tunnel. You've blamed her, and you've blamed yourself." She paused. "It's been ten years. Sigrid and Jurgen are free. Don't you think you've carried that blame long enough?"

It was true. Wolf's efforts on behalf of Sigrid and Jurgen had paid off: they'd been released thanks to a program that allowed Western nations to pay for the return of political prisoners. Sigrid had served eight months, but Jurgen had languished in an East German prison until just last year, while lawyers on both sides of the border argued over his culpability in the death of Uwe Spranger.

Jurgen and Wolf were now reunited and ran a small garage together somewhere in Kreuzberg. Uli had written to them on Jurgen's release, and although Jurgen had made it clear he didn't hold a grudge against Uli for the time he'd spent in prison, it was obvious that Wolf still did.

Inge threaded her fingers through his and lifted his hand to kiss the back of his palm. "You need to forgive yourself, Uli. This is how."

He shifted Inge gently out of his grasp and twisted to open the bottom drawer of his bedside table. He pulled out three letters he'd kept hidden, still sealed in their envelopes, the latest postage stamp bearing the year 1964.

He turned on the bedside light once more and handed them to Inge.

"Well," he said, "I suppose we can start here."

48

APRIL 1972

The shop was quiet, Lise and Gerda each lost in their work as they cut and pinned, stitched and sewed. After more than ten years of working together, their days had taken on an easy, companionable rhythm, their movements around the studio set to the staccato hum of the sewing machine.

Lise watched as Gerda pinned a polyester fabric to a dressmaker's figure with steady hands. She knew without asking what Gerda's next move would be: she stepped away from the form, pins wedged between her lips as she scrutinized the fall of the fabric.

"It looks nice," Lise offered, and Gerda cracked a tight smile before responding through the corner of her mouth.

"Wrong. You see how it's not quite symmetrical on the shoulders?" She returned to the form and began tearing out the pins, letting the polyester slide between her fingers. "This fabric doesn't hold its shape like it should..."

Lise returned to cutting her own fabric for a summer dress she'd been commissioned to make. Even after so long, Gerda still saw Lise as her protégée, talking through the changes she made as if Lise were still a novice.

"Always the perfectionist," she said.

"Why not? I was trained by the very best." Gerda looked at Lise, serious and mocking at the same time. "And so are you. Perfection is our gift to the world."

"And what a gift it is." To Lise, Gerda's friendship was the real gift, one she'd come to appreciate more and more with each passing year. After Rudi's birth she'd appointed herself something of a grandmother to Rudi and a surrogate mother to Lise: in the dark days following the failed escape, Gerda had turned up at Lise's door with *jägerschnitzel* and *kartoffelsalat* in hand, chalking up Lise's constant tears as "baby blues" while she rummaged through Lise's kitchen and bathroom for fresh nappies and formula.

She'd been there, too, during the early days of Lise's relationship with Horst, offering advice and wisdom to help Lise in her first days as a wife, back when Lise still pretended to care about her relationship.

"Do you want me to try my hand at it?" Lise set down her shears and approached the form.

Gerda shook her head. "If you could just hold that piece down..." she said, and Lise dutifully pressed down on a pleat as Gerda set her pins.

"Rudi's birthday is coming up," Gerda said conversationally. "What are your plans to celebrate?"

"Is that your way of asking for an invitation to his party?" Lise asked, and Gerda winked. "Ten years old...how time flies. It feels like only yesterday I brought him home from the hospital."

"Children have a tendency to make the years move faster."

"Just a bit." She shifted her finger along the fabric so Gerda could continue pinning. "He asked for a camera for his birthday. A Prakti, like his uncle's. Last year it was toy trains, this year he fancies himself a photographer." She smiled, thinking of how

Rudi had played with Paul's camera on their last family picnic, snapping photo after photo until he'd reached the end of the roll and then simply watched the world through the viewfinder. "Horst thinks we ought to get him something more practical. He worries that Rudi's getting spoiled."

"And why shouldn't he be spoiled?" Gerda replied staunchly as she slid the final pin in place. "Get him the camera. I can find some film for him, a friend of mine works at *Sybille* and owes me a favor. Will you need help with the dinner?"

"It shouldn't be a problem. It's just going to be family. And you, of course." She stepped away from the form, brushing stray threads from her hands as she returned to her table. Little though she relished the thought, Paul and Anna would be coming to Rudi's birthday dinner—Paul would be in her home, scrutinizing her marriage, her possessions, her son. She did her best to keep him at arm's length, enduring family dinners and outings for Papa's and Horst's sakes, but she hadn't—couldn't—forgive him for his part in what he'd made her to do Uli, all those years ago.

He'd tried, of course, to weasel his way back into Lise's good graces, but the bond between brother and sister had snapped, irrevocably. To Lise, Paul had become nothing more than polite company: Horst's drinking buddy, a necessary endurance at birthdays, weddings and funerals.

The realization saddened her. Had they really once been thick as thieves?

The bell above the shop door tinkled as it opened, pulling Lise out of her reveries to see Papa coming in with a checkered suit jacket over his knees.

"Rudolph!" Gerda hastily patted down a few wisps of her coiffured hair.

Lise circled the table and bent to kiss his cheek. "What a welcome surprise," she said. "To what do we owe the pleasure?"

"I've a commission for you." He set the jacket on the counter. "It recently came to my attention that the cut of my jacket is irredeemably out of date. I wonder whether the two of you might take a look at it."

"You know I could have done that for you at home," Lise pointed out. "You didn't have to come all the way here."

"Maybe I just wanted an excuse to visit my favorite girls."

Papa's gaze slid to Gerda and his smile broadened as Gerda flushed a deep crimson. Though Papa and Gerda had enjoyed a close friendship over the years, they'd never gone so far as confirming that they were anything more—at least, not to Lise. But they'd been blushing in each others' company for over a decade. Glaciers moved at a quicker pace.

"You know, I think we have some cookies in the back," she offered. "Perhaps you might want to stay for a cup of tea, Papa."

"Tea. Yes, of course." Gerda's cheeks were still furiously bright. "You get started on the jacket and I—I'll put on the kettle."

She retreated to the back room, and Lise addressed Papa in a low voice. "Your *two* favorite girls, hmm?"

"And what if she's one of them?" Papa gazed down to the door at the back of the shop where Gerda had disappeared. "I've concluded that I've spent far too long sitting on my feelings. I ought to declare myself before some other gentleman comes along with a better offer."

Gerda's earlier question about Rudi's party took on new significance, and Lise leaned down to kiss Papa on the cheek. "I'm relieved to hear it. Now—" Lise raised her voice and picked up the jacket "—what do you suppose we should do with this?"

"Well now, that's why I've come to the experts," Papa replied. "I've noticed that the young men are sporting different lapels."

A letter slipped out of the jacket's pocket, and Lise bent to pick it up as Papa continued talking.

"—I thought perhaps you could alter the width so that it looks a little more contemporary..."

His voice slid into the background as Lise studied the return address. The letter had been sent from a West Berlin address, the crooked writing unmistakably familiar.

"And of course, it would stand to reason that I would need to have the trousers altered as well to go with the jacket... Lise?"

She looked up to catch Papa's sharp gaze and he mimed putting the letter in a pocket. "Altered trousers, don't you think?"

Lise could hear Gerda returning from the back room and hastily jammed the letter in her apron smock.

"You were right, Lise, I found a packet of Wikanas in the cupboard," Gerda said brightly. She'd recovered her composure just, it seemed, as Lise lost hers. "But if you take yours with milk, Rudolph, I'm afraid you're out of luck. We've run short."

Lise looked up, her heart pounding. "I'll go to the shop," she offered. "You two stay here and chat. I won't be a minute."

She stepped out the door and crossed the street, barely noticing the cars as they passed. Why had Uli written to Papa? How had he gotten Papa's address?

She sank onto a park bench and ripped open the envelope with trembling hands as she began to read.

5 APRIL, 1972

Dear Lise,

Your father visited me recently and while I hadn't intended on reaching out to you, I find that I have some things I need to say—things I ought to have told you years ago, but which my heart and pride wouldn't let me.

What happened on that terrible day was as much my failure as it was yours. For a long time, I held you solely responsible for what happened, until Inge and I had our daughter, Gretchen. You had to make a terrible decision. I see that now. And when I look at my daughter, I know without hesitation that I would have made the same one if I'd been in your place.

If you've carried around the weight of this all these years, I apologize. I've been carrying it too, in my own way.

I've missed out on our son's life, and that is something I bitterly regret. With your permission, I would like to write to him.

With warmest regards,
Uli

Part Five

49

SEPTEMBER 1979

The cemetery was quiet and lushly forested, sunlight casting dappled shadows onto crumbling, ivy-clad headstones that made Lise feel as if she'd fallen back in time. Thanks to its historical reputation as a graveyard for suicides, only a handful of modern memorials dotted the grounds, but Lise understood why Inge had chosen Friedhof Grunewald-Forst as her final resting place: with its mighty evergreens and blanket of browning leaves, it would have reminded Inge of the magnificent Swedish forests of her childhood.

She lifted her face to the sun, listening to the respectful murmurs of the other mourners: Inge's colleagues in Médecins Sans Frontières; friends and relations that Lise had never had the opportunity to meet. She tilted her head back down and caught sight of a familiar face amidst the strangers: Jurgen, his ruddy face now hollowed but recognizable nonetheless. Recognition dawned in his eyes, and she looked away, her cheeks burning, as he whispered something to Wolf.

She wouldn't inflict herself on them; not when they'd suffered so much on her behalf. But despite the difficulty in acquiring a temporary visa—and despite her own sense of profound discomfort—she'd felt it necessary to come today and pay her respects to the woman she'd once regarded as a sister.

Uli stood at a shining new headstone with his arm around a dark-haired young woman: his daughter, Gretchen. She'd inherited her father's height and coloring, and Lise couldn't help comparing her to Rudi: she was a year younger, but nearly as tall as him, with Inge's striking features and Uli's deep-set eyes.

Gretchen stared down at the casket, and Lise's heart went out to her. She'd had time to prepare for this moment, but Lise could see only too well the pain behind her composure. She knew what it was to grow up without a mother—and even at sixteen, a girl needed her mother. How would Uli cope with Gretchen's grief as well as his own?

"Lise." Jurgen and Wolf had made their way across the cemetery, and for a craven split second, she thought of pretending she was somebody else: an old relation, an unlikely doppelgänger. But she gripped her handbag and met Jurgen's smile with a nod.

"You look well," she said as Jurgen leaned in to kiss her on the cheek. He was shorter than she remembered, and stockier; behind him, Wolf hung back, still tall and handsome, with a trim moustache.

"So do you. I wondered whether you'd heard." Jurgen glanced at Uli with a sigh. "Cancer is a cruelty. She was far too young."

"She was. Uli started writing to me a few years back—we corresponded mostly for Rudi's sake. But when he told me about her diagnosis..." She broke off. "Just terrible."

"Terrible." Jurgen jerked his head in the direction of a massive horseshoe of flowers set near the headstone. "It's a shame Axel isn't here. He'd have liked to see you. He's teaching at Cambridge, now...couldn't get away."

"Is he?" Lise looked down, dizzy at the mention of her old

friend. "Please—please give him my regards when you next speak to him."

"I see you finally made it across the Wall, then," Wolf offered stiffly, and Jurgen twisted round to glare at him.

Lise blanched. "I— It's a temporary visa," she stammered. "Just a few hours so I could—I could pay my respects in person."

Wolf's eyes narrowed, and Lise thought of elaborating—of telling him how the application had taken weeks; how the border guard who'd issued the pass had told her, with an ominous look, that he expected her to return for her son's sake—but then with a final glance at Jurgen, he turned and wandered off into the crowd.

Jurgen watched him go with a frown. "He doesn't mean it like that," he said, though Lise, her cheeks growing hot, doubted it. "He's just a little on edge."

She'd imagined a thousand times what she'd say to Jurgen if she ever saw him again, but somehow every apology, every explanation and excuse, turned to dust in her mouth.

"I—I want you to know I never—never intended—"

"I know," Jurgen said. He spoke without heat or bitterness, but Lise teared up all the same.

"They—they had my son and I—I couldn't—"

"I *know.*" Jurgen collected Lise's hands in his and squeezed, his brown eyes soft. It was clear that there was no need for her to elaborate further: not when he'd endured his own cruelties at the hands of the Stasi. "I've said this to Uli and I'll say this to you. What I did that day, I did for myself. For my family. Wolf will never truly understand the position you were in, but I do. Really." He paused, and Lise thought back to the show trial she couldn't bear to watch, but had read about in the papers: Jurgen, sentenced to life in prison; Paul, one of the many who'd testified against him. "I know that you didn't have a choice, but I did. It was my choice to go in that tunnel. It was my choice to stay."

"But at the expense of your own freedom..."

"My family's freedom was worth mine." Jurgen smiled. "My niece Willa was almost three when we brought her through to West Berlin. She's at university now, finishing a degree in international relations. She plans to work for the United Nations and help refugees all around the world. That wouldn't have happened if she'd stayed in East Germany." He squeezed her hand once more. "It's all in the past, Lise."

From his place at Inge's headstone Uli cleared his throat, and Jurgen gave Lise one final smile before going to stand with Wolf. She'd endured so many sleepless nights imagining Jurgen's fate at the hands of East German prison guards. Would she have come out as decent, as gracious, if their roles had been reversed?

There was so much of his story he hadn't told her—so much that wasn't hers to know.

But could forgiveness really be that simple?

Uli looked up to address the crowd. "She would have hated this," he began, and a few people let out weak chuckles. "All these people, making such a fuss... You know what she was like. *Tell them to raise a glass of something half-decent, and then get on with things.*"

He changed his tone to approximate Inge's voice, and even in jest it broke Lise's heart to hear an echo of her old friend. Something in the impression seemed to have broken a small part of Uli, too, and he bowed his head for a moment before lifting it again, composed once more.

"You know, we had plenty of time to prepare for this day, but somehow it still doesn't seem quite real." He rubbed his hand along his chin, and the gesture was one Lise had forgotten was his: the memory catapulted her back in time to the night they'd met, Lise and Inge and Uli and Wolf, together at a dance hall.

"My wife was...she was many things," he continued. "A doctor. A mother. A truly truly terrible singer. I had the privilege of seeing so many different facets of the remarkable woman that was Inge Neumann." For a single, wrenching second his gaze landed on Lise. "But perhaps her most winning trait was her friendship. She was a loyal friend. I know, perhaps, that loyalty isn't the most highly rated of the virtues. It's something that's taken for granted. Something squandered too quickly in a moment of doubt." He smiled. "The trouble with loyalty is that it can too easily be seen as weakness, but as everyone here can attest to, my wife was anything but weak. You see, to her, loyalty was a matter of argument and debate. Of getting those she loved to look at every side of a position they might be defending and ask: *am I truly in the right here*?"

Uli paused as if caught in the grip an old memory.

"Of course, to some, loyalty means something else entirely. It means blind faith. Automatic acceptance," he continued. "Question Everything—that was Inge's motto. To her, that was true loyalty. Because loyalty isn't about standing by your friends when you know they're wrong. It's about standing shoulder to shoulder to help them make things right."

Lise thought of the letters they'd shared over the years since they'd started writing to each other again: polite correspondences that kept each other at arm's length, mainly focused on Rudi and Gretchen. Inge had been as much a part of those letters as Uli himself, and at first it irked her to know how much Inge shared with Uli—to know that she'd had so much more of Uli than Lise ever did. In her least charitable moments, Lise had even resented Inge her happiness, as if Inge had stepped wholesale into the life she'd planned with Uli. But then in her better moments Lise could see that Inge's relationship with Uli was something else entirely.

Perhaps theirs had been the love story all along.

How could she resent Inge for that?

Lise hung back after the funeral was over, letting the other mourners pay their respects and filter out of the cemetery in groups of twos and threes. She watched from the shade of an alder tree as Uli exchanged words with Jurgen and Wolf: as he'd done earlier, Wolf held back while Jurgen spoke, and Lise wondered about how their friendship had fared over the years. Was today a reunion for the three of them as well?

Finally, once Gretchen wandered off in the linked arms of what looked to be her schoolmates, Lise stepped forward to join Uli at the headstone.

"I was hoping we'd have a moment to chat," he said. "I worried that you'd have to rush off. Thank you for coming."

Lise laid a rose on the freshly turned earth, then rested her hand briefly on the sun-warmed stone. INGE NEUMANN. "I hope you don't mind my being here."

"Of course not." Uli smiled. "She would have been glad you're here. *I'm* glad you're here."

From beyond the cemetery's stone fence, she heard a ring of laughter: Gretchen and her friends, the noise so joyful, so natural.

"I remember when Inge and I were like that," she offered. "Joined at the hip. I'm glad Gretchen has her friends to lean on."

Uli sighed. "She's been so stoic, but it's been hard on her. We're coping as best we can."

For the second time that day, Lise felt as if she was crushed beneath the weight of unsaid words. There was so much she wanted to say to Uli; so much that felt wrong to raise at a moment like this.

He spoke again. "How's Rudi?"

She dug in her handbag and pulled out a photograph: Rudi, seventeen years old, sitting between Papa and Gerda at the dinner table.

"My. Quite the hairstyle," Uli said as he took the photograph, his eyebrows raised high into his own messy bangs, and Lise laughed.

"The Mohican? It's his latest fashion statement." Her shoulder brushed against Uli's arm as they studied the photo together. "I'm afraid our son has become something of a rebel. He questions *everything*." She smiled, thinking of how Horst viewed that particular trait as a failure, but in Inge, Uli had seen it as a virtue. "I think half the reason he does it is to annoy his stepfather."

"It's youthful exuberance." Uli studied the photograph closely, curling the edge of the paper over the ridge of his thumb. "What child doesn't rebel?"

Lise thought of the shouting matches and school meetings; the visits from Volkspolizei with Rudi in tow. "I know he doesn't mean anything by it, not really. But rebellion…it's different, where we live. It's dangerous." She paused, weighing whether to admit the extent of Rudi's difficulties. "He's been sent to a-a reformatory. For his antisocial attitude."

Uli looked up, alarmed. "No."

"He's out in two months' time. Not that it will do him any good."

"He won't…they won't…?"

"I don't think he'll be harmed, if that's what you're asking. It's indoctrination, more than anything. Reeducating him about the merits of socialism, that sort of thing. But Rudi is… he's ungovernable." She smiled, trying to make lighter of the situation for Uli's sake. "I mean that with the highest of compliments to him."

Uli still looked troubled, and Lise regretted saying anything at all.

"I don't want you to get the wrong impression. He's a good boy. Smart. Stubborn. He's wonderfully artistic—quite the photographer, as a matter of fact. He just…he questions what he shouldn't."

"If he's asking questions, then you've put him on the right path." Uli held up the photograph. "May I?"

"Of course. I brought it for you."

He tucked the photograph in his pocket, his wedding ring glinting in the light as he patted it safe against his heart. "And—and you? You're happy?"

She thought of Horst and Rudi; Papa and Gerda. Her work, which she'd grown to enjoy; her marriage, which she hadn't.

Her letters to Uli had never mentioned anything beyond postcard platitudes, because she knew the envelopes were steamed open and scrutinized for any hint of criticism of the state. She held her tongue and controlled her actions, for fear they might come to the attention of those who might consider her ripe for "reeducation" herself; always conscious of the invisible, pervasive surveillance from those watching, waiting to find enemies in the shadows.

Finally, she spoke. "I'm as happy as I've a right to be."

Uli seemed pained by her answer. "Everyone has a right to be happy."

She could feel the dam of her reserve threatening to burst, everything she wanted to say to him—everything she needed to say—ready, there on the tip of her tongue. She'd lived so long in anticipation of seeing Uli once again, but the moment felt so wrong. How could she speak openly when she had no choice but to return to East Berlin, to Horst and Rudi, in an hour's time? How could she tell him she'd never stopped loving him, here, standing over his wife's grave?

A flicker of something came over Uli's face as he watched her wrestle with what to say.

"I—I want to explain, Uli, I want you to know… They were going to take Rudi from me. I couldn't abandon him, I couldn't—"

"I know."

"Do you?"

He stepped closer and looked up past Lise, toward the echoing laughter of Gretchen's friends. "You were put in an impossible situation. And you've been a good mother to our son. Of that I have no doubt."

Lise, too, stepped closer. For so long Uli had lived in her mind as a young man, but this Uli had lived an entire life without her:

he was someone completely different, completely new, and she searched for signs of the person he'd been in his gray eyes, his deep dimples. A trim beard now hid those dimples from sight, but she knew they were there, beneath the salt and pepper; she knew his heart was just the same, beating in an older chest.

She would never ask the universe for a thing again as long as she lived, if only she could commit this newer, older face of his to memory.

He brushed his hand against hers and her stomach lurched at the electricity that still sparked between them after all these years. "Lise, I want you to know—if our lives had turned out differently..."

She pulled away: this was a path too painful to tread. "I—I need to go," she said, her heart breaking anew at the hurt in his eyes. "My visa is going to expire, and Rudi—Horst... And Gretchen, no doubt she's in need of you."

Her whole body ached for want of him; from the pain of holding back. But Uli nodded, his jaw working hard, and he studied Lise's face as closely as she'd studied his. "Of—of course," he said, the crack in his voice so low that Lise might have imagined it. "Thank you for coming. For—for taking the time. Let's not...let's not wait so long again."

"Eighteen years," Lise said, trying to sound as though she'd not marked each one down in the calendar of her mind. "Let's hope our paths might cross sooner than that."

"Next time, let's split the difference," said Uli, and his joke was as half-hearted, as futile, as hers. "We'll plan to meet in eight years."

"Then four. Then two..."

"Half lives," he whispered hoarsely. "That's what they call it. We'll meet again in the half lives of our separation."

"Half lives." Lise pressed her lips to his cheek, her tears mingling with his before she pulled away. "That's when we'll meet again."

50

Uli pushed sizzling pork chops across a cast iron-pan, the pop and hiss of frying meat drowning out the sound of Phil Collins's voice from the living room. He studied the caramelizing edge of fat along bone, knowing full well that he'd had other, easier options for dinner, but the act of making his own meal suited him: it gave him something to do other than think about the day's events. There would be other nights in the weeks to come for him to tackle the mountain of Tupperware containers in the refrigerator, brought over by friends and family who didn't know what else to do for grief but feed it.

He smiled, thinking of Inge. What would her prescription be for a diagnosis of grief?

It wouldn't be food; it wouldn't even be sympathy. *Do something,* he heard her say, and in his imagination, she was sitting at the kitchen table, healthy and happy, pushing her curtain bangs gracefully out of her face. *There's nothing to be gained by wallowing in it.*

He pulled himself out of his reverie as Gretchen stepped into the kitchen—lured, no doubt, by the smell of dinner. She'd changed out of her funeral dress into Levi's jeans and a T-shirt, looking thankfully like herself once again: she'd been so tense, so poised, during the long days since Inge had left them: a child grown up too soon, rather than the teenager she deserved the time to be.

He held out his good arm and Gretchen wrapped her arms around his middle, pushing her dark hair out of her eyes to reveal the cheekbones she shared with her mother.

"What do you think?" He held up one of the pork chops for her inspection, and Gretchen shot him a wry smile.

"I think it's the same meal you made for us two days ago," she said. "And last week...and the week before that."

"Yeah, well, I've never been much of a chef." He set the chop back down in the pan with a pang. This was what he'd cooked for Inge all throughout their marriage: his one dish, the one he made for her every Mother's Day.

He cleared his throat. "How about you find a cookbook you like, and we'll learn together?"

"I like that idea." Gretchen pulled away and stuffed her hands in her pockets. "Mind if we start tomorrow? Only, Christa and her mom invited me for a sleepover tonight, and I thought it might be nice..."

He flipped the pork chops, considering. On the one hand, the thought of facing an evening alone was unbearable—but then, perhaps that was why she needed to go.

Do something.

He covered his disappointment with a smile. "Of course, *liebchen*."

"You're sure?"

He waved the fork, sending the rich scent of pork wafting through the kitchen. "Absolutely. You were wonderful today, and you deserve to have a break from it all. Besides—" he indicated the frying pan "—that means more food for me."

She left a short while later, kissing Uli on the cheek before skipping out the door with a rucksack in hand. He took the frying pan off the heat, and once he switched off the exhaust fan, he realized the cassette he'd been playing in the other room had reached its end.

The silence made him feel oddly bereft at Gretchen's absence. Shouldn't he have asked her to stay, given them a chance to grieve together? To share their memories, their pain?

Let her be, Inge's voice answered in his mind, and Uli knew that she was right. They'd grieved for a long time, him and Gretchen both—they'd grieved for two long years of Inge's illness, watching her slip away bit by bit.

He fixed himself a plate for dinner and poured a glass of pinot noir, then wandered into the living room to change the tape.

This was the room he'd done his best to avoid in the days following Inge's death: it was where the nurse had set up her bed, her monitors, her IV drip. Much as he'd hated the sight of the medical equipment, it had been so much worse to come home on the day it had all been removed.

He sat on the couch with his plate in his lap, feeling the familiar groove in the cushion from where he used to sit, elbow crooked on the armrest so he could hold Inge's hand in his.

She'd been so tired on the day she'd come home from the hospital, after she looked at her medical charts and concluded, with expert pragmatism, that there was nothing more that could be done for her. She wanted to be here, with Uli and Gretchen, and Uli had spent as much time with her as he could: for three months they read books and listened to music, watched television and slept, Uli curled up on the couch so that if she woke in the night, she wouldn't be alone.

They'd talked, too, in those last three months: about Inge's hopes and dreams for Gretchen; about old memories and unfinished business.

He took a sip of wine, recalling one of the last conversations he'd had with her.

He'd written to Lise at Inge's request, to tell her about Inge's turn for the worse. He closed his eyes, recalling how he'd propped Inge up in bed so she could read the letter before mailing it: how frail her hand had felt in his, the bones grown brittle without muscle and fat to soften them.

She'd rested the letter in her lap once she'd finished, turned her cheek to the pillow so she could look Uli in the eye.

"Is it still there?"

"I'm sorry?"

He could have counted the blue veins beneath Inge's eyelids as she blinked, slowly. "What you felt for her. Is it still there?"

He'd hesitated before answering. "What difference does it make?"

"It makes all the difference." Inge smiled, and Uli could see the effort it took for her to do so. "When I'm gone—" She held up a hand to stop his protestations. "When I'm gone, I want you to finish what we started all those years ago. I want you to bring Lise home."

"Inge, I..." Uli trailed off. "This isn't the time for this."

She quirked her eyebrow. "It's the only time for it," she replied, her voice strengthening as she spoke. "When we were married, you promised me that you'd be loyal in body and in spirit. And you have: we've taken that loyalty and built a wonderful marriage. But you and I both know that Lise has always been the love of your life."

Guilt ripped through Uli's chest as cleanly as a sword. "*You're* the love of my life," he said fiercely, willing himself not to break Inge's hand as he held it, seeking to tether her here, to life. To him.

"I know *that*." She rolled her eyes, giving Uli a glimpse of her old sense of humor. "But I've not been the only one. We've had a beautiful life together, you and I. I couldn't have asked for a better husband. And Lise will be a wonderful wife to you when I'm gone."

Uli pressed his eyes shut, feeling a hot rush of tears down his cheeks. "I don't *want* another wife," he replied. "I want you."

"My darling, I'm afraid the choice isn't either of ours to make." Inge's laugh quickly turned to a cough. "And I know you, Uli. You're a romantic. A two-legged stool. You need the support of someone else to stand upright. Why shouldn't it be her?"

Uli let his head drop. "I can't—I can't think about this," he muttered. "It's been so long, we've—we're entirely different people. She's still in East Germany, she—she's married, for God's sake."

"All the more reason to bring her across the border," Inge replied. "I've spent a lot of time thinking about this, Uli. I've read her letters. I know how much the two of you loved each other back when we were young. How hard you fought to be together." She laid her head back on the pillow and directed her gaze to the ceiling. "I think it's one of the reasons I fell in love with you. You were so romantic. So faithful. Who wouldn't have fallen in love with someone like that?"

There was a knot deep in Uli's throat as he listened to Inge. She'd never tried to replace Lise in his affections; she'd never said a word against Lise, in all the years of their marriage. Her loyalty to Lise was as heartbreaking as her fidelity to Uli.

How had he ever deserved the love of a woman like her?

"If there's even a chance that there's still some feeling between the two of you, you owe it to yourselves to find it. You owe it to yourselves to be happy." She paused and ran a limp finger down Uli's hand. "What's more, I know that she'll be a good stepmother to Gretchen. She'll treat our daughter with the same kindness that I would have treated her son, had our positions been reversed. And that, to me, matters more than anything."

Uli wiped a stream of tears from his cheeks as he sat in the darkened living room—so quiet, so still, without Inge there to bring it life. Yet still, her final request echoed in the silence.

"It's time I give you back to Lise," Inge had said, and in his mind's eye she looked as she had on the day he'd married her: young and beautiful, bathed in a golden glow. "If you still feel for her what you felt all those years ago, I want you to bring her home."

51

NOVEMBER 1979

Lise waited outside the entrance to the Plötzensee youth reformatory, the jangling bulk of her car keys a comforting weight in her hand as she looked up at the building's bricks and bars. Flanked by sprawling walls, Plötzensee had been the city's most notorious prison under the National Socialist regime, and although the East German government had acknowledged the institution's sorrowful past with a memorial garden where the prison's guillotine had once stood, the rest of the facility had been turned over to the Ministry of Education to be used as a reformatory—a *youth workhouse*, in Politburo parlance.

She looked up at the barbed wire that topped Plötzensee's brick walls, uncomfortably aware that the official distinction meant little. Bars were bars, no matter the age of the person they were holding.

Antisocial behaviour: that had been the reason Rudi had been sent to Plötzensee in the first place. His refusal to carry on with youth programs; his frequent shirking of classes. He listened to Western music—rockers like The Clash and Joy Division, whose cassettes had been smuggled across the Wall by punks like him who dressed in outrageous clothes and criticized the government, threw up their fingers at the soldiers guarding Brandenburg Gate.

Perhaps Lise ought to have paid closer mind to Rudi's antics, recognized that he'd fallen in with the wrong crowd. But she'd met his friends, and they were all like him: thoughtful and restless, railing against a society that refused to try and understand them. If the punk movement had been around when the Wall had first gone up, Lise had little doubt that she would have been among their number.

After what felt like forever, the doors to the reformatory swung open and a young man walked out, carrying a limp duffel bag. When she'd last seen Rudi—on the day he'd been sentenced to five months in Plötzensee—he'd still looked like himself, in contraband Levi's and studs, his hair gelled high in a spiked Mohican. But the boy who walked toward her now was dressed in gray trousers and a white jacket, his dark hair a shaven stubble. He drew closer and Lise could see that the nose piecing he'd given himself last year—one that had nearly given Horst a heart attack when he'd seen it—was gone.

Her heart broke for him. As much as she found her son's sartorial choices shocking, she loved how comfortable he was expressing himself: how, at seventeen, he knew himself enough to stand out from the crowd. As a child, he'd flipped through the pages of her magazines and watched Western television, studying the styles to determine who he wanted to be beyond the neckerchiefs of the Pioneers or the cookie-cutter offerings of Präsent 20 clothing stores. She liked to think that perhaps her work with Gerda had inspired him, in some small way, to cut up his clothing and pin it back together in clashing prints and riotous patterns, which shouted to anyone who saw him that he was someone different, a person with something to say.

But that, of course, was exactly what had led him here.

She held out her arms and he stepped into her hug, his shoulders tensing for a brief, horrible moment before he relaxed into her embrace.

He drew away and knuckled his eyes with a clenched fist.

"They burned my clothes," he mumbled, looking down self-consciously at his trousers. "My jeans…my favorite T-shirt. It took me ages to find that leather jacket, I don't know where I'll get something else like it."

"We'll get you another one." She pressed her fingers to his cheek, studying his face—so similar to his father's—for signs of distress. Despite what she'd said to Uli at Inge's funeral, she knew that Rudi's sentence had been serious, nor did she put it past the "educators" within Plötzensee's walls to resort to corporal punishment. "How are you? Are you okay? Did they feed you enough?"

"They fed me fine, Mum." He pulled away, pushing his glasses up the bridge of his nose before throwing his duffel in the trunk of the car. "Can we go?"

She shot one final look of loathing at Plötzensee before driving down the street.

"I brought you something," she tried. "Glove compartment."

He opened it and pulled out his old Prakti camera, and to Lise's satisfaction, the ghost of a smile crossed his lips. "Thanks," he said, stroking the shutter button with a gentle finger.

"Your grandparents are coming to dinner tonight," she continued as she navigated the Trabant over the Spree. "Paul and Anna, too. A little welcome home party."

What little glimpse she'd had of the old Rudi dimmed. "It's not like I was on holiday, Mum."

She stopped at a traffic light, unnerved. He'd always been one for talking a mile a minute, asking endless questions and wearing his heart on his sleeve. But he crossed his arms, shoulders hunched as he leaned against the window, and Lise wasn't sure what to say to ease him open.

"Rudi...what do you want to do with your life?"

He shrugged. "Does what I want really matter? It's not like I'm going to be able to go back to school. They don't let guys like me take photos for *Neue Zeit*." His expression was bleak as he stared out the window. "In that—that place—they told me to report to the Fleishkombinat Berlin—the meat processing facility. You're looking at their newest factory worker."

The news wasn't entirely unexpected: like all young people, Rudi didn't have a choice when it came to his employment. But a factory floor seemed such a waste for a young man like him: someone with creativity and potential; someone too smart to accept the limitations put upon him without question.

But with higher education now out of his reach, factory work was Rudi's only choice.

"But—but if you had the chance? If you had the opportunity to do anything you wanted?"

"Careful, Mum." Rudi's voice was flat, expressionless. "You don't want anyone to accuse you of being a hostile influence."

The traffic light turned green and Lise shifted gears to carry on. Out of the corner of her eye she could see Rudi lean his head against the window, arms crossed tightly across his chest as he closed his eyes, and she pressed her lips together, determined not to cry.

As she walked up the stairs to her apartment, Lise wished she could have canceled the party that Papa and Gerda had convinced her to throw—that she might open the door and find blissful silence. The shadows under Rudi's eyes were evidence enough that the last thing he needed was a crowd, but when they opened the door and walked in, he gamely rose to the occasion.

"What a welcome," he said as Gerda pulled him into a tight hug. To Lise's surprise, a banner hung in the living room, made of embroidered scraps of fabric that spelt out Rudi's name: one of Gerda creations, no doubt.

"We *missed* you," Papa said.

"Look at you, all skin and bones...what did they do to your lovely hair? Come with me, I've something to show you..." Gerda fussed as she led Rudi toward his bedroom, and Lise smiled at her stepmother's warmth. She and Papa had married two years ago in a small ceremony attended only by their children, and Gerda had joined Papa in retirement last year: Lise, now, ran Die Nadel und der Faden on her own, though she'd put in an application for an assistant. These days Papa and Gerda spent most of their time at the datsche, tending to Papa's carefully cultivated vegetables.

In the kitchen, Anna was setting out a plate of sausages on a platter while her son, Kurt—a thirteen-year-old carbon copy of Paul—leafed through a copy of the Young Pioneers handbook in the corner.

"How is he?"

"Well enough." Lise sighed. "Quiet. But that's to be expected, I suppose."

Anna tilted her head as she finished filling the plate. "I'm sure he learned a lot," she replied. "He's had his difficulties, but hard work will set him on the right path." She looked out the pass-through as Rudi and Gerda returned from the bedroom, Rudi wearing a denim vest and—crucially—a smile. "Goodness, without all that metal in his face you can see what a handsome young man he's become."

Lise's smiled tightened and she trailed Anna into the living room where Rudi was modeling the vest. Gerda had worked on it for weeks, fashioning it out of old pairs of Wisent jeans, and Lise loved her all the more for her efforts: wearing it, Rudi looked little bit more like himself.

"Of course, you'll have to find the patches on your own," Gerda was saying as she fussed with the fit. "But I'll be happy to sew them on for you, even the ones with profanity..."

Lise exchanged an amused glance with Papa. Marrying her had been the best decision he'd ever made.

At the far end of the room, Horst stood by the television, beer in hand as he conversed with Paul. He hadn't approved of the idea of a welcome home party for Rudi, but he'd not stood in Lise's and Gerda's way as they planned it.

He didn't have to like it—but Lise was profoundly disappointed that he'd not made even the scantest effort to acknowledge Rudi's return.

"Dear?" She rested a hand on his arm and looked up at Horst with a bright, bitter smile. "Aren't you going to say hello?"

Horst slid his flat gaze from Paul to Lise, looking mildly irritated at the interruption. "Of course." He lifted his pilsner and raised his voice. "The prodigal son. Rudolph, I hope your time at Plötzensee has taught you the respect and discipline you've always lacked. There's nothing shameful about learning the value of hard work."

Rudi was frozen in place between Gerda and Papa. "Thank you," he said stiffly as Horst drained the last of his beer.

He set down his empty glass. "A civil response," he said, addressing Paul rather than Rudi himself. "Perhaps I ought to have sent him to Plötzensee long ago."

Rudi's shoulders slumped beneath his denim vest, and Lise snapped.

"Horst!"

"What?" Horst looked from Rudi to Lise with an all-too-familiar expression that Lise loathed: the one he wore every time he tried to get Lise to side with him over her son. "All I'm saying is that the workhouse seems to have done its job." He turned back to Paul, but not before throwing one final aside over his shoulder. "By the way, Rudi, your conscription notice came while you were away. It's in the kitchen."

Leave it to Horst to twist the knife in deeper. Though conscription was mandatory for all young men in East Germany, it still seemed a cruelty to tell him today.

Paul lifted his beer. "Congratulations, my boy," he said genially. "I loved my time in the People's Army. Best years of my life."

Rudi looked from Paul to Lise. "I… I don't want to serve in the army," he said frantically. "I can object, can't I? Can't I object?"

She put her hands on Rudi's shoulder, alarmed to feel him trembling. "It's just a formality," she replied. "An interview and a medical examination. There's no guarantee you'll get called up, not for a few years, at least. It's just…it's just putting you on the list."

"But I—I'd have to shoot people." Rudi's eyes were wide. "If I'm stationed at the Wall, I'll have to shoot people—"

"I wouldn't worry." Horst exchanged a glance with Paul. "The Wall is where they send only their most loyal troops. Given your reputation you'll be stationed in some backwater, I'm sure."

Rudi's panicked expression faded into something worse: resignation. Without another word, he turned on his heel and strode out of the apartment, shutting the door with a quiet click.

Lise was horrified. For all his difficulties, Rudi was still a child, and Horst the adult in the room. How could her husband have thought his words appropriate?

But then, why had she expected anything different from him?

"I—I suppose he's excited to see his friends," Gerda said, more to fill the shocked silence than anything else. Wordlessly, Anna crossed to switch on the radio, then began passing appetizers around.

"Was that really necessary?" Lise snapped. "He's been home for five minutes. The least you could do—"

"I told you many times I don't have any interest in giving him a warm welcome," Horst replied, infuriatingly even-tempered. "Pretending as though being released from juvenile detention is some great accomplishment… This is what comes of indulging his bourgeois inclinations."

Though Lise was ready to jump down Horst's throat for his callousness, she could feel Paul beside her, watching, judging. "I—I need some air."

She stepped out onto the balcony, trembling with unspent fury as she leaned over the railing to watch Rudi storm out of the building and down the road. *My fault*, she thought as she watched him go. It had been unfair to put him on display so soon after getting out of Plötzensee, pushing him into a room filled with people and expecting him to entertain small talk; it had been unfair to allow Horst to spring the news of his conscription on Rudi without warning. She'd meant this afternoon to be a show of support, to demonstrate to Rudi that he was loved, valued—but what good was that, when she should have known that Horst would spoil it at the first opportunity?

She debated whether to go find Rudi and apologize, then thought better of it. He would be searching for his friends by the Brandenburg Gate.

The door slid open, and Paul walked out. "I thought you might need this," he said, balancing a glass of wine on the balcony railing.

Lise wiped her eyes before accepting the wineglass. "Thank you. I'm fine, Paul, you can go back inside."

He hesitated. "Lise, are you sure you're all right?"

"I'm just tired. Really. Go inside, Paul."

To her intense irritation, Paul sat down in the folding chair that Lise had placed amongst her dahlia pots. He'd tried, over the years, to repair the bond that had broken between them back in '62, but never by doing the one honest thing that might have made peace for Lise: never by discussing what had happened. It was as if their conversation within Stasi headquarters had never happened—as if Lise had imagined the whole thing and created the rift between them out of spite. Lise did her best to put up buffers, using the rest of her family to keep Paul at arm's length, but Paul persisted, clumsily, in trying to be the big brother he'd once been to her. Had he even sent Uli the letters she'd written for him? Or had they merely papered his way to promotions up the Stasi ranks?

"The conscription notice really doesn't mean anything," he

offered. "He's got plenty of time before he might be called up. He's not even eighteen yet."

"But he will be called up someday." Lise knew that Paul was the worst person to voice her concerns to, but she had to say them aloud or else she'd burst. "You didn't hear him in the car, how—how hopeless he feels. And now they might take him away, send him off to some—some faraway regiment..."

Behind her back, Paul let out a heavy sigh. "You're his mother. It's only natural for you to feel nervous," he said. "But it could be the making of him, you know. Away from here, away from those antisocial elements he spends his time with...it might be just what he needs to mold him into a proper, productive citizen."

The Rudi that Lise had driven home from Plötzensee seemed to be only half the person he'd been before he went in. After he served his eighteen months with the military, what would be left of him?

But she'd divulged too many doubts to Paul to voice that thought aloud.

"Perhaps you're right," she said carefully. "I just... I just want him to be happy."

"That's all I want for you, too." Paul got to his feet and stood beside her, resting his elbows against the balcony rail. "I know you and Horst have had a difficult time of things recently. Perhaps Rudi's return can be a new beginning for the three of you. As a family."

She'd tried to be conciliatory, but Paul's measured tone set her teeth on edge. "So, you're a marriage counselor as well as a Stasi agent now, are you?"

Paul was silent for a long moment. "I just want you to be happy."

There it was: Paul's old refrain, come back to haunt her like the chorus of a bad song. Why did he feel that Lise's happiness was his responsibility?

She knew the answer to the question as soon as she'd asked it, but that didn't make it any less irksome.

"We're fine, Paul." She turned, gripping the glass tightly by the stem. "Why do you feel the need to interfere in my marriage? I never ask about yours."

"I wish you would," Paul replied softly, and there was a note of regret in his voice that nearly gave Lise pause. "I miss you, Lise. I miss our friendship."

"Don't," Lise snarled. "Don't pretend like you ever cared about our friendship when you were the one who tore it apart."

"Then how about we have a real conversation about your son," he replied, and his tone was no longer soft, no longer tender. "He's been out of control for years, and if his reaction to Horst just now is any indication, his stay at Plötzensee won't have changed that. I know you won't believe this, but I've worked hard over the years to keep Rudi out of trouble. To keep him safe."

"By grinding down his spirit—"

"By calling in some important favors." He looked up with a hard stare. "Why do you think Rudi's gotten away with his delinquent behaviour for so long? Because I've been able to intervene. Because I've protected him from the worst consequences of his actions for years."

He paused as if waiting for Lise to say *thank you.*

"When Rudi was arrested, I was able to pull some strings and have him sent to Plötzensee rather than somewhere worse," he continued. "But if he continues acting out, my influence won't be enough to save him. He's nearly eighteen years old, and if he can't get himself under control, the military will be the least of his concerns." His expression darkened, and Lise knew that for all his meddling Paul was deadly serious. "If you can't get him to fall in line, there will come a day when I can no longer protect him."

52

DECEMBER 1979

Uli stepped into the entrance hall, greeted by the fragrant smell of something wonderful simmering on the stovetop. He crossed into the kitchen and found Gretchen at the stove, chopping herbs with a cookbook balanced beneath her cutting board.

"Rigatoni with a lamb ragù sauce," she said by way of explanation, holding out a wooden spoon for Uli to taste. Two months ago, they'd embarked upon a culinary project, working their way through cookbooks with recipes from places they'd traveled with Inge: Italy and France; Burma and Tanzania. Some evenings, like tonight, they traded off cooking duties, but the nights Uli liked best were those when he and Gretchen cooked together, sharing memories, ingredients and ideas.

The sauce was fragrant and rich—beautifully balanced and indulgent in a way that Uli, with his rudimentary kitchen skills, hadn't quite figured out how to re-create.

"Onion, pancetta, lamb, and...?"

"Red wine." Gretchen smiled. "You have to build the flavors, layer them one on top of the other: sauté the onions and garlic, brown the lamb separately..."

He nodded, marveling at Gretchen's natural ability. Irresistibly, he pictured her ten years older, running her own restaurant in the heart of Berlin; earning a Michelin star, traveling the world in search of culinary inspiration...

Or you could just let her enjoy cooking. Inge's voice broke into his mind, amused and exasperated. Uli loved thinking about Gretchen's future, and at sixteen her future was still limitless. She might decide to follow in Inge's footsteps as a doctor, or Uli's as an engineer; or perhaps her newfound passion for cooking might one day result in that Michelin starred restaurant.

In any case, it was good to see Gretchen discovering new talents that made her happy.

"Red wine," he said approvingly, and pressed a kiss to the top of Gretchen's head before inspecting the label. "Not one of my good bottles, I hope?"

She shot him a withering glance. "What do you take me for? The sauce needs another twenty minutes, and you're making the salad. Ingredients are in the fridge."

Uli rolled up his sleeves before pulling a head of lettuce and half a tomato from the crisper. "How was your day?"

"Good. I went to Kreuzberg with Christa and Pamela."

Uli looked up, frowning. "I'm not sure I like the idea of you spending time in Kreuzberg."

Though her back was turned, Uli could all but hear Gretchen roll her eyes. "It's not your posh Kurfürstendamm, but it's not dangerous. It's cool. Different."

Uli began chopping the lettuce, hardly mollified by his daughter's words. Kreuzberg butted up against the Wall and was a hotbed for dropouts and radicals and punk rockers—and though Gretchen was responsible enough, she was still, at sixteen, a girl.

"I just don't think it's a good idea to spend time there," he began, and Gretchen sighed.

"You can be so *square* sometimes, Papa," she said, filling a large pot with water. "It's perfectly safe, and besides, I was with friends the whole time." She hefted the pot back to the stovetop and added an ocean's worth of salt. "Friends. Remember those? You used to have friends before Mum died, but now you spend all your time alone."

"I'm not *alone*," Uli replied, trying to sound as if Gretchen's observation didn't sting. "I spend time with you, don't I?"

"And it's the dream of every teenage girl to have a father who thinks he's her best friend," Gretchen muttered, though her tone was friendly rather than resentful. "Seriously, though. What about those friends of yours who came to the funeral? Those old guys—I think they were a couple?"

"They're not *old*," Uli replied, "but they are a couple."

Wolf and Jurgen had paid their respects at the funeral, but did that make them friends again? Jurgen had seemed to think so: he'd shaken Uli's hand, even invited him to join them for a beer sometime. Had the invitation been genuine, or given out of pity? Did the distinction truly matter?

There had been a healing, of sorts, in seeing Jurgen and Wolf again, but Uli wasn't sure that meant they could all pick up where they'd left off. Jurgen, it seemed, had moved on, but Uli would always feel guilt over the part he played in Jurgen's incarceration.

Was that enough to prevent them from renewing a friendship?

Gretchen dumped a box of pasta in the water. "I still can't believe what the four of you did," she said wonderingly. "Digging a tunnel to East Berlin, it's like something out of a movie."

"Not a very good movie," Uli replied as he mixed ingredients for a salad dressing. Two years ago, Gretchen had discovered a newspaper clipping about the tunnel when researching a school project, and she'd been captivated by the idea that her parents had orchestrated an escape from East Berlin ever since. Uli and Inge had told her the basics of what had happened, but they'd never told her the full extent of the pain and heartbreak that had ensued from their efforts. To Gretchen, it was a madcap adventure, something she might read about in a paperback novel. "We failed."

"You got twenty-four people out of East Germany. I'd hardly call that a failure."

In her words Uli could hear an echo of what Jurgen had told him at the funeral: that theirs was a victory, even if it had ended in defeat.

Seven years of my freedom in exchange for twenty-four lifetimes, Jurgen had said, with that old twinkle in his eye. *I'd consider that a fair trade, wouldn't you?*

"I suppose," Uli said aloud.

"You got all those people out of East Germany...but not *her*." Uli looked up to find Gretchen leaning against the kitchen counter, a tea towel slung over her shoulder. "That's what it was all for, wasn't it? Mum told me."

"That wasn't your mother's story to tell." Uli was struck by the realization that Inge had shared this part of their life—this part of *his* life—with Gretchen. He'd mentioned Rudi, but only in the scantest of terms, explaining him as the result of a broken engagement. In his heart of hearts, Uli doubted that he would have ever told Gretchen the truth about Lise, if left to his own devices—but then, that was exactly why Inge had.

So I can't back out of my promise, he realized with equal parts awe and anger.

"Would you do it again?"

He cleared his throat. "Don't be absurd. Digging a tunnel was hard enough when I was in my twenties. Not to mention completely reckless..."

"There are other ways to get people out of East Germany," Gretchen began, but Uli stopped her with a glance.

Behind her, the pasta had bubbled on the stovetop too long,

drops of water splashing out onto the hot edge of the coil with a hiss.

"You're scared," she said softly.

"You're damn right I'm scared." Resentment burned, hot and sudden in his chest, at Inge for putting him in this position. Though his final promise to her still echoed in his mind, seeing Lise at the funeral—enduring the unbearable cacophony of the conflicting emotions she'd unearthed in him—had thrown the insurmountable cost of such an endeavor into stark relief once more.

They'd endangered lives. They'd ruined one, taken another, in their pursuit of each other.

For all her worldliness, Gretchen shared her mother's blind idealism. How could she truly understand what she was asking?

"You're being naïve, Gretchen. Besides..." He pictured Lise's brown eyes, filled with tears, pressing a photograph of Rudi into Uli's hands. "We don't even know if she wants to come."

Gretchen crossed her arms. "Don't you owe it to her to ask?"

53

FEBRUARY 1980

Lise stepped out the door of Die Nadel und der Faden, flipping the small sign on the door to Closed before locking it and setting off down the sidewalk, an empty string bag under her arm. She'd spent the day working on an evening dress for one of Gerda's longtime clients, and though she longed to step into the current of a hot shower and wash away the day's work, there was a part of her that wished she could stay here, working late into the night.

She turned onto Schönhauser Allee to join the long queue of people waiting outside the supermarket, feeling, with momentary guilt, a sense of relief at the wait: it would afford her another twenty minutes of calm before she needed to return to the battlefield that had become her home. Rudi had accepted his factory job at Fleishkombinat Berlin with sullen compliance, but only last week he'd received the call they all knew was coming: he'd been drafted into the People's Army and was to report to the Military District Command shortly after his eighteenth birthday.

Horst had greeted the news with predictable sanctimony, but Lise had been nearly as dismayed as Rudi: the thought of her son spending eighteen months in the army was more than she could bear. She pictured him with Horst's regulation haircut, his beloved camera wrenched from his hands, losing the last shred of himself to become a soldier as beholden to the state as his stepfather and his uncle.

It was clear to Lise that Rudi was suffocating beneath the weight of living in a country where his every decision was made for him: his education, his work, his life. She remembered what it had felt like to fight against the unstoppable current that was East Germany: to struggle her way in the hopes of finding some solid, distant shore. But when she'd allowed herself to be borne away on by the tide, she'd felt, oddly, relief. Though it wasn't what she would have ever chosen for herself, her life, undeniably, became easier once she stopped fighting.

She'd resigned herself to her fate. But now she was watching her son break against that same tide. Living in East Berlin was killing Rudi's spirit, and he would fight against the current until it drowned him.

The queue shuffled forward, and Lise followed suit. There was no future for Rudi in East Germany.

His future lay with Uli, in the West.

But how could Lise get him there?

From somewhere behind her, a voice broke through her thoughts. "Excuse me, have you a light?"

"I'm sorry, no."

"Are you sure?"

Lise turned to find a pair of familiar eyes, staring at her from the set of an unfamiliar face. The girl looked at Lise, a cigarette perched between her fingers, eyebrows raised in polite inquiry.

"I… I may have one back in my shop," she stammered, holding out her arm to chivvy Inge's daughter away from the queue. "If you'd like to come with me."

★★★

They walked north along Schönhauser Allee, deeper into the countercultural enclave of Prenzlauer Berg. Gretchen looked so much like her mother, up close—the same high cheekbones and sharp chin, the same lilt to her stride as she stepped over the sidewalk curb. But she could see Uli, too, in her pale complexion and dark hair; in her dimpled cheeks and crooked smile. She couldn't help feeling like she'd been catapulted back in time, to the day Inge showed up at the door to Gerda's shop with a grin. *I'm Swedish. I can get a day pass, remember?*

She led Gretchen onto Pappelallee, past small restaurants and goldbroilers and kneipes like the one on Bernauer Strasse where she used to sit with Uli and Inge, dreaming of their lives after graduation.

"Does your father know you're here?"

"Of course he knows," Gretchen replied. "He wasn't thrilled about it, but he knew I was going to do it one way or another."

"I see." Lise turned onto Raumerstrasse: overhead, artists and dropouts stood on the dilapidated balconies of crumbling apartments, sharing cigarettes and bottles of liquor. "And does he know you came here to meet me?"

"He does." Out of the corner of her eye, Gretchen gave her an appraising look. "You know, I saw you at Mum's funeral, standing there in the back. Why didn't you introduce yourself?"

The question made Lise feel as though she, not Gretchen, was sixteen years old.

"I wasn't sure it was my place," she replied gently. "I didn't want to confuse you or upset you." She stared down at the sidewalk, thinking of the tears in Uli's eyes as she'd said goodbye; the tears in her own as she passed back through the border checkpoint. West Berlin itself had felt like an oasis, vibrant and bustling, and she'd longed to remain there, to slip her identity card out of her wallet and drop it in the Spree, shed her name and become someone new.

If it hadn't been for Rudi, she would have done so.

"I don't know whether it did any good, turning up like that."

"Of course it did," Gretchen replied. "You were friends with Mum. She spoke so fondly of you."

"She told you about me?"

"At the end, mostly." Gretchen smiled. "We talked a lot, in those last few days..."

She trailed off, her smile fading, and Lise longed to take her hand and give her the comfort she'd so sorely missed as a motherless child, herself. "I know it may not seem like it now, but you were so lucky to have had your mum as long as you did." She thought of her own mother, gone too long; of Gerda, who'd stepped into the role long after Lise had thought she stopped needing it. "I lost my mother when I was just a little girl—too young, really, to have any proper memories of her. But you... you have so many wonderful memories of Inge. And that's something, Gretchen. I hope you know that."

Gretchen was silent a moment. "I worry that I'll forget who she was. That I'll forget what she looked like, or sounded like..."

"People think that memories fade with time, but I'm not sure that's the case," Lise replied gently. "You know, I've got a thousand stories about your mum that you've never heard before. We went on a road trip once, hitchhiked our way to Prague when school was on break for the summer..." She shook her head, laughing at the memory of Inge in the front seat of a stranger's Mercedes, her long legs stretched out on the dash as she grilled the driver about his views on Vietnam. "Inge was always able to talk her way into anything."

Gretchen looked thoughtful, and Lise, with a sudden maternal urge, hoped she'd not given her any silly ideas about climbing into strangers' cars.

"What I'm trying to say is that you have your memories of Inge, and I have mine. And when we share those memories with each other, our understanding of her grows clearer."

They stepped into a parkette lined by graffiti-clad apartment buildings: off in the distance, she could hear the drifting chords of a violin. From somewhere nearby, someone laughed, and Lise looked up at a nearby building to see a pair of young people, two punks like Rudi, perched facing each other on the edge of a windowsill, their dangling feet touching as they talked.

"Your mother won't ever be forgotten. Not by you or me, and not by your father." She pictured Inge, twisting Uli's engagement ring from her finger for Lise; Inge, braving the scrutiny of border guards as she danced on both sides of the barbed wire. "She was too vibrant a person for her memory to ever grow dull. Does that—does that make sense to you?"

Gretchen craned her neck to watch a pair of pigeons swoop overhead, twisting and buffeting in the blue. "It does."

Every day, Lise walked through East Berlin with the certainty that there were a thousand sets of eyes upon her—Stasi officers and informants, tracking her every move—but for some reason she felt as though they'd slipped into the city's inner lining. Here, somehow, she felt hidden away from the scrutiny of others, and the feeling, though illusory, was intoxicating; as if she'd shed years of suspicion and paranoia from her shoulders, and could simply be the Lise who Inge had once known; the Lise who Uli had loved.

Finally, she spoke again. "Why are you here, Gretchen?"

Gretchen followed Lise's gaze up to the pair of lovers at the window. "Dad tells me I've got a brother, here," she said. "I'd love to meet him someday."

54

It had been years since Uli had visited the West Berlin neighborhood of Kreuzberg. Stories, repeated in the newspaper and by Uli's well-heeled neighbors in Halensee, about the immigrants, criminals, Bohemians and layabouts lured there by low housing prices had long ago given him enough pause to skirt the neighborhood. But this afternoon he'd climbed into Inge's old Volkswagen 1300—the car she'd bought back in the late sixties, which she'd refused to sell, even long after they'd bought a sensible Ford Taunus—and driven down Kreuzberg's winding streets, finding not the city's underbelly but a bustling community where street markets stood side by side with family restaurants and cafés perfumed with the intoxicating scent of Turkish coffee.

He turned up Dresdener Strasse, slowing as the neon-lit windows of bars revealed men dancing with men, and he looked back at the road, feeling suddenly, unbearably old. He thought back to the disapproving noise he'd made when Gretchen had said she'd come here: since when had he let the opinions of others dictate where he went? Though the buildings in Kreuzberg were shabbier than those in Halensee, the neighborhood was just another part of the city he loved. Why had he avoided it?

He pulled up outside a small auto body shop next to a kebaberie and looked at his watch, wondering idly whether he had time to stop in for a *döner.* But this, he knew, was his own feeble attempt at a stalling tactic, and he stepped out of the car before he could lose his nerve and drive away.

The auto body shop was a modest concern—a family business with two wide garage doors and twin lifts painted a cheery shade of blue. A Mercedes sedan sat on one of the lifts, midway through what Uli suspected was an axle repair; the other bay was empty, tools hanging neatly on the garage's metal walls.

"I'll be with you in a minute," someone called from the back room, and Uli inched further into the garage to study the curlicued certification above the cash register. Next to it hung a photograph of two men, one stocky and one tall, standing side by side in front of the shop with matching smiles.

They'd made a good life for themselves, Wolf and Jurgen. Uli only hoped that his visit wouldn't throw all they'd built into disrepair.

After a few more minutes, Wolf emerged from the back room.

"It's you," he said, and to Uli's relief his tone wasn't hostile. He wiped his hands on a rag and stowed it in the back pocket of his coveralls which, Uli was impressed to note, were emblazoned with a faded badge from Ferrari.

Wolf noticed him staring. "I was on the pit crew a few years back," he said by way of explanation, waving a hand at another photo on the wall: Wolf, shaking hands with Niki Lauda. "Nice guy. A little curt, but nice."

"Were...were you there when he crashed? At the Nürburgring?" Uli didn't follow Formula One racing all that closely, but like the rest of the world he'd been captivated by the story of Lauda's crash at the 1976 German Grand Prix: how Lauda's car had swerved off the tracks and burst into flames; how another driver managed to drag him out of the wreckage of the car.

"I was." Wolf sighed. "Horrible business. But he returned to racing, even after all that..." He trailed off. "Jurgen's upstairs, I can go get him if you like."

"As a matter of fact, it's you I came to see." Uli stepped forward, breathing in the heavy scent of motor oil. "I wanted to apologize. To you, personally. I know Jurgen and I, we've—we've made our peace, but I...I wronged you that day, too. No matter how Jurgen feels about it all, I—I should have stayed behind. I should have gone back for him and I'm...I'm sorry."

A poignant look flickered across Wolf's face. "If you'd gone back for him, I would have had three friends locked away in an East German prison, rather than two." He sighed and glanced back up at the photo of Lauda. "I know now how hard it is to stand on the sidelines and watch a tragedy unfold without any ability to stop it." He held out his hand. "It's all forgiven, Uli. Everything that happened...it's in the past."

Uli took Wolf's hand and let out a breath he hadn't known he was holding—then, instinctively, he pulled Wolf into a tight hug.

Wolf patted him on the back. "You've been holding on to sadness for too long, my friend," he said, and Uli let out a choked laugh. It was true. He'd spent so many years walking through West Berlin always looking over his shoulder, for hope or for fear of seeing Wolf or Jurgen—of having this very conversation.

He'd avoided this apology for so very long, convinced that when it happened it would all go wrong.

He'd never considered the possibility that it could go *right.*

"I think that's true," he conceded as he took off his spectacles to wipe the glass clean. "Inge always did say I have a tendency to brood. Losing her has put a lot of things into perspective, I suppose, and it's made me realize that I've left too many conversations unfinished. You and Jurgen. Lise and Rudi."

Wolf leaned against the wall. "I was surprised to see her at the funeral," he said, crossing his arms over his chest. "She looks… defeated. Like Jurgen did, after he was extradited back home." He glanced upward, and Uli knew he was listening for Jurgen's heavy tread on the stairwell. "Jurgen's told me a lot about what happened to him when he was in Hohenschönhausen and knowing what I know now about—about the Stasi, my heart goes out to her. It really does."

"Lise *has* been defeated by it," Uli replied. "She and Rudi both. My daughter went to see them last week and they…they can't stay in East Berlin." He reached into his pocket for the keys to Inge's Volkswagen and set them on the table. "Wolf, I know I have no right to ask this of you, but I need your help."

A genuine smile crossed Wolf's lips. "I was hoping you'd come to say that," he replied. "It's worth a hell of a lot more than an apology."

55

MARCH 1980

The woods around Lake Flakensee were brown and peaceful, scented with the balsam sweetness of conifers that stretched high to the brilliant blue sky. After several hours of hiking, Lise had left the crowds behind: here, in the higher altitude of the rolling Kranichsberge mountain range, she could hear nothing but the sound of the forest around her and the crack of her footfalls on the weathered path.

She lifted her cheeks to a warm column of sunlight that fell through a break in the trees, listening as wind breathed a song through bare branches. This was a trail Lise knew well: only a short car ride from the datsche, hiking through the Rüdersdorfer Heide was a favourite weekend activity for her, and she could always count on finding some new marvel to admire in nature: the call of a bird or the fall of a feather; a patch of jewel-like moss forming a miniature mountain range on a fallen log.

Today, however, Lise marveled at something else. Up ahead, Rudi lifted his camera to take a photo, and Lise followed his sightline to find a hawk nestled in the branches of a Scots pine.

He was patient, focusing the camera's lens as the bird cleaned its feathers; then Lise heard the *click, click* of the shutter as the bird took flight.

He directed his camera at Lise, and she smiled, shaking her head as he took another photo. "I would have appreciated some warning," she said, raking her fingers through her tangled hair. "I must look a mess."

"Candid photos turn out best." He set the Prakti back against his chest, the sun catching on the camera's metal body. "You should see the one I took of Renate the other day."

Out here in the wilderness—away from Horst, away from his looming enlistment and talking about his girlfriend—Rudi seemed at peace: he looked, for the first time in months, happy. She could see in his unguarded smile the boy she'd raised: energetic and intelligent, joyful and artistic.

She could see, too, the man he had the potential to become, one day. A man like his father, compassionate and thoughtful.

"Come on, there's a lookout ahead," he said, and he charged on down the path, Lise following in his footsteps.

When Lise had asked for the datsche this weekend, she was grateful that no one else in the family had staked a claim to join them: Papa and Gerda had gone to Berlin to attend the opera and left them with a stocked larder and freshly washed sheets, while Paul and Anna, who were known to turn up on occasion with Kurt to visit, were vacationing in Lake Balaton with some friends. Even Horst had thought it best to stay in the city, hoping that Lise might take the opportunity to speak to Rudi properly—to get to the heart, he said, of what was troubling the boy.

Lise had agreed, but she didn't need to talk to Rudi to know what was wrong.

Last night, Lise had listened to the sound of Rudi snoring upstairs in the loft that she still thought of as Paul's. There were so many memories tied up in the datsche: watching Rudi crawl toward Papa, using the spokes of his wheelchair to pull himself upright for the first time; helping Paul dig up harvest after harvest in the garden. She'd even made good memories with Horst here: he'd proposed to her on the sandy banks of Lake Flakensee, held Rudi in his arms and vowed to be a father to her son. Whatever else had happened between them, she knew that in that early moment, Horst had been entirely genuine in his wish to make the three of them a family.

Up ahead, Rudi had reached a fork in the trail, and he glanced back, unsure which way to go.

"Go to the right," Lise said, and Rudi hesitated.

"You're sure? The left leads to that lookout we once went to with Kurt—"

"Trust me. Head right."

They continued onward, Lise's throat tightening with every step as she overtook Rudi on the path. She glanced behind her shoulder, listening for the sound of other voices, other people, as she turned onto an even smaller footpath which led to a narrow service road.

"Mum?"

"Follow me." She could feel her heart pounding as she quickened her pace to take the lead. Up ahead, a tall man waited beside an idling blue Volkswagen, parked on the shoulder beneath a heavy thicket of trees. He looked up and tossed the butt of his cigarette into the dirt.

"Wolf." Lise wasn't sure whether to hug him or shake his hand. "Thank you for doing this."

Wolf crouched over the wheel to twist the dial on the radio, faint music flickering in and out of the static. "Let's just say I've grown tired of Jurgen having all the heroic stories." A song crackled to life and Lise heard a pop from somewhere near the car's back seat.

Rudi drew closer. "Mum, what's going on?"

"Your father and I called in a few favours," she said, "but all I need to know is this: Do you want to live in the West?"

Rudi's eyes lit up, and he answered without hesitation. "Yes."

Wolf pushed the driver's seat forward, then leaned in and lifted the back bench seat to reveal a small compartment. "I modified the engine block to give you a bit of room, but it's going to be a tight squeeze," he explained. "Hop in."

Lise blinked back her tears as she pressed a kiss to Rudi's cheek. "There's a bottle of water and a sandwich in your rucksack," she said. "Good luck."

"But what about you? Aren't you coming, too?"

Her heart broke at his wide-eyed assumption that there was some other space in the car meant for her. "There's not enough room, *liebchen*," she replied, trying to keep the pain from her voice as she watched him crawl into the car. "But we'll see each other soon. I promise."

He hesitated. "But what will you do? What will Horst say—"

"Leave Horst to me," Lise replied with a bravado she didn't truly feel. "Please, Rudi. We don't have much time."

He tucked himself into place, looking impossibly young, impossibly fragile. The border guards at all the Berlin checkpoints were trained to search cars for hidden compartments just like this. How could she even think of sending her son across the border in the rattling void of a Volkswagen?

Given his imminent conscription, what other choice did she have?

"This compartment will only open if the radio is tuned to the correct station," Wolf told Rudi. "You'll be safe, I promise."

He made as if to close it, but then Rudi threw up his arm. "What about my stuff? What about Renate, I can't leave without saying goodbye—"

"Renate will understand." She pointed to the camera that still hung around Rudi's neck, knowing they'd lingered too long on the road. "You've got what's most important. Take it and become the photographer you've always wanted to be." She pressed her lips together and attempted a smile. "I love you, Rudi. Tell your father I said hello."

She watched the car drive off and wiped away her tears. Slowly, she turned and walked back down into the trees.

56

Uli sat out on the balcony, watching as dusk fell over the stuccoed buildings along Halberstädter Strasse. From within the apartment, he could hear Jurgen and Gretchen in the kitchen, laughing over some joke at the stove, and he was grateful that Jurgen had come: he was a welcome distraction for Gretchen as Uli sat in silence, smoking a rare cigarette to calm his nerves.

He got to his feet at the sound of a car turning onto the quiet street, then sank back in his chair, deflated, as a sleek convertible rolled past the building. He wasn't looking for the fancy cars that tended to frequent Halensee—muscular BMWs and boxy Volvos, Mazdas and Mercedes in bright colors that faded to gray in the evening light. Instead, he was waiting for Inge's old Volkswagen, the car he'd given to Wolf three weeks ago when he'd asked for a favor he knew he would never be able to repay.

He pictured the Volkswagen with its new alterations, passing through the near-impenetrable mass of the Berlin Wall. Wolf would take the border crossing at Invalidenstrasse, Uli knew, and he could all but see the car waiting to cross Sandkrugbrücke;

Wolf's knuckles, white on the wheel. While other, bigger border crossings like Checkpoint Charlie were reserved for use by foreigners and diplomats, Invalidenstrasse was one of the few designated crossings for West Berliners—busier by far than Sonnenalle or Chauseestrasse, which, Uli hoped, would make for less scrupulous border guards, weary after the end of long shifts.

He knew that the Grenztruppen had ways of searching for hidden compartments in the vehicles that passed from East to West, on high alert for desperate citizens attempting to escape the GDR by any means possible. He'd heard of all manner of ingenious escapes, some of which bypassed the Wall altogether: people hiding in hollowed out surfboards tied to roof racks; flying over in hot air balloons or scuba diving through heavily guarded canals. Wolf's conversion of the Volkswagen felt remarkably risky to Uli, but he trusted in Wolf's abilities, both in retrofitting the car and in keeping his nerve. He'd made the compartment inaccessible to anyone who didn't know about the trick with the radio; he'd changed the air pressure in the tires so that the car wouldn't look like it was carrying a second person. He'd even reinforced the front bumpers so that if all went wrong, he would be able to smash hell-for-leather through the barrier—but that thought made Uli want to reach for a second cigarette.

Not for the first time, he wished that he could have been the one to go to East Berlin to retrieve Lise and Rudi himself. When he'd been arrested, Jurgen had given up Uli's name as one of his coconspirators, but he'd been able to keep Wolf off the Stasi's radar; as a result, although Uli was permanently banned from entering the GDR, Wolf was able to pass back and forth.

The sliding door opened and Jurgen stepped out, carrying two bottles of Coca-Cola.

"I thought you could use a refreshment," he said, offering Uli one of the bottles. "Gretchen's made it quite clear that I'm a better bottle washer than I am a sous chef. I'm to return to the kitchen once she's made a mess of all the dishes." He opened his soda and settled into the chair opposite Uli's, looking so serene, so unruffled, as he stretched his legs out.

Uli traced a finger along the bottle's design and started to prize up the label with a short fingernail, hearing Inge's voice, chiding and affectionate, in his mind: *use a glass, for goodness' sake.*

Below, another car—a Volvo, Uli determined with a disappointed glance—crept up the road.

"How did you do it?"

Jurgen glanced over. "Do what?"

"When you were in prison…how did you get through all those years, not knowing if you would ever make it back to Wolf?"

Jurgen leaned back, looking thoughtful. "The same way you did, going down into that tunnel every day for half a year." He held out his bottle, and Uli lifted his own to knock the two together. "I just had to believe we would find each other again."

From behind them, a shadow interrupted the spill of light from the living room, and Uli looked up to find Gretchen leaning against the doorframe. "Anything yet?"

"Not yet." Without Jurgen to distract her, Gretchen seemed anxious as she shared in their balcony vigil, and Uli stood to wrap her in his arms. Whether Wolf succeeded or not, he needed to be strong for her. "They'll be fine, liebchen. Everything's going to be fine."

She glanced down the road at the sound of another car turning onto Halberstädter Strasse, and Jurgen got to his feet.

"Well," said Uli as Inge's blue Volkswagen trundled slowly into view. He dropped the cigarette butt into his bottle of Coke. "Come on."

He descended the staircase on shaking legs, gripping the banister so tightly he was amazed that he didn't peel it off the wall and carry it with him out into the street. Parked beneath the glow of a streetlamp, the car's interior was bathed in shadow, but he could make out Wolf, bent over the dashboard as he fiddled with the radio dial.

He gripped Gretchen's hand. "Is it all— Are you both—?"

"One minute." Uli heard a *pop* and Wolf unfolded his lanky frame from the small car as Jurgen hustled to the passenger side door to help shift the back bench seat.

A tall young man in a denim vest, a plaid shirt and black trousers emerged from the cavity beneath the seat, pale and unsteady after so long crouched in the dark. In the light Uli could see him properly for the first time, and his heart swelled at the sight of his dark curls, the glint of a ring set in a nose that so perfectly resembled Lise's.

Rudi stumbled forward, no doubt suffering the effect of pins and needles, and Uli caught him, held him upright as he pulled him into a hug that was seventeen long years in the making.

He pulled away, knowing that the resemblance between them was strengthened by their shared tears.

"Gretchen," he said. "Meet Rudi. Your brother."

57

Though it was only just past dawn, Lise was wide-awake, watching as sunlight began to breathe life into her bedroom's willow-print wallpaper. This early, there was nothing to distract from the peace of the morning: no footsteps from the apartment above or music, leaching through the walls; no blaring television programs from the living room. Nothing but Horst, snoring softly beside her.

She'd spent fifteen years of her life waking up in this apartment, accumulated fifteen years of memories here, and not all of them were bad. Watching *Sandmännchen* with Rudi when he was six years old, curled in her lap; hosting dinners for Papa and Gerda at the square table, laughing late into the night. Sharing a glass of schnapps with Horst at Christmas, long after Rudi, wriggling with glee at the prospect of Father Christmas, had gone to bed; feigning outrage after Horst discovered her cheating at a board game and carried her off to the bedroom over his shoulder.

Why was it that now, at the end of the road, Lise could think of nothing but the good in the life she'd built here?

She'd returned from Lake Flakensee five days ago, feeling as if she'd sawn off one of her arms. Horst, being Horst, hadn't been overly concerned when Lise came home without Rudi: she'd told him that Rudi had decided to spend a few days with his girlfriend, and Horst had accepted the story without argument. She spared a thought for Renate, Rudi's girlfriend, but she didn't dare enlighten her as to Rudi's disappearance: it was too dangerous to let her know that he'd had to make a decision on a moment's notice.

Assuming, of course, that he had made it across the Wall. There was no way for her to know—it was too risky for him or Uli to send word now. No, she needed to take it on faith that Rudi and Wolf had made it to West Berlin without issue. Faith in that was the only thing that kept her going in those moments when all she wanted to do was cry at her son's absence.

Beside her, Horst rolled onto his back with a sigh, bare chested and unguarded in sleep. Here in bed, Horst had always seemed so much softer to Lise than when he was fully awake: more human, somehow, less the automaton she'd thought him to be so many years ago.

When they'd first married, Horst had shown Lise that softer side of him, but over the years he'd calcified, somehow. Now, at forty-seven, he was the Party man he'd always longed to be, loyal to the State and the Stasi in a way that cut at the heart of what he might have had with Lise.

Between his allegiances and hers, there had simply been too many others in their marriage bed for them to have ever truly succeeded as a couple.

Lise lay a hand gently on his chest and Horst let out a contented sigh, then batted his eyes open, his voice rasped with sleep. "What is it?"

She kissed his cheek. "Nothing, Horst. Nothing at all."

After Horst had left for work, Lise retrieved her handbag and filled it with only the barest essentials: photographs of Rudi and

Papa and Gerda; the letter Paul had given her on his wedding day to Anna. She debated whether to leave Horst a note, but decided against it—what was there left to say, when her actions would speak so much louder than her words ever could?

She took one more look around the apartment, then checked her watch. It was still early enough for her departure to coincide with regular commuters, her little Trabi blending in with the thousands of other cars bustling around the city as she made her way to Lake Flakensee, where Wolf would be waiting for her. She pictured her little shop, sitting empty: her half-finished commissions, waiting on hangers for a new dressmaker to finish them. Her clients wouldn't understand her decision to flee, but Gerda, she knew, would.

She picked up her car keys, then a knock at the door turned her blood to ice.

There was nothing she could do but open it: not when there was no way to escape from seven storeys up; not when whoever was outside had no doubt heard her bustling in the entrance.

She opened the door, hands trembling.

"Good morning, Lise. I'm sorry to call on you so early." Paul paused, and although somewhere in the back of Lise's mind she knew he was waiting for an invitation inside, she was too shocked to do anything but stand stock-still.

He cocked his head, his expression grave. "I would prefer not to have this conversation on the landing," he continued. "May I come in?"

She trailed him into the living room, her heart pounding at his formal demeanor. She'd not seen him since the afternoon of Rudi's party.

It might be nothing, she thought, fruitlessly. *Maybe he needs to borrow a cup of sugar.*

He glanced down the hallway as they crossed into the living room. "Horst's left for work, I take it?"

"You know Horst." She let out a dry laugh. "He likes to make an early start to the day."

"I do." Paul lifted his chin, eyes darting around the apartment. "And Rudi? It's been a few days since you last saw him, isn't that true?"

There was no point in lying; not to Paul, who still, so many years later, knew her best. In an instant, she felt as if she was back in that interrogation room, watching Paul slide a typed confession toward her. How could she be here again, on the brink of her future with her brother barring her way?

But there was a difference between the Paul of the past and the Paul of the present: a rounding of his shoulders, an uncertainty behind his eyes. Lise stepped closer, realizing what Paul was trying, and failing, to hide.

He'd *asked* where Rudi was; he'd not *told* her. And Lise was certain that if Rudi had been caught trying to cross the border, Paul's demeanour would be quite different.

Was it a bluff?

Did it matter?

She'd signed away her life in exchange for her son, once. But if Rudi had made it safely to West Berlin, there was nothing Paul could hold over her: no bargaining chip he could use to force her hand.

She closed her eyes, relief washing over her in a merciful wave. "He's with Uli, then. Good."

Paul's expression barely changed. "After everything I've done for you," he muttered. "After all the love I've shown you...and this is how you repay me."

It felt like the refrain of an old song: one that Paul had long sung, but Lise was only now hearing the words correctly. "What love?" she replied. "How is any part of what you've done for me love, Paul?"

"I've protected you!" Paul took a step forward and then another, his face growing red as Lise stepped out of his path. "I've protected you from so much, Lise—from prison, from losing your child, from your own recklessness. I've taken care of our father, I've found you a *husband*, I made sure you were given a job in that shop rather than a factory..." He trailed off and ran a hand through his hair: still thick and blond, still the hairline of a twenty-year-old. "If you only knew the true extent of everything I've done for you over the years... I've not said a *word*, and you've given me nothing but resentment and anger in return. I've never asked for anything other than your happiness."

She heard Paul clearly for the first time in years; now, it was his turn to listen.

"I've never been happy." Lise felt as if a dam was ready to burst within her, spilling out all the emotions she'd held so tightly, unable to express them for fear of reprisal, for fear of rejection, of danger—but now that fear was gone. "I've not been happy. Not once since the Wall went up. You took a lifetime of happiness from me." She looked up, trembling with her own sense of conviction. "I've lived a life *you* wanted for me, Paul, rather than one of my own choosing."

Paul gaped at her, his face grown so slack that Lise thought, for a moment, he might have gone into shock. "But I—I protected you."

Did he truly not see the difference? When they were children, Paul had always been the one there to save her from bullies and nightmares, always ready to be the knight in shining armor. It was the reason, Lise knew, that he'd become a police officer.

Lise had no memories of the war, but Paul had been old enough, in those last, desperate days, to remember the invasion of Berlin: the arrival of the Red Army, the carnage that had been visited upon the city thanks to the arrogance, the hubris and cruelty of their parents' generation. He'd been powerless to stop the chaos that had followed, but he remembered it, as a child: it had been the foundation of his dreams of gallantry.

Pity formed a crack in the concrete she'd poured around her heart. Paul had become a hero out of desperation, and it was desperation which had driven him his whole life.

Desperation had made him into a monster, and he'd mistaken it for love.

"I never asked for your protection," she said finally. "I have spent the last twenty years suffocating under your control. It's been killing me my whole life, Paul, and it was going to kill Rudi, too." To her surprise, the realization had stopped her from trembling. "Please, Paul. Let me be with my family."

His face crumbled. "*I'm* your family," he replied, and she could hear in his voice the child he'd been, back when he'd vowed never to feel powerless again.

"You gave up the right to call yourself my brother when you chose the State over me." Lise's heart broke for him, but she stood firm. "And now I'm choosing my family over you. It's time for you to let me go."

Paul stood between Lise and the door, his expression unbearably slack, unbearably anguished. He gripped the doorjamb between the hallway and the living room, immutable and solid, and Lise glanced up at the clock hung on the wall beside him. Time was running out: she needed to meet Wolf.

She positioned her handbag over her shoulder and took a step forward, and then another, daring Paul to remain in her way.

58

In the nineteen years since he'd signed the lease, Uli's apartment on Bernauer Strasse had gone through very little in the way of material changes. He'd replaced the moth-eaten sofa and chair at some point in the mid '70s but had retained the faded wallpaper in the living room; he'd added a new television at the request of one of his tenants and retiled the bathroom two winters ago after a burst pipe had brought up the linoleum. But he'd kept the essentials of the space intact: the eggshell blue in the kitchen and the headboard in the bedroom; the fireplace, with its hulking andirons.

His last tenant had moved out last year and, given everything that had passed in the months since, he'd not gotten around to relisting the place with a rental agent; now, he doubted whether he would. Instead, he'd stocked the kitchen cupboards and brought over fresh linens, made up the bed and set up a cot in what he'd once intended to be a nursery.

This apartment was, he knew, too close to East Berlin for Lise and Rudi to feel comfortable staying here, but to him it was still a home—one from a past life he'd found impossible to forget. He and Gretchen could stay here for the time being, and let Lise and Rudi get their feet under them at the apartment in Halensee.

Jurgen, sitting on the couch, switched on the television, allowing the sound of *Der Alte*—a rerun of yesterday's episode—fill the air between them. There wasn't much to say, beyond the obvious: they'd both been here before, waiting in the unbearable silence.

At least he'd not subjected his children to this tense vigil. Instead, he'd given Rudi and Gretchen tickets to the Jethro Tull concert at Deutschlandhalle arena, as a means of letting them get to know each other better, but also as a convenient excuse to keep them busy. He'd not told either of them that Wolf had gone back into East Germany today for Lise, nor did he think it wise to enlighten them. It seemed a particular cruelty, especially for Rudi, to make them join in the agonizing wait.

In the days since his arrival, Rudi had spoken little, but he'd taken in West Berlin and its inhabitants with a wide-eyed amazement that Uli, given everything Lise had told him about his son's restless nature, suspected was only temporary. Uli hadn't taken him yet to register with the West German authorities as a refugee—not until Lise made it safely across the border—but he'd shown Rudi around the small neighborhoods of West Berlin so he could take photos with his old camera, burning through roll after roll of film. Uli couldn't wait for him to have them developed. What would they reveal of this unique chapter in Rudi's life, when he'd lived on both sides of the Wall?

Though they'd exchanged letters, Uli knew he had a mountain to climb in gaining his son's trust. There was so much he wanted to explain, so much he wanted to share, but building an honest relationship with Rudi would take time and difficult conversations. Right now, he and Rudi were strangers to each other, both showcasing their best sides with self-conscious deference. But one day, Uli hoped, Rudi's careful manners would give way to who he really was—not as a stranger but as a son, with all his scars and flaws.

Jurgen leaned forward, staring at the television without truly watching it. "They ought to have been back by now," he muttered, and Uli took a sip of his beer, resisting the urge to check his watch. Wolf had left for East Berlin hours ago, and they'd had no word from him since: when he'd gone to get Rudi, he'd been back much earlier in the evening. Had he been arrested at the border? Questioned, for his unlikely return visit to East Berlin in the space of a week?

He got to his feet and opened the curtains, letting in a view that was drastically different from what he'd once known. In 1962, the Wall that Uli had once crawled under had been a long stretch of concrete slabs, patched together and topped by lines of barbed wire, backed by bricked-up apartment buildings and guards watching from timbered towers. Twenty years on, the Wall had morphed into something else entirely: a hulking monstrosity that spanned nearly half the width of a city block, merciless and terrible in the perpetual daylight cast down by tall lampposts.

It began in East Berlin as a snaking, whitewashed mass of concrete, immediately followed by an electrified signal fence, meant, no doubt, to trap anyone who might have succeeded in jumping over the inner wall. From there, a strip of metal spikes and hedgehog tank traps sat joined together in a long line on either side of a sentry footpath, dotted every few metres by the lampposts that burned through the night. Raked sand covered the entirety of the so-called "death strip"—the better, Uli knew, to see the footprints of anyone who might dare try to dash across to the final, insurmountable obstacle: the Wall itself, a high concrete barrier topped with a cylinder of concrete meant to prevent anyone from gaining purchase on the top with their fingers.

It was hateful and grim, overlooked by square watchtowers manned twenty-four hours a day by armed guards. Looking at it from his high perch, Uli saw in it the utter terror it was meant to convey; the sheer futility it communicated to anyone who dared try to cross it.

He shifted his gaze to the Western side of the Wall where artists, activists and dissidents had used the vast expanse of concrete as a canvas to scrawl political slogans, colorful art and messages of hope. The sights sparked a small fire in Uli's mind: that whatever East Germany wanted the Wall to say, there were still those determined to make it stand for something different.

He drew back from the window, letting himself consider the possibility that tonight they might succeed where twice they'd failed. Once Lise made it across, what would come next? He knew better than to think that they might simply pick up where they'd left off, all those years ago, but there was still something there between them: much though he'd tried to deny it at the time, it was still there between the lines of the letters they'd sent back and forth; it had been there on the day of Inge's funeral.

He pictured the life they could build together, here in West Berlin or anywhere else that Lise might want to go. But, as with Rudi, it would be a long road for the two of them to find each other again—a road they would travel only if Lise was willing. But for now, he let himself believe in the future they could have here, beyond the inhumanity of East Germany; far beyond the time and space of the half lives they'd spent apart.

Finally, a small blue Volkswagen pulled into view, flashing in and out of pools of light cast down by the streetlamps that dotted Bernauer Strasse, and Uli turned away from the window.

"They're here."

He was lightheaded with anticipation as he tripped down the staircase, following in Jurgen's brisk wake. There was still every possibility that Wolf was alone in the car: that Lise had been detained before she could make contact with Wolf—or worse, that she'd changed her mind. He followed Jurgen out into the street just as the Volkswagen disappeared around the corner. They began to sprint as they turned onto Wolgaster Strasse, and the realization of why Wolf was still driving made Uli run all the faster: even though the guards in the watchtowers along the eastern edge of Bernauer Strasse stood with their backs to the West, he didn't want to park anywhere they might be seen.

He was panting by the time he caught up with the Volkswagen on Stralsunder Strasse, his chest heaving with the exertion of running faster than he had in years. In the darkness he listened to the fluttering static of the radio, the unmistakable baritone of Elvis's voice momentarily audible before Wolf twisted the dial further. From within the car, he heard a muffled pop and rushed forward to help Jurgen ease up the back seat of the car.

A woman shifted within the depths of the Volkswagen's concealed compartment, her blond hair dishevelled, one arm crooked over the strap of her purse. She eased herself upright, blinking in the golden light of the streetlamp, and took Jurgen's and Uli's hands as they helped her out onto the sidewalk.

Unlike Rudi, Lise didn't stumble as she straightened to her full height; she had Uli's hand around her waist, and it was Uli's knees that were turning to water; Uli's eyes that were filling with tears.

He sagged with relief, and she pulled him close.

"Lise," he said. "Welcome home."

epilogue

9 NOVEMBER, 1989

Lise sat back on the tufted couch at the apartment on Bernauer Strasse, listening to the sound of voices through the closed curtains as Gretchen pulled a fragrant strudel from the oven. She looked up, impressed by the decorative changes that Gretchen had made, now that the apartment belonged to her: she'd replaced the peeling wallpaper with fresh, white paint and swapped out the ancient sofa for a sleek sectional; she'd torn out the pass-through window so she could install a wide harvest table that would give her the sort of counter space that a professional chef required.

The apartment was different now, but Lise could still see the old bones of the place she'd once thought would be her own. Gretchen had highlighted some of the charm of the ancient building, painting the ornate trim an electric green that she'd carried onto the kitchen cupboards and decorating with antique finds she'd picked up with her boyfriend in Kreuzberg. The pièce de résistance, however, was a spectacular work of art above the fireplace: a black-and-white photograph taken by Rudi on his

Prakti camera, blown up to majestic proportions, of an eagle taking flight, its wings outstretched as it launched itself from the branches of a Scots pine.

Uli had been doubtful when Gretchen had announced she planned to redecorate the apartment—but then, he'd always been more precious about the place than Lise. From the outset, she'd seen the need for Gretchen to put her own stamp on things, and the result was a delightful mishmash of old and new.

Gretchen emerged from the kitchen with three plates of strudel and Lise accepted hers on the couch, balancing the dish atop her knee.

"Well, I think it's safe to say that your efforts with interior decorating have paid off," she said, lifting her glass of wine in a toast.

Gretchen sank down into the occasional chair. "I'm pleased with it," she replied, then gestured to the closed curtains with her fork. "If only there was something I could do about the view."

Outside, the voices grew louder, accompanied by the snippet of a song, and Uli, next to Lise, grinned. "It's nice to know that the neighborhood still has some spark to it."

"It's all the students," Gretchen explained. "Foreign exchange students like it here. They think it gives them a bit of cachet, living next to the Wall. It's a story they can tell when they go home to England or Japan or wherever. There's a decent little kneipe a block away, so I'm always hearing crowds at odd hours."

Lise set down her empty plate and leaned into Uli's arm, tilting her head to meet his knowing look. Whenever she thought of sitting in Siggi's all those years ago, it was always at a full booth: arriving with Inge after hours spent at the library, ready to wash away all their heavy studying with a cold pilsner; Uli, youthful and exuberant, waiting to pull her into his arms.

Uli was still exuberant; however, Lise doubted whether either of them could be called *youthful*, anymore. As one of a handful of a mature students at the Free University, Lise still studied late into the night, but she did so now from the comfort of her home, where Uli was ready with a glass of red wine when she finally put down the books. Her days were soon to become even more hectic, once she began her hospital rotations; but she knew that Uli would be there, supporting her as she pursued her long-held dream of becoming a doctor.

It was hard to believe that this was her life now; impossible to think that it could get any better. When she'd crossed the border nearly a decade ago, she'd known that she was giving up a certain future for the unknown, and that there was a possibility that what she found in West Berlin wouldn't be what she wanted. She and Uli might have decided that they were ill-suited, after all; Rudi's troubles might have continued to plague him. She might have missed Papa and Gerda too much to be truly happy, or decided that the pursuit of the collective good in the socialist east outweighed the struggles of seeking personal happiness in the capitalist west.

She looked back on the girl she'd been and was proud of the woman she'd become; proud of the life she'd built here for her and her son, the precious family she'd created with Uli and Gretchen. Rudi now traveled the world as an award-winning photographer, snapping photos of urban landscapes that sold in galleries across Europe, while Gretchen, a celebrated sous-chef, was preparing to open her own restaurant in Wedding. Lise was even able to visit regularly with Papa and Gerda who, under the more flexible travel laws afforded to pensioners, visited West Berlin every few months.

They kept her updated on her old life: how Horst had remarried a year after she'd left, to a chess player who was clearly much better suited to his sedate lifestyle; how Paul and Anna's son, Kurt, had become a nuclear physicist in Dresden.

They spoke, too, of Paul. Three years after Lise had left East Germany, he'd had a nervous breakdown, which had forced his early retirement from the so-called "police service." Now he spent his days as a mail carrier—a job which, given how physically fit he'd always been, Lise suspected suited him.

She thought often of Paul, and though the memories were painful, she could, with time and distance, acknowledge the good: the love and affection they'd shared in their youth.

What was it that had finally made him step aside and allow her to reunite with Uli? She still wasn't entirely sure. Perhaps it had been the same realization that so many socialist governments had come to in the past ten years, as their citizens' demands for freedom became too loud to ignore and the Iron Curtain had begun to fray: that control was impossible to maintain forever.

Or perhaps it was simply that he had finally understood, at the end, what love truly looked like.

She set aside her empty plate and studied the sparkle of her engagement ring, tucked away for nearly two decades, finally paired on her finger with a gold wedding band: the commitment she and Uli had made to each other, so many years ago, finally fulfilled.

She had the life she'd always dreamed of; one she'd freely chosen.

And that, to her, made all the difference.

"Goodness," Uli said as the crowd outside the window grew louder. Behind him, Gretchen's telephone rang, and she got up to answer it. "Are you sure it's students?"

Gretchen listened for a moment, frowning. "It's Rudi," she said, holding a hand over the receiver. "He's in Rome, he says he's been trying to get in touch." She held out the phone to Lise. "Here—"

"Mum?" Rudi sounded panicked and excited all at once. "I've been trying to call you for the better part of an hour! For God's sake, turn on the news, open the window—"

She frowned. "What is it? What's happened? Uli—" She put her hand over the receiver. "He's telling us to open the curtains."

Rudi's voice was audible even with the phone away from her ear. "It's open! The border is open!"

Gretchen reached for the television remote and fumbled to turn on the news while Uli flung open the curtains, letting in the bright white of the streetlamps that ran along the Wall. Slowly, Lise advanced to the window, letting the phone—Rudi still rambling on the other end—slide from her hand. He would understand that she had to see it for herself. She had to confirm it with her own eyes.

She drew close to Uli's side and stared down, stunned, at the Wall. Below, crowds had gathered in front of the concrete barrier with ladders and ropes, determined to climb to the top of the graffitied surface and straddle it, letting their feet dangle in East and West.

The sight was enough to turn her knees to water. There had been mass demonstrations in East Germany for months, for years, calling for freedom of movement and an end to socialism: similar demonstrations of malcontent in other Eastern Bloc countries, Hungary and Czechoslovakia, had led to revolutions only weeks earlier. But to see it happening, here, was beyond what Lise had ever imagined: to her the Wall was a permanent scar, a permanent state of division.

Uli snugged Lise closer. "Are we dreaming?"

"Listen." Gretchen turned up the volume on the television to drown out the growing chorus of songs and car horns. On the television, an American reporter—Tom Brokaw—stood before the crowded Brandenburg Gate, the screen behind him filled with hundreds of people pulling each other up onto the Wall, as he strove to make himself heard.

"Tonight, the Berlin Wall can no longer contain the East German people," he said, and Uli and Lise looked at each other in amazement. "A new policy announced by the East German government tonight has granted East German citizens freedom of movement. East Germans may now leave for short visits or to the West permanently through checkpoints."

She pressed a trembling hand to her lips as Brokaw elaborated on what that meant. Freedom of movement—freedom of choice. Freedom to cross the border, to leave East Berlin of one's own volition—to travel, to live where one chose, with whom one chose.

It was an astonishing thing: so humble, perhaps, to those who had not experienced its lack.

"It's true, then," she muttered as a stout Trabant turned, its lights flashing, onto the quickly filling street. She dabbed at her cheeks, barely noticing that she was crying; behind her Gretchen had picked up the phone and was filling Rudi in on what they were seeing. "It's—it's true. I can't believe it."

Out of the corner of her eye, she could see Uli, watching her closely. "Are you all right?"

"We need to go down there," she replied. "We need to see it for ourselves!"

They descended onto Bernauer Strasse and joined the biggest street party Lise had ever seen. Strangers hugged in the streets, openly weeping as they joined hands; someone whizzed past on a skateboard, music blaring from a boom box they'd hoisted onto their shoulder. They lost Gretchen within minutes of stepping onto the sidewalk, and Lise clung to Uli's hand as they ventured into the fray, worried that if she let go, she might not find him again until morning.

She'd always thought of a revolution as a violent, bloody thing—a cleansing fire, righteously burning as it devoured the core of a fetid, unjust regime. But tonight felt more like fireworks than fire: peaceful and beautiful, but no less a revolution.

As they drew closer to the Wall, someone pressed a bottle of champagne into Lise's hand and she drank deeply, joyfully. Close up, the Wall had already begun to show signs that the checkpoints were swiftly becoming meaningless: people had brought hammers and chisels, pickaxes and sledgehammers, and were tearing down, with tools and hands, the concrete barrier that had separated east from west.

Someone offered Uli the use of sledgehammer. He held it out to Lise.

"You deserve this more than I do," he said, and Lise took it, weighing the sledgehammer heavily in her hands.

She knew that hers wasn't the final blow that brought down one of the panels of the Berlin Wall, nor was it Uli's idea to gather long wooden boards and pieces of drywall to lay down over the sanded strip between the border walls; but soon she was walking through No Man's Land, striding against the current into the East, Uli at her side.

Together, they walked along familiar old roads with a bottle of champagne in hand, Lise's feet taking them along a path she knew so well she didn't need to consider where they were going. They turned onto Ruppiner Strasse, smiling and shaking hands with the hundreds of East Berliners flooding west; passed Schönholzer Strasse, the faded buildings looking so gray, so modest, to her Western eyes. This was a journey of a lifetime, one which took five minutes to walk and seventeen to crawl: a route that she ought to have been able to take every day of her life, between the man she loved and the family she adored.

She knew before turning onto Rheinsberger Strasse that she would find him there, sitting on the stoop of number 56. He was dressed in a white shirt and dark trousers, and in the light of a streetlamp she could see the new lines carved around the corners of his eyes; lines that hadn't been there on that day nine years ago when he'd finally stepped aside and allowed her to pursue a life of her own choosing.

Paul stood and tucked a hand into his pocket. He hesitated on the stoop and glanced from Lise to Uli and back again, a question in his expression which Lise, for a moment, wasn't sure how to answer.

Uli squeezed her hand and she smiled, then took a step toward her brother.

postscript

19 JULY, 1979

My dearest Lise,

When your father reached out to Uli, it felt, in no small measure, like providence. How else can I explain the serendipity in it all?

Two years after you and Uli start communicating once more, I get diagnosed with a terminal illness.

Either the universe has a sense of humor, or I do. Perhaps it's both.

I'm not angry about it. In fact, I'm glad. It's given me the chance to say some things that I would rather not take with me into whatever comes next.

They say that when you reach the end, your past flashes before your eyes. I've not reached that point yet, but when I close my eyes, I see a certain future.

You and Uli will be together someday. Soon, I hope, but I'm not quite so clairvoyant as that. I've known my whole life that you two belong together, but somehow, I got caught up in your love story.

Take care of him for me. For god's sake, don't let him wallow.

He's developed something of a habit for it ever since I got ill. Give him reasons to smile. Good Christmases. Single malt whisky.

Sing to him when you're in the car. He'll make a big show of pretending that you're off-key, but it makes him laugh.

I know without asking that you'll take care of Gretchen. She's going to have to make so many memories without me. Help her where you can, but above all, love her.

I hope you know how much I love you still. All these years later, my memories of our friendship remain undimmed. Even today, I count you closest in my heart.

It may not feel like it now, but you and Uli have an entire lifetime to live together. Live it, and know that you go with my blessing.

All my love,
Inge

*****

author's note

Just three weeks after the fall of the Berlin Wall in November 1989, US President George HW Bush and Soviet General Secretary Mikhail Gorbachev declared an end to the Cold War; by October of the following year, Germany was reunited as a sovereign, democratic state. Though the fall of the Wall can't be considered the beginning of the end to Communist rule in Eastern and Central Europe, it was without doubt the most momentous moment in its collapse: as the most enduring image of the Iron Curtain, the Wall symbolized the split between East and West, and stood as an embodiment of tyranny to those who lived in its global shadow. Its demise was seen as a new dawn in Europe.

The first time I went to Berlin I followed the city's cobbled streets along the twisting divide between east and west. Though the lines demarcating the city's four zones of occupation—drawn up in the rubble of the Second World War—made sense at the time they looked, to my eyes, all so arbitrary: as though someone had walked a meandering path from block to block and left barbed wire in their wake. I live in downtown Toronto, and while writing this novel I pictured what it would be like for my city to be divided as the Wall divided Berlin: to look out my window and see concrete splitting Bloor Street in two; to stare out at the CN Tower like Uli might have looked at the Berlin Fernsehturm, a few blocks and yet a world away.

We still live in a world that builds walls; a world where families can still be separated by political, physical and psychological divides. While writing this novel I was struck by the stories of real people who were willing to put themselves in mortal danger for the chance at a better life. During the Berlin Wall's thirty years of existence, 140 people died or were killed as a result of trying to flee East Germany, most falling victim to the GDR's "shoot to kill" order given to border guards. While many would-be refugees fled East Berlin by swimming Berlin's canals or hiding, as Lise and Rudi do, in the cavities of cars, others found more intriguing methods of escape: by flying over the Wall in hot air balloons and makeshift airplanes; by hiding in hollowed out surfboards or in shipping containers.

There were those, too, like Uli, who journeyed eastward in the hopes of rescuing loved ones. Uli's tunnel is heavily inspired by the experiences of a group of Free University students who dug two tunnels beneath Bernauer Strasse—incredibly, NBC obtained permission to film one of the escapes, resulting in *The Tunnel*, a 1962 documentary which, if you have the time and the inclination, is a gripping account of how the students defied the odds to rescue twenty-six East Germans.

Those who tried to escape did so in countless daring ways, but they all had one thing in common: a determination to flee from a country that couldn't give them the life they wanted.

For those who are interested in learning more about the Berlin Wall, I invite you to consult the *Chronik der Mauer* and *Stiftung Berliner Mauer*, two excellent online resources that provided me with unique insights into the sorts of lives that Uli and Lise would have lived. While I read too many books and articles to count on the subject, five books were particularly foundational in my research: *The Berlin Wall: A World Divided, 1961–1989* by Frederick Taylor; *Berlin: Life and Death at the Center of the World* by Sinclair McKay; *Checkpoint Charlie: The Cold War, the Berlin Wall, and the Most Dangerous Place on Earth* by Iain MacGregor; *Stasiland: Stories from Behind the Berlin Wall* by Anna Funder; and *Tunnel 29: The True Story of an Extraordinary Escape Beneath the Berlin Wall* by Helena Merriman.

As an author of historical fiction who considers herself firmly entrenched in the early twentieth century, it stuck me multiple times through the course of writing this novel that the Wall came down in my lifetime—that, little though I knew it, I lived through that momentous moment in history. It's comforting, I think, to consider history as something that exists within the pages of a book, but then that's the remarkable thing about it: we're always living through history. Whether or not we're fully aware of it in the moment, we're living through events that future authors will write about; the sort of history that future readers will learn of and think, "isn't that extraordinary?"

I hope this book serves as a reminder that we have a responsibility to shape our history for the better.

acknowledgments

It's a cliché to say it, but sometimes those old clichés ring true: it takes a village to raise just about anything, and a book is no exception. In many respects, this was the hardest novel I've ever written, but then they're all hard in their own ways—they're all special too, and it's the encouragement of the people listed in these acknowledgements that helped me write through the hard to reach the special.

First, I'm so grateful for my publishing team. My agent, Kevan Lyon, who has supported my writing career from the very outset; April Osborn, my editor, who gave me the opportunity to live my dream as a published author, along with my entire publishing team at MIRA—particularly Nicole Brebner, Puja Lad, Evan Yeong, Elita Sidiropoulou, and Rebecca Silver. My thanks as well to Mary Jane Wells, my extraordinary narrator who made me cry real tears when I listened to her performance of my novel... quite a feat, given that I knew every plot twist in advance!

Special mention must be given to Edith Turnbull, C.L.F., my

research assistant, without whose academic and emotional support I would not have written this novel.

My thanks as well to Christine of Christine's Couturier Boutique in Toronto, whose expertise and stories in Swiss dressmaking helped give structure to the dressmaker's judy that was Gerda; and to Mary Revell and my mother Dana, whose stories about talking their way into nightclubs by pretending to be renegade nuns inspired my favorite scene in the novel.

To my community of author friends (you know who you are), and most prominently the Lyonesses: thank you for being the sorority sisters I never had. To the Yorkville cocktail club: Mohammad, David, Amber, Rawan and especially Josh—thank you for being incredible friends and sounding boards for my flights of fancy. My thanks as well to Emma Ingram, Aaron Vomberg, Michael McCain, Jill Kantilberg, Rachel Thorne, Nastasia Nianiaris, Mandy Bean, Natasha Campbell and Mike Schneider.

To Derek, Brenda, Alec, Hayley and Logan, who endure my historical rants and questionable fashion choices with good grace, and Coretta, who told me to pick up a shovel and start digging somewhere near Bernauer Strasse—thank you for your many indulgences. And my eternal thanks to my parents, Doug and Dana, whose love story is the most remarkable one I know.

Finally, to you, my reader. Thank you for allowing me to leave my imagination in your pleasant company.